Super Secret Space Squad

Jonathan Coleman

Super Secret Space Squad by Jonathan Coleman

Copyright © 2023 Jonathan Coleman

For permissions contact: jonathan.i.coleman@gmail.com

Cover by Zachary Malich.

ISBN: 978-1-957674-02-5 (print)

Published by The Ocean Deep Publishing

13833 Dumfries Rd, Manassas, VA 20112

Printed in USA

First edition 2023

For my grandparents, Tom and Mary Jo Coleman, who were the first to read this story in its infant stages, and for Ms. Dyche of the Colgan High School Creative Writing program, who helped me bring it to full maturity.

Pride goes before destruction, and a haughty spirit before a fall.
-Proverbs 16:18

Your scientists were so preoccupied with whether they could,
they didn't stop to think if they should.
-Ian Malcolm (Jeff Goldblum), Jurassic Park

CHAPTER ONE

RESEARCH OUTPOST THETA-FOURTEEN—OUTSIDE CHICAGO, ILLINOIS, USA

"Recalculate."

Albert Nurmen pushed his glasses further up the bridge of his nose as the numbers on his holoscreen blinked in and out of existence.

One by one, the lines of equations resolved themselves. Albert's eyes flicked back and forth, left to right then left again, noting the outcomes of each as they came. With each solution presented, a new wrinkle took shape on his already furrowed brow.

Soon his gaze landed on the lower right corner of the screen, where a frustratingly meager double-digit figure flashed twice before fully stabilizing.

"No, no, no," Albert bit out, pacing back and forth in agitation. "We should be seeing a much larger yield by now. What are we missing?"

A lighthearted chuckle echoed around the small side room, followed closely by the patter of approaching footsteps. A voice followed close on their heels—the tones of his beloved wife and lab partner, Rebecca.

"I thought we agreed we were taking a temporary pause," she reminded gently—not as an accusation, but merely a statement of fact.

"We're on to something major here, Becca," Albert said stiffly, without tearing his eyes from the vexing data before him. "The alloys we used in our recent trials proved effective for redirection and even capture, yet our input energy continues to far exceed its return output. Our next priority has to be finding an explanation for the discrepancy."

"No, our next priority has to be getting as far away from the whole thing as possible," she shot back in a tone laced with thinly veiled anxiety. "You know it's not a good idea to be attached to this project at the moment."

Albert relaxed his shoulders, recognizing the truth in her words. "I know. We were just so close. If we had only had more time, we could have cracked the whole thing."

"I certainly don't disagree. But, really, who's to say what could have been? This … stuff, it's never shown much regard for our hypotheses. Full of surprises, that's what it is."

Albert huffed in exasperation. His wife laid her hand on his shoulder, and he tilted his head back to finally meet her eyes.

Physically, they couldn't have differed more. He was short and stocky where she was tall and slight. She kept her auburn hair tied back in a tight bun, but he preferred to let his rogue salt-and-pepper curls hang free. Even where personality was concerned, they remained in contrast. Albert prided himself on his dedication to his tasks, often losing himself in his theoretical models for hours at a time, while Rebecca possessed a carefree and spontaneous nature. Yet they had always shared a deep emotional bond that allowed them both to perceive each other's mental states, meaning Rebecca knew exactly how frustrated Albert was just then.

Cold, hard facts hadn't worn him down, so she resorted to an attempt at levity. "Besides, how can you expect us to conduct a proper study now that Prang's cut our staff by eighty percent?"

That finally sobered him.

There had been other technicians and radiologists working out of this facility, as recently as two days ago, until they had all abruptly been recalled. Albert understood why the order had been given and, somewhere, deep inside himself, he

8

could even sympathize. On the surface, though, he knew it must be quite plain that the setback in his research infuriated him.

"An order born almost solely from unfounded speculation," he said. "Far be it from me to speak ill of Admiral Prang, but under the circumstances, I would suggest that he is being either overcautious or …"

His energy drained out of him. He knew that the last word he had intended to speak—*senile*—was entirely unfair. Prang's mental faculties were doubtlessly in perfect working order, the evidence for his thought process clear as day.

Rebecca squeezed Albert's shoulder to reassure him, even as her eyes darkened. "I still don't like it. Ever since Epsilon Station went dark, everything's felt off."

Albert scoffed—a dismissive sound, yet in his heart, he knew he didn't mean it. Was it truly her he was attempting to convince? Or himself?

It didn't matter, his next words would accomplish both.

"Nonsense, dear. The loss of so many agents is tragic, but we have no definitive proof that it was an attack. Anything is possible as long as we don't know the facts."

"And that's what worries me. All this not knowing. I hate how I keep finding myself looking around every corner like a horde of enemies is going to jump out and attack."

A pang of bitter irony came over Albert. Their roles had now fully reversed, leaving it up to him to comfort her.

"Who could go up against the 4S?" he said. "We have the backing of most of the world's nations."

"All of which could be revoked in an instant if they discovered what we've been keeping from them," she shot back.

"You're worrying too much. They need us. They didn't act fast enough to solve this planet's problems, so the only way forward is to find another," he said.

"Fine. Then what about co-opting our work? There are potentially limitless uses for it," she reminded him.

"And even we haven't figured out how to practically accomplish any," said Albert. "The 4S has its pick of the cream of the scientist crop, and if we can't achieve that goal, who else is better equipped?"

"We can't assume we alone have the answers," Rebecca said. "The 4S is far from infallible, and even we haven't gotten all that close to figuring this out yet. If someone were to get a hand on our blueprints, they could be reverse engineered."

"But this hypothetical someone may not exist at all," said Albert. "The incident at Epsilon could have simply been an accident. And even if someone had accessed its files, nothing in them could have compromised this station or any of the others. We're safe here. Even our own son is unaware of our true career choices."

At that, Rebecca had to smile. "Speaking of our son, how do you think it looks when you prioritize your work over him?"

Albert rounded on her in mock indignation, jabbing her playfully in the ribs with a closed fist.

"That," he scolded, "was a low blow. Jax is an adult by several years, and I trust him to take care of himself." He stirred and seemed to compose himself. "Even so, it would be best to keep up appearances. We should be getting back. Have you wiped all the data logs yet?"

She took two steps forward, thumbing a button on the side of his holoscreen to erase all its saved data and power it down. "Just did. Now there's nothing left in this facility that could reveal what we were researching."

"Perfect." He clasped her hand between his own for several seconds before letting go. "Now then, we might as well try some of this *blending in*, don't you think?"

And he led the way from the room.

*

Instinct, more than urban planning, guided Albert as he steered the small electric car through the bustling streets of their hometown. When one lived among so many identical prefabricated dwellings, as the Nurmens did, they tended to develop a sort of snow blindness. For that reason, Albert had long since committed their homeward route to muscle memory.

He and Rebecca had made their home in a settlement

of the sort that had been springing up all over the globe for the last several hundred years. Ever since the twenty-first century, climate change and rising sea levels had threatened to consume more and more of the world's dry land. Fortunately, new carbon-capture technologies and sustainable energy sources had vastly slowed the progress of global warming, although it had already progressed too far to be completely reversed. Millions of people had become climate refugees—colloquially referred to as Roamers—and the world's governments had quickly built hundreds of new towns to house them all. Even four hundred years later, much of the Earth's population still lived in those cramped shantytowns.

Such a town naturally stood out as the perfect place for two people who didn't want to be noticed to hunker down. The hustle and bustle lent itself particularly well to anyone hoping to get lost in the shuffle. Additionally, proximity to the city and to its spaceport meant consistency of work and good quality of living for the Roamers, and even Albert's own son Jax assumed that the same trend applied to his parents.

In reality, Albert and Rebecca worked for the 4S, or the Society for the Settlement and Security of Space. Admiral Prang, its current leader, wholeheartedly believed that a new home and a brighter future for humanity lay out among the stars. His enthusiasm had infected all those below him, including the Nurmens themselves. The energy source they had been studying had the power to be a force for good, and so long as it remained firmly under the thumb of the pure-hearted Admiral Prang, Albert truly thought the 4S could realize its potential.

For so long it had seemed to be a foregone conclusion that Albert's idealized future would come to pass. Now, for the first time, an enemy force actively moved to prevent it. As much as Albert tried to pretend otherwise, he knew that it was the only explanation for the strange occurrences centered around the Epsilon base and the disappearance of its staff. If it came down to him to prevent those enemies from gaining control of his life's work, he would fight to his last breath.

But this was no time for such morbid thoughts. However the assailants had discovered the Epsilon base, there was no reason to assume that they had divined the location or purpose of any of the other hidden research stations scattered across the solar system. The stations operated as a network, each working on a small portion of the overall experimentation so that no one who stumbled across one would know everything about the project. Even so, they contacted each other and shared data and results through unofficial means, often through the personal communicators of the science officers, leaving nothing logged in the official station records that would reveal there was more than one. For now, and hopefully for a long time, the Nurmen family was and would remain safe.

Albert swung the vehicle into a hard left turn, pulling into the small garage attached to his home, a perfect cube constructed of gray metal. It stood two stories high, with two rows of double windows on each side, one on top of the other. In the front, a door stood in place of the bottom two windows.

The garage, meanwhile, was a smaller single-story cubic structure snuggled against the side of the house. The entire building stood in the center of a small lawn, the half-acre parcel of land that each Roamer family was granted to maintain. The grass in the Nurmens' yard had been freshly mowed while they were out, until it stood only half an inch tall, just as Albert liked it. He had Jax to thank for that, of course.

Turning his key to shut off the engine, Albert opened the door and stepped out. Grabbing a remote control from a low table in the back of the room, he closed the garage door. As it ground its way downward, he stepped around the car to open Rebecca's door and help her step out. She giggled at his chivalry and accepted his outstretched hand as they moved into the house.

Albert held the door open, and together they stepped into their living room. Sparse as far as furniture was concerned, it contained only a television screen mounted on one wall and a couch against the other with a coffee table in front of it. The couch was currently occupied by their son Jax, a sandy-haired young man of twenty-five years, lanky and lean but muscular. He rose to his feet when he saw them, placing his plate of snacks on the coffee table.

"Hey," he said. "How was work?"

"The usual," Rebecca told him, in a valiant attempt to be vague.

Jax seemed to accept this. He popped a cracker from his plate into his mouth, standing still while he chewed and swallowed. By the time he had finished, he had forgotten about his parents' working lives.

"I cut the grass today," he said eventually.

"I noticed," Albert said. "Well done."

"Thanks," Jax said. "Oh, and the recycler's full again. Someone's going to have to take it to the processing facility tomorrow."

"I can handle that," said Albert. Perhaps, if he spent some time around the complex where recycled materials were converted into energy and new products, he might gain some flash of insight as to how he might solve his lingering questions regarding his own work with energy.

"Cool," Jax said, with enviable nonchalance. Clearly he hadn't spent his day being anxious about unidentified enemies and the evils they might carry out. His lack of concern just gave Albert more reason to believe in a world where all people could be so carefree.

Whatever will come will come, however we may feel about it, he reminded himself. *We can only control how we respond. If those who attacked Epsilon hope to do the same here at Theta, let them try. After all, there's too much at stake here for us not to fight for it.*

*

Late that night, Albert sat up in bed, holopad in hand. He kept the screen brightness low so as not to disturb Rebecca, who slumbered beside him.

Albert, for his part, had no interest in rest. He knew what his wife would say if she saw him: something about how he needed to let it go, no doubt. But he had never been the type of person who could turn away from a problem once he became embroiled in it. He preferred to work at it from every angle until the solution finally revealed itself.

So Albert scanned the same lines of data over and over again and attempted every method he could imagine to make them all correlate, searching for the unknown variable that must have escaped his notice. At last, he had to pause when he realized how dry his mouth had become. He flicked his eyes downward to the clock on the bottom corner of the screen, realizing that he had been analyzing the lab data for two whole hours. Maybe there really was some truth in Rebecca's claim that he was too invested.

Ever careful not to disturb Rebecca, Albert sat up in

bed, laid the holopad facedown, and reached down to pull on his slippers. He headed out of the room and down to the kitchen to fetch himself a glass of water.

When he reentered the room, he noticed a blinking red light emitting from his holopad. He turned the device over and gasped when he read the alert on the screen.

"Rebecca," he hissed. "Get up."

"Wass goin' on?" she mumbled into the mattress.

Smirking in benign amusement, Albert took hold of her shoulder and shook it gently until she rolled over, blinking up at him from eyes sticky with sleep. She looked from him to the wall-mounted digital clock, which displayed a time far too early in the morning for any human to function, then back up at her husband.

"Albert …" she moaned weakly. "This isn't funny."

"I'm not trying to be funny," said Albert. "You need to see this. It's the perimeter sensors."

Instantly, Rebecca sat up in the bed, sweeping her hair out of her face and disentangling herself from the sheets. She knew what Albert meant.

They had had to calibrate the sensors very precisely, so they weren't alerted to every small animal crossing into their yard. If the devices had been activated now, it meant that they had picked up something large: a human being, most likely.

Albert keyed for a visual, tapping his fingers against the side of the tablet as he waited for it to be pulled up. When it finally appeared, he gaped in dismay as he recognized the dark shapes of not one, but several, people moving across their lawn.

"We've got company," he announced bluntly.

Rebecca's strained face displayed panic for only a moment before she regained her composure. "We've prepared for this," she said. "Lock the doors."

Albert tapped a button on his holopad. "Done."

"Great," she replied. "But that won't buy us much extra time. We need to hurry."

14

"Agreed."

"Get dressed for some foot travel," she advised. "We can't take the car without being noticed, but if we move fast on foot there's a good chance we can slip away in the dark. If we can make it to the lab, we can take the escape vehicle from there."

"Of course," he said, already hurrying toward the dresser.

"When you've done that, wake up Jax," she told him. "We can't leave him behind."

"He'll have questions," said Albert.

"All of which can be answered once we're safely away. Just get him. I'll grab the emergency packs and meet you in the garage."

While she spoke, Albert had stripped out of his pajamas and shrugged his way into a shirt, jeans, and a pair of sturdy shoes. He was already halfway across the room before Rebecca noticed him leaving.

"Wait!" she called.

He paused and turned to face her. She stepped up to him, took hold of his shoulders, and leaned down to kiss him on the lips.

"I love you," she whispered as she pulled away.

"I love you, too," he told her. Neither one would let the other head into danger without knowing how appreciated they were.

With those four words, it was back to business.

Jax's bedroom was right at the other end of the upstairs hallway, and it didn't take long for Albert to reach its door. He stretched out his hand in preparation to swing it open, then hesitated.

So far, he hadn't allowed himself any time to process just how quickly their plans had deteriorated. If it came down to it, Albert would gladly lay his life down for his family, but that should never have been necessary. Then again, hadn't he practically asked for a fight?

But there would be time for dithering when all their lives were no longer in jeopardy.

Taking a deep breath, he swung Jax's door wide open.

CHAPTER TWO

NURMEN FAMILY HOME—ROAMER CAMP IL-048—
OUTSIDE CHICAGO, ILLINOIS, USA

By sheer stroke of fate, Jax had already been awake for several minutes by the time Albert barged into his room. It had been a balmy day, and the humidity had continued into the evening. Unable to get comfortable under his bedsheets, Jax had eventually opened his window halfway. With a slight breeze now circulating around him, Jax had returned to bed, satiated for the time being.

He had just begun to sink into sleep when the window snapped closed.

Jax sat upright, just in time to see a metal screen sliding over the inside of the window. He had never seen it do that before.

While Jax's mind raced in consternation, his father entered the room.

Without the light cast from the window, Albert Nurmen was merely a silhouette in the darkness of the hallway. Jax had to blink several times before he recognized him.

Albert took two steps forward, and Jax crossed the distance to meet him.

"What's going on?" he asked before Albert could explain himself. He flung out an arm to point to the window. "I used to be able to see out of there, you know."

"Security measures," Albert said tersely. It sounded to Jax as though his father couldn't believe what was happening any more than he did. "The kind we hoped would never have to come online."

The news hit Jax like a truck. His understanding of the situation shifted from 'strange technological glitch' to 'possible crime in progress'. But that still didn't make any more sense.

"That can't be right," he protested. "Nothing ever happens around here. Definitely nothing that would warrant 'security measures'."

Albert grasped Jax's shoulders, and their eyes met. A fierce sense of urgency reflected in Albert's gaze, so much so that Jax found himself unable to pull away.

"Jax, we don't have time for this. People with very bad intentions are outside the house as we speak. Your mother and I have bought us some time, but it won't accomplish a thing if you insist on delaying us all with inane questions. Get dressed, and meet us in the garage as soon as you can. Time is of the essence."

Jax acquiesced with a simple nod. His father had always been logical and scientifically minded; he never overstated or exaggerated any situation. If he believed that things were about to hit the fan, so should Jax.

Albert pulled away and left the room, closing the door behind him to grant Jax a measure of privacy. Jax moved to the dresser, exchanging the loose-fitting clothing he had worn to bed for a simple T-shirt and cargo shorts ensemble. Next came his shoes, then his holowatch from the night table.

He took the stairs two at a time on his way down. When he reached the garage, he found his mother pulling a faded backpack from a previously hidden compartment in the ceiling while his father sifted through the contents of two more such bags on the floor nearby.

Rebecca placed the third bag on the pile next to her husband and crossed the room to enfold Jax in a brief hug. "Good, you're here. We have to go soon, or they'll be on us before we can cover our tracks."

As if to emphasize her point, a loud crash came from somewhere close by, as though some heavy object had collided with the wall.

"Quite right, dear," Albert agreed, straightening from where he had been squatting in the background. "Our supplies are in order, so let's be on our way."

"Supplies?" Jax asked. "What supplies?"

"We're going to have to go away for a little while," his mother explained. "We might not come back for a few days. Think of it like a family trip. These bags have everything we need to lie low for a while."

At that, something inside Jax gave way.

"Lie low?" he asked incredulously. "This is seriously starting to freak me out. Are those people outside the criminals, or are you?"

"That's not fair and you know it," Rebecca retorted.

"Well, then, what am I supposed to think?" Jax shot back.

Albert moved to stand between the bickering pair. He locked gazes with his wife for a moment, sharing a look Jax couldn't see.

"Your questions are valid," Albert said, turning to Jax, "and your anger as well. For the moment, all you need to know is that your mother and I have access to critically sensitive information that must not be allowed to fall into the wrong hands. Those hands, of course, being the ones currently besieging our home."

Another boom shook the house, louder and more forceful than the last.

"Hence," Albert continued as though nothing had happened, "we must maintain our hold on it at all costs, even if that means getting as far away as we can and living in anonymity."

"So, we're just going to run and hide?" Jax asked.

"As undignified as that makes it sound, yes," Albert replied. Then he softened his voice and expression. "I promise you, you will have all the answers we can give you once we are on the other side of this potential crisis."

"Good luck with that," Jax muttered. "We can't even get out of the dang house. The second we open the door, they'll be on us, and you'll lose that oh-so-valuable information just like that. The car might give us a little more protection, but we'd have the same problem if we tried to use it."

"Then it's lucky we have another option." Rebecca's tone was flat—not exactly sarcastic, but it sure sounded like it.

Jax spun to face her. In the time that he and his father had been in conversation, his mother removed a panel from the wall to reveal a hidden switch. She flipped it, and a floor panel in the corner of the room slid aside to reveal a ladder leading down into a tunnel.

Albert reached into the three bags and pulled a small portable flashlight from each. He handed one to Jax, one to Rebecca, and kept the third for himself. Then, gathering up the backpacks, he dropped them into the tunnel. It took only a few seconds for the sound of their hitting the ground to echo back, meaning the tunnel couldn't be too deep. Jax's mind compartmentalized that, but the greater part remained flabbergasted by the revelation that there was any tunnel at all.

"How …" He breathed out in wonder. "How long has that been there?"

"It came with the house," said Rebecca. "It'll get us where we need to go, and that's what counts."

She replaced the wall panel, fitting it snugly into its place, then headed down the ladder.

Albert motioned Jax to follow her. For a moment that seemed to stretch into infinity, neither of them moved a muscle. Then came another thunderous, earsplitting crash, accompanied by the creaking of stressed metal. The door was beginning to give way.

That was enough to snap Jax out of his indecision.

"Go!" his father urged him. "This is our only chance to make it out."

"All right," Jax said. "But you owe me some explaining, and don't you forget it."

Despite the gravity of the circumstances, Albert couldn't quite stifle a chuckle. "I would never."

Satisfied for the moment, Jax lowered himself into the tunnel. Not long after, Albert joined him and his mother at the bottom.

Albert flipped another switch on the wall, and the floor panel slid closed above them, enveloping the family in darkness.

"It's all up to us now." Albert's voice rang through the tunnel, echoing into the distance down the long corridor. "We've activated every possible safeguard. All we can do from here on is trust that our own bodies and minds will carry us through."

Rebecca switched on her flashlight, the beam catching several motes of dust that had been shaken loose by the raiders' battering ram. Jax and Albert turned their own flashlights on soon after, and the family found themselves in a tunnel hewn from the earth. The stale air indicated that it hadn't been used for some time.

Jax turned his light in the only direction they could go: onward. "Where to now?"

Albert took the first steps into the shadowed unknown.

"We'll make one stop before we leave the city. After that, we'll keep going. We don't look back. And we hope with every ounce of being that we aren't followed."

*

As she jogged through the escape tunnel, Rebecca's thoughts swirled, trapped within a fog of half-formed questions and statements that should have been impossible.

The network of research stations should have remained secret from even the vast majority of the 4S. And yet, in the last few weeks, some malevolent force had struck two of those stations, leaving one in ruins and seeking to similarly cripple the other.

Still, the Theta station had had the advantage of forewarning. It was why Prang had recalled the other scientists when he did. And the Nurmens had been operating under deep enough cover that they should have blended seamlessly into their local community. But the raiders had still seen through every protective measure they had undertaken.

How could it all unravel so quickly? Rebecca pondered, even as she pushed on, never allowing her burgeoning doubts to slow her pace. *They knew where we were—and not only the lab. Even if they had discovered the Theta outpost by chance, there's no way they should have been able to find our home, unless—*

Rebecca breathed out in shock, her sharp exhale masked by the steady rhythm of her pounding footsteps.

They've broken into the 4S database. Not just the public one—they've been snooping through the High Command's private files. How much do they know?

It was now all the more imperative that the Nurmens survived their ordeal. Admiral Prang had to be informed of the massive security breach his pet project had suffered.

The tunnel sloped gently upward as the Nurmens neared its end, eventually stopping in front of a blank metal wall. They took the first few seconds to get their breath back after their frantic run. Rebecca listened for sounds of pursuit. When she heard none, she nodded to her husband, who flipped a switch that caused the 'wall' to slide aside and reveal the path forward.

Stepping out into the starlight, they found themselves at the base of the small hill into which their escape tunnel had been built. Before them stretched a massive forest, with the broad trunks of its trees coming together with their gnarled, leafy branches to form a tangled web of mystique and intrigue. As far as secret base locations went, this one was a classic.

Albert took a slow, deliberate look at their surroundings. It took less than a minute for his gaze to settle on something beyond the trees, and for him to give a satisfied nod.

Jax, meanwhile, turned in a full circle—once, twice, three times, taking it all in. Rebecca's heart went out to her son; though he would never voice it aloud, he must be growing increasingly frustrated with his lack of context on the events that had transpired around him.

"There's nothing out here," he said bluntly. "Not even a trail that could lead to something."

"Ah," Albert said, "that's what we want you to think, isn't it?"

He led the way into the mass of trees. Darkness quickly

swallowed them as they struggled on, only the occasional flicker of starlight illuminating their way. Without a clear path, it was slow going as they ducked and weaved their way through the underbrush and around low-hanging branches. After what seemed like an eternity of maneuvering deeper and deeper into the woods, they reached their destination.

They stopped in front of a gray stone cliff carved by weather and erosion. Though not exactly imposing in its height—only twenty-five feet or so high—its slope precluded any wanderers from simply pressing on to the top, and without many viable hand- and footholds, there was no way anyone could scale its mass without the proper equipment. Fortunately, with Rebecca's and Albert's official clearances, there would be no need for such tedious athletics.

Jax snorted loudly, making his exasperation known at last. "A dead end. You cannot be serious."

Rebecca took a step toward him, clasping his hand in hers and draping her other arm across his back. "Jax," she began, "we've asked a lot of you tonight. I know it's wearing on you. Keeping these secrets for so long, even from you—well, it pained us, every day."

"What are you trying to say?" Jax asked with a scowl.

"What we are about to reveal to you is extremely sensitive," she went on. "Only a very select few know the full extent of what we've been involved in these last thirty years, and ordinarily protocol would dictate that you remain in the dark. But the situation changed very suddenly, in ways we weren't prepared for, and now the protocols are just going to have to be bent. Your father and I have a responsibility now to ensure that word of tonight's events gets to the right people, and I assure you that, once we've fulfilled that, we will tell you everything we can." She looked into his eyes, awaiting his reaction.

Jax pulled away from his mother, taking two steps back. Rebecca's heart ached for her son, but he had to work this out for himself. At last, he gave a small shrug, marginally relaxed, and nodded once.

"Okay," he prompted. "Show me this thing."

Albert moved to a point on the cliff where a reasonably large stone jutted forth. It blended well into the rest of the cliff face, though this particular rock was rounded in front—not so much that it stood out from the rest, but enough to allow the machinery it concealed to work effectively. Albert pulled out a keycard and held it steady until a faint chime sounded. With a faint scraping noise, the rock retracted into the cliff face until its surface was even with that of the cliff. In front of Rebecca and Jax, a door hidden in the rock lifted to reveal the entrance to a small room.

Rebecca walked into the newly opened chamber, and Jax followed. Albert joined them a moment before the door slid closed. They stood in darkness for only the next few breaths before the lights kicked in, bathing the room in a warm, ambient glow. The gunmetal-gray walls sparkled under the light, as did the set of double doors on the other side of the room.

As soon as the lights came on, Jax began asking his inevitable questions: "What is this place? Where are we?"

"It's a sterilization chamber," Albert said. "All laboratories have them. The scientists are subjected to a perfectly healthy level of radiation until all germs from the outside world that might disrupt the quality of their work are burned away."

"How long does it take?" Jax asked.

"It's barely an inconvenience. Any second now ..." Rebecca replied.

As she finished speaking, the doors at the far end of the room hissed apart, and they continued onward.

The room they entered next was far larger, yet just as austere. It spanned a hundred and fifty yards from end to end and stood three stories high. A metal ledge running the entire length of the room demarcated each new level, with several doorways to adjoining rooms along each one. Currently, the expansive laboratory floor stood empty; the machines that the researchers had used had been extracted or destroyed to avoid giving away the purpose of the lab.

Jax stared down from the railing, his expression somewhere between interested and disappointed.

"You said this place was a lab," he observed. "But it's empty. What kind of experiments could you possibly do in an empty room?"

Rebecca evaded his question. "Feel free to take a look

around," she encouraged. "But don't be long. We're still on crunch time here. Meet us at the elevator on the opposite side of this place in three minutes."

Jax grunted in assent and moved off down the ledge to one side of the chamber. Rebecca took advantage of his distraction to steal a few private moments with her husband as they set off down the other side. There were words to be shared between them that could wait no longer.

"Do you know what all this means?" she asked, carefully modulating her voice so as to avoid an unwanted echo in the vast chamber. "They came to our home. Not the lab."

"Which means they knew we were working undercover," he replied.

Rebecca, stunned by the idea, struggled to get her next words out. "But … how? That information was highly classified. And why target us, or the 4S, at all?"

Albert shook his head ruefully. "Believe me, I want to know why this is happening as much as you do. Based on the fate of our Epsilon Station counterparts, I'd assume our visitors desire to force information out of us, or to silence us forever. More than likely, it'll be both."

Rebecca's throat went dry. She had to struggle to speak her next thought. Hearing Albert speak the danger of their circumstances aloud had only made it that much more tangible. "We have to get in contact with Prang."

"I agree," said Albert. "These people after us have far more information than they should. We have to plug the leak in our communications."

They picked up their pace as they headed to the elevator. When they reached it, Jax was already there.

From the looks of it, he had made no particularly earth-shattering discoveries, but, then again, Rebecca hadn't truly expected him to. This level contained mostly bunks for the staff who had spent their lives inside the base. It truly did cut Rebecca to the quick, leading her son on like that, but she couldn't let it bother her. The time for truth would come once they had made it to a safe haven.

"Off we go," Albert beckoned, pressing the button to

open the elevator. Once they were inside, he pressed the button that would take them all the way down to the basement.

The elevator doors opened onto a small room from which two separate hallways branched. One led to the storage rooms, packed with supplies; the other led to a garage with a large, unmarked van. Rebecca led the way into that garage—and pulled up short in horror.

Their intended escape van was mostly in one piece, though the hood had been removed completely to allow access to the engine beneath. Said engine had been smashed up and pockmarked all over with dents. Fluid dripped from it in several places, and a scattering of broken and twisted scrap lay all across the floor. The vehicle's most essential component had been damaged beyond repair.

"Sabotage," Albert spat. "I should have known we wouldn't get away so easily."

They could take time to put it back together, certainly. The lab was well-stocked with the necessary components, but there was hardly time now to effect repairs, when their pursuers could swoop in at any moment. If they had already gotten into the lab once, there was nothing on site that would stop them from doing so again.

"No," Rebecca breathed. "They've done us in."

"What do we do now?" Jax asked. "Tell me there's still a backup plan. If this data you're guarding is so important, you can't just give up!"

That snapped his parents back to reality.

"We'll go into the city," Albert declared. "Lose ourselves in the throng. We need to stay hidden until we can find a safe way out. We already have everything that we need in our packs."

Albert's idea was a good one, and, perhaps more importantly, their only one. Rebecca nodded. "Then what are we waiting for?"

Albert crossed the garage, the other two close behind, and flipped a switch on the wall. The garage door opened agonizingly slowly onto more of the same old forest. The Nurmens emerged into a narrow valley that should have been their road out. Turning in the opposite direction, they climbed to the top and used the new vantage point to locate the glittering lights of the city a few miles away. Once they had, they set off right away, with even greater urgency than before.

As they sprinted, Rebecca thought she could hear a whooshing sound from somewhere behind her, then again on her other side. Albert's head rotated ever so slightly at the second instance, confirming to her that he had picked up on it, too. Jax remained oblivious so far.

Over the next fifteen minutes, Rebecca counted seven more noises from various directions. When they broke through some trees into a large clearing, she reached out a hand to tap Albert's shoulder, signaling him to halt. They both knew exactly what was about to happen.

Their gazes simultaneously honed in on Jax, who had noticed that they had stopped and now came back their way.

Albert and Rebecca shared the sort of look that only two concerned parents ever could. Their enemies had crossed a line when they had put Jax in danger, dragging an innocent young man into a conflict he had no part in. If there was any chance they could spare him from what was to come, they owed it to him to try.

When Jax reached her, Rebecca squared herself and faced him, affecting her best encouraging yet hardened expression.

"Jax, I want you to listen to me very carefully," she ordered. "Keep running until you've reached the city limits. Don't look back. Don't stop for anything or anyone. I promise we will be right behind you, but you need to go, now."

"But—" he protested.

"Now!" Rebecca repeated, putting as much power behind it as she could without giving in to her rapidly growing desperation.

Jax seemed to recognize something in her face or her voice, something that told him it would be best for him to heed her advice. It almost looked as though it physically pained him when he turned and hurried away, fading rapidly into the shadows that pooled among the trees. Rebecca waited for several long seconds to be sure he hadn't gotten second thoughts, then turned to her husband. He took his cue right off the bat.

"You can come out now," Albert called. "We know you're there. Let's get this over with."

In an instant, a small mob of human figures swarmed the clearing. The newcomers were clad all in black, including full face coverings, leaving not a single identity exposed. They formed into a tight circle surrounding Albert and Rebecca. In the heat of the moment, her hand found his, and reassurance seeped into her as he held it tightly in his grip.

The figure closest to them spoke. "Albert and Rebecca Nurmen, your reckoning has come." His voice was masculine but slightly robotic, as if it had been filtered through some kind of mouthpiece.

Rebecca couldn't hold back a groan and an eye roll. "Oh, please. Can we cut the theatrics and just get this over with?"

Another figure spoke, its voice clearly female yet distorted the same way as her counterpart's. "Very well. But you're clearly failing to grasp the full potential of the forces at work here. You seek to contain power that should be set free."

"And what exactly would you do with it?" Rebecca shot back.

"It is futile to attempt to contain a power of this kind," the woman responded. "For too long the universe has languished in rot and stagnation. With the data from your laboratory, our mission will begin in earnest, and this world will be the first to be scoured."

"Do you even hear yourself?" Albert asked in disbelief. "There are forces at work here that none of us understand. Not me, not the 4S, and certainly not whoever you think you are. Whatever you hope to gain by unleashing those forces, surely the risks outweigh any benefits."

"The risks and benefits are not yours to decide," said the woman, "so long as you cling to your moral compunctions. But it doesn't matter. We do not need you, only your research findings. Such data belongs in the hands of those who can see the full scope of its potential."

"If that's what you want, you're too late," Rebecca gloated. "The information you came for is already safe with Admiral Prang. He's already preparing to hunt you down and eliminate you. Do what you will to us; it won't matter. Your mission is over."

For a long moment, the group of figures went silent, and Rebecca almost dared to believe they were safe.

That instant of hope was when their fates were sealed.

"Then we have no further use for you," the man intoned. "Farewell, Nurmens. You could have been so much more."

Two of the masked assailants stepped closer to Albert and Rebecca, the rest of the circle tightening to compensate for their absence. From holsters at their waists, the figures drew short metal batons, hefting them as they approached the Nurmens like ghastly specters.

There would be no escape, Rebecca belatedly realized. This had been their attackers' intention all along, to drag them into exactly this situation. They would take the Nurmens out, and then they would move on to the entire 4S. And, if Rebecca and Albert died here, the 4S would remain blissfully unaware of just how much danger it was in—perhaps until it was too late.

And Jax … What would happen to him?

The attackers raised their clubs above their heads, and all non-immediate concerns were banished.

Rebecca closed her eyes before the fatal blow struck. In the few seconds of serenity she had bought herself, she called up a mental image of her son's face, firmly enshrining it in her mind.

It was the last thing she saw before her consciousness surrendered to the void.

CHAPTER THREE

OUTSIDE CHICAGO, ILLINOIS, USA

The night lay perfectly still, as if this one moment had been captured and held in place between two invisible fingers. Under the shade of the forest canopy, the darkness had deepened until Jax could barely see ahead of him. The chittering of the night creatures mingled with the distant white noise from the city. A chill breeze blew, rustling the dead leaves littered across the ground, and Jax pulled his knees closer into his chest, burying his tear-stained face in the space between them.

For all intents and purposes, the world around him ground to a halt. In the midst of it, he curled up in a shallow dip among the oak roots, waiting for it all to come back to life.

It had all happened so fast ...

He had obeyed his mother when she had ordered him away, but he hadn't liked it. As soon as he felt sure that no one had followed him, he had doubled back, finding a hiding place within a close-knit copse of young trees where he could observe the interaction undetected.

When he watched his parents being slaughtered, it had taken all his self-control to beat back the impulse to scream. His tears had still streamed freely, blurring his vision for a time. Only when the tromp of heavy boots had signaled the raiders moving away did Jax pull himself together, wiping his eyes until his vision cleared again. He feared that the raiders would rip him from his hiding place and beat him to death like they had his parents, but they had remained in a single group and headed away from him.

When they had disappeared into the distance, Jax had allowed himself an immense exhale of relief. After several minutes had passed without their return, Jax had at last stepped out from his hiding place. Glancing around him to double- and then triple-check that the coast was clear, he had made a break for it. He had run until he could run no longer, and collapsed at the foot of the oak tree.

*

He must have fallen asleep, because he snapped awake to a long, low droning sound, which grew steadily closer as he listened. Blinking to take the weight off his eyelids, he lifted his gaze to the sky. The stars had barely begun to blink out in the predawn light; among their lights he made out a cluster that formed the outline of a small space shuttle moving toward the spaceport.

For a brief minute, Jax's surroundings plunged back into darkness as the shuttle cast its shadow. The whine of its engines built to a deafening crescendo, and the wind of its passing whipped Jax's hair and clothes around him.

Then, just as quickly as it had come, it was gone, and the stillness of the forest returned.

As long as spaceships kept coming and going above him, Jax would never fall back asleep. He shouldn't want to, either, not as long as he didn't know whether the raiders were still nearby. He had sat there feeling sorry for himself for long enough. If life really did go on, he'd have to figure out something meaningful to do next with his own.

Standing and stretching his cramped limbs, Jax picked his way through the trees. After a few false starts, he found himself back in the clearing where his parents' corpses lay.

The bodies remained undisturbed. Dried blood crusted the forest floor beneath their skulls, where it had seeped from the bludgeon wounds that had been their end.

Jax lingered for a few minutes—still and silent at first, then with tears and words spilling forth unbidden.

"I'm sorry," he began. "This should never have happened. I should have stayed. I could have fought with you. I could have done something."

He choked back a sob on those last two words, breaking down into a blubbering mess. His parents had given up everything to protect him. Joining them in death wouldn't honor their sacrifice, but surviving and thriving would.

Whatever he did, he would need supplies. But could he risk going back to his house?

Then he looked down and saw his parents' backpacks still hanging off their limp bodies. This would be awkward …

Jax tried a few times to turn his parents' bodies over before he overcame the instinct to cringe away. He opened their backpacks and stuffed the contents into his own. Next, he emptied their pockets, claiming two key cards and one personal communicator. He took a step back, not wanting to contaminate the crime scene any further.

Jax keyed the frequency code for emergency services into the comm. The device buzzed once, then five seconds later, then five seconds after that, indicating an outgoing signal. Jax placed the unit atop his father's chest, leaving it there as a homing beacon for the responders.

He knew that whoever answered that distress call would take good care of his parents. He hated to leave them like this; they deserved so much better. Then again, if they had gotten what they deserved, their corpses wouldn't be lying here to begin with.

For as long as Jax remained in the clearing, his tears kept coming. Eventually, he had none of those left, either. He closed his eyes, fixing the scene in his memory.

Jax would make sure his parents hadn't died in vain.

First, however, he had to figure out what exactly they had died for.

Despite the seriousness of the situation, he couldn't help but crack a small smile at the irony of his predicament, one that vanished as quickly as it had come. He didn't have time to be amused; he wanted to get down to business.

And he knew just where to begin.

*

Tom Ubert watched his fellow ensign Ara Kendall pace beside their Reconnaissance Transport shuttle, blinking as the harsh light of the sunrise. Even this early in the day, the spaceport tarmac already emanated heat at them.

Tom brushed his dreadlocks back from his forehead. He fought the urge to wipe phantom sweat from his brow, knowing full well that there couldn't be any so soon. He had grown too accustomed to the modulated climate of the space cruiser they called *Home Base*.

Making a mental note to get out more, he shook his head to clear away the stray thoughts.

Focus, he chided himself. *First-mission jitters are a fact of life, but you can't control the temperature.*

The ship's ramp clattered as the third and final squad member, Billy Vurk, hurried down it. His coppery red hair glinted as he emerged into the light.

No sooner had Billy's boots hit the ground than the ramp retracted into the shuttle's undercarriage. The entrance hatch slid closed and, with a dull metallic *thunk*, the magnetic-lock seal took effect.

"Ship's locked down," said Billy. "Where to now, Tom?"

The other two gathered around Tom before he even spoke. No one had officially elected or installed him as leader of this mission team, but his friends had always been willing to defer to his cool-headed logic. Despite the disparate paths they had taken since their academy days—Tom as a mechanic, Ara as an archivist, and Billy as a pilot—the camaraderie they had established there had survived and thrived. Tom didn't consider himself a leader, but he did see himself as keeping the others steady.

He pulled a holopad from one of his pockets and a small data chip from another. Inserting the latter into the former, he booted up the pad. Two images filled the screen: a red-haired woman and a man with long, messy black hair. Tom turned the tablet toward Ara and Billy.

"You know as much as I do," he told them. "Prang wants these two, and he wants us to bring them to him."

"They're science officers, apparently," she replied. "I cross-referenced their names with the 4S personnel register, and they were there. But they haven't been assigned to *Home Base* or any official 4S station for nearly thirty years."

"Are you suggesting …?" Tom couldn't bring himself to finish the thought.

"I'm suggesting"—Ara stressed the word—"that someone went to great lengths to keep their whereabouts hidden. That's all."

"That doesn't make any sense," Billy said. "Why would Admiral Prang send two scientists out here for so long without telling anyone?"

"How about we stop arguing and go find out from the scientists themselves?" Tom asked. "There's probably a perfectly innocent explanation."

Ara nodded, and Billy too looked mollified. Tom tapped the right side of his screen, replacing the images of the Nurmens with a satellite map of the spaceport and its surroundings, including a Roamer settlement some eight miles away. He rested his pointing finger on it.

"The Nurmens live here." He pointed to a blue dot signifying the exact dwelling. "Our job is to get over there, find them, and bring them back with us."

"Simple as that?" Billy's face twisted with doubt.

"Simple as that," Tom confirmed. Even so, he was all too aware of what potential prospects hinged on their success. This was the first mission they had ever undertaken for the 4S. They had to complete it, and prove their worth to the High Command, or they might never be given another. That would have been stressful enough, even without all the secrets swirling around these Nurmens. To Tom, it felt like they had been initiated into some top-secret conspiracy.

Tom switched off the holopad and removed the data chip before stowing both in his pockets once again. "Let's get started," he said.

Billy and Ara fell into step behind Tom as he led the way toward the spaceport's main terminal.

The cool of the air conditioning washed over Tom all at

once as he entered the building. He tugged twice at his collar to try and get some airflow under his uniform.

Ara headed straight for the nearest registration console to enter their ship's specifications and landing zone.

"Finished!" she called after a few minutes. "We're all sorted out."

"Great, thanks!" said Tom. "Let's get going."

Tom and Billy had just started to move toward the door when she spoke again.

"Hold on. What's that?"

The two men paused and turned on their heels.

"What is—"

Tom never finished his sentence. His gaze tracked hers to a holoscreen on the wall, currently playing the morning news.

"…reports of a tragedy which struck the Roamer resettlement camp just outside the city in the early hours of the morning," the grim-faced anchor said. "Local emergency services followed a beacon into the forest, where they discovered the bodies of one man and one woman, both of whom had died from head trauma. Currently it is unknown whether the deaths occurred due to homicide or a simple accident, and Chicago residents are advised to be on their guard against a potential criminal element."

"The victims have been positively identified as husband and wife Albert and Rebecca Nurmen, whose house in the community was broken into last night. The fate of their son Jax, who lived there with them, is currently unknown. Authorities have opened an investigation …"

Tom tore his eyes from the screen to find Ara and Billy awaiting his reaction. For one excruciating moment, they all stared at each other in panic.

Billy broke the silence first. "Well, that can't be good."

"We're …" Tom had to force the words past his lips. "We were too late."

"So now what?" replied Billy. "Are we just supposed to

go back, shrug our shoulders, and say *oh well, we tried*?"

Tom took a long deep breath. "No. I refuse to believe there's nothing we can do."

"You may be right, Tom," Ara broke in. "There might just be a way we can still salvage something from this mess."

"Go on," Tom prompted her.

She delivered her words slowly and methodically. "The Nurmens are dead. Whatever Prang wanted them for is probably dead in the water now, too. We can't fulfill the original mission requirements, but regulations have always given the mission commander relative freedom to change the objective where they deem it prudent-"

"What's your point?" Billy asked.

"Let me finish," Ara told him. "Like I was saying, we can't bring the Nurmens to Prang anymore. But we can bring him information, and that will turn this mission from a total bust into … well, something slightly better. After all, if someone is going around killing 4S agents, that's the sort of thing High Command needs to know."

Tom nodded once. "That's all well and good, but how exactly are we supposed to get that information when nobody knows what happened last night?"

"Almost nobody," Ara corrected. "This Jax character might know something. He could at least tell us what his parents were doing last night."

"They said Jax is missing," Billy pointed out.

"Which is different from gone," Tom said. "Even if he left the city, he couldn't have gotten far."

"So we go after him," Ara said. "Sweep the area. It's the only way we'll ever unravel this mess."

"Just what I was thinking," Tom confirmed. "All right, then. Let's find this Jax."

*

The sun was already well on its way into the sky by the time Jax came to rest on a ridge overlooking the rocky slope that concealed his parents' lab. Leaning against a moss-covered boulder and crossing his arms in front of him, he let his eyes rove back and forth as he took in the lay of the land.

He picked his way carefully down to the valley floor until he stood level with the secret door. He pulled his mother's key card from his pocket and held it above the secret scanner until the door lifted to admit him.

He had barely crossed the threshold when he heard a faint rustling and snapping of twigs from behind him. He whirled around, but the forest had already fallen silent, and the door slid closed before Jax could locate the source of the sound.

Unsettled, Jax paced back and forth across the room. He tried to tell himself that it had only been some forest creature, but it didn't really help. He knew that his parents' killers were likely still in the area, and he knew that they had already proven their ability to get into the lab.

The doors to the lab slid open, and Jax cautiously stepped out onto the ledge. The large open space was as deserted as it had been before. For the moment, he allowed himself to relax. His senses remained on high alert, but, until a real danger presented itself, there was nothing he could do but get on with his mission.

He had searched this top level, albeit briefly, when he had last been there, and had encountered nothing but living quarters. That told him that, at some point, there had been more people than just his parents operating here, but it didn't reveal what they had all been doing. Those answers, Jax presumed, would lie at the heart of the complex, where the work had been done.

Jax rode the elevator down to that level, exiting directly onto the open floor. He had already known the room would be empty, but now he saw it was so clean that there wasn't even any lingering dust left to show where equipment had lain.

It was all just … gone.

In increasing desperation, Jax headed down to search the storage rooms around the garage with the wrecked van. There, he found several cases of spare parts, and even rudimentary science equipment, but nothing that could tell him what specific experiments his parents had been conducting.

At last, Jax found himself on the middle level of the lab. The rooms there were apparently office spaces, with dormant holoscreens and empty desks. Just like the rest of the lab, however, the offices contained nothing that could have compromised the scientists who had used them.

In the room opposite the elevator, Jax discovered what had to be the lab's central computer. If there was any hope left that he could find out what had happened, it would be on that device.

When Jax booted up the computer, it came to life almost instantly. When he opened the data drive, however, he found it completely empty. The entire device had been wiped clean.

Jax banged the palm of his hand on the tabletop in frustration. Recoiling slightly from the pain and shock of his action, he took several deep breaths and fought to regain his composure.

No sooner had he accomplished this then there came a sound of boots scuffing against the floor from somewhere very close by. Jax turned toward the door and froze.

There stood a redheaded young man, no more than one or two years older than Jax himself. He wore a two-piece uniform consisting of a dark orange shirt with blue sleeves and blue pants.

"Sorry," he apologized, only seeming half sincere. "Is this a bad time?"

Jax did his best to keep up a peaceful facade. "Who are you, and what do you want?"

"I'll take that as a yes," the newcomer quipped.

Jax took a step toward him. "How did you get in here?"

"Oh, that?" the man replied. "It was easy enough, once you showed us the way."

"You followed me?" Jax bellowed.

This young man didn't resemble any of the raiders from the previous night, but that didn't preclude him from being one. They had all hidden their faces and disguised their voices. Jax's suspicion rose even higher. Had the murderers returned to finish him off?

"Billy?" came a woman's voice from somewhere outside the room. "Is that you there? Who are you talking to?"

"I think I found him, Ara!" the redheaded man called back.

A few seconds later, the owner of the second voice strode through the doorway and into the room. It was another young person close to Jax's age, this one a brunette woman, wearing the same orange and blue uniform. She assessed the situation before her with a keen, scrutinizing glance which finally settled on the young man, who Jax realized must be Billy.

"What have you gotten yourself into now?" she asked him.

"I didn't—" Billy protested.

But her attention had already shifted to Jax.

"Look," she began, "whatever my colleague here has led you to believe, we come in peace. We only want to help you, and we think you can help us, too."

"Do you really expect me to just believe you?" Jax asked. "All of the other strangers I've seen in the last twenty-four hours played a part in my parents' deaths."

"Your parents' deaths?" the woman echoed. "I guess that makes you Jax Nurmen, then."

"How astute," Jax grunted. "What's it to you?"

"She told you already," said Billy. "We came here to find you."

Jax sighed. "Fine. Say that's true. What do you get out of it?"

"It's about your parents," she told him. "We need to know how they died."

That was the straw that broke Jax's back.

Jax saw red as he raised a shaking hand to point at the other two. "My parents were murdered! They died to protect this place, and I'm not afraid to do the same. So, whatever you think you're doing here, it ends now!"

"Whoa, dude! Take it easy there!" Billy held up his

hands. "We don't want to hurt you."

Blinded by rage, Jax barely registered the plea. Raising his fist, he wound up and aimed a punch at the side of Billy's head.

It never landed.

Something sharp pressed into the back of Jax's neck. His body went limp, all his muscles tensing then rapidly deflating. His sense of balance fell away, and he toppled over backwards.

He fell into the waiting arms of the one who had stabbed him: another young man close to his own age, with dark skin and long black hair, who wore the same uniform as the other two.

"Nice one, Tom," said Billy, his voice muffled by the ringing in Jax's ears. Whatever they had slipped into his system, it had obviously been potent.

The man called Tom lay Jax gently on the floor as his vision began to blur. Before he fell into slumber, he noticed a glinting silver emblem on Tom's left chest, an image of a vague triangular shape imposed upon a circle. He knew he had seen that logo before …

Then his eyes slid shut, and he could notice nothing more.

CHAPTER FOUR

UNKNOWN LOCATION

Jax's sight was the last of his senses to return to him. His head throbbed, and his back ached where it had hit the ground. Too weak and stiff to move much yet, he resigned himself to lie still, trying as best he could to gain a handle on his situation.

Although he still lay on a cold metal floor, he felt comfortable assuming that he had not been left where he had fallen. His parents' laboratory had stood empty and virtually silent, yet this new place hummed with the sounds of machinery on standby.

This epiphany came in the span of the few minutes that went by as Jax recuperated, regathering his strength after the sedative had sapped it. Once he had enough in reserve, he heaved himself up until he lay on his left side. Stretching out that arm as far as it would go, he swept it around in a circular pattern and encountered no obstacles. Another few minutes elapsed before he could shift onto his right side. Repeating the process there, he achieved the same results.

Satisfied that no danger lay waiting in his immediate vicinity, he forced his eyes open. For a moment, his surroundings remained as dark a void as before, and he feared that he hadn't succeeded. Then, the haze gradually sharpened into clear, recognizable shapes.

Jax found himself in a decently sized room, sprawled limply in the relative center of a wide aisle. Based on the shelves that lined the deep blue walls, the space seemed to be a storeroom. Crates and containers of various sizes and shapes stocked those shelves. Each one was labeled with both a string of numbers and, below that, a few words presumably describing its contents, such as *Instant Meals* or *Coolant Valves*. Currently, only a few dim emergency lights shone down from the ceiling: enough to read the closest labels but not enough to see to either end of the room.

A chill ran down Jax's spine at the realization. Perhaps his celebration of safety had been somewhat premature. This location was certainly not one he recognized, though he could hazard a guess as to its intended purpose.

Once, as a child in school, he had viewed a three-dimensional holographic model of a nuclear fallout shelter dated to the First Cold War. The inner workings of that shelter had much resembled the room where Jax now found himself. There, the provisions had been stockpiled so that the desperate inhabitants could outlast any apocalyptic eventuality.

Here, Jax could only guess what sort of endeavor was being supplied, though he doubted it could be so dire. Even based on what little of the world he had seen, he trusted it not to fall apart the second he was out of commission. So, then, if he hadn't been placed here for his own well-being, there could only be so many other reasons for it, not all of them good.

Questions flew into Jax's head three at a time. What, then, was the purpose of this place? Why had he been dumped here so unceremoniously? Where were the strangers who had accosted him? And how was he supposed to get out?

Spotting his backpack lying at his feet, Jax dragged it toward him. A quick rifle through its contents confirmed that all the items he had collected from his home had been left inside. He chose to take that as a good sign. He might well be needing some of those supplies in the near future.

Jax heaved himself to his feet and slung one strap of the bag over his right shoulder. Every muscle in his legs shrieked in protest. It took a few seconds for him to regain feeling in his lower body, but it held his weight beneath him from the start. He flicked his eyes from side to side, debating what part of the room he should check out first. Even if he couldn't find a way out just yet, it would be better to know that nothing was lurking in the shadows.

Jax made up his mind and started off. Stumbling at first, then taking longer strides as he regained his balance, he ambled along for several minutes, observing the sides of the room as he went. He saw no branches leading off from the main aisle, nowhere an attacker could hide and spring from, but also nothing that could tell him where he was. There were no markings that might hint at his ultimate location, but he still perceived himself to be alone, and took comfort in that fact.

Squinting, he made out the outline of a hatch set into the wall. It ran floor-to-ceiling in height, and the entire length of the space between the two ends of the shelves. A simple keypad had been mounted on the wall to its left.

New hope flooded into Jax as he realized that this could be his way out. He just had to figure out how the controls worked.

Experimentally, he reached out a finger and pressed one of the buttons. The entire face of the keypad flashed an angry red, signaling that the hatch was locked.

That did not bode well. Jax took a deep breath, reminding himself not to jump to conclusions. Without knowing what lay beyond this wall, he couldn't be sure there wasn't some perfectly valid reason to lock the hatch. Still, he had to consider the idea that whoever had brought him here might not want him to leave. If that turned out to be the case, he would need to be warier.

Jax turned and strode back across the room. Eventually he came to the other end, where he found another wall, this time with a door set into it rather than a hatch. The door was small, built solely to accommodate human personnel rather than heavy machinery. Unlike the cargo hatch, this door had a window set into its top half. Keeping low to avoid detection, Jax peered through the window.

The room he saw was smaller and emptier than the one in which he had awoken. The only furnishings were the table in the center and the ring of chairs around it. Instead of shelves, a counter ran the length of one wall, with a microwave unit and a drink dispenser atop it. It looked like a kitchenette or common room, with a hallway directly across from Jax's location.

The room also had three rectangular window panes nestled in each wall. Looking through the one closest to his door, he saw a black backdrop scattered with various tiny white pinpricks of light. That would be the night sky and the stars.

So, he was above ground. That was a start. His chances for escape or release had just increased exponentially. He stepped back toward the center of the room, pondering. There had been no way for him to tell where exactly he was, but that would come later. Where he was didn't matter until he found out why he was there. But how to do that—?

Suddenly, a nearby noise jerked Jax from his thoughts. He spun to face the door as a puff of displaced air signaled its opening. He wasn't entirely sure what he planned to do. Should he stay, or should he make a break for it? At this point, though they both had their advantages, either venture seemed equally likely to end in disaster.

That split second of indecision was enough for the dark-skinned man from the lab, the one apparently called Tom, to step across the threshold.

"Good morning, sunshine!" Tom called. "I thought you'd be up by now. Motion detectors don't lie."

Jax lunged forward in one fluid movement, grabbing Tom's shoulders and shoving him up against a shelf.

"Where am I?" he demanded. "What's this about? Take me back to where you found me, immediately."

Tom struggled to free himself from Jax's grip but found little success. In the end, he chose to simply let his body go slack. Jax appreciated the gesture, although it did leave him wanting, in a strange way.

"Take it easy, dude," Tom replied, answering none of Jax's questions. "I can explain, but you have to bear with me."

"Give me one reason why I shouldn't beat you to a pulp for what you did to me," Jax growled.

"You're angry," Tom observed. "That's understandable. The deaths of both your parents at once … well, I can't even imagine what that must—"

"Leave my parents out of this!" Jax roared.

He hadn't meant to; in the heat of the moment, it had slipped out. He took a breath, reminding himself to stay calm and composed. He needed answers, and shouting wasn't likely to help him get them.

"All right, no parent talk," Tom continued, as if nothing had happened. "Fine by me. You asked where you are, right?"

Jax made no reply in word or in motion. Tom, for his part, mercifully took the hint and got on with it.

"It's probably better for me to just show you," he said. "If you don't mind letting me go?"

Jax pondered this question for a moment. This Tom was a stranger, with unknown intent, who had dragged Jax off to a mysterious location. At this point, he was just as likely to shoot Jax in the chest as he was to treat him to a five-course meal.

But, then again, he had entered the room unarmed, hadn't he? If Tom had truly wanted to harm Jax, he wouldn't have let himself be caught off guard.

Slowly and carefully, Jax unclenched his fists, letting them hang at his side once more. Tom smoothed out his wrinkled shirt and looked directly into Jax's eyes.

"Come over to the window," he said. "And promise not to react too strongly?"

Jax simmered silently until Tom shrugged in deference. "Look, just come and see."

Beckoning Jax to follow, he strode into the next room and over to one of the windows. Jax hesitated only a second before accompanying him. He took a good long look and found that he could see a dull blue sphere below them, with one of its several muddy greenish-brown patches in full view.

Jax had seen pictures of a similar object in books he had read on the history of space travel. Its visual appeal had dulled somewhat since the nineteen-hundreds, but it was unmistakably the planet Earth. And if he could see the whole thing, that could only mean—

"We're in space?" Jax demanded incredulously. He turned to face Tom, anger flooding back into him. "What made you think that was a good idea?"

Tom held up a hand to forestall another physical attack. "Relax. We haven't technically gone anywhere. It's a geosynchronous orbit," he explained. "This ship will remain above this exact spot on the planet and rotate at the same speed it does."

"That's all well and good," Jax replied, "but last I checked, I didn't choose to fly myself into orbit. This was all against my will, meaning you and your friends have some serious explaining to do. I want to hear it all, right now."

Tom shook his head slowly. "You're perfectly within your rights there. I wish I could give you a straight answer, but the truth is I just don't know. I can tell you that the orders came straight from the desk of the big man himself—Admiral Prang of the 4S."

At the last word, Jax found his eyes drawn to the badge on the corner of Tom's uniform, the symbol of a rocket circling a planet. It was the same badge he had observed before he had passed out. So, these were 4S agents. Jax knew he had recognized the badge, but the confirmation of his theory only heightened his concern.

As the old saying went, when one door closed, another opened. If doors were questions, Tom's revelation had opened more than just one.

"And this admiral of yours just told you to kidnap a guy?" he pondered aloud. "And here I thought you were legitimate."

"That's a gross oversimplification," Tom replied. "Yes, our mission was originally a standard personnel extraction, but you can hardly call that kidnapping. And remember, we gave you multiple chances to come quietly, but you forced our hand. Sedation was the only option we had left."

Jax clenched his fist in frustration. He hated to admit it, but Tom did have a good point. There was no way he was going to say that out loud, of course. Instead, he voiced another thought which had simultaneously occurred to him.

"Hold on," he said. "Back up. You called this a personnel extraction, but I've never been one of your personnel. Shouldn't you be out looking for the real guy instead of wasting your time and resources keeping me in your closet?"

"We hit a slight stumbling block, and you're our best way around it," Tom explained. "You're right, it wasn't you we came for. It was your parents."

Jax's mouth hung open, his next furious retort having died at the back of his throat. It took effort for him to shut his jaw and gather enough presence of mind to grind out, "Go on."

Any other day, Jax would have rejected Tom's proposition outright. But he wanted answers, and this was the only way he could see himself getting any. Whatever Tom said or did next, Jax would deal with it when it came.

Tom's eyes went wide for a fraction of a second, then dilated just as quickly.

"It was as much of a surprise for us as it was for you," he began, speaking just a bit too quickly at first. "I know I called it a standard extraction, but it was really anything but straightforward. For one thing, if Prang wanted them to return to base, they could have done so on their own at any time. Their names are registered in the 4S database, and as science officers they had the credentials to get aboard an outgoing vessel with no trouble. The fact that Prang sent us in means he wanted it on the down low, and that's not how it should go. Transparency has always been the name of the game where the 4S is concerned. It's how we let the world know that we're doing it all for them."

Finally, Jax began to see the truth. The disparate pieces of the puzzle had finally come together. Much as he struggled to reconcile his mental image of his parents with their newly revealed position in one of the world's most prestigious organizations, he had to admit that it was the only way to explain a lot of what had happened over the last few days.

"Okay." Jax bit out the word. "I'm hearing a lot about you and them, and I can see why you'd want to take them with you. But let's forget about my parents for now. That doesn't tell me why I'm here right now." He jabbed his finger at Tom. "What does your admiral want with me?"

"It's … complicated," said Tom. "Your parents were always our primary objective, but your name was on the list as well. We thought that was a bit weird, since you're obviously not a part of the 4S, but who were we to question our orders? You have to understand, Prang could have given the mission to anyone with seniority, but he chose a couple of lowly ensigns. If it was a test, we didn't want to jeopardize our chance of passing."

He ducked his head, lifting his hands. "But I'm rambling again. The fact is, we just don't know what Admiral Prang wants from you. That's why we're still hanging around here. The mission went south almost before we began, and now we need to reassess the situation. We've sent a message off to Prang, asking him whether he still wants you to come with us, but we haven't heard anything, and it's been a full day now."

Jax snorted, still much more than a little disgruntled. He couldn't detect any hints of duplicity in Tom's face or voice, which led him to guess that the man truly believed what he was saying. Loath as he was to admit it, Jax could actually empathize with Tom's confusion.

Jax let out a long sigh. "Very well," he huffed. "As long as we're both searching for the same answers, I'll hang around for now. But if I decide that those answers don't align with my best interests, you won't like what I'll do next."

Tom didn't reply for a few seconds, but the sheer relief in his eyes spoke volumes on its own.

"Fair enough," he replied at last. "But I'd advise you not to be too hasty. Like I told you, the 4S isn't looking to harm anyone."

The two young men stood there in uneasy silence, neither one seeming sure of what to do next. Tom flexed his fingers in and out while Jax stared out the ship's window impassively. Now that he and Tom were more or less on the same page, Jax found to his surprise that most of his initial anger had abated, and he could take a more rational approach to his surroundings.

Somewhere down there was his home, or at least the place he had been taught was home. Clearly, his parents hadn't been the unassuming ordinary folk he and all those around them had been led to believe. They must have been important to this Prang person for some reason, given how determined he appeared to be to keep their retrieval a secret. But would he really show the same zeal for Jax himself? Jax, who had nothing to do with the 4S, especially with his parents now gone? And, if not, where would he go?

Suddenly, the silence broke as the clatter of boots against the floor turned Jax's and Tom's eyes. From the front of the room, where it led into a narrow hallway lined with smaller rooms, a young woman had just emerged. She was another of the agents Jax had seen in the lab. He tried to recall her name—Amanda? No. Ava? That seemed closer.

Tom nodded in her direction, and she returned the gesture coolly. Tom opened his mouth, but Jax spoke before he could.

"I remember you," said Jax. "Ara, wasn't it?"

Her focus shifted fully onto Jax. "That's me," she said. "Good to see you're awake. Has Tom gotten you up to speed?"

"I think so," Jax told her, at the same time as Tom cut in with an "I tried."

"Perfect," Ara said briskly.

Unlike her fellow 4S agent Tom, this one was all business. Jax thought he could grow to like her.

"Any word from *Home Base*?" asked Tom.

"Nothing yet," replied Ara. "Billy's in the cockpit watching the comms in case anything comes in. I've been searching through the personnel files to see if I can find anything more on these Nurmens and their work, but so far, I've come up dry. I don't suppose you would know anything about what your parents were up to?" She posed this last question to Jax.

Jax shrugged ruefully. "I'm in the dark as much as you," he stated. "They had a whole underground laboratory, but I guess you've already figured out they were scientists. I couldn't tell you what they were researching though. One of the raiders mentioned that the lab's computer had been wiped clean, so there's no chance of anyone getting data from that thing."

"It was the first place we checked, anyway," Ara confirmed regretfully. "But wiping it does make sense. If their research was such a big secret, it stands to reason they wouldn't want it falling into enemy hands."

"But the 4S doesn't have enemies," Tom objected. "First of all, no one else has the spacefaring capacity. Not even the most major world powers could set up a separate space program, not with the amount of funding and resources they're already pouring into this one. And even if they did, it would just be doing the same things we already are. Why have several separate agencies if they all want the same thing?"

"You do make a good point, Tom," conceded Ara. "but until we have some concrete answers, we're always going to find ourselves asking the same questions. It's a vicious cycle, sure, but we can't escape it yet."

"If you want my opinion," Jax ventured, not bothering to wait and see if they actually did, "the whole thing's fishy. If even such a respected humanitarian group as the 4S can keep secrets, anyone can. It's definitely counterproductive for anyone to try and sabotage you guys, but someone's trying anyway. I saw them with my own two eyes. Or are you going to tell me I didn't?"

"The murders of your parents are evidence enough to support your claim," Ara assured him. "It's all a muddled mess, and if even an outsider can see it, something unusual is definitely going on. Still, there's nothing I hate more than incomplete data, and these circumstances more than qualify as such."

Jax couldn't find a rejoinder for that, and apparently neither could Tom. The conversation seemed to be going in circles anyway.

Jax stared out the window at the planet below, his slight frown deepening into a withering scowl as he watched.

Why did this have to happen to him? Why had his parents lied to him for so long? Couldn't they have trusted their son? Had any of his previous life even been real?

Jax grunted. This wasn't getting him anywhere. He could only carry on and see where this new path led. He hated it, but it was the only option.

Jax took a few deep breaths to calm himself, and while it didn't really help, his face did relax just a little.

Then, all of a sudden, Jax snapped out of his torturous inner thoughts at a new noise from behind him. He, Ara, and Tom spun toward the head of the room as a new set of footsteps clattered toward them. The third 4S agent from the lab, the one with the red hair, came running up to the rest.

"Billy?" said Tom. "What's up? Is everything okay?"

Something had clearly excited Billy. He moved at a fast clip into the room and panted as he came to a halt in front of his comrades. "Message from Prang," he told them. "It's marked urgent."

"What did he say?" asked Ara.

Having delivered his news, he bent forward, planting his

hands on his knees as he fought to get his breath back.

"Well?" Ara demanded after several seconds. "If it's that urgent, spit it out. What does he want?"

Billy straightened up, his composure returning. "He wants us to return to *Home Base* as soon as possible," he said. "I've already got the coordinates set in the navigation system."

"Okay," Tom said slowly. "But what about—?"

"I'm not done," Billy interrupted. He turned to face Jax, raising a finger to point at him for added emphasis. "There's one more thing: we're supposed to bring him."

Really, Jax thought with an inward groan, he should have expected that.

CHAPTER FIVE

4S SHUTTLE RT-587—LOW EARTH ORBIT

Tom clapped his hands once. "Well, that settles that, then."

"It does not!" Jax said venomously. All his initial anger rushed back at the casual assumption that he would comply. He had been willing to hear these people out; he had even begun to sympathize with their uncertainties, but he still hadn't gone so far as to trust them.

Jax's circumstances had been rapidly fluctuating over the past forty-eight hours, through the workings of forces beyond his control. It was time for him to take back control.

Tom offered no reaction. He stared placidly ahead, gazing into Jax's eyes with an utterly stoic expression.

Out of the corner of his eye, Jax noticed Billy move off in the direction he had come in from, presumably heading back to the ship's cockpit. Without breaking his staring contest with Tom, Jax clamped his hand around Billy's arm, stopping him in his tracks. Jax slowly tightened his grip, and he couldn't deny the shiver of satisfaction that coursed through him when Billy let out a pained grunt.

"Take it easy." Tom said slowly. He lifted his hands, displaying their empty palms. "Whatever you're thinking of doing, don't."

"I could say the same to you," Jax said.

"We aren't going to do anything," said Ara.

"Good," Jax replied. "You've done enough already."

"However you feel about our actions, our motives are true," said Ara. "We only wanted to talk. We still do." She paused. "I'll admit, our methods were hasty. We shouldn't have sedated you, and we shouldn't have dragged you all the way here."

Tom turned his head away from Jax to gape at Ara. His mouth moved, but no sound came out. Jax could barely see Tom's face from his angle, but the gist of his message seemed to be *What are you doing?*

Ara didn't answer him.

"We've all had a pretty crappy few days, haven't we?" she said to Jax. "We didn't get off on the right foot, but I do believe we were starting to come to an understanding."

Privately, Jax wasn't so sure. Yes, as far as he was able to look into it, their story checked out. Their uniforms, equipment, and vessel looked consistent with what he knew of the 4S. And, despite the fact they had drugged him and left him unconscious for a full day, he had recovered already, with no leftover injuries or side effects.

Yet he was unwilling to believe they had come that close to a mutual understanding. He couldn't bring himself to accept their story just because they had asked him to. They had shown up out of the blue and dragged him away from his home for reasons they conveniently weren't able to explain. Now they were asking him to blindly follow them into the unknown, and he wasn't about to do that with so much still up in the air.

"I'm not asking you to believe us wholeheartedly," Ara continued. "I'm only asking you to listen. We all may be guilty of overreacting, but I hope we can scrub the record clean and try one more time to have an honest conversation."

And there it was. It seemed that all the cards were on the table. Perhaps Ara did wish to negotiate. If this was all some kind of performance, it was a remarkably good one.

Jax looked around the room, taking everything in. The situation could certainly have been worse. None of the 4S agents were armed, so any fight that broke out would be strictly hand-to-hand.

If it came to that, Jax felt sure he could hold his own. Billy was scrawny enough that he wouldn't present a challenge, and while he didn't like the idea of attacking a woman, he could easily take out Ara as well. That left only Tom. With his large, callused hands and muscular build, he would make a formidable opponent.

Focus, Jax told himself. *You can afford to try bargaining here.* If these people were going to hurt him, they would have done so already. He could give them the benefit of the doubt, and if worse came to worst, he at least had a chance of coming out on top.

"Very well," he said. "Say what you have to say, and I'll listen. But the ship stays here the whole time. You don't take me anywhere unless I agree first."

Ara and Tom exchanged a look, clearly uncomfortable with the delay. He raised an eyebrow. She nodded once.

Tom's shoulders slumped. "Okay, fine. We won't leave. You'll get a fair hearing as long as we get one in return."

A stalemate was more than acceptable for Jax. Jax released Billy, giving him one last serious stare to emphasize the delicacy of his position.

Wisely choosing not to rise to the bait, Billy walked over to stand by his comrades, flexing his arm as he tried to regain feeling.

A long moment passed. Ara, Billy, and Tom looked tentatively at one another, then at Jax. When Jax saw that they weren't going to make the first move, he elected to break the ice.

"Let's get one thing straight here," he started. "I don't trust you. You've treated me well enough, and I recognize that. On some level, I'm even grateful. But before I can really accept that you're sincere, I'm going to need some more answers."

"We've already told you everything we know. We came for your parents, on the orders of Admiral Prang. When we got there, they were dead, and we needed to know how. The only way to do that was to get your side of the story," Ara said.

"You came for my parents," Jax repeated. "Funny you

should use those words. Some other people came for my parents, too. And it didn't end well when they did."

"If you're accusing us of somehow being involved, you couldn't be more wrong," said Ara. "We weren't sent to kill your parents. In fact, I'm starting to think we were sent there to save them."

"And you did such a good job, didn't you?"

Ara snorted. "Jax, I'll say this bluntly. You're being needlessly difficult here, and it's really getting on our nerves. We have our orders, and we fully intend to carry them out. The only question here is how much dignity you want to still have when we present you to Admiral Prang."

Jax let loose a low growl from between clenched teeth. So they weren't going to back down. Taking a mental step back, he inhaled a breath and slowly released it. Threats and intimidation would only get him so far, and whatever credence these 4S agents had been willing to give him was rapidly running out. Blinded as they were by their collective sense of duty, was there any way they could be convinced to just leave him alone?

"Fine. I digress," he said. "But are you really going to overlook how bizarre your orders are? Or does the 4S regularly bring in random guys off the streets for social calls?"

"You make a good point," she replied, "but you're being willfully ignorant. Like we've said, we have personnel listings that show your parents as official 4S agents. They may be vague, but what reason would anyone in our High Command have to falsify official documents? This is more than a social call. Something big is at play."

"Maybe so," Jax agreed. "I still can't discount the possibility that this is all some sort of setup. Unless you can definitively prove it isn't, I reserve the right to be skeptical."

Tom narrowed his eyes in thought. "As much as I hate to bring this up, what choice do you really have? For better or worse, you're hundreds of miles above the planet in a spaceship we control. What other option do you have except to go where we take you?"

"I could overpower you," Jax asserted. "I could take your ship, fly back down to Earth, and figure things out for myself. You might need me, but I sure don't need you."

"It's not that easy," Billy told him. "Flying a spaceship isn't like driving a car. There's all kinds of extra gauges and meters, and it's not the sort of thing a civilian can just instantly learn. I spent a full year and a half studying shuttle controls before they even let me near a simulator."

Tom's tone hardened. "But by all means, go ahead and try. Even if you managed to take us all out, you'd still be stuck. Whether you end up coming along or staying behind, you need us. Don't forget it."

Jax stomped his foot against the floor. Without access to the ship's controls, he had no way of knowing if they were right. He could call their bluff, certainly. He could go on the offensive and see what happened. But was it worth the risk of becoming trapped aboard this shuttle, with no way out?

As Jax pondered his predicament, of all things, the memory of his mother floated to the forefront of his mind. Rather than evaluating the situation on its own merits, he began to wonder what she would have done in his place. Rebecca Nurmen had always been a compassionate woman, seeking to see the good in others and give them the chance to show it. Her husband Albert had been much the same. While Jax had always considered himself a realist, often to the point of pessimism, it was their outlook rather than his own that he suddenly found himself falling back on.

Is this what they would have wanted for me? To live the rest of my life as some paranoid lunatic? He wanted more than anything to believe that there was closure somewhere out there. He just wished it wasn't constantly being dangled just out of his reach like some carrot on a stick.

And yet, how much could he truly accomplish on his own? By all accounts, there was no evidence left in the lab or elsewhere that could assign a motive to the murderers.

As much as Jax tried to stamp out the thoughts, one in particular kept coming back to him. Sooner or later, he would have to throw away his convictions and take a leap of faith. And who better to help him solve his parents' deaths than the admiral of the world's preeminent space force, who had apparently ordered the project they had died to cover up?

Jax let out a sound halfway between a scoff and a sigh, conceding at last. "Screw it. I accept your logic. I'll come with you."

"You will?" Tom asked.

Jax nodded.

Surprise flickered across Tom's face. His whole body stiffened in shock before he relaxed again, his handle on the situation regained.

"Perfect." Tom visibly relaxed. "Now it's really settled."

"But," Jax held up a finger to forestall any further action, "you still haven't told me what it is that I'm supposed to do when I get there."

Tom, Ara, and Billy looked at each other, as though none of them were sure how to respond. Maybe they truly didn't know. The part of Jax's mind that could still be called pragmatic was willing to admit that they had never given any indication that they knew why their admiral wanted Jax around.

"It seems simple to me," Ara said. "Your parents were murdered. Murder is a crime. As the only witness to said crime, your testimony would go a long way toward justice being served."

Justice. The word seemed to drape around Jax's shoulders like a suffocating winter scarf, a mildly uncomfortable weight he couldn't remove without exposing himself to something colder.

In all the turmoil of the previous two days, he had almost forgotten that something as mundane as the legal system still applied to his situation. He doubted that his parents' killers were the kind of criminals who could be dealt with in a trial by jury. This whole affair seemed to be bigger than a simple criminal case.

Jax huffed out a breath. "Whatever. Just be aware that I'm still on alert. The second something seems off, I'll know."

"Yes, yes, you're very scary," Ara scoffed. "We'll try our best not to be suspicious. But we need to get underway. We've wasted enough time as it is, and the admiral is expecting us."

"Right," Tom agreed. "Billy, go fire up the shuttle."

Billy, lurking on the edge of the conversation, started and recovered just as quickly and headed off down the hallway he had come from.

Tom and Ara turned to Jax.

"What do you want now?" Jax asked.

"Come on. You'll want to see this," said Ara.

"See what?" Jax demanded.

Neither answered, but he trailed after them regardless as they followed Billy down the hall, figuring it couldn't do him any harm.

The area between the shuttle's common room and its cockpit was divided into eight small rooms, four on each side of the corridor. As Ara explained it, those were the bunkrooms for the ship's crew.

"This class of shuttle can accommodate up to sixteen people," she said. "As you may have noticed, we're flying extremely light here."

They moved past those rooms and into the cockpit itself, somewhat larger than Jax had expected. A short aisle ran down the middle, with four rows of two chairs each on either side. Each chair was padded for comfort, dark blue leather stretching over a bare metal frame.

A final solitary chair sat at the front of the room, with a control console wrapping around it on the front, left, and right sides. The sculpted slab of metal was covered in such a mess of buttons, screens, levers, and dials that Jax had no idea where he should look first. It was no wonder Billy had taken so long to figure it out.

Their pilot sat in his chair, his back to the others as he faced the ship's front windshield head-on. The clear glass screen wrapped around the entire cockpit, beginning halfway up the wall and ending at the roof of the ship.

As Jax lifted his eyes to take in the view, he was struck just as much by what he didn't see as what he did. It was all so empty. There was no planet Earth lazily rotating before them, there were no other spaceships, just unobstructed open space and the stars that populated its vastness.

"Okay," Billy said. "Looks like we're far enough out of Earth's gravity. Everyone ready?"

"You may want to sit down for this part," Tom advised

Jax.

Jax shrugged and plopped himself down into the nearest chair. Tom and Ara each chose a seat as well. All three had strapped themselves in before Tom gave a simple, "Ready" in response to Billy's question.

Billy pushed a lever forward, and, all at once, the starscape beyond the windows blurred. The distant glowing stars turned to streaks as they leaped toward the shuttle at an alarming pace. Jax thought they might hit the ship, but no impact came. Utterly confused, he blinked rapidly to clear his vision, but nothing changed.

Tom and Ara chuckled, clearly amused by his reaction.

"Calm down," Ara told him. "It's all right."

"What's all right?" asked Jax. "What's going on here?"

"Lightspeed travel," Tom explained. "It's not as glamorous as the old sci-fi flicks made it out to be, but it gets the job done."

"But … how?" Jax could still barely believe his eyes.

"It's just what it sounds like," Tom said. "The ship moves at the speed of light, meaning we can cover the distances between planets in hours or days now instead of months. We're locked into a localized stasis field so the velocity doesn't rip us apart, and the navigation system's running pretty fast itself so we avoid any interstellar objects or gravitational masses. Crashing at this speed would be a disaster, but don't worry, the risk is minimal."

Jax couldn't help but be skeptical. "How can you know that?"

Tom shrugged. "Well, no one's died in a long time, anyway."

*

The shuttle's voyage had been underway for roughly seven hours. After the initial shock and awe from his first taste of lightspeed had worn off, Jax had retreated back into his sullen persona. With nothing left to do, and no more arguments left to be had for the moment, the fatigue of his recent misadventures had caught up with him all at once. It had been more than twenty-four hours since Jax had had an opportunity to change his clothes or clean himself. Although he remained adamant in his desire to have as little to do with the others aboard as possible, he chose to take advantage of the downtime and avail himself of their various facilities. It was like Ara had said: he should keep at least some of his dignity if he was going to meet with the leader of the 4S.

Billy, Ara, and Tom had proven to be accommodating and gracious hosts. They had set him up in one of the unoccupied bunkrooms, where he had spent the first few hours of their journey sitting alone and stewing. When he had emerged, they hadn't held back in sharing the plentiful rations they kept stored in the back of the shuttle. They had even let him take a shower, though the only extra clothing they had had on hand was a spare 4S unitard. From the moment he had shrugged his way into the dull orange jumpsuit with blue sleeves and pant legs, he had been fighting an internal battle not to see it as an omen.

Jax sat upright on the mattress as a chime from the door announced the arrival of a visitor. He spun towards the sound, sliding off the edge of the bed so he could be on his feet when the other came in.

Jax shook all the dark thoughts from his head in time to watch the door slide open. Tom stepped inside, though Jax saw Ara outside in the hall.

"I hope I'm not interrupting anything?" asked Tom, in a commendable attempt at politeness.

"You're not," answered Jax.

Tom acknowledged him with a nod.

"We're getting close to our destination," he stated. "In about fifteen minutes, we'll stop running at lightspeed and enter the sector of space where *Home Base* is. We're going to have to keep a bit of a distance when we revert to realspeed to prevent any accidents, but once we make our way over to the cruiser the docking process won't take long."

"Great," Jax muttered.

"We just came to tell you in case you felt like joining us in the cockpit," Ara called from her place in the corridor. "No one ever forgets their first glimpse of the *Home Base*."

Jax sniffed. "Might as well."

Tom stepped back to give Jax room to pass through the door. Before doing so, Jax grabbed his backpack from where he had left it at the foot of the bed, wanting to keep it on hand in case the situation went south. It might have been a futile gesture, given that there was nowhere else for him to go except out into space itself, but it comforted him to have something from his parents to hold on to.

Because Jax had taken one of the bunkrooms closer to the rear of the shuttle, the three of them had some walking to do before they arrived at the cockpit. When they reached it, Tom and Ara sat down near the front while Jax remained in the doorframe, leaning against the wall on one side as he watched the stars zipping by.

"How's it looking, Billy?" asked Ara.

"We're on schedule," Billy said. "Six minutes to breakout, and at the exit point I've calculated we'll be docked with *Home Base* in about half an hour more."

Jax crossed his arms over his chest as he watched the exchange. He could ask himself whether he had made the right choice—indeed, he had spent several of the last few hours doing exactly that—but that question was no longer relevant. He had cast his lot with the 4S, and the next move was theirs to make. Any musings on what that move might be would only lead him in circles.

The lack of certainty chafed, an itch that Jax could identify but not scratch.

"One minute to breakout!" Billy called.

Jax took a seat near the front of the cockpit. He wanted to get a good look at this *Home Base* of theirs, inexplicably curious as to whether Ara's sentiments had been true.

The floor of the ship shuddered briefly beneath his feet as the shuttle reverted to a normal speed. Beyond the windshield, the blurred view of the starfield snapped back into focus all at once, each individual point of light now maintaining a fixed position around them.

Jax searched among the myriad stars for any sign of a massive space cruiser but found none. Then his gaze settled on a particular glowing dot, indistinguishable from the millions of identical dots around it except for … was it blinking?

Seeing Jax's confusion, Ara pointed at the offending light.

"Yep," she said, "that's it."

When Jax gave no reply, Tom offered further clarification.

"It stays lit up so we can always find it in the dark of space. Once Billy locks onto its homing beacon, we'll be over there before you know it."

"Already done," Billy said. "I'm moving us in."

Tom grinned at Jax. "See? Before you know it."

The thousands of stars around them moved and shifted, more languidly than before. The shuttle cruised at a good pace, crossing countless miles of space in mere minutes, but lightspeed was no longer necessary. Jax fixed his eyes on the single blinking dot, looming larger and larger by the minute.

Soon the cruiser came into view. Jax had known what to expect, but the sheer size of it still astounded him. The shape of the *Home Base* resembled that of the space shuttles of the early twenty-first century, but massively scaled up to accommodate all the necessities of an international federation of space explorers. Its fuselage was flat on the bottom but rounded on top, tapering to a cone in the front and housing no less than ten hulking engine nacelles in the rear. Above those engines loomed a blunted triangular fin atop the cruiser, which Jax knew housed the offices of the 4S's administrative staff. Two triangular wings extended from either side near the back, providing additional room for 4S activities. The entire cruiser was painted in blue on the bottom and orange on the top, bisected by a thin line of gray.

Jax whistled in appreciation before he fully realized he was doing it. Thankfully, none of the others called attention to it, and even Jax quickly put it out of his mind. Emotion was all well and good, but he needed his mind to stay in the present then more than ever.

Billy pulled up just short of reaching the cruiser, bringing their ship to a full stop while they were still a few miles out.

"Okay," Jax asked, "what now?"

"I'll just call them," Billy answered. He flipped a switch on the control board, bringing the diode above it to life, displaying a warm blue light with an accompanying beep. Billy leaned down to talk into a miniature speaker, signaling to some person or persons on board the other craft.

"This is Shuttle RT-587 to 4S Hangar Control. We've just returned from a mission, and we request clearance to dock with *Home Base*."

Static issued from the ship's comm for several seconds before a deep male voice came through.

"Shuttle RT-587, this is Hangar Control. Please transmit your clearance codes."

"Copy that, Control. Sending codes now." Billy fiddled with a data screen to the right of the comm and tapped a button beneath it.

At last, the voice of the Hangar Control worker rang through the cockpit again.

"Shuttle RT-587, you are cleared for landing in Docking Bay 94. Follow the approach vector outlined on your screen and do not deviate from the prescribed course."

Billy deftly manipulated the various buttons and screens all across his control panel.

"Vector is received and locked into our system," he confirmed. "Shuttle RT-587 is commencing its approach."

The ship accelerated slowly, rotating ninety degrees to orient itself with the cruiser. Billy maneuvered them along the length of the immense vessel until they hovered about a quarter of the way back from its front. Slowly and carefully, Billy lowered the shuttle down toward the bottom of the cruiser until Jax was almost certain they were going to pass under the cruiser and come back up on the other side. Only then did Billy turn the nose of the shuttle toward the *Home Base* for the docking to begin.

As the small shuttle closed the distance to its mothership, Jax was treated to an up-close-and-personal look at the hull of the 4S' mobile headquarters. The nearer they got to their assigned hangar, the more narrow the view became. Soon,

Jax could make out the open hatch that would admit them, and the empty space beyond in which their ship would rest. Not long after that, they were inside, the starscape replaced by blue-paneled walls washed in sterile white light.

The shuttle touched down on the hangar floor with remarkable grace and delicacy, so much that Jax barely felt it happen. Half a minute later, the bay door slid closed somewhere behind them with a dull clang.

All of Jax's nerves were suddenly alight with tension. He knew what that sound meant. The trip was over; it was time to get down to business.

This is it. No backing out now.

CHAPTER SIX

4S SHUTTLE RT-587—DOCKING BAY 94—4S COMMAND CRUISER *HOME BASE*

Jax moved to get up, then sat quickly back down again at the shake of Tom's head.

"Not so fast, pal," the technician warned. "See, when they opened that door to let us in, all the oxygen in the hangar got sucked out into space. Now that they've closed us inside, we have to wait for them to pump more in. Otherwise, we wouldn't be able to breathe once we stepped off the shuttle, which would just be embarrassing for everyone."

Jax shrugged, leaning back in his seat to make himself that much more comfortable. If nothing else, he could at least get behind the idea of not dying. The 4S had waited this long for him, hadn't they? They could stand to wait a little longer.

They sat in silence until the controller's voice rang through their cockpit once again. "Shuttle RT-587, your hangar's atmosphere has reached equilibrium. Your crew may now safely exit the craft."

"Copy that, Control. Over and out." Billy flipped the comm switch into the down position, severing the transmission, and the blue light above it faded out. Billy turned to the others, a smile spreading across his face.

"Well, we're here. Let's not keep 'em waiting."

With Jax already having his backpack on his person, and the 4S agents apparently having no personal luggage to speak of, it didn't take long for all four to disembark via the boarding ramp behind the cockpit.

As Jax had observed upon their entry, the hangar bay around them was as empty as could be. Blue-walled and windowless, it had obviously been designed for function over visual appeal.

Their shuttle sat in the center of the room, ringed by a circle of orange lights. It was the first time Jax had seen it from the outside, and despite the obvious difference in scale, he noted its resemblance in shape and color to the main 4S cruiser. Uniformity and simplicity in design seemed to be the virtues the organization emphasized. Really, it wasn't all that surprising. Flashy decor was unlikely to do much good for a person stranded between solar systems.

Ara, Tom, and Billy headed toward the back of the room, and Jax followed, not wanting to get left behind. There, set into the rear wall, they found a door leading into parts unknown. The door had a small inset window, but the space beyond was dark, denying Jax even the faintest glimpse of what he was in for.

When Ara touched a button on the wall-mounted keypad, the door slid open with a faint scraping of metal on metal. Jax would have thought nothing of it had the noise not persisted after the door was fully ajar.

He spun around to see the circle of flooring on which their shuttle rested sink into itself, the ship disappearing into a lower level of the titanic cruiser. He watched it go, mesmerized despite himself.

Tom—of course it was Tom—caught him staring and came to stand beside him.

"I hope you didn't get too attached," he said. "You might never see that particular shuttle again."

Jax could only stare back bemusedly.

Tom elaborated. "It's standard procedure. After every voyage, the ship goes in for some routine maintenance and servicing. Since I work down in the repair bays, I might get the chance to work with it again. Next time you go into space, though, you'll probably have an entirely different ship."

Jax sniffed and moved away towards the exit. It wouldn't do, he decided, to be showing too much interest in the 4S. After all, he still didn't know why they had brought him here. They did good work, he'd admit, but that good work didn't usually involve abducting unsuspecting mourners from a crime scene.

Ara and Billy had already walked through the door. Jax and Tom caught up with them, stepping into the next room.

Whatever Jax had been expecting to find there, another empty space wasn't it. The adjoining room was much smaller than the hangar bay, but it had been decorated just as minimally, with the same blue walls and the same lack of windows.

Almost before he had taken in his new surroundings, the door behind him closed with a hiss and a clunk. He whirled around, not liking where this was going. He looked frantically for a way to reopen the door, at least so he could know it was possible, but found no control panel anywhere on the wall. The door on the far wall had no keypad either.

Jax tapped his foot against the floor as his eyes darted back and forth. There had to be some way out.

Ara glanced over and picked up on his obvious discomfort.

"Calm down," she told him. "We haven't been locked in—at least, not forever. It's required for all returning agents to spend some time in a sterilization chamber before reentering the *Home Base*."

Jax relaxed at that, but not completely. His parents had had one of these chambers in their lab, and that one hadn't hurt him. This setback might have been harmless, but it was still infuriating.

At last, the door across the room slid open, and the party continued on.

The next room they walked into was smaller than either of the others had been. Jax didn't like that at all. As they had traveled farther into the *Home Base*, he had begun to feel more and more like he was being boxed in. Nothing expressly bad had happened to him yet, but he couldn't help imagining the weight of all the millions of tons of metal pressing down on him.

The third room had no extra doors. Jax was beginning to think that it was just his luck that they had ended up at a dead end when he noticed the rail that ran from a tunnel in one wall to another in the opposite wall, disappearing into darkness at both ends. They stood on a platform about two feet above that rail. Despite the size of the room, it was large enough to accommodate their small group comfortably, and a console with a small screen and a big orange button served as its only decorative feature.

Ara walked briskly over to the console and pressed the button. The screen blinked to life, displaying two words: *Stop Requested.*

For the first five minutes, nothing else happened. Then Jax saw a light at the end of the tunnel, growing brighter and stronger as it crept toward the platform. At last, a sleek, orange tramcar emerged into their small antechamber, pulling three more behind it.

The tram had no driver, no visible means of control, yet it came to a smooth stop in front of them. Ara, Billy, and Tom took seats in the second car, and Jax opted to join them there, not wanting to be left behind. Once each of them had clipped the two ends of their seat belt together, the tram started off again.

Their journey took them past at least ten more platforms, all unoccupied, before Jax lost count. They only made one other stop, where they collected two women who took seats at the very back of the last car. For as much time as they spent passing barren platforms, though, they spent an equal amount traveling through pitch-black tunnels. When at last they came to a halt at the end of the trip, Jax's eyes threatened to water from the constant transitions between dark and light. He took a second to compose himself, not wanting anyone to get the wrong idea, then gazed around to see where they had ended up.

Their tram had parked itself in the middle of a vast open space, one even wider and deeper than the hangar bay, though it boasted the same blue walls and ambient lighting.

Glancing behind him, Jax could see the tunnel from which they had come. At the mouth of that tunnel, the single rail split into eight, each separate track stretching all the way to the back of the room, where they came to a stop shortly before the rear wall. Each was divided from the next by a platform, and each platform had an elevator where it met the wall. At that moment, there were trams parked on six of the eight tracks in the room.

In the time it took for Jax to observe all that, the others had already disembarked. They now stood waiting for him not far away. Shaking his head to clear it, Jax unbuckled his seat belt and strode over to them.

"Well, Jax?" Tom asked. "Ready for your first taste of the 4S?"

"Does it matter?" Jax shot back. "You've already told me I have nowhere else to go."

Tom put his hands on his hips, unsure at first what to make of such a rejoinder. At last he chuckled lightly, clapping a hand on Jax's shoulder. "No, I guess it really doesn't."

Jax pulled away almost as soon as Tom touched him. "Cut the crap. Just get this show on the road already."

"Okay," said Tom, now mildly exasperated. "No need to get snippy."

He walked up to the elevators and pressed the button that opened the one on the left. He stepped inside, beckoning the others to follow with a sweep of his hand.

"Right this way, then."

*

The terminal had been an oasis of calm, but the room one floor above it was a bustling hub of organized chaos.

It seemed to Jax that the room they found themselves in must have taken up at least a quarter of this level. One entire wall was devoted to a massive screen displaying various listings of times, dates, and names. A long row of desks stood below, with an attendant stationed every ten feet. Tables and benches filled the remaining floor space, and several dozens of 4S agents milled about, attending to various tasks.

"This is Beta Hub," Ara said. "*Home Base* has two of these, one at the front and one at the back. The Hubs are where 4S agents assemble before missions, and where they reconvene afterwards."

Jax grunted. "That's great and all, but what do we

actually do now? Where do we go from here?"

Ara hesitated. "I'm not sure. Admiral Prang said he'd have a contact here to meet us, but he didn't tell us how we'd identify them."

As they waited, trying to figure out just what they were supposed to do, a man appeared from the crowd and strode over to them. He was dressed in the 4S uniform like everyone else in the Hub, with light brown skin and dark brown shoulder-length hair. He grinned as he approached them, his green eyes bright and cheerful.

Billy, Ara, and Tom stood at attention and saluted him.

"Captain Ramón," Ara greeted him. "Hello, sir."

"Hello yourselves, Ensigns," the captain replied. His eyes fell on Jax. "And would this be the young Mr. Nurmen?"

"I would hope so," said Tom.

Jax couldn't determine what he felt more strongly just then: appreciation that he wouldn't have to interact directly with this unfamiliar 4S officer, or resentment that Tom had taken away his chance to speak for himself.

"We performed three separate DNA tests, and they all told us that's who this guy is," continued Tom.

Jax shuddered. The idea that these 4S agents had taken genetic material from him while he had been lying unconscious rubbed him the wrong way. What other lines might they have crossed?

Ramón, meanwhile, kept grinning obnoxiously.

"Perfect," he said. "No problems getting here?"

"Before or after the people you actually wanted were killed?" Jax bit out.

Ramón didn't answer for a moment.

"Point taken," he said at last. "But there are more important people than me waiting to hear about it. Admiral Prang is anxious to meet you, Jax. Come along now."

The captain led them back into the elevator they had rode up in. Once the doors had closed, he pressed the button marked *Admiral's Office.*

As the party rode in silence, Jax did his best to look at anything except his companions. He knew they must be watching him intently, but he wasn't about to indulge their curiosity. When the elevator came to a stop and the doors opened with a soft chime, Captain Ramón stepped out first; the others followed. Jax went last.

They entered another waiting room, albeit a significantly smaller one. Several seats laid out before them, and the walls to each side had a pair of double doors set into them. Each set of doors had a nameplate affixed to the wall next to them. The one on the left read *Alpheus Prang, Admiral*, the one on the right read *John Pitt, Vice Admiral.*

Directly across from their group, a young man stood behind a blue metal desk, working away at a control panel laid out before him. The receptionist looked up, eyes roving across the small group as they approached. When he noticed Jax, he squinted for a few seconds, as though he could sense something was off, but then he gave a miniscule shrug and moved on.

Jax wondered for a moment why he wouldn't seem more out of place to this stranger, until he looked down and remembered he was wearing a 4S uniform. The implication that he had been reduced to nothing more than a nameless grunt among thousands chafed him, but he forced himself to let it go.

The young man's gaze lingered on Ramón longer than it did on Jax. As he registered the captain's identity, he straightened to attention and saluted.

"Good evening, sir."

"At ease." Ramón waved his hand, and the receptionist complied.

"We're here to see the admiral," Ramón continued. "I believe we're expected?"

"I'll have to check that, sir."

"Of course," the captain told him warmly. "No problem at all."

The man behind the desk tapped a few commands into his computer. "You're on the list. He'll see you immediately."

"Then we'd better not keep him waiting," said Ramón.

The receptionist pressed another button, and the doors on the left wall opened with a buzz. Ramón led his charges through, sparing a nod of gratitude for the receptionist.

Beyond the doors, the group was met with a large, brightly lit room, with two of the walls lined with shelves stocked with various odds and ends: paper books, small metallic statuettes, potted plants, and the like. The third wall, the one opposite the doors, was entirely taken up by a floor-to-ceiling window looking out over the vacuum of space.

A grand wooden desk sat in the center of the room, surrounded by an assortment of chairs, and two men sat at the desk. The one closer to the new arrivals looked to be in his late forties, with dark skin and close-cropped black hair. He carried himself with a commanding air.

The other man, seated on the other side of the desk in the fanciest chair, was even more distinguished. His pale skin had begun to wrinkle with age, his face framed by an impeccably groomed mane of silver hair, but his eyes burned bright with youthful vigor. He wore a variant of the common 4S uniform fitted with blue-tasseled epaulets over the shoulders.

All the 4S agents in Jax's group stiffened when they saw the two men and collectively raised their arms in salute.

Ramón spoke to the older man first.

"Admiral Prang." Then he turned his eyes on the other. "Vice Admiral Pitt. Allow me to present the mission personnel of Operation Homeward Bound"—he indicated Ara, Billy, and Tom—"and their last remaining passenger." He gestured to Jax.

"Welcome, my friends," Admiral Prang said warmly. "There's no need to stand on formalities. Come, sit, and tell me everything about your mission."

Everyone gratefully sat, except for Jax. He cast a disapproving eye around the room before settling into a chair, trying not to appear too complacent. He wanted to be ready to move at any moment.

If Prang took any offense at Jax's disdain, it didn't show on his features. He simply studied Jax with an entirely neutral expression until he spoke again.

"You must be Jax Nurmen."

Really? Jax thought. *What gave it away?* He was, after all, the only person in the room who Prang wouldn't have known beforehand. Miraculously, he kept himself from airing any of his sarcasm.

All he said was, "Yes. Jax Nurmen. That's me."

"Wonderful," said Prang. "I suppose you're wondering why I wanted you here."

"Wow. How'd you guess?" Jax replied dryly.

Once again, Prang took no umbrage. He actually smiled, somehow amused by Jax's obtuseness.

"It might interest you to know," he said, "that your parents were working on a project for me even before you were born."

There it was: the confirmation. Hearing it from the lips of people his own age had been one thing, but hearing it from the renowned leader of this international space force was another.

His parents had been working for the 4S. His life had been a lie.

Jax glanced over at Billy, Tom, and Ara beside him, making every effort to keep his expression neutral.

"That's what they told me," he said. "But what does it have to do with me? I wasn't in on it, and they died before they could tell me what it was."

"A terrible tragedy indeed," Prang agreed. He glanced down at his feet, seeming to compose himself, then looked up once more.

"It pained them to keep you in the dark, you know. They always wanted to be able to share their secrets. If they hadn't died so abruptly, they would have done so, too.

And that brings us to my next point. This is the reason that I brought you here. I know it will likely hurt to relive the memories, but I need to know everything you can tell me about the night your parents were murdered."

Jax couldn't speak. He didn't want to speak. Explaining

what had happened would put him right back in the midst of it all over again. He had thought he had started to work through his grief, but he knew then that all he had really done was push it aside to focus on the other issues at hand. Now, Prang's words about his parents had brought it all surging back.

Then, somehow, his mouth opened without him consciously willing it, and then he was spouting off words, unable to stop himself once he had started.

"I can't tell you much. It was the middle of the night, and all of a sudden my dad burst into my room and told me we had to leave. We all went through this secret tunnel that led out into the woods, and they took me to this secret bunker thing they had hidden inside a cliff. I think they thought there was some kind of getaway vehicle inside, but it was destroyed by the time we got there. We tried to escape on foot, but they … they didn't make it."

"And you stayed together the whole time?" the admiral asked. "Curious that the killers should take their lives but spare yours."

"Okay, not the whole time," Jax amended. "Just right up til the end. They sent me ahead of them. I guess they were trying to protect me. But I wanted to see what would happen, so I snuck back around to watch. Then a bunch of people came out of nowhere and—" He couldn't bring himself to finish the thought.

"A bunch of people?" said Prang. "How many? Can you describe them?"

"Probably fifteen or so," said Jax. "I didn't get a good look, but it probably wouldn't have helped much more if I could. They were dressed all in black, head to toe, and they all had their faces covered. It looked like they were having some kind of conversation with my parents, but I couldn't make it out. Obviously, it didn't end too well."

"Obviously," Prang said dolefully. "What did these attackers do afterwards?"

"They just left," said Jax. "They walked off, and I never saw them again."

"Intriguing." That was all Prang could say. "And you're absolutely certain there's nothing more you can tell us? Any information at all could go a long way toward helping us solve this dreadful crime."

"That's all I know," said Jax. "These murderers came out of nowhere and went right back when their job was done. They did a pretty good job covering their tracks and sneaking around. Good luck finding them," he finished, somewhat derisively. It wasn't as though they had much to go on.

"I daresay we'll need it," said Prang. "Thank you for the information, Jax. You've done us a valuable service."

"Great," said Jax, not meaning it at all. "But now what am I supposed to do? I don't belong here, so where do I go?"

"About that," Prang began. "The 4S—"

Vice Admiral Pitt swiveled in his seat to face Prang. "Admiral, if I may?"

"Certainly," Prang told him. "Speak your mind."

"Perhaps it would be wisest to not overburden them," Pitt rumbled in his deep baritone. He pointed to a clock on one of the shelves. It displayed the time *2230*. "After all, they've just returned from a long voyage, and there is nothing more to be said that cannot be saved for a later date."

Prang's eyes narrowed in thought, and his mouth compressed to a thin line.

"Er … quite right," he finally conceded. He turned back to his audience. "I'm terribly sorry, but the Vice Admiral is right. It really is quite late, and I'm sure you must be tired."

Jax could see right through the flimsy excuse. If it had been so important for Prang to speak to him, why couldn't the admiral make time for that encounter? What was he trying to hide?

At the same time, however, the adrenaline Jax had been running on recently had finally started to fade. He wanted nothing more than to curl up and sleep for days.

Prang rose from his chair. "Captain Ramón, if you would please lead them to the dormitory? See that our young friend Jax finds himself a room, if you would."

Ramón stood. "Right away, sir."

"Ensigns, Jax, go with him," Prang went on. "We will speak again when the time comes, but for now, there are demands on both your schedules and mine. Rest up, and carry on your duties as normal tomorrow."

"Yes, sir," the three ensigns said as one, crestfallen but accepting.

Jax, however, wasn't about to let himself be tossed out so quickly. He had barely begun to get what he had come for. He raised a hand in objection. "Hold on. What about me? I don't have any duties. Do you expect me to just sit around?"

"Fear not," Prang assured him, "I have taken your situation into account. You'll be able to get into all the facilities aboard our *Home Base*—those not reserved for officers, that is. Your fellows here will be able to show you everything there is available. You won't have to worry about being bored."

His words did little to reassure Jax, since boredom had never been his issue in the first place. But despite Prang's passive appearance, Jax could still somehow sense that the admiral wouldn't be telling him anything more just then.

"I guess I should say thank you, then," he said.

"It was the least I could do," Prang said. "I owe it to your parents' memories to help you in whatever ways I can."

And who says I need help? Jax thought. But Prang had already proven he would be dispensing no more answers that night.

Jax dipped his head in acquiescence. Prang smiled at him in response and turned to Ramón.

"At your convenience, Captain," he declared. "They're all yours."

Ramón led the way from the room. Tom followed, laying a hand on Jax's shoulder to steer him after Billy and Ara. Jax looked back as they walked to see Prang and Pitt watching him. Pitt's eyes were dark, while Prang's remained as placid as ever. Neither moved or spoke; they simply stared after the departing group.

Then the doors slid closed between them, and Jax's next adventure began.

*

  Admiral Alpheus Prang settled himself once more into the high-backed leather chair behind his mahogany desk. From across the room, the eyes of Vice Admiral Pitt tracked his movements in stony silence.

  "Well?" Prang asked. "You clearly have something to say. Out with it."

  Pitt restrained himself for several moments before his retort burst out of him.

  "You can't possibly still want to go ahead with this! How can you be sure it'll end even remotely well for us?"

  Prang sighed deeply, steepling his hands on the desktop in front of him. "Surety is a luxury in this economy of ours, Pitt. Making a decision and knowing its outcome are almost mutually exclusive."

  "That's hardly reassuring," Pitt retorted. "It's a bad business either way. Your passion project—"

  "The project was in place long before I rose to lead it, if you recall," said Prang. "I expanded upon it, but it's hardly mine alone."

  "Your passion project," Pitt continued slowly and deliberately, "is hemorrhaging personnel. Two outposts have been eradicated by now, and we have no idea how much data is in the wind. Surely you cannot still be thinking of going ahead with your crazy scheme!"

  "What better time would there be?" replied Prang. "The mystery remains unsolved. The loss of the Nurmens is unspeakably tragic, and my 'crazy scheme' has certainly become more complicated for it, but the problem needs to be addressed while any catastrophe can still be mitigated."

  "And yet you would fill the void with an unreliable civilian? He may be the Nurmens' son, but he has no ties to the 4S. His appointment would be conspicuous, and we don't even know that he won't reject it outright before that issue arises."

  "I have full confidence in Jax Nurmen," Prang confirmed. "He may yet prove to be an invaluable asset."

  "The boy is impetuous," Pitt protested. "He allows his

mind to constantly vacillate between trust and mistrust because he lacks a firm grip on his emotions. Your secrecy is just as likely to turn him against our cause as it is to convert him."

"I disagree," said Prang. "I strongly doubt there's any love lost between him and the other side. He'll see this through for closure, even if his loyalty is never fully realized."

"Is this what we've sunk to?" Pitt's tone was beginning to waver, his emotions welling behind a facade of professionalism. "Emotional manipulation? Blackmail?"

"Be fair," Prang cautioned. "Trust in his conviction. This will be the purpose he desperately desires."

Pitt straightened to his full height, curling his hands into fists. He raised one trembling arm and leveled a finger at Prang. "Admiral, with all due respect, I can't help you if you refuse to see that this requires so much more than just blind faith!"

Throughout the entire exchange, Prang never once raised his voice or showed any signs of anger. Even after Pitt's insubordinate outburst, he remained unmoved.

"There is a wide gulf between blind faith and jumping at shadows," he said. "If we had it your way, we would eat ourselves alive before our enemies could get us."

At that, Pitt seemed to deflate. His rigid stance dissolved so quickly that Prang feared he might actually fall to the floor. His accusatory finger retreated to the shelter of his side, like a snake darting back into its hole.

"Apologies, Admiral. I spoke out of turn. Please forgive my lack of discretion."

"You have nothing to apologize for, Vice Admiral," Prang said. "Your dissent can be very instructive. You aren't wrong that I'm frequently in danger of losing myself in my own idealism."

"Then you must see how disastrous this plan could be," Pitt ventured. "You're patching the holes in the project, but you have no way of knowing if it will be enough to keep it afloat."

"That may be," Prang said. "Still, we must keep trying. If not us, then who?"

"I suppose you have a point," grumbled Pitt. "But I

would still hesitate to—"

Prang raised a hand to silence his second-in-command. "I have considered all the angles, and I have determined that this is the best choice. Your opinions have been noted, and I will do my best to take them into account. For now, though, this discussion is closed."

Pitt seethed for a moment, a look of barely contained anger flitting across his face. Then, just as suddenly, the strained expression was gone, and the vice admiral stood up straight again, filled with renewed purpose.

"With your permission, sir, I'd like to personally oversee the efforts to integrate Jax Nurmen into our organization."

"That would be a great help," said Prang. "Please see to it at once."

Pitt offered a formal salute and turned his back on his superior as he walked away.

When he was nearly at the door, he suddenly stopped and whirled around, affixing Prang with one of his famous stern glances. "Admiral, you know I respect you more than any other man alive. But I want you to know that I won't let that loyalty keep me from doing my job. If I'm ever unsure of your judgment, I will call you out on it."

A heavy silence hung between them. Then Prang smiled a thin smile, and all was forgotten.

"I would have it no other way, my friend."

CHAPTER SEVEN

COMMISSARY—4S *HOME BASE*—DEEP SPACE

Jax stirred a liberal amount of seasoning into his Instant-Meal stew in an effort to add some real flavor to the bitter sludge. The red powder sank into the broth, vanishing among the meat and beans. Once he thought it had permeated every inch of the bowl, Jax raised a bite to his lips. After testing its temperature with his tongue, he gulped it down before even giving himself a chance to see if his flavoring efforts had borne fruit.

Only when his stomach let loose an ungrateful gurgle did he realize that the table around him had fallen completely silent.

Jax glanced up, fully expecting to find Ara, Billy, and Tom staring at him, or perhaps sharing a smile at his expense. To his surprise and relief, their attention was focused somewhere else entirely. All three had turned to face the nearest doorway, where Captain Ramón had just entered the room, heading for them.

Jax almost did a double take. He hadn't seen the captain since he had first arrived on the *Home Base*, almost a full three weeks ago.

That couldn't mean anything especially good. From what Jax had been able to pick up on, senior officers didn't take time out of their schedules to fraternize with low-level recruits.

Any professional communications were handled electronically. Whatever had drawn Ramón to them that day was more than likely both important and unusual.

Could it be something to do with Jax's continued presence among the 4S? Despite his promises, Admiral Prang had sent no further messages regarding Jax's role in his plans, and he had grown more and more suspicious with each passing day. The way Jax saw it, Prang had no excuse for not reaching out sooner.

Jax shook the thoughts out of his head for the moment. There was a more immediate conversation to be had.

When Ramón reached their table, Ara, Billy, and Tom stood to offer him a crisp salute. Jax rose from his seat but made no further movements.

The captain greeted them with a polite nod. "Ensigns Kendall, Vurk, Ubert. Jax Nurmen. Good afternoon to you all."

"Good afternoon, sir," the three ensigns chorused.

Jax remained warily silent.

"Please, let's sit," Ramón said.

As the others sank back into their chairs, he claimed the one remaining seat. This placed him directly across the table from Jax. Jax locked eyes with the captain for several drawn-out seconds. Neither moved or spoke, and their expressions remained neutral throughout. All the same, Jax was glad when Ramón broke eye contact to look around the table and confirm that everyone had made themselves comfortable and ready for his news.

"Now, then," he began, "how are the four of you getting on?"

"We're doing well enough, sir," Ara said. "Honestly, we're all a bit restless, especially Jax, but that's to be expected, isn't it?"

Ramón chuckled lightly.

"Indeed it is," he assured her. "In that case, I come bearing good news." He paused to throw a conspiratorial glance around them, leaning closer even though no one else was in earshot. "The four of you—yes, even you, Jax—are to report to Briefing Room 201 at exactly fifteen hundred hours for a rundown of your next assignment. Am I clear?"

Ara, Billy, and Tom dipped their heads in assent. Jax, still not trusting Ramón entirely, neither moved nor spoke.

"Very well. Carry on, then." Ramón started to rise from his seat.

A look of confusion crossed Billy's face. "Why would you tell us like this? Why not send the message by holopad as usual?"

"A good question." Ramón said, resettling himself in his chair, "though one I unfortunately cannot answer. But I'm sure the Admiral and his staff have their reasons. All the rest of us can do is walk the paths we've been set upon. I have no doubts that your briefing will make it all abundantly clear."

He pushed back his chair and stood, casting a glance at his watch. "And in the meantime, there is much to be done. Until the meeting, my young friends."

Then he melted into the bustle of the crowded room. When two minutes had elapsed without his return, Billy was the first to break the silence.

"Well, that was ... weird," he finished lamely.

"You said it," agreed Jax. "I haven't been here nearly as long as you all, but I've seen enough to know that wasn't how it's usually done."

"This is more stringent secrecy than I've ever heard of from the 4S," Tom said. "We can usually afford to be upfront about all our activities. I don't want to think about what it means if we suddenly can't."

"Well," said Billy, "if they want this off the books so badly, it's got to be something really sensitive. Maybe some kind of secret project that Prang just hasn't revealed yet."

"It might be," cut in Ara. "But there's only one way to find out. We just have to go to this briefing, and sooner or later, we'll know everything."

*

Against his better judgment, Jax wholeheartedly looked

forward to the upcoming mission briefing. Admiral Prang had been extremely cagey during their initial meeting, speaking few words and conveniently finding himself unable to elaborate on his plans for Jax. As the weeks since that night had begun to pile up, Jax had woken every morning with constantly decreasing hope that that day would be the one where Prang called him back for a follow-up.

Nevertheless, Prang had kept his word on one thing, and had granted Jax unhindered access to all public areas aboard the 4S *Home Base*. Before his first full day aboard was up, Captain Ramón had delivered Jax a key card that provided as much. He had been told that, given his lack of training and his place outside the 4S command structure, it was the best they could do for the moment.

Jax had tried to ask what *for the moment* meant, but Ramón had hurried off, spouting off a half-cocked excuse and leaving him to fester in the quarters they provided—large enough to not be cramped, only ten feet from end to end. The only amenities were a bed and a desk with a chair, and Jax had only had to spend five minutes in the bland space before he knew it would drive him stir crazy if he didn't get out of there.

The challenge had been figuring out how to fill his time. Days aboard the 4S cruiser were long and regimented. The ship's lighting operated on a diurnal cycle. Between 2300 and 600 hours, the lights all across the huge vessel switched off while its occupants slept. The rest of the day divided into hours-long work shifts with the occasional mealtime or rest break. The system worked well, Jax had to admit, or at least it worked well until someone who had no work to do came along.

Jax ate his meals in the commissary at the appointed hours, and hung out with Ara, Billy, and Tom whenever the three had downtime, but those diversions only lasted so long, and sooner or later he always found himself back on his own. At first, he had been anxious that he would be found out, or perhaps accused of negligence or dereliction. However, he soon discovered that the sheer amount of personnel the 4S kept on staff, coupled with the sheer amount of work there was to be done, didn't leave many people with time to go hunting down strays and stowaways. As soon as Jax had realized he would be safe from prying eyes, all his worries had melted away, and a sense of numbness and resignation had crept in to replace them. That sense had only grown stronger the longer Jax went without hearing from the admiral.

His "fellows" had at least had their various daily tasks to keep them occupied throughout those long four weeks. Tom toiled away for long hours deep in the 4S' repair bays, keeping all their technology functioning. Ara cataloged files in the vast 4S archives, making sure each one was stored so as to be accessible when necessary. Neither of them had complained even once that they felt unmoored or disaffected.

The ensign whose situation was most akin to Jax's was Billy. As he said to Jax one day, it wasn't unusual for a pilot to be without a task for several days or even weeks at a time. The 4S kept more pilots than ships on hand in case of emergencies, so not every member of the Pilots' Corps could be out on a mission at once. Still, Billy did admit that an entire month of being grounded was at least slightly out of the ordinary.

Jax had used their downtime to his advantage, and had enlisted Billy to help him get better acquainted with all the *Home Base* had to offer. Tom and Ara had chipped in where they could, as well. Tom had supplied him with a spare holopad he had obtained from the quartermaster's office, and Ara had shown him how to request files from the archives. Jax wasn't privy to any especially sensitive data, but he was able to fill his time by reading up on the 4S' history and purpose.

If he was going to be spending so much time among them, he told himself, he might as well know what they were all about.

All the while, Jax had known that there was something more for him out there. He had long since grown tired of Admiral Prang stringing him along, tempting him with information but never divulging it. By the time he and the others made their way into their assigned briefing room, he was ready to get the whole ordeal over with.

When he saw that it was Ramón, not Prang, who would be briefing them, his enthusiasm started to wane.

"Right on time," the captain said. "Perfect. Let's begin."

Ara, Billy, Tom, and Jax took seats at the circular table in the middle of the room. The table was strangely beautiful to look at, in an aesthetic sort of way. Blue metal covered most of its exterior; it had a translucent top with some kind of control panel built in.

Ramón remained standing. He cast a glance at the

door, then shrugged and moved over to the table. He positioned himself in front of the keypad, entering a command.

The table's entire surface came to life with a soft blue glow. An image materialized out of thin ai, springing up where there had previously been nothing but empty air. Jax moved his chair back a few inches in surprise before he realized it was only a hologram. The others in the room did him the courtesy of not noticing.

Jax studied the hologram closer. It displayed a space station with a spherical core and an outer shell made up of blue hexagonal plates. Four dark orange pylons extended from it, each one set at a ninety-degree angle with the last, forming the shape of a plus sign. Two more pylons jutted out from the top and bottom. All six were connected by pylons running diagonally between them.

Ara, Tom, and Billy gazed at the image in wonder.

Sensing that he was the only one who had no idea why this space station was so significant, Jax decided to speak up. "What exactly are we looking at here?"

"Voyager Station," Ramón explained. "This is the 4S's premier scientific outpost, where the bulk of our research and development is conducted. It's named that way because it sits at the spot where the Voyager probes are believed to have passed out of this solar system, to represent the promise of new horizons."

At any other time, that would have been inspiring. But Jax didn't care for sentiment. All he wanted was for Ramón to get to the point.

"And how does this concern us?" Jax asked.

"I was getting to that," Ramón said. "Effective yesterday, the four of you have been reassigned to this station. You'll be traveling there today, and you'll be living and working out of there for the next little while."

"Us?" Billy asked. "Really? But only the 4S's major science bigwigs work there."

"Yes and no," Ramón said. "It's true that the station is entirely devoted to experimentation, but they do keep a small staff on hand to deal with day-to-day operations: archivists to organize their data, mechanics to keep their technology in working order, and pilots to … well, to pilot. The bureaucracy must go on."

"And we'll be part of that now?" Tom said.

"Correct," Ramón said. "You'll be leaving on today's supply run. There'll be a few other personnel transferring in with you as well."

"Okay," Ara said, "but why us? Us specifically, I mean. None of us have distinguished ourselves in any way that would get us appointed to such a prestigious place."

"Admiral Prang apparently disagrees," Ramón said. "He told me himself that he was proud of the way you handled the Nurmen mission. Even though the parameters changed on the fly, you all kept a level head and did the best you could with what you had."

His answer appeared to pacify Ara. Her expression became pensive.

Jax, meanwhile, couldn't stay silent.

"All right, then, that's them sorted, but what about me? I'm not a 4S agent. I have no idea why Prang wants me here. He's kept me in the dark for weeks! And now he just expects me to move myself over to this station just because he said so? How does he expect that to work?"

"Because," came a deep voice from the doorway, "we need you, Jax."

They all spun to see the dark figure of Vice Admiral Pitt stepping into the room, each 4S agent offering the customary salute. At the imposing sight, a large part of Jax's insolence rapidly died.

"Oh?" he asked, innocently enough. "Why is that?"

Pitt looked over to Ramón. "How much have you told them, Captain?"

"Not all that much, sir," Ramón said. "I told them where they'll be going, but that's pretty much all Admiral Prang gave me to work with. I thought you'd be here to make the hard sell."

"My apologies," said Pitt. "I was waylaid by a minor

inconvenience on my way down. But you didn't need me to perform your duty, and you've performed it. I'll take it from here, if you don't mind."

"Of course," Ramón said with a sweep of his hand. "Be my guest."

The Vice Admiral nodded curtly and began to pace a slow circle around the table, taking in each of the four young people sitting there. He came to a stop right in front of Jax.

"Admiral Prang is currently searching for personnel to staff an upcoming venture. This is a project that has been in the works for some time, and your parents actually had a hand in the initial stages. Unfortunately, they're gone now, which does leave us with some holes to fill. Your perspective on the night of their deaths has already been invaluable, and the admiral has expressed hope that you would be willing to assist us in a more hands-on role."

Jax opened his mouth to interject, but Pitt wasn't done talking.

"You would not be joining us in any official capacity, unless that becomes your wish. Your task would be to continue helping us identify and track down the group that raided your house. It would involve staying at 4S installations, and traveling with some 4S missions, but you would retain your autonomy. If you choose to leave at any point, Admiral Prang will accommodate you. You would be able to return to Earth and resume a civilian life, and we would never contact you again. We don't want to force you into anything. We want to find closure for all parties involved."

Some part of Jax knew that he should be skeptical. Pitt still held his cards close to his chest. Despite his grandstanding, he still had much to reveal.

At the same time, whether by meticulous planning or just dumb luck, he had found all the right buttons to push to make Jax compliant. The Vice Admiral hooked him the moment he had mentioned his parents. All he had wanted ever since the attack on his home had been to see his parents' killers face justice. Could he really be blamed for latching on to someone who had promised to help him do so?

"Say I agree," he said. "Say I decide to help you out. If I go to this space station, will you finally let me know just what it is I'm supposed to do?"

"All will be revealed in due time," Pitt said.

Jax couldn't tell if he meant the answer as a yes or a no. Either way, he had already made up his mind. Come what may, he would track down the murderers, even if it was the last thing he did.

"All right," he said. "You've convinced me. I'm in."

I'll play along with your charade for now, he added in his head. *I'll indulge you. But I can only tolerate secrecy for so long, so this had better be worth it.*

Vice Admiral Pitt didn't seem to pick up on any of Jax's private thoughts. "Very good," he said. "The admiral will be pleased."

He swiveled on his heels to face Ramón. "You may take them to their shuttle, Captain. The mission leader will know to expect them. She is scheduled to leave in one hour, so you should make it with plenty of time if you don't dawdle."

"Don't worry, sir. They'll be aboard on time," Ramón replied.

"See that they do," Pitt said, and he stalked out of the room.

The captain turned to face the others. "There you have it. Any further questions?"

No one voiced any, and after a few seconds of silence Ramón clapped his hands once. "Right. All that's left is to get you to your ride. Follow me."

He entered a new command into the table's keypad, and the hologram vanished. Ara, Tom, and Billy rose from their seats and headed for the door.

Jax stood too, but he hesitated before following them. Was he really going to go through with this based on nothing but a bunch of vague promises made by strangers? Then, once again, an image of his parents flashed into his mind. He saw them surrounded by masked assailants, he heard the crunch of blunt objects against their skulls, and the desire for vengeance burned white-hot within him.

Jax forced his feet into motion, and the group was on its way.

Ramón led them down to Beta Hub by way of a series of hallways and elevators. After some brief haggling with one of the desk attendants, he had secured them all a spot on one of the trams headed for Docking Bay 183. They stood in the sterilization chamber for the required time and exited into a lively maelstrom of activity.

4S agents filled the hangar. They worked moving containers of supplies from a pile in one corner to a shuttle sitting square in the center. The shuttle's rear hatch lowered to allow people to scurry in and out, depositing their cargo on the shelves and heading back for more.

The person who seemed to be running the show was a woman who stood in the middle of the crowd, waving her arms and barking orders to keep the work moving along. She stood at average height, with tan skin and frizzy red hair. She hadn't yet noticed Ramón or the young people with him, but the captain walked briskly over to her nonetheless, and Jax and the others followed.

As they drew closer, the woman finally noticed them. She broke off from a conversation she was having with a trio of men carrying crates to salute Ramón. When she spoke, it was with a coarse Irish accent.

"Good afternoon, sir. What brings you to this stretch of the *Home Base*?"

"Official business, Lieutenant," Ramón replied. "I'm escorting these fine young folks to join you on your journey."

He turned to face Jax and the ensigns.

"This," said Ramón, "is Lieutenant Macgregor. She's in charge of coordinating this supply run to Voyager Station."

The lieutenant gave Jax and the others a brief once-over. "So these are the last-minute additions old Alphie snuck onto my manifest?"

"Admiral Prang," Ramón replied, stressing the title, "did ask me to express his sincerest apologies for the short notice. Still, when both the Admiral and Chief Research Officer put their signatures on an order, there's not much that we down the chain can do to avoid it."

"Aye," agreed Macgregor. "Weird, that. These buggers must be important. I don't suppose the Admiral told you anything about that?"

"Not a word," Ramón answered dolefully.

Macgregor shrugged. "Oh, well. Orders are orders, just like you said."

"I'm glad we're on the same page," Ramón said. "So you'll take them on?"

"I'll have to put them to work, sir," Macgregor said. "You know how I feel about slackers."

"That won't be an issue," Ramón said. "You should have a full rundown of their capabilities and areas of expertise in your inbox."

"I've seen it," said Macgregor. "A pilot, a technician, an archivist, and a … how did they put it?" She paused while she searched for some unknown word. "A special correspondent."

Special correspondent? Jax wondered what that meant. Had Prang relegated him to some kind of advisory role? What did he expect him to provide? Jax, who knew next to nothing about the 4S, and had already offered up all the information he could regarding his parents' murders?

Macgregor remained unconcerned. "I reckon it won't be too hard to fit 'em into the crew. Should go off without a hitch."

"Wonderful," Ramón said. "Admiral Prang will be pleased. I'll leave you to it, then."

With that, he was off, pulling out his holopad to type something into it as he walked. Lieutenant Macgregor turned to scrutinize her new charges.

"The Admiral clearly believes in you," she said, "so I guess that means I do, too. Just do your best not to disappoint us, all right?"

None of them were sure how to respond.

Finally, Tom spoke up. "Uh … we'll try, ma'am."

That seemed to mollify her.

"Aye," she said. "You do that. I'll be back soon to give you the full rundown." And then she, too, moved away, calling to someone across the hangar to "Be careful with that pallet!"

Jax looked around at his companions, seeing his own questioning reflected in their faces. It occurred to him for the first time that he had never once thought to ask their opinion on any part of their current situation. They had had many lengthy conversations about Jax, and what Prang's designs for him could have been, but none of the others had ever seemed concerned about their futures. Perhaps they hadn't foreseen that their fate would be inextricably linked to Jax's, or perhaps they had. It didn't matter, because it had happened either way.

Jax realized now that their lives had been upended just like his—perhaps not to the same extent, but they, too, were undeniably undergoing a change. Whatever their expectations for their future careers had been, their new appointments hadn't factored into it.

In any case, the four of them were now decidedly all in the same boat. Admiral Prang's machinations had sent them all spiraling down an unexpected new path, and none of them could know what lay at its end. And yet, if they wanted any answers, they had to walk it.

And that was exactly what Jax intended to do. If he had even the slightest chance of uncovering what Prang wanted, he had to seize the opportunity before it was gone.

"Voyager Station, here we come," Jax said, so softly that only he could hear. "Let's just hope you don't turn out to be another total bust."

CHAPTER EIGHT

4S SHUTTLE RT-616—EN ROUTE TO VOYAGER STATION

"Shuttle exiting lightspeed in T-minus two minutes," their pilot intoned over the intercom.

Jax sauntered over to the nearest chair and sank into it. This journey, just like his last aboard a 4S spacecraft, had been as smooth a ride as he could have hoped for. Even so, the deceleration from lightspeed at the end of that first trip had still left his stomach churning mildly for several hours. Perhaps it would become easier with time; Ara, Billy, and Tom had not complained nor seemed affected. For the moment, Jax chose to simply be glad of the extra comfort.

The pilot's voice came again, tinny and crackling as it passed through the speakers. "Return to realspeed in T-minus one minute."

Jax gazed out the window as the ship began to slow. The stars feverishly sprinting past them slowed accordingly, their blurry images sharpening through the glass. At last, they had resolved completely into fixed points of light drifting lazily by, and the ship was once again solely under the power of its own engines.

Jax clambered to his feet, finding to his satisfaction that his stomach was notably calmer than it had been the last time.

Ara came to stand beside him, casting her gaze across the starscape before turning it on Jax.

"How are you feeling?" she asked.

"Eh, I'm fine." Jax shrugged his shoulders, feigning nonchalance.

Under the surface, however, his mind raced. The sooner he got on board the station and found out what his purpose there was, the better. Ara didn't need to know that.

Luckily, the ship's speakers buzzed once again before either of them could say another word. This time, it was Lieutenant Macgregor's voice that came through.

"All right, crew," she barked. "We're commencing our approach into Voyager Station space. Should be about twenty minutes until we've docked. I want everyone on this ship to be ready to disembark and offload the cargo by then. And I want this shuttle shipshape. The 4S has an image to keep up, aye?"

The lieutenant said nothing more, and the ship fell silent.

Jax continued staring out the window as their shuttle cruised through the darkness. He sensed Ara peering intently at him, as though trying to gauge the validity of his last statement, but she never spoke any of her thoughts aloud. After a few seconds, she turned away to gaze alongside him at their rapidly approaching destination.

As the station loomed larger and larger in their view, Jax had to admit—to himself, at least—that he was impressed. It was massive in scale, perhaps even dwarfing the size of the *Home Base*. The miniature hologram that Ramón had shown them in the briefing could never have done it justice.

Rather than heading for the station's spherical core, their pilot set a course for the docking pylon extending downwards from the bottom. They idled halfway down the structure before the massive bay door opened to let them in. The shuttle alighted smoothly inside the hangar, and that was that.

Once they had touched down, Lieutenant Macgregor barked an order over the intercom for the crew to disembark. Jax and Ara were two of the first to do so, and they stood together as they waited for the rest of the shuttle's complement to offload themselves.

Sometime during the process, Billy and Tom emerged from the throng to find their way over to them. There wasn't much time for them all to make small talk, however, before Lieutenant Macgregor came striding down the ship's boarding ramp to assume command of the situation.

"Right," she said. "Everyone, line up. We'll be having guests in a few minutes, and they'll be telling us what to do with the supplies we brought. I want us all to be looking our best when they get here."

No sooner had the crew formed up as requested than there came the hydraulic hiss of an opening door and the footfalls of several human beings.

All the 4S agents straightened up and fixed their eyes on the source of the sound. Three men approached from the other side of the room. The elevator doors slid closed behind them.

Each of the new arrivals wore an orange lab coat with blue pants and sturdy black boots. The silver emblem of the 4S on their lapels glinted under the harsh overhead lighting. When Jax took a closer look, he noticed that the man in the middle had metallic braces running from his waist to his feet, painted in standard blue to blend in with the uniforms of his fellow scientists, but their wearer's pronounced limp wasn't so easily disguised.

The man with the braces was clearly the leader. The other two stayed a pace behind him. The man in front was older than either of them, with a wrinkled brow and piercing gray eyes. The entire top of his head was bald, though he did have a close-cropped ring of white hair running along the sides.

The middle newcomer wasn't physically imposing, and yet he had no trouble commanding the attention of the 4S' low-level grunts. Even Jax, with no prior knowledge of this man's identity or credentials, couldn't help but be awed by his sheer presence.

"That's Gregory Fletcher," Tom whispered in Jax's ear. "He's Chief Research Officer for the entire 4S, which makes this station his own little kingdom."

"Ah, all right, then," said Jax, hopeful that he had found someone who could finally give him the answers he wanted. He interlaced his fingers and extended his arms palms outward in front of him. After a few seconds, he let them drop back to his sides, notably more relaxed and uncharacteristically optimistic. "Let's go to court."

Gregory Fletcher ambled slowly across the hangar, his leg braces impeding his speed. Each time he took a step, a dull clunk echoed off the walls. His two attendants moved with him the whole way, one on each side, but he never showed any signs of collapsing. By the time Fletcher had arrived at the place where the shuttle's crew stood, Lieutenant Macgregor was ready to meet him.

The Chief Research Officer spoke first. His nasal tone would have made his words almost comical, but the slowness and care with which he spoke offset the effect.

"Lieutenant Sheila Macgregor, I presume?"

The lieutenant let her hand fall back to her side. "Aye, sir, that would be me."

Fletcher acknowledged her with a crisp nod. "You've brought in the scheduled supply run?"

"Yes, sir," said Macgregor. "Everything's accounted for."

"Marvelous," replied Fletcher, in a flat tone that failed to adequately convey the sentiment. He turned to survey the rest of the ship's crew. He gave them a brief once-over, grunted, and returned his full attention to the mission leader.

"Doctor Jennings here," he said, indicating the scientist on his left, "will assist your crew in unloading and storing the supplies. But you will spare me Ara Kendall, Jax Nurmen, Thomas Ubert, and William Vurk. They will be coming with me."

"Those four?" Macgregor said. "What d'ya want with 'em? Just a bunch of green recruits, ain't they?"

"Be that as it may," Fletcher drawled, "their presence here was ordered by Admiral Prang. He also asked that I directly assist them in … adjusting to their new posting. I don't suppose that will be a problem?"

Lieutenant Macgregor straightened to attention. "No, sir. Of course not."

"Very well, then." With a sweep of his hand, Fletcher indicated the shuttle she had arrived on. "I imagine your crew will need you."

Chagrined, Macgregor glanced in the direction of his gesture. "Ye—yes, sir. Right away, sir." And she started off back towards the ship.

Once she was out of earshot, Fletcher turned to his second companion. "Doctor Melville? My holopad, if you please?"

The younger scientist rooted around in his satchel before drawing out a small personal tablet. He handed it to Fletcher, who placed his thumb on the designated scanner. The screen lit up, and Fletcher scrolled for a moment before tapping the screen once. He lifted his eyes to face the small crowd that remained gathered around him.

"As I'm sure you're well aware," he said, "Admiral Prang has asked me to quarter you four here on this station. The tasks you undertake during your stay will be integral to a future project of his."

The way he stressed the words *future project* gave Jax the sense that, under other circumstances, he likely would have said more. That made two occasions where high-ranking 4S officials had mentioned this "project", and yet neither one had actually explained what it was. Vice Admiral Pitt had avoided the topic, and now it seemed that Doctor Fletcher intended to do the same.

"What tasks will those be, sir?" asked Ara.

Doctor Fletcher spoke to each of the three ensigns in turn, pointing his finger at each one in their turn.

"Ara Kendall, you will work alongside the archivists to collate and organize our library of records. Thomas Ubert, you will work in the maintenance depot, ensuring that this station's machinery runs smoothly. William Vurk, you will join our pilots' corps, transporting supplies and staff to where they need to go."

Ara, Billy, and Tom shared a look that indicated either confusion, dismay, or both. Even Jax knew that the jobs they had been assigned were identical to the ones they had performed back on the *Home Base*. Why, then, had Prang considered it so imperative that they do those jobs halfway across the solar system instead?

But Fletcher wasn't finished. There was still one new arrival he hadn't mentioned.

"And you"—he pointed to Jax—"will be under my direct supervision. Admiral Prang has special plans for you …"

*

"Again."

Groaning, Jax picked his limp self up off the floor. As he wiped the sweat from his brow with the back of his hand, his gaze tracked along the wall, up to the small inset window at the top and the speaker from which his observer's voice had issued.

"Again?" he echoed. "I've already made it through this death trap three times today! Surely I don't need to do it again."

"Must I explain this yet again?" Fletcher retorted wearily. "Admiral Prang has instructed me to assess your physical and mental capabilities. If you are to undertake the challenge you have been assigned—"

"What challenge?" Jax asked. "I've been here two weeks, and I still have no idea what the challenge even is!"

"All in due time," Fletcher replied. His nasal voice, made even tinnier as it filtered through the speaker, was really getting on Jax's nerves. "If I were in your shoes, I would be making a more earnest attempt to prove myself, thus avoiding the humility of being cast out and returned to where I came from."

At this point, Jax admitted to himself, *that might not be so bad.*

He had dared to hope that Admiral Prang had finally decided to give him the answers he sought. His placement so close to a prominent figure like Dr. Fletcher seemed to indicate some grand purpose in the works.

Instead of comforting revelations, however, Jax found only pain and exhaustion as he was put through his paces day after day, forced to run a gauntlet of various physical and mental exercises. He knew that he was being tested, but he couldn't guess exactly what results the 4S was looking for from him, but it was test enough for him to resist the urge to simply walk out. The tantalizing promise of eventual clarity had kept him going, but the continued excuses of Prang and his fellow higher-ups were quickly wearing thin.

Jax opened his mouth, but before he could speak, his stomach lurched as the floor dropped away. It wasn't just a feeling, though—his feet had indeed left solid ground. The grip of artificial gravity had released him, along with the menagerie of metal scraps and space rocks littering the floor around him.

"This trial will begin in thirty seconds," Fletcher warned. "Do make this quick, Nurmen. Hard as it may be to believe, I too have several places I would rather be."

The goal of the exercise was simple: at the heart of the debris field lay a palm-sized metal orb, the smallest object in the room. Like its bulkier counterparts, it would be floating randomly throughout the room. Jax's task was to reach it as quickly as possible, pry it open, and press the button inside, which would alert Fletcher and his team of controllers to power down the anti-gravity generators.

Jax took one deep breath, then another. He tensed his muscles, casting his eyes around for something he could latch onto to set himself in motion …

Fletcher spoke again. "The exercise begins now."

The objects around Jax accelerated out of their previously lazy orbits. A jagged slab of blue metal passed below Jax. He bent to grab for it and dragged it toward him. Such a maneuver would have been nigh impossible under any other circumstances, yet here, Jax's weightlessness worked to his advantage.

Positioning the metal beneath him, Jax kicked off, lunging for a small asteroid twenty feet away. He ducked as another piece of shrapnel passed over his head, almost overcorrecting as he tried to regain his intended trajectory. Scrabbling for a handhold and finding purchase, Jax clung there for several minutes as he searched the room for the orb.

There it was—halfway across the room, near the ceiling. But how to get up to it?

Jax dragged himself up until he stood atop the jagged rock. It wobbled and shook beneath his feet, almost unbalancing him before he could grab another rock floating close by. For a few heartbeats, he hung there by his fingertips.

A thick metal beam slammed into his side. All the breath in Jax's lungs escaped him. He tumbled backwards toward the wall.

Regaining control of himself, he kicked off from the wall as hard as he could. Where had that orb gotten to? There, in the corner!

"Stop dithering. Keep your focus!" Fletcher admonished.

What do you expect me to do? Jax wondered incredulously. *Grow wings and fly?*

Jax let his momentum carry him forward, ducking and weaving as flying objects crossed his path. Spotting the same rock he had been hurled from earlier, he oriented himself to skim across its top, digging in his hands and feet to keep from sliding any further forward.

The orb still lay where he had last seen it, languidly bobbing between twisted metal panels. A smaller rock bumped into one of the panels, sending the orb spiraling off to Jax's left.

Abandoning his caution, Jax threw himself forward, fingers outstretched. He barely wrapped them around the orb before it drifted fully out of reach. His fingers fumbled with the catch, but in the end, he pried its halves apart and slammed his open hand down on the button.

It was over. A chime rang through the chamber, and Jax felt an invisible grip guiding him slowly back down to the floor. On his way down, he twisted the two halves of the orb back together and tossed it away, leaving it to find its own space among the clutter.

"Congratulations, Jax Nurmen," Fletcher said. "You completed the trial in twelve minutes and forty-seven seconds. A new personal best. Until dinner hours commence, the rest of your day is yours."

"Finally." Jax clambered his way across the flotsam as he made his way to the exit door. His arms felt as though they were on fire, and his legs might as well have been turned to putty beneath him as his body readjusted to the presence of the station's dense core.

Jax passed through the door into the antechamber. He trudged past the stairs to Fletcher's control booth and a row of seats against the other wall, registering it all peripherally as he made his way to the corridor that connected the chamber with the rest of the station.

The hallway was not especially crowded at this time of day, with most personnel occupying themselves with whatever project had found its way onto their lab stations or workbenches. On his way to the elevator, Jax passed only two researchers, swaddled in their orange rubber lab coats, engaged in animated conversation. They walked in the opposite direction, though, and the elevator was empty.

Jax valued the silence as it transported him to the Hub at the top of the station. From there, it was only a short stroll to the dormitories.

As he passed through the common area, Jax passed Billy and Tom engaged in a holographic chess match at one of the game tables. Tom considered the board for several moments before tapping a command into his keypad. One of his pieces moved onto a square occupied by one of Billy's, and Billy's piece fizzled out of existence. Billy slammed his hand down on the table in frustration.

Jax continued past without sparing them a second glance, hoping to make it into one of the shower stalls before too many others returned for their scheduled afternoon break. He accomplished that goal without issue, and once he had, he stood still for a moment, allowing the ice-cold water to run down his body and cool his aching muscles.

As the sandpapery bar of soap scrubbed the day's sweat and grime from his skin, Jax let his mind wander back to the question of what he was supposed to be doing. His arrival on Voyager Station had done nothing to lift the shroud of secrecy that Prang had so carefully folded around his master plan. All Jax knew was that the relentless training regimen Doctor Fletcher had been putting him through was meant to get him ready for whatever that plan entailed. If Jax was going to be used, he felt he had a right to know what for.

When he had cleaned himself, he turned off the water and reached for a towel. He shivered as the coarse fabric scraped along his skin, no smoother than the soap had been. He swore he would never get used to that.

All the while, Jax asked himself what was stopping him from simply taking a ship and heading back to Earth.

There was the problem of skill, of course—Jax simply had no idea how to fly a spaceship, and he doubted he would be able to convince any pilot, even Billy, to desert their post just so he could abscond. And even if he could go home, there was nothing for him there anymore. As long as he was here, he could at least enjoy the knowledge that he had a purpose to fulfill, however nebulous it presently was.

As Jax shrugged on a clean uniform, he once again reluctantly decided to remain in this infernal holding pattern. He would see Prang's full hand if and only if the admiral chose to play it. Jax could summon neither threat of duress nor emotional plea to sway the hastening of that time.

Jax dumped his old uniform and his towel in his assigned laundry bin, then headed back out into the common room. Billy and Tom's chess game had been powered down, but both of them remained at the table with Ara. Billy had leaned back in his seat, staring ruefully at the deactivated game board, while Tom had shifted his focus to something Ara showed him. Their backs were turned, denying Jax a glimpse of whatever that something was, but from the urgent mutterings he could pick up from them he sensed that it had to be important.

Ara looked up as Jax strolled over to join them. "Ah, Jax, there you are. New orders just came through."

She held out a holopad. Jax accepted it and sat down, drawing it toward himself so he could read the words:

*

<u>TO</u>: ENSIGNS ARA KENDALL, WILLIAM VURK,

AND THOMAS UBERT, AND JAX NURMEN

<u>FROM</u>: ADMIRAL ALPHEUS PRANG

*

THE AFOREMENTIONED AGENTS ARE TO ASSEMBLE

AT THE TOP OF VOYAGER STATION'S UPPERMOST PYLON

BY TWENTY-THREE HUNDRED HOURS TONIGHT.

*

Jax grunted, pushing the tablet back toward Ara. "Look

at that. He did it. He managed to be even vaguer than last time."

"The upper pylon is full of docking bays just like the rest," said Billy. "Maybe Prang wants us on a research ship."

Their going out into space was a likely conclusion, given the hours Fletcher had made Jax spend in the anti-grav chambers. Still, Jax hated the thought that Prang had brought him to the 4S only to ship him off again. And what could he offer the 4S in terms of research anyway? He wasn't his parents. He didn't care much for science.

"The late hour is the thing that concerns me," Tom said. "Any research expedition would depart when most personnel are still awake. The 4S has nothing to hide."

"Except when they do," Jax reminded him. "There isn't a lot that Prang's asked us to do so far that's been normal, is there? He clearly wants to keep this secret. This is just another link in that chain."

"Good point," Ara said. "I can't think of any reason we'd need to do all this skulking around, though. Like Tom said, all 4S operations should be entirely above board. What can it mean if they suddenly aren't?"

"I don't know," Billy replied, "and right now, I don't really care. All this mystery talk makes me hungry, and there's still an hour until dinner. I need something to distract me."

Billy's stomach rumbled as if to emphasize his point. The other three laughed good-humoredly, and the moment of levity, brief as it was, proved enough to break the tension among them.

"How about we finish our game?" Tom asked. He pressed two buttons underneath the table, the first to power it up and the second to restore the board to the way it had been arranged when they had paused their last match. "It was my turn, wasn't it?"

Ara and Jax watched as Tom and Billy picked their game back up, Tom outmaneuvering Billy at every turn to win quite handily. Afterwards, they went on to complete their evening routines: dinner, a few more hours at their work stations, and finally reuniting back at the dormitories. From there, they headed off toward the station's upper pylon and their mysterious destiny.

CHAPTER NINE

HANGAR BAY U-01—UPPER PYLON—VOYAGER STATION

The elevator doors slid open to reveal two people standing in an empty room.

Jax and the others might have assumed there had been some mistake and returned to their dormitories had those two people not been Admiral Prang and his Chief Research Officer, Gregory Fletcher.

Ara, Billy, and Tom snapped to attention. Even Jax found himself standing straighter. He resisted joining the others in their obligatory salute, but his whole body suddenly felt reinvigorated, all his drowsiness falling away.

Admiral Prang spread his arms wide.

"Hello there, my young friends," he said. "Thank you for joining us."

Jax stared back, unsure what to make of those words: a warm greeting, without a hint of malice, clearly meant to put them at ease. All the same, Jax couldn't help feeling like the other shoe was about to drop.

"I must apologize for keeping you from your warm beds at such a late hour," continued Prang. "I had hoped we could all take a ride together."

He indicated the hangar floor behind them with a flourish, where an orange and blue space shuttle sat waiting. Identical in shape to all the other 4S ships Jax had seen, its only difference was its size, seeming to be about half the size of the shuttle that had first brought him to the *Home Base*.

"A ride, sir?" said Billy, a slight hesitation in his voice. "Why? Where to?"

Prang chuckled. "There's no need to worry, Ensign. I only want to talk, and I daresay this particular conversation is long overdue."

Jax perked up. If Prang's admission could be believed, if it meant what he thought it meant, the truth that had evaded Jax for so long would finally be revealed. Was he really about to hear the true story of what his parents had been up to, and why they had died for it?

However, part of Jax's mind remained unsure, and he thought he knew why.

"So why not just tell us?" he said, trying to make the question seem offhanded. "What's there to be said that can't be said here, or anywhere else on the station?"

"Ah," said Prang. "I should have guessed I wouldn't be able to sneak that past you all."

He clasped his hands together.

"The simple answer is that I wanted us to have an extra bit of privacy. Besides, I thought you four might welcome the opportunity for a short ... excursion. Being cooped up on this station can wreak havoc on the brain."

Jax glanced to his side, and saw his own mild confusion reflected in the faces of his three companions. When it became clear that none of them knew what to say, Doctor Fletcher took a step forward.

"You should all be honored," he said. "It is not every day that one gets to go aboard the admiral's personal shuttle."

Jax didn't care if it was an honor. He was tired of jumping through hoops. If Prang was finally going to reveal his big plan, he should reveal it right there and then.

Looking around him, however, Jax sensed that his

companions no longer shared his reservations. Billy gazed at the shuttle with wide eyes, as though he could already imagine himself at the controls. Ara nodded in appreciation, and Tom looked the whole ship up and down, taking in every part of its design.

Realizing that he had become the sole objector, Jax caved. "Fine," he said stiffly. "If that's how this is going to be, I'll play along."

"Wonderful," said Prang.

He dipped a hand into his pocket and produced a small remote control. His ship's boarding ramp lowered at the click of a button. He swept a hand toward it in invitation to the others.

"Shall we be going?"

Jax could have rolled his eyes at Prang's theatrics, but he forced his frustration down with a deep breath. He shouldn't do anything that might jeopardize his chances of learning why Prang needed him so much. For the sake of his parents' memories, for the possibility of finding a way to bring their killers to justice, he could suffer a few more delays.

Jax was the last of their small party to board the shuttle, and the ramp slid closed behind him. He turned to take in the ship's interior, and found it not very dissimilar to the other 4S ships. It contained a cockpit, crew quarters, a small common area, and a storeroom.

Doctor Fletcher went to the cockpit, while Jax, Ara, Billy, and Tom followed Admiral Prang into the common room and toward the table.

"Feel free to sit. This may take a while," he said.

Jax made his way to a chair. His three companions joined him, expectation showing in their wide-eyed, non-smiling faces. Prang remained standing. Jax scanned Prang's face, hoping to find some clue as to what he wanted, but Prang simply stared placidly at the ensigns. Jax crossed his arms above the tabletop and waited for the admiral to start talking.

The moment didn't come.

Jax tried to be patient, but after about a minute he had had enough. He had promised himself that he wouldn't be too insolent, but he had waited too long.

"Okay," he burst out. "What's this all about?"

"I will tell you everything, don't worry," said Prang. "Please, indulge me for a few more minutes."

Jax grunted but didn't protest further. He and the others remained silent and listened as the shuttle's engines hummed to life and built to a crescendo. Billy interlaced his fingers and pulled them apart repeatedly, as if looking for something to do with himself. Tom appraised the shuttle's interior with a mild scowl on his face. Ara simply sat up straight in her seat and patiently waited for Prang to speak again.

Once their voyage was underway, Fletcher came in from the cockpit to stand beside Prang.

"I've set the course, sir. The autopilot system will handle the rest," he reported briskly.

Prang nodded once. "Very well, then. Let's get down to business."

Prang ambled around the table until he could stand directly in front of Jax, leaning down slightly to look the younger man in the eye.

"Tell me, Jax," he said, "are you familiar with the story of the Garden of Eden?" He looked around at the other ensigns. "Are any of you familiar with it?"

For the first few moments, no one responded.

Finally, Jax tentatively said, "Should I be? I'm not really all that religious, to be honest."

Prang sighed deeply. "Few people are, in these times. Still, this particular story is one that has always interested me."

Jax didn't know whether to gape in confusion or snarl in frustration. This was not at all how he had expected this conversation to go. Prang had been promising some kind of grand revelation for weeks, but now that he stood before them, all he could do was tell stories. Jax wanted to groan, to protest, to declare this entire affair to be a colossal waste of his time. Then, somehow, he restrained himself at the last possible moment. Prang was building up to something, and Jax would ruin his chance to learn what that something was if he got angry now.

"Really?" he said, innocently enough. Despite his best

efforts to remain calm, a small degree of irritation bled into his tone. "Why is that?"

Prang chuckled. "Don't worry, Jax, I don't bring this up lightly. I sincerely think that this story is valuable context for why I've brought you here."

Jax calmed outwardly, though his internal resentment didn't fade so quickly. Still, he didn't see what he could do to change anything. If he wasn't going to be able to persuade the admiral to get to the point, all he could do was listen.

"The Garden of Eden, to put it simply, was paradise," said Prang. "It was a time before war, before violence. The Earth was clean and unspoiled, and humanity lived in harmony with itself. All religious symbolism aside, the vision of such a place continues to inspire people to this day, myself included."

This is going nowhere, Jax thought. Hoping to speed the conversation along, he butted in with a question. "But how does this apply to us?"

Doctor Fletcher shot Jax a withering scowl, but Prang just smiled. "You're entirely correct; I should get to the point. Allow me to remedy that. If we consider the entire span of time in which humans have lived on Earth," he began, "our society has only been industrialized for a short time. And yet, how long did it take before we began to ruin our pristine planet? An even shorter time. We filled our oceans with rubbish and our skies with smoke, all in the name of progress.

"And yes, we came to our senses. We made a valiant effort to turn back the clock. With all our various carbon capture programs and new sustainable energy sources, we even made a fair amount of headway. But it was still too little, too late. The founding fathers of the 4S knew that we would eventually have to find a new home for the human race, but they also knew that we needed to ensure that humanity didn't upend the ecosystem of its second planet like it did with its first.

"Ever since it was created, the 4S has been studying alternative energy sources. Not just the ones you might be used to, such as wind or solar power, or even nuclear energy. We have long been trying to find a way to convert the ambient cosmic energies of the universe itself to fuel our society. We could draw our power straight from the space around us, without needing to disrupt the ecosystem we live in.

"And that," he finished, "brings us back to the subject of Eden. As I said, the concept of such a place is attractive to many people. Many 4S admirals and researchers have aspired to create such a society somewhere beyond Earth, even though a fully suitable planet has never yet been found. Even so, the 4S has never stopped trying to make the dream a reality. Our efforts have come to be known as the Eden Project."

"So why are you telling us this?" asked Ara. "Do you want us to join the research teams? If that's the case, only one or two of us would be particularly helpful."

"I agree," put in Jax. "If it's science you're looking for, you've got the wrong Nurmen."

A grin flitted across Prang's face, before it vanished just as quickly.

"You're half right. I would very much like to have you four working as auxiliaries to this project, but I don't want you toiling away in a laboratory. I have another assignment entirely for you."

"What kind of assignment, sir?" Billy asked. "I'm a pilot, Tom builds machines, and Ara works with records. Jax doesn't even have a job or a position right now. None of us are officially attached to the Research Division. What could we possibly do to help them?"

Prang shook his head wryly. "Quite a lot, actually. Think of it as essentially a scouting mission. I would be asking you to gather information for me on … well, a variety of subjects. That's all I can say at this point."

"Scouting for what? New research sites?" asked Tom.

"Not quite," replied Prang. "Your mission could potentially involve travel into unknown space, though."

A look of mild concern crossed Ara's face. "How long would we be scouting? Would we have to abandon our regular tasks?"

"No, not as of now," said Prang. "You'd continue on with your duties as usual, but I would call upon you when I had need of your services."

Ara, Billy, and Tom all seemed satisfied with that, and they voiced no further questions. Jax, however, still had several.

"So we're some kind of special task force, huh?" he asked.

"You could say that, yes," said Prang.

"And just how many of these 'special task forces' are you planning to set up?"

"Yours would be the only one."

Jax snorted. He had been afraid of that.

"So what's the catch?" he asked. "This whole thing seems off."

Doctor Fletcher's expression soured. He took a threatening step toward Jax, but the admiral held up a hand, and he relented.

"Go on," Prang prompted Jax.

"Okay," said Jax. "You called us up to a hangar when you had plenty of good briefing rooms back on the station, but even that wasn't private enough for you. You still felt the need to pile us all into this shuttle and took us out to empty space. None of that suggests that this is a normal conversation. You obviously have something you want to keep secret."

"And what might that be?" said Prang. "Enlighten me."

Jax grunted, realizing too late that he had backed himself into a corner.

"You've got me there," he admitted. "I don't really know what it is you're up to, but I know it has to be more than just scouting."

He raised a finger as a thought suddenly occurred to him. "Hold on. I'm here as well, so this has to be something you want me to be part of. And there can only be one reason I'd ever be involved in a 4S operation. This relates to my parents' deaths, doesn't it?"

Prang sighed a heavy sigh. "You got it in one. I wanted to break it to you a little more gently, but we were going to get there in the end either way."

He took one step back, his line of sight expanding to encompass all four people seated at the table.

"I'll admit, I wasn't entirely truthful with you before," he told them. "The fact is, we have a situation on our hands that requires immediate action. I'm inviting you to be part of the 4S' response. But, as Jax made clear, we're out in space for a reason. We've come out here to be alone, because what I'm about to say is for your ears only."

"So this is sensitive information, sir?" Ara asked.

"Indeed," Prang said gravely, "You must understand that what I am about to show you must be kept strictly between us. I don't consider myself a vindictive man, but if any of this information were to be leaked, I would have no choice but to bring you up on charges."

"I think I speak for all of us when I say we understand, sir," said Ara. "We won't breathe a word to anyone. You can trust us."

Billy and Tom nodded along earnestly. Jax nodded once. If Prang was asking for their silence, he must be about to reveal the good stuff.

Prang tapped keys on the table's control panel. A hologram of some kind of structure shimmered into existence. Formed from two rectangular modules joined by a short pylon, it rotated lazily to allow all the viewers to get a good look. One of the modules was slightly larger, but both were adorned with several strange fins that seemed to be solar panels of some sort. It might have looked even more intriguing if the end of one of the modules hadn't been completely blown out, leaving the inside exposed to the elements.

"This is—or, rather, was—Epsilon Station," said Prang. "It's one of several scientific research outposts attached to the Eden Project. For security purposes, I can't reveal exactly what its particular task was, but it's a moot point by now anyway. About three months ago, the 4S lost contact with Epsilon. The squad we sent in to check it out reported that the entire station had been cleared out. All the research staff had vanished, and the central computer had been wiped of all data."

He pressed another button, and the hologram faded out. "At the time," he went on, "we had no idea how any of that had happened. It wasn't until the attack on Theta Outpost—which was Jax's parents' laboratory—that we realized that someone was deliberately targeting our facilities. We still have no clues as to the ultimate fate of Epsilon's personnel, but we know that these unidentified raiders fully intend to cause violence. Their murder of the Nurmens certainly seems to prove that. Therefore, unfortunately, it isn't too far out of the question that all the scientists stationed on Epsilon have been … lost for good."

Jax let his gaze travel around the table. Ara's eyebrows had risen, Billy's face had gone pale with shock, and Tom seethed with barely concealed anger and disgust. They all knew what Prang was implying, and they understood that they had just been given access to extremely privileged information.

The only question left was: why? Why were they the ones being informed about these events, when there must have been dozens of people more qualified to do something about them? Jax wasn't even part of the 4S, and Ara, Billy, and Tom were still very low in rank. What right did they have to know anything they had just been told, and what were they supposed to do now that they did?

Jax didn't even know what to think anymore, so he asked the first question that jumped into his mind. "So my parents were involved in this project?"

"Yes," said Prang. "They were some of its most dedicated advocates. They truly believed that the work they were doing would one day make the world a better place. It's a dreadful shame that they'll never live to see that day."

"But you admitted you were just studying radiation," Tom cut in. "Why all this secrecy for something so basic? Who would it harm if the truth came out?"

"I wouldn't say this is all a complete secret," said Prang. "After all, even the general public knows that the 4S has been experimenting with cosmic radiation. The specifics of the project have been withheld in some cases, especially after the Epsilon and Theta incidents, but the basics of the project are hardly unknown. Does every 4S agent need to know everything the 4S does?"

"I suppose not," said Tom.

"We simply hoped to avoid causing a massive stir before it was necessary," Prang went on. "When Epsilon went dead, we hoped it was an isolated accident. When the Nurmens died, we realized that it wasn't."

"So what is happening, then?" asked Ara.

"I won't lie to you, friends. There is an enemy force actively moving against the 4S. Fortunately, they have only made two attempts so far, but at least one of those has had lethal consequences. We cannot just sit around and wait for that to happen again. If we can be preemptive and stop them from causing any more damage, that is what we're going to do."

"But why us?" asked Billy. "What makes us such good candidates? There must be loads of 4S agents out there who would be better."

"Nonsense," said Prang. "I daresay you're all perfectly qualified for this mission. On top of that, you complement each other, and you function well as a team. Ensigns Kendall, Vurk, and Ubert, you three shared a great friendship in your years at the Academy, and I've seen your efforts to adopt Jax into your group. It's best to have a squad that's familiar with each other on a sensitive mission like this. Additionally, you each have several individual qualities that make you a good fit for the task."

He turned to Billy. "Ensign Vurk, you may not have been the highest-ranked pilot among your graduating class, but you stood out among them nonetheless. You never worried about being the fastest or the best, but you always took the time to double-check your route and you kept a cool head in the face of obstacles. You're the kind of pilot that isn't concerned with showmanship, and discretion could end up being crucial to your new assignment."

Billy grinned in a way that seemed half sheepish and half prideful. "Thank you, sir."

Then Prang looked at Ara. "Ensign Kendall, our Chief Records Officer himself told me that you were one of his brightest up-and-coming record keepers. He says you're exceptionally skilled at analyzing data, finding key points, and even making extrapolations. Your ability to rationalize and interpret the world around you is exactly what this squadron needs."

"I'll do my best, sir," Ara replied. She kept herself perfectly composed, with no excess emotion showing through, but the glint in her eyes betrayed her true reaction to Prang's compliments.

Prang turned to Tom. "Ensign Ubert, you've shown prowess in repairing ship systems on 4S transport shuttles, and every mission team needs a mechanic. I don't expect your squad to encounter any major problems, but I want someone on hand who knows how to fix up a shuttle. The less people we have to involve in this before it's absolutely necessary, the better."

Tom thanked the admiral for his praise, but his expression didn't entirely match that sentiment. His forehead creased as he mulled over Prang's words. Jax guessed he must thinking something along the lines of, *Why would we ever have to repair our ship in secret?*

"Are you expecting us to encounter some sort of danger?" Tom asked, keeping his voice neutral.

"No, not at all," Prang said, a bit too quickly. "As always, there are precautions in place, but we wouldn't be doing our due diligence if we didn't prepare for the most extreme eventualities."

He had answered Tom's question, but he had simultaneously not provided any answers at all.

Finally, Prang made his way back over to Jax. "Jax Nurmen," he said. "You aren't part of the 4S, and I won't force you to become one, but I would like to make you a proposition."

Jax looked the admiral in the eye. "Go on."

"Very well," said Prang. "You probably know that I originally wanted to retrieve your parents and take them out of danger. What you couldn't have known is that I wanted to bring them on as liaisons with the Research Division for the squad I'm building now. Obviously, you can't fill that role, so Doctor Fletcher will handle that side of things for now. Still, I do think there's a place for you here.

"I've been watching you go through your training on Voyager Station, and your results certainly seem promising. You may not fit into any single one of our divisions, but that just makes you all the more versatile. This team we're putting together will more than likely have to adapt on the fly, and flexibility is key for situations like that. With all that in mind, I would like to invite you to join this team along with the three ensigns here. Will you accept?"

Jax hesitated for several moments as his thoughts churned in his brain.

"I don't know," he said. "How do I know this will be any

different from before? I've been living among the 4S for a month and a half now, but. Are you going to actually draft me now?"

"You wouldn't be an official member of the 4S unless you want to," said Prang. "For appearances' sake, you would be classified as an ensign, but you would be free to leave at any time. This team could conceivably function without you, but I thought you would appreciate the chance to find closure for your parents' deaths."

Closure. It was the lure dragging Jax ever further into the thick of this whole mess. But he had wanted to do something for his parents, hadn't he?

"So why'd this take so long? Could you really not have told me this the first night we met?" he asked.

"You're right," said Prang. "I certainly could have told you there and then, and I do sincerely apologize for not being more forthcoming. As you have seen, this is a matter that must be approached with absolute secrecy. Laying the groundwork for your assignment took longer than I expected, I'll admit. Still, I wanted to give you a chance to acclimate to the 4S before broaching this subject, and I needed some time to assess your capabilities as well, to ensure you would be a good fit for the project."

Jax let that information sink in, allowing himself another moment to digest it all. By all appearances, Prang was being honest. The admiral really had only wanted to test his mettle.

More like test my patience, Jax thought.

But none of it changed anything. His choice had been made long ago, ever since Jax had sworn on his parents' graves all those weeks ago that he would see their killers brought down. He didn't know when, where, or how, but he knew that day would come.

And when it does, I'll be there to watch it all.

"All right," he said at last. "I'm in."

"Brilliant," said Prang. "You've made the right choice. I fully believe you'll be a credit to this operation."

"Great," Jax said, only half sarcastically. *Let's just hope you know what you're talking about, admiral.*

Once more, Prang addressed the four of them: "Your squad's mission will be to investigate any leads the 4S might discover on our enemies. You'll have full access to any resources you might require, but your role is only to observe and report back to us. You are not to take offensive action; my officers and I will decide how to respond to the information you uncover. You will simply be our eyes and ears."

He turned to Doctor Fletcher, who had observed the entire conversation without speaking once. "Doctor Fletcher, do you have any words of wisdom to offer?"

"I do, thank you," Fletcher drawled. "You've all heard the admiral. The future of the Eden Project, and perhaps even the 4S itself, is at stake. Your surveillance will be our first line of defense, so be thorough, but be careful. In the end, the most important thing is that you survive. Your task force may very well prove indispensable, but only so long as you remain focused on your mission."

"Quite right, Doctor," agreed Prang. "Ensigns, you are undertaking crucial work. Thanks to you, we may never have to lose any personnel before their time again."

"That's all well and good," said Jax, "but where are we supposed to start? The people who killed my parents went to ground immediately afterward, and it sounds like the people who attacked Epsilon Station did the same. How are you going to find these leads you want us to follow?"

"It will be difficult, yes," said Doctor Fletcher, "but rest assured, we are not without clues. Any number of people could conceivably locate and attack Theta Outpost on Earth, but Epsilon Station wasn't on Earth. The fact that our mystery raiders found both would indicate that they must have some amount of spacefaring capability. The equipment and facilities they would need for that would be difficult to conceal, and there are only so many hidden spaces left in our solar system. Eventually, they'll give themselves away, and your job will then be to find and expose them."

That seemed reasonable to Jax. It was as good a place to begin as any other, at least.

"Thank you, Doctor," said Prang.

He turned back to the ensigns. "I should reiterate that you are not to reveal yourselves to the enemy if it can be avoided, and you are certainly not to go into live combat. We must do all we can to settle this without further bloodshed. If your circumstances ever take a turn for the worse, get away as quickly as you can. That is an order. You aren't properly equipped to fight, and I don't want you throwing your lives away in some useless display of bravado. Am I understood?"

"Yes, sir," the ensigns replied.

"Very good," said Prang. "I'm glad I've made myself clear. Now I'll open the floor to you. Do any of you have any further questions?"

None of them did. After a few moments had passed in silence, Prang clapped his hands once.

"In that case, I think we're done here. Doctor Fletcher, would you mind setting us a course back to Voyager Station?"

"Of course, sir," replied Fletcher, heading off back to the cockpit. Prang watched him go before turning his attention back to the others.

"As for you," he began, "you all will be free to go once we've docked. You'll return to your duties as we discussed, and I'll contact you again when—"

He was interrupted by a slightly muffled chime from somewhere on his person. He raised a finger to his audience.

"If you'll excuse me for a moment?" he asked.

No one thought it prudent to object.

The ensigns looked at each other while Fletcher stood off on the other side of the room.

"So we all agree that something's off, right?" asked Tom.

"Like what?" said Billy. "This whole thing is pretty cool, if you ask me."

"*Cool* isn't the word I would use. There's an enemy operating right under Prang's nose, and he wants to send three of his most inexperienced agents, along with one guy who isn't even an agent—no offense, Jax—instead of the more qualified professionals?"

"It makes a certain amount of sense. If Prang mobilized

all his forces, people would know something was up. We ensigns can stay undetectable and gather information without being too visible and causing a mass panic," put in Ara.

"So? Maybe there should be a panic! The Nurmens' death was reported on live television. People know what's happening, even if they don't know the full extent. This is the perfect time to get the bigger guns involved!" said Tom.

"Lighten up, will you?" said Jax. "Don't knock it until you've tried it. Let's just wait until the first mission, and see how that goes. Maybe it won't be so bad."

"And maybe pigs will fly," Tom grunted.

As they talked, Prang pulled a holopad from his pocket, his gaze narrowing as he read something on the screen. The wrinkles on his forehead deepened as he went on, until he finally raised his head and turned to Doctor Fletcher. His expression was as studiously neutral as ever, but it was clear that he hadn't liked what he had just read.

"We'd better get them back to the station quickly, Doctor." His voice had taken on a slight inflection of urgency. "It seems their first task has arrived sooner than expected …"

CHAPTER TEN

COMMAND MODULE—4S REFINERY CHAIN—
ASTEROID BELT

Ara rose from her seat when the shuttle landed in the center of the docking bay. She joined the throng of passengers as it made its way down the boarding ramp. They formed an orderly line heading toward the doorway at the far end of the room. Ara found herself a spot near the middle of that line and waited patiently as it slowly pushed her closer and closer to the exit.

The transport had departed from the 4S lunar colony's administrative complex at 0530 hours and reached the fringe of the asteroid belt after a half-hour journey. From there, it took another twenty-five minutes before they reached the command module for all 4S mining operations in the area. The shuttle docked in the module's hangar, and its passengers, all of whom were 4S staff assigned to manage and maintain the asteroid mining equipment, offloaded themselves. The entire process had taken just over an hour to complete.

When it was her turn to pass through the door into the station, Ara pulled out a data chip, one of two that Doctor Fletcher had given her. She inserted it into a port on the wall. When the light above the door flashed green, she collected her chip and passed through into a sterilization chamber. She walked out into the base once she had completed the requisite time within it.

Ara tuned out all the noise of workers making their way

to their various work stations. She found herself listening for the voices of Jax, Billy, and Tom. She had grown so used to having them around for the last several weeks that she had forgotten that 4S operatives from separate divisions didn't usually work together for so long. Now that the others weren't around, even a crowded room seemed oddly quiet.

Eventually Ara came to a point where the hallway split into two branches. A sign mounted between them pointed the way to her destination, the module's central computing hub.

Ara chose that path, holding her head high and humming a jaunty tune as she walked. Enough people going her way made her seem inconspicuous, but she felt out of place anyway. Unlike all the other people she had arrived with, she didn't work in the asteroid-mining branch of the 4S. In dress and mannerisms, she was the equal of any other person there, yet she couldn't help but feel like she was about to be exposed as some kind of stowaway.

She did her best to shake those thoughts from her head. *I'm here on orders from the admiral himself. The information I'm retrieving could help save the entire 4S. I have as much right to be here as anyone else, even if I am working under the radar. There's nothing to be afraid of.*

As usually happened when she was stressed out or anxious, Ara's thoughts went to her family back home on Earth. They had always believed in her; now she merely needed to find that belief within herself.

The Kendall clan of Roamers had always been one of those few that still chose to live up to the designation. Preferring not to be shackled to any one settlement, Ara's father had led his family all across the United States: finding work and shelter wherever they could, but never staying in one place for too long. The jobs they worked had been diverse in nature, ranging from building to disaster relief to even domestic help.

From the moment Ara had been old enough to join her father and brothers at work, she strove to be their equal in physical strength and productivity. She had succeeded more often than not. Once it became clear that her true skills lay in datawork, however, her mother frequently stole her away to help with the family's budget as well as the various other legal forms their temporary work agreements often required. Ara and her mother had spent many a late night poring over the holopad the Kendalls used to keep track of their monetary resources, ensuring there would be enough for spending and saving. Ara's mother swore one day that it seemed like her daughter had been born to handle spreadsheets.

Ara's family always told her that she was destined for greater things than a Roamer's life. Once she had expressed interest in joining the 4S, they all worked tirelessly to scrounge up the funds needed to send her to the 4S Academy and get her trained as an archivist. They did everything they could to give Ara a chance at success, and she owed everything she now had to them. Thinking of them had always conjured up nothing but happy memories and feelings of safety.

In the present, Ara let the image of her family bring her the peace she so desperately needed. She forced herself to relax, trying to act as casual as everyone else around her. She could do this. She would complete this mission. She just wished it wasn't such a strange one …

*

Jax had been the first to voice his opinion, laced with what Ara was coming to understand as his trademark cynicism.

"So much for being some kind of special task force. All we're doing is running Prang's errands," he griped.

"Give him some credit, Jax," said Ara. "This is real life, not some action-packed fantasy. Being part of a space force isn't always going to involve shoot-outs or heroics. We all have to do the jobs we're given."

Jax snorted. "And that's another thing. How come we got this job anyway? If Prang really wants this data, he should be able to just put in a request and take it."

"I'm not so sure about that," cut in Billy. "He told us he didn't want to cause some kind of uproar. This definitely seems like the sort of thing that would cause an uproar."

"He's admiral of the 4S!" said Tom. "He shouldn't have to resort to spying and sneaking around to learn things."

Ara shook her head in irritation. This conversation had gone on long enough. In her opinion, could haves, would haves, and should haves didn't matter anymore. Everything had already changed irrevocably. They might as well get used to the way things suddenly were.

"Don't get so worked up," said Ara. "We won't be breaking any rules. Prang's given us full clearance to access the data. We're just being a little … creative with how we do it."

"We shouldn't have to be," Jax said. "I'm with Tom on that. I know Prang made a big deal about keeping this secret, but it still doesn't feel right. 4S personnel have already been murdered. Shouldn't everyone be on high alert by now?"

"Admiral Prang doesn't want to cause panic," Ara said. "I, for one, am choosing to believe that he knows what he's doing. If the whole 4S was aware of what's been going on, it would only lead to more paranoia. We're only going to stop these criminals by staying calm and collected."

"I get that," Tom said, "but that doesn't explain why we're doing this current mission. I still think Prang doesn't need us to do this for him."

"But shouldn't we follow orders?" asked Billy.

"Not blindly!" Tom said. "With or without enemies, the 4S doesn't need to keep secrets from its people. Admiral Prang is playing a dangerous game, and I won't be surprised when it comes back to bite him later on."

"*If* it comes back to bite him," Ara reprimanded. "Not *when*."

"Yeah, yeah. Whatever you say. Can we please just get on with it?" said Jax.

Ara couldn't help but agree.

"Fine," she huffed. "I'm not staying here to beat a dead horse. I don't know about the rest of you, but I need some sleep."

She spun on her heels and stalked out of the shuttle's cockpit. Once she reached her bunkroom, she splashed some warm water on her face, stripped off the outermost layer of her 4S uniform, and flung herself onto her mattress. She fell asleep almost as soon as her head touched the pillow. Her slumber was quiet and dreamless, and yet she could never entirely shake the feeling that Tom hadn't truly been wrong.

*

The next morning, Ara walked alone through the corridors of the control station. Her boots clicked against the hard metal floor and the conversation with the others played on a loop in her mind. As much as she had tried to be the voice of reason, she couldn't quite bring herself to believe her own arguments.

As Tom liked to claim, the 4S had always been remarkably transparent. The vast majority of their records were accessible even by those of the lowest rank, and a great number had even been made available to the general public. Ara knew for a fact that the admiral had secure channels he could use for any private transactions. Her presence aboard the mining station seemed unnecessary, and she had always hated being deceptive, even for a good cause.

Calm down, she thought. *Prang's reasons aren't important right now. Focus on your orders. You know what you're here for. Just do it.*

The 4S had long kept up a tradition of strip-mining the multitude of asteroids scattered across the galaxy for raw materials such as metals, minerals, and sometimes even water. Using small mining ships equipped with powerful lasers or switching to robotic probes with drills when a more close-up approach was required, the 4S miners broke the floating rocks into smaller chunks and harvested them for whatever they could provide. The precious ores traveled via cargo ship to shipyards and factories across the solar system, where they would be put to use in projects run by both the 4S and its many outreach and aid programs.

Every 4S ship, whether cargo transport or passenger shuttle, contained a program built into its onboard GPS system that transmitted its location to a central computer. That computer was located within the command module that controlled the various refinery stations scattered throughout the asteroid belt. The precaution helped the 4S to retrieve any ships that broke down and became stranded in space.

The news Admiral Prang had received at the end of his conversation with Ara's team had been strikingly unusual: one of the ore transports had failed to reach its destination. That news was strange enough on its own, even without the added fact that the ship's transponder had gone dead, leaving the 4S unable to locate it.

"This is an unprecedented situation," Admiral Prang had said. "It may yet prove to be a simple mechanical failure, but with murderers on the loose, we can't afford to make premature assumptions. I can't say what our enemies might want with a shipment of metal, but if this is their handiwork, we need to know."

His news had immediately sparked controversy among Ara's team, none of whom knew what to do about it. Tom and Billy had doubted the need for so many precautions, while Jax and Ara had argued that the mystery needed to be solved.

"Thankfully," Prang had continued, "the ship's last known location should still be backed up in the database. Getting that location will be the first step in tracking down the missing shipment and, hopefully, saving the crew."

"But what does that have to do with us?" Ara had asked.

"The data will need to be downloaded physically from the archives on the main 4S refinery," Prang had replied. "That will be your task. I'll grant you access to the command module, and you'll retrieve the data and send it to Doctor Fletcher and myself for analysis."

The second data chip Doctor Fletcher had given Ara had been specially encrypted to perform that exact task. It contained the usual subroutines to extract data from the command module's central computer, and it would simultaneously purge the system of any indication that the download ever occurred. She would give Admiral Prang a copy of the requested data and no one monitoring the recording system would have picked up on her actions.

Ara entered the hub and took a seat at the first available computer stations and plugged the data chip into the computer. Her fingers flew across the keyboard, pulling up archived flight data. She isolated the data she was after and queued it for download.

Ara involuntarily gasped as lines of text scrolled across her screen. A technician working at one of the other nearby computers raised her head to stare, but Ara carefully controlled her expression and offered a warm smile. The other woman smiled back and returned to her work.

Ara exhaled in relief. She didn't have the luxury of time for small talk or the ability to reveal what she was up to.

Ara had to get this data back to the others and transmit

it to Admiral Prang, because, if she had read the data correctly, things were about to get a whole lot more complicated.

*

Jax glanced up at the sound of rhythmic tapping to see Billy drumming his fingers against the cold metal tabletop.

"Will you cut that out?" Jax snapped. "I can't hear myself think."

"Sorry," said Billy, dropping his hands to his sides. "Nervous habit."

Jax sniffed. "Whatever. Just don't do it right now, okay?"

"Calm down, both of you. The ship will land any minute now. Ara will be back soon." said Tom, eyes fixed on the wall clock across the room.

Their mission team had arrived on the moon base in the early morning hours. Billy had flown through the night while his shipmates slept. Once they had landed in their assigned docking bay, Ara had gone to board the personnel transport with the asteroid miners while the others found themselves a room in the base's dormitory. Billy had slept for most of the day while Jax and Tom had done their best to entertain themselves with the sparse amenities the 4S outpost had to offer. Once their pilot woke in the late afternoon, the trio made their way to a table in the base's cafeteria, near the docking bays, where they could wait for Ara to return to them.

Jax pulled a soggy French fry from the carton they had ordered half an hour ago and choked the now-cold potato mash down his throat.

"Let's just hope she got what we came for," he said. "I'd hate for this whole day to go to waste."

They didn't have to wait much longer; Ara entered the room roughly five minutes later and made her way over to the last open seat at their table.

"Hey, boys." she winked lightheartedly. "Did you miss me?"

Her attempt at humor didn't land.

"Did you get it?" Jax asked.

Ara rolled her eyes and drew out a data chip out of her pocket. "Of course I got it. Have a little faith."

"And you didn't run into trouble?" asked Tom.

"What trouble?" Ara said. "I was acting on direct orders from the admiral. If anyone has a problem with that, they'd be the one in trouble."

'It still rubs me the wrong way, and I don't see why you all aren't more concerned," said Tom. "The 4S—"

"Stop whining, Tom," cut in Jax. "It's alright. She got what we needed, and she got away. Now we have bigger things to worry about."

Tom didn't look at all mollified, but he voiced no further objections.

"Now, then," Ara said. "Let's go make a call."

They returned to their temporary quarters in the moon base, where they gathered around Tom's bed. Tom reached underneath to pull out a small blue metal box, the third piece of technology Doctor Fletcher had produced for the team. It contained a secure holocommunicator that allowed them to communicate directly with Prang while emitting an invisible energy field neutralizing any nearby surveillance devices for the length of that communication. Tom had objected to such a device at first, but Ara had been able to convince him to relax his stance and see the need for it.

Placing the box down on his mattress, Tom pressed the button to call the admiral. After a few minutes of waiting, a miniature holographic image of Admiral Prang appeared, hovering an inch above the box.

"Good evening to you, ensigns," he said. "I trust you completed your mission?"

"I have the data, sir." Ara stepped in front of the group to place herself in Prang's field of vision. "I'll transmit it now."

She inserted the data chip containing the missing transport's flight data into a port on the side of the box. She straightened up and watched as Prang's gaze shifted to something near him that they couldn't see.

"Data received," he finally said. "I'll have Doctor Fletcher and his team get to work on it immediately. Thank you very much for your work, Ensign Kendall."

"No trouble at all, sir," Ara replied, giving him a respectful salute.

"You've all done extremely well so far," said Prang. "Now get some rest. It will take us a few hours to analyze this flight data, and we may need your services again once we've finished. Sleep while you can, and we shall speak again soon."

With that, the admiral cut the transmission from his end, and the hologram fizzled out of existence.

"I don't know about the rest of you," said Jax, "but I'm thinking of taking Prang up on his offer. I may not have done all that much today, but sitting around and waiting is still really exhausting." He let out a huge yawn to emphasize his point.

"I say Jax has the right idea," Tom said. "Anticipation really wears a person down."

With that, they split up, each one returning to their own dorm room. Jax fell asleep long before the base's lights automatically dimmed at 2300 hours and woke up at 0630 the next morning when they came back on again. He and the others ate breakfast in the cafeteria and returned to the dormitory's common room to wait for Admiral Prang to contact them again.

The call came at around noon. Tom was the first to notice the blinking blue light on the box and quickly alerted the others. They clustered around the device in tense anticipation.

Billy flipped the switch to accept the communication, and the blue hologram of Admiral Prang once again appeared.

"Good morning, my friends," the admiral began. "I trust you have all rested and recovered from yesterday's mission?"

"We're ready to go whenever you need us, sir," said Ara.

"Wonderful," replied Prang. "That's exactly the news I was hoping to hear. It just so happens that I have the beginnings of your next mission already.

"We've analyzed the data you extracted, but unfortunately, it doesn't offer much in the way of explanation. The security camera footage from the ship's hangar bay doesn't show anyone except the assigned crew anywhere near the vessel, and the ship departed on schedule with no issues whatsoever. We checked over the footage for evidence of tampering, but we couldn't find any."

"So what now, then?" asked Billy. "This ship is just … gone?"

"Not entirely," replied Prang. "Its present whereabouts are most certainly unknown, but that isn't the most important part of this story. We still hope to recover the ship, its cargo, and its crew if that is all still possible, but we aren't just concerned with the ship's physical location. The other part of this mystery is how it got there."

"It must have been a mechanical failure," said Tom. "If the transport wasn't sabotaged, there has to be a simple explanation. It's unusual, sure, but this should just be another routine recovery operation."

"The data would certainly seem to bear that out," agreed Prang. "Unfortunately, it isn't that simple. The ship may have left its hangar as planned, but it doesn't seem to have followed its planned course."

"What are you saying, sir?" asked Tom.

Prang took a moment before speaking. His next words were conveyed with the level of gravitas that only a man living under extreme duress could muster.

"Based on the data you four recovered," said Prang, "we have every reason to believe the missing ship has been hijacked."

<u>CHAPTER ELEVEN</u>

4S ADMINISTRATIVE COMPLEX—LUNAR COLONY SITE L-12—EARTH'S MOON

The three ensigns stood thunderstruck before the hologram of their admiral, each one processing the revelation in their own way. Jax watched them all, curious to see who would react first.

Ara proved to be that person. Surprisingly, her reaction wasn't one of outrage, but one of reluctant resignation. Then again, she had already seen the data.

"I assumed so, sir." Her words ended in a heavy sigh.

Tom whirled to face her.

"Hold on. Back up. What do you mean, you assumed?" he said.

"What do you think?" she asked. "I already knew the ship didn't end up where it was supposed to. I didn't know about most of the other stuff Admiral Prang mentioned, but I always knew that."

Tom shook his head in exasperation. "Okay, fine. That's not the important part, anyway." He stiffened as he faced Admiral Prang, and it looked as though it took him some effort to keep his voice even as he went on. "With all due respect, sir, you must be mistaken. How could a 4S ship be hijacked?"

Jax decided to take Tom's side on that one.

"It doesn't make sense to me, either," he said. "If we know that no unauthorized people touched the ship, it should have gotten where it was going."

"Maybe it got intercepted," said Billy. "Some other ship could have picked it up while it was still in open space."

"Or the pilots lost their way," said Jax.

Billy scowled at those words, but Jax ignored him and continued, "Or maybe their ship took them to the wrong place."

Seething, Tom stepped forward and squared up to Jax.

"That's out of the question," he said hotly. "The 4S uses only the most state-of-the-art navigational systems. If there were any major issues with the autopilot system, incidents like this would be a lot more common. But this is the first one in years. Maybe even decades. So it almost definitely isn't operator error."

Jax shrugged lazily. "Keep your head on straight. I was only trying to help."

Tom growled once in the back of his throat and turned away.

"That's enough, you two," Prang said sternly. "You've both raised good points, but we simply do not have enough conclusive evidence to know the reason the ship went off the grid. Until we do, every opinion shall be considered equally valid."

"Of course, sir," said Tom. "Can we at least stop using the word hijacked prematurely, though?"

"Your point is taken, Ensign Ubert," said Prang. "Perhaps I chose my words too hastily. For the moment, let us consider the shipment to simply be lost in transit."

"Can I say something?" asked Jax.

Prang nodded. "Of course. Please speak your mind."

"All right, then," Jax began. "I think we're focusing on the wrong thing. Like you said, we don't know why the ship is … well, wherever it is right now. But you still haven't even told us where that place is."

"You are correct," said Prang. "Allow me to rectify that." The four ensigns all inched a little closer to the blue box as Prang continued, "The transport was last seen in the vicinity of our solar system's sun."

"The sun?" Jax asked incredulously. "What was it doing there?"

"It does seem illogical. Are we sure it didn't just fly into the sun and burn up in some freak accident?" said Ara.

"We cannot know for certain that it didn't," Prang said. "However, the ship was well out of range of the sun's heat when its transponder cut out. Our current working theory is that it must have docked with one of our abandoned solar power facilities."

"Wait, what?" Jax said. "Solar power facilities? Abandoned? What's that about?"

"You heard correctly," said Prang. "The 4S did indeed once consider using solar energy to power its technology, and several orbiting modules were constructed to house the collectors. Even so, the project was determined to be uneconomical in the face of alternative energy sources, and it was shut down just shy of its official launch. The modules have been lying derelict ever since, and many of them would be large enough to house a cargo shuttle."

"Is that going to be our next mission, sir?" asked Ara. "Do you want us to scout those solar modules?"

"Indeed," said Prang. "I want you to do some reconnaissance and see if you can find the lost ship somewhere in that area. If your mission is successful, leave a homing beacon behind and I will send out a retrieval team. However, if you see anything amiss, you are to turn back immediately and report it directly to me. Am I clear?"

Each of the ensigns before him gave a grave nod of understanding.

"Very good," Prang went on. "How soon can you four be ready to leave?"

"Whenever you need us to, sir," Ara told him.

"Very good," said Prang. "I've requisitioned a scout ship for you. I'm told that it will be ready for launch from Docking Bay Forty-Seven within twenty minutes. The hangar crew will know to expect you. The journey should be relatively short and easy, and the relevant coordinates will be uploaded to your onboard navigation system shortly. Any questions?"

The four ensigns glanced at each other before Tom answered.

"No, sir. We're ready and waiting."

"Then let's not waste any more time," said Prang. "Go now, and good hunting."

*

The small scout ship dropped out of lightspeed at a good distance from the sun and the solar power collection modules. Ara, Jax, and Tom crowded into the cockpit as Billy gradually accelerated toward the nearest module.

Jax scanned the open space beyond the windshield. His eyes roved back and forth, but he couldn't make out anything between the shuttle and the orange sphere of the sun countless miles away.

More free-floating structures came into view, rotating around the massive ball of gas. Painted in bright blue and orange colors to stand out against the stark blackness of space, the boxy cubic modules sat desolate and forlorn, their vivid exteriors a disorienting contrast to their empty interiors. Jax tried to imagine the area around them swarming with ships, but couldn't quite manage it.

The comm unit on Billy's control panel began to chirp repeatedly, as though it were receiving a signal.

"What's that?" Jax asked.

"I don't know. Let's find out," Billy flipped the switch to open the comm channel, but no sound or voice came through. Instead, a simple line of text scrolled across the screen next to the speaker, too small for Jax to make out. Billy turned his head to read it.

"What's it say?" asked Tom.

"It's some kind of automated warning," said Billy. "It says that no ships without proper shielding should pass beyond the outer ring of modules."

"What would we need shielding for?" Jax asked.

"Solar flares can get pretty nasty. Anything left unprotected gets burned up real quick," said Tom.

"Great," Jax muttered. "As if this wasn't already complicated enough."

Ara spun in her seat to face him. "Don't worry. This actually narrows down our search parameters by quite a bit. Cargo transports don't have good solar shielding either. It would be too expensive to put it on large ships like that. Any ships like our missing one would have to stay beyond the outermost ring of modules, so only the outermost modules would be built to accommodate them."

"Unless the hijackers deliberately took the ship in deeper so we couldn't follow," objected Jax.

"That's unlikely," Ara replied. "Solar flares are notoriously unpredictable. The hijackers would be gambling with their cargo and their lives. I hardly think they'd want to risk losing either."

"Can we please not assume there are any hijackers? Can we not just give this case the benefit of the doubt?" asked Tom.

"All right, all right," said Jax. "Either way, which module do we start with?"

Billy projected an image of the modules' inner workings up onto the ship's windshield for all his comrades to see. "I've already scanned most of them. If there are ships or people inside any of them, we'll know."

Twelve of the thirteen modules captured in Billy's scan consisted of the same interior design: one large hangar bay built for cargo ships in front and a smaller hangar bay for shuttles in the rear. The wall dividing the two rooms contained a small hatch through which the solar panels could be transferred.

Unfortunately, none of the modules showed any signs of activity, either the infrared thermal signatures of living beings or surges of electrical power from technology.

One module stood out from the rest, showing nothing except blackness within it. No matter how much Billy fiddled with the intensity and direction of the shuttle's scanners, the ensigns remained unable to peek inside it.

Jax laid a finger on the dark shape. "What's going on with that one?"

"I'm not sure," said Billy. "Our sensors can't pierce its shell."

"How come?" Jax shot back. "Do we need to get closer?"

"It's within scanning range like all the rest. If we can't see inside, it's because something over there is stopping us," said Billy.

Jax turned to face Ara and Tom.

"I suppose it's too much to hope that the 4S built it that way," he grunted.

"It's unlikely," said Ara. "I've never heard of the 4S using cloaking technology in any of their major facilities. I hate to say this, but it has to have been a deliberate addition. And the only people with anything to hide are the ones we're tracking."

"And that module's definitely large enough to hide an ore carrier," put in Tom.

"So that's it, then," said Jax. "If our missing ship is anywhere in this place, it'll be there. So what do we do now?"

"We need visual confirmation," said Ara. "As long as we're here, we might as well get it. Either we'll find the ship, or we won't. This could all still be some wild goose chase, but we can't go back to Prang without actual evidence."

"I can take us in," said Billy. "The docking facilities on that module look intact."

"What about the rest of the structure?" Ara asked.

Billy took another look at his screen. "It all seems stable. It can't have deteriorated that much. The 4S builds these things to last, even when they don't use them."

"Sounds safe to me," put in Tom. "Take us in, Billy."

Billy set the shuttle in motion, plotting a trajectory that would take them right to the one module they had been unable to scan. Ten minutes later, they hovered in space in front of the module's docking bay door— a door that remained frustratingly closed.

"And just how are we supposed to get inside?" Jax asked. "There's no one in there to let us in."

"Relax," Billy told him. "4S stations include automatic docking protocols, too. All I have to do is transmit our ship's clearance code"—he tapped a few commands into his control panel, and after a few moments the door began to slowly slide open—"and we're in."

Jax snorted as Billy looked back at him with a smug expression on his face.

"Whatever. Just hurry up and get us in there," said Jax.

Once the shuttle touched down in the large empty hangar,, the ensigns waited for the door to close and the module to fill itself with breathable air again. As soon as it was safe, the team disembarked. Jax looked around him and couldn't help but think that all their worries had been for naught. The room was completely bare, with no other people or ships besides those that had just landed.

"There's nothing here," Tom observed. "Seems like a waste of time."

"I don't know if it's that simple," said Ara. "Whoever put the cloaking tech on this module was obviously trying to cover something up."

"But if no one's here, then it's already over and the people got away," Tom said. "That's worse than this being a wild goose chase."

"That doesn't make much sense. All the clues lined up. The transport should be here," Billy insisted.

"We must have misread the information," said Tom. "Someone must have made a mistake."

"Admiral Prang said the data hadn't been altered," Ara objected. "The ship has to have come here."

"Then maybe we're just on the wrong module," said Billy.

"You scanned all the other ones," Tom reminded him. "Did any of them have a ship inside?"

A thought occurred to Jax. Taking one involuntary step back, he scanned his surroundings with a fresh perspective. It seemed as empty as before, but something in the air had shifted irreversibly.

"Hold on," he said, turning to the others. "Doesn't this all seem too easy?"

"What do you mean?" asked Tom.

"You saw the scans," replied Jax. "Whoever set up shop here last wanted to keep whatever they were doing secret. We know the 4S wouldn't have included cloaking technology in the original design, so someone else must have added. It all seemed like a pretty good place to hide a stolen ore shipment, right?"

"We discussed all this back on the ship. What's your point?" asked Ara.

"My point," said Jax, "is that all that effort seems to have been wasted. Whoever put the cloaking in place made a big show of hiding something, but there's nothing here."

"Maybe they've already left," suggested Billy. "Maybe they got what they wanted from this place and took the ship somewhere else. They disabled the tracker, so they could be anywhere by now."

"That's a possibility," Jax said. "The way I see it, there are two options. Either Billy's right and the shady stuff already happened, or—"

The air shimmered as a human figure faded into view from where it had previously been camouflaged against the blue metal. Six more figures emerged and joined the first in creeping slowly toward the startled ensigns. All seven were clad in black from head to toe, with even their faces covered. The sight of a group of such people was familiar to Jax, and seeing it again chilled him to the bone.

"—or it's a trap," he finished.

*

One of the dark figures lunged at Jax, moving so swiftly that he barely dodged left. The attacker skidded to a halt.

For a split second, Jax looked around him and saw Billy, Ara, and Tom entangled in their own tussles. Then Jax's attacker barreled toward him, and Jax tuned out everything else.

Jax deflected the masked man's first punch, then the second, ignoring the stinging feeling in his arm. He kicked out with one leg; the masked man staggered but didn't fall. The man shook his head, chuckling softly.

"You're good, kid," he told Jax in a filtered, robotic voice. "But you ain't good enough."

His kick brought Jax to his knees. He smacked Jax's face, knocking him to the floor.

Jax touched his hand to his face, relieved to find no blood. When he tried to rise to his feet, the man kicked him back down.
"What are you doing?" Jax burst out. "Who are you? Are you the ones who stole the ore shipment?"

The man paused in his attack.

"Oh, yes. That. We never cared about the ore. It was necessary, but not the end goal."

"Then why do it?"
"What does it matter?" the man shot back. "You won't be around to find out."

We'll see about that, Jax thought. Taking advantage of the break in the fight, Jax rolled onto his side and began to push himself up.

A memory struck him. The last time he had seen his parents, they had been in the same position, at the mercy of a figure cloaked all in black. Was this how Jax would honor their legacy? By dying as pointlessly as they had?

No. He wouldn't. He couldn't.

Feeling a surge of newfound energy coursing through him, Jax jumped to his feet and swung his fist into the masked man's stomach. The man stumbled, allowing Jax to dart away and find Tom nearby.

Tom, locked in his own struggle against a hooded figure, spared a moment to glance at Jax, silently inviting him to join the fight. Together, they coordinated their attack: Tom went high, and Jax went low. Tom's attacker, distracted by Tom's fists heading for his face, failed to notice Jax's boot going for his knees until it was too late. The man stumbled into a wall with a loud thud and sank to the floor.

Jax and Tom shared a glance, relief and apprehension mingling in their expressions. With all the other masked raiders busy, the two shared a few words as they caught their breath.

"We can't keep this up too much longer," Jax huffed.

Tom nodded. "It took two of us to get rid of one of them. But they're keeping us divided. Makes us easier to pick off."

"So what do we do?" Jax asked. "Can we even stop them?"

Tom's eyes widened as he stared at something behind Jax. Startled, Jax whirled around, only to see the first man charging at him.

Tom's gaze flicked toward the hangar's empty control room. "I-er, I might have an idea. But I'm not sure it'll work."
"Go!" Jax stepped forward to meet his opponent's attack. "We have to try!"

Jax didn't see what Tom did next. His mind was occupied with his resurgent battle.

Jax and the masked man. But Jax was tiring. The man was bigger and stronger, and Jax couldn't detect any weak points in his body or technique.

Jax went on the defensive, parrying the masked man's strikes without making too many of his own. He allowed himself to be driven back, until suddenly he stood beside Billy and Ara, facing off against a cluster of raiders. The two ensigns had clearly been able to hold their own; neither one looked any worse for wear than Jax felt, and both were still on their feet. Like Jax, however, both looked to be tiring. Tom was still nowhere to be seen.

The first man laughed.

"It's over," he said. "You can't escape. Give up and this will all be over quickly."

"Never!" Ara snarled, aiming a punch at the closest figure. The masked woman stepped to her left, and Ara doubled over, swinging wildly at empty space.

"Resistance is futile," the masked woman said. "None of you will make it out of this hangar."

The circle of attackers closed in around the ensigns. Jax frantically searched for a gap they could break through and escape, but there was none.

One of the masked men paused. The others paused with him.

"Hold on," he said. "Weren't there four of these guys?"

Something clattered loudly behind. Jax spun around to see that Tom had felled two of their enemies. He stood over their prone bodies, clutching a piece of metal piping he hadn't had earlier.

Tom beckoned with his hand for his comrades to follow him. "This way. Hurry!"

Jax, Ara, and Billy clambered over the masked bodies to follow Tom before their other attackers could retaliate. Tom led the others into the control room and slammed the button to shut the door. It slid closed just as the raiders reached it; the ensigns were safe for the moment.

"What's going on?" Ara asked.

"And what did you do to those two guys?" asked Billy.

Tom shrugged. "Relax. I didn't kill them, but they won't be getting up again anytime soon."

"But what are we doing in here?" asked Ara.

Tom looked at Jax. "Remember the plan I mentioned?"

Jax nodded.

"Great news," Tom said. "I've been able to restore the electricity in this hangar, which means we can pull that plan off."

"I don't follow," Jax admitted after several seconds of silence.

Tom gestured toward the hangar's control panel. "Right. Here's how it goes. We're going to fight our way back out there—"

"Back?" Billy asked incredulously. "Didn't you hear

them? They said they'd kill us, and I for one believe them."

"Don't worry," Tom soothed. "All we need are a few minutes, and I have a way to buy us that time." He strode over to the control panel and began fiddling with the buttons. "This station, just like every other one, uses a built-in gravity generator to counteract the Zero-G environment in space. If we can turn it off, we can put those guys out there out of commission long enough for us to get to the ship and blast off."

"It would take us out of commission too," Jax said.

"I've planned for that," Tom said. "Billy, your job will be to get on board our shuttle. Use the magnetic docking clamps and anchor it to the floor, then fire up the engines. We'll need you to be ready as soon as the rest of us make it to you."

Billy gulped once, then nodded. "I can do that."

"Good," said Tom. "The rest of us will need to buy him time. I've set a timer, so the gravity generator will disengage in three minutes and turn on again one minute later. We need Billy to be on the ship by the time the gravity goes off and ready to fly when it comes back, or else we'll have accomplished nothing."

"It'll be difficult," said Ara. "We'll only have a narrow window of time. But it's our only shot. We have to take it."

"I agree," Jax chimed in. "It's not a bad plan. Let's do it."

Tom reached under the control panel and came back up with two more sections of pipe. He handed one each to Jax and Ara.

"These'll give us an edge. We can't match them in strength, so we'll have to fight a bit dirty to compensate," he said.

No one had a problem with that.

"All right, then," Tom said. "Are we all ready?"

"We are," said Ara. Billy and Jax inclined their heads in agreement.

"Good," said Tom. "I'm opening the door in five … four … three … two … one …"

With that, he slammed the button again, and the door began to slide open. The five remaining masked attackers poured in, but Jax, Ara, and Tom were ready to meet them.

"The timer's started!" Tom yelled above the chaos. "We need to get to the ship!"

Even though Tom had already taken out two of their enemies, the 4S agents were still barely outnumbered. Even so, their improvised weapons helped them drive back their enemies. In no time at all, they pushed the masked men and women back into the main hangar.

Billy hid behind his three friends as they slowly but surely moved toward their ship. When he saw an opening, he rushed for the shuttle's ramp and made it onto the vessel while the attackers were still preoccupied. Jax, Tom, and Ara fought on, keeping themselves between their opponents and their shuttle, until they heard the ship's engine hum to life.

"How much longer?" Ara asked Tom.

"Any second now!" he replied.

Jax felt a slight jolt run through him, and his feet began to lift off the floor. Looking around, he saw every single person and loose object in the hangar rising into the air.

Jax forced himself to relax, remembering the hours he had spent in Voyager Station's antigravity simulator. Moving his arms in broad strokes, he propelled himself closer to the shuttle where it still rested on the floor. Ara and Tom did the same, releasing their metal pipes to lighten their weight. With any luck, they wouldn't need them when the artificial gravity resumed.

All at once, Jax hurtled back toward the ground. He hadn't been high enough to suffer any serious damage when he collided with the cold metal floor, but his bones ached as he clambered to his feet.

Jax sprinted for the ship's ramp, followed closely by Tom and Ara. Ara reached it first and scrambled aboard, with the other two only a few steps behind. The masked attackers tried to follow, but, disoriented from the gravity disappearing and reappearing, they had no chance. The ramp closed and locked long before any of the raiders made it anywhere near it.

Seconds later, the hangar door opened and the shuttle shot forward into the stars. None of the ensigns looked back to see what had happened to their foes, but Jax didn't think they could survive the vacuum of space.

As their ship sped away from the sun and the modules orbiting it, Ara spoke up.

"We have to go back," she said. "We can't leave until we find the ship."

"The ship isn't there!" Tom argued. "Don't you get it? It was a trap! Who knows? Maybe all of those modules are crawling with people who want to kill us. We barely got away from one set, so why should we take our chances with another?"

Ara held up her hands. "All right, all right. I see your point. But what do we do now?"

Her question hung in the air for a very long time.

CHAPTER TWELVE

4S SCOUT SHUTTLE S-349—DEEP SPACE

For two hours after their confrontation with the mysterious figures in black, Billy kept the ship cruising at lightspeed. He hadn't bothered to input a destination and none of the others had come to him to suggest one. Their current and only priority was to get as far away as possible from the abandoned facility.

As he stared out into the starfield, Billy started to think that there might have been something in Tom's complaints after all.

Their team had been ambushed, their assailants lying in wait before they had arrived. The whole ordeal had been a trap.

Billy had wanted to believe that Tom's worries over the missing ore shipment amounted to nothing more than fear-mongering or stress wearing on his friend's brain. The cargo ship's loss couldn't have been deliberate, Billy had told himself. The alternative had been unthinkable. After all, the 4S was doing a valuable and necessary service for the entire world. How could anyone, no matter how depraved, have chosen it as a target?

But clearly, someone had. The knowledge chilled Billy's spine. He may not have been as rational as Ara or a true believer like Tom, but he knew what that meant.

They knew we were coming, and they didn't want us to leave. Our enemies are organized—and they know far more than they should.

Billy forced himself to relax, trying to tell himself that he was safe for the moment. All his teammates were safe. If anyone would know what to do about their situation, it would be Admiral Prang. They would reach the *Home Base*, and everything would be all right.

As he repeated these calming words over and over in his mind, Billy believed them more and more. The world gradually came back into focus. His breathing slowed, and the tension throughout his body eased. A host of sensations flooded into him all at once, grounding him once more to his immediate surroundings.

Billy winced at an aching pain in his hands. He looked down to find them clenched around the blue metal joysticks that controlled the shuttle's steering. He gripped them so strongly that his knuckles turned white. Had he been gripping the sticks the whole time?

Billy uncurled his hands with tremendous effort, flexing his fingers in and out to restore feeling in them. He allowed himself a slight grunt as the motions sent pain shooting up his forearms.

He observed the instruments on his control panel. Thankfully, the shuttle had taken no damage in the attack and all its systems remained fully operational.

At least there's one silver lining, thought Billy.

Boots scuffed the floor behind him. Billy turned to see Jax standing awkwardly in the doorway of the cockpit, with crossed arms and a sour expression. Jax raised his eyes to the windshield and the stars careening by beyond it.

"We're still running at lightspeed?" he asked. "Where are we even going?"

"I don't know," Billy admitted with a sigh. "Away, I guess."

"Fair enough." Jax crossed the cockpit and plopped himself down into a seat close to Billy's console. "Some scouting mission that turned out to be, am I right?"

Billy couldn't find the right words to respond, so he settled for a simple, "Uh, yeah, I guess."

Jax waited for a few moments before finally asking, "How are you feeling?"

The question took Billy by surprise. For as long as he had known Jax, the other man had never struck him as the conversational type. To hear him directly ask for Billy's opinion signified a major break from that trend. Had their recent life-or-death experience changed Jax's outlook, or was it simply shock talking?

Regardless, Billy found his words pouring out of him. "Honestly, I'm scared. Something big is going on out there and here we are in over our heads and I never would have signed up for this if I knew this was what we would be getting into and—"

Jax let out a sardonic chuckle as Billy broke off, panting as he caught his breath. "You're not wrong," he said. "I knew I'd run into those guys again eventually, but I never expected it'd play out like that."

"I take it those were the same people who killed your parents?" Billy asked.

He regretted the words almost immediately. The attack on the Nurmens' lab had always been a touchy subject for Jax, and Billy could vividly remember several times when Jax was ready to bite his head off for even alluding to it. Billy braced himself for the inevitable outburst.

But Jax didn't seem to care. He looked more tired than angry. What was going on in his head? Had the fight knocked all the fight out of him?

"I don't know," he said slowly. "I mean, the guys we saw that night were dressed the same, but I never saw any of their faces either time, and they modulated their voices to make them unrecognizable. Even if they weren't the exact same people I saw that night, I think it's safe to assume they're working together."

"Then it's true," came a voice from the door.

Jax and Billy whirled around to see Tom making his way up the aisle toward them. He took a seat in the row behind Jax and propped his feet up on the chair in front of him.

"What's true?" asked Billy.

"It's all connected," explained Tom. "These mysterious enemies are behind everything that's happened. First they attacked Epsilon Station, then they killed the Nurmens, and now they came for us. I don't know what they could possibly be hoping to gain, but they clearly have an agenda."

Billy stayed silent. Tom wasn't saying anything that he hadn't already been thinking. Jax, meanwhile, stared out the windshield with a pensive expression on his face.

"The people who killed my parents mentioned something about looking for data," Jax said. "I didn't hear the whole conversation, but they definitely wanted information they thought my parents had. Maybe these people want the research the Eden Project is doing."

"But why would they kill to get it?" asked Tom. "Especially when it was always going to be made available to everyone eventually. What do they think they could do with it that the 4S isn't already doing?"

"It's not a perfect theory," said Jax. "I'm just stating what I know. But enough about their motivations. What about ours? What do we do after everything that just happened?"

"I'd say that's obvious," said Ara, walking up to join them, holding the blue box. "We tell Admiral Prang. He needs to know."

"We'd have to drop out of lightspeed to do that," said Billy. "Are we sure it's safe?"

Ara mulled that over for a few seconds. "Not entirely, but I think we have a good chance. We're a good distance from the sun by now, and it didn't look like anyone was following us."

"Then let's do it," said Jax. "We can't run forever."

"You're right," agreed Tom. "Billy, let's stop here."

"Okay," said Billy. He flipped a switch, and the shuttle came out of lightspeed. Billy ran a quick scan of the area and found they were entirely alone, surrounded by empty space.

Ara led everyone to the shuttle's common area. She placed the box on the table and opened a comm channel to the admiral. When Prang's hologram finally fizzled into existence, the four ensigns breathed a collective sigh of relief.

"Greetings, friends," said Prang, nodding as they all saluted him. "How is your mission going? Did you find the cargo ship? We haven't seen a homing beacon."

"We have bad news, sir," said Tom.

"How bad?" Prang asked.

"About the worst it could be," said Jax. "We didn't find the ship, but we found some guys who attacked us. We barely made it out with our lives."

"You went into combat?" Prang said.

"It wasn't our choice, sir," Ara replied. "We were set up. We thought we might have located the ship, but it turned out to be a sneak attack."

"I see," Prang mused. "Is there anything else I should know?"

"Probably that they looked exactly like the guys who killed my parents," said Jax.

Prang sighed. "I feared something like this would happen sooner or later," he said. "I only hoped we would be in a better position to respond. There's still so much we don't know about our enemies."

"But they sure know a lot about the 4S," Jax said. "They found two of your secret research stations, and they killed at least that many of your personnel. They managed to steal an entire shipment of metal ore, and they knew you'd send people out to look for it. It can't possibly all be coincidence at this point."

"You're quite right, Jax. I've been living in denial for too long," said Prang. "I can't ignore the facts anymore. I hoped that what happened at Epsilon Station could have been a tragic accident. The murder of your parents proved beyond a doubt that the 4S has enemies, but I never would have thought that they could predict our moves."

"How would they pull off something like that?" asked Billy.

"Hacking, maybe," suggested Ara. "If they tapped our communications or bugged our briefing rooms, they could learn all kinds of things. Knowledge is power, and we know these people have the power to act on their knowledge."

"But that doesn't make any sense," objected Tom. "What reason would anyone have to attack the 4S? We're a humanitarian organization."

"Unless they're not attacking the 4S," Ara said slowly. "Before that missing ore shipment, no other normal 4S missions had problems, right?"

"Normal? What are you talking about?" asked Jax.

Prang seemed to understand. "She's right. Whoever is working against us clearly has one very specific goal: the destruction of the Eden Project."

"But now they're going after the entire 4S?" asked Billy. "Seems like a pretty sudden shift."

"It would mean changing their entire modus operandi," said Ara. "Before today, they stayed off our radar for so long because they only attacked bases not many people paid attention to. There's only a limited amount of sabotage they can pull off against the 4S' public operations before someone catches on."

"It all seems pretty foolish," Jax said. "The 4S may not be a military, but it's got the entire world behind it. Trying to take it out would be suicide for just about anyone."

"And there's something else," put in Tom. "How are they getting around? They must have spacefaring capacity, but no one except the 4S should have that."

"It isn't about what they *should* have, Tom. We need to be focusing on the fact that they clearly do have it, whether we like the idea of that or not," retorted Ara.

"Is it really that impossible?" asked Jax. "Couldn't there be a chance you just missed the signs that someone else was moving in on your turf?"

"No way," replied Tom. "The 4S would have noticed something like that. We've got people flying all over the solar system each day."

"Not necessarily," said Billy. "There's a lot of space out there to lose someplace in. It's like the ocean back on Earth. We've only explored a small part of it."

Prang raised a hand to his chin. "Lost in space …" His eyes became distant, unfocused, staring at something none of the ensigns could see, or perhaps at nothing at all.

The four ensigns looked at each other.

"Is he okay?" asked Billy.

Concern flickered across Tom's face. "I don't know. He doesn't usually space out like this."

"Should we say something?" Jax asked. "Would that be out of bounds?"

"Let's not be hasty. Maybe he'll snap out of it on his own," said Ara.

Prang broke out of his reverie as he registered Ara's words. "My apologies, you four. I just remembered a tidbit of history that may prove useful in solving this dilemma. Would you all like to hear a story?"

"If you think it would be relevant, sir," Tom answered hesitantly.

"Oh, I very much believe it would," said Prang. "Some thirty-odd years ago, not long before my time as admiral began, the 4S sent a long-term scientific expedition beyond the boundary of the solar system to study the cosmic energies at work there. The mission was connected to the Eden Project, and the scientists' goal was to trace the potential sources of the cosmic rays and particles zipping about in our galaxy."

"I think I've heard about this one, sir," said Ara. "The team never came back, did they?"

"Unfortunately, they didn't," Prang replied. "Well, they returned, just not in a way any of us expected. Roughly three months into their assignment, their ship's GPS transmitter went dead. When a search and rescue squad reached the science team's last known location, they found the research ship drifting, dead in space with an entire chunk of its hull blown out. None of its crew survived, except for one lone man. The cause of the disaster was put down to a failure in one of the research instruments. By all appearances, the device had overloaded with energy and couldn't contain it."

"So what does this have to do with the mission today?" cut in Tom.

"Patience, Ensign," Prang said. "I'll get to that. But first, I can't tell this story without mentioning the research team's leader, Doctor James Simmons. That man was nothing short of a prodigy. While he was still enrolled at the 4S Academy of Science and Technology, he designed a new engine that helped our shuttles run with twenty-five percent more energy efficiency. When he officially joined the Research Division, his prestige only increased. At one point, he was even considered as a candidate for the Chief Research Officer position alongside Doctor Fletcher. Since sustainable energy was always his passion, it didn't surprise anyone when he became part of the Eden Project's think tank. It was a terrible shame that his story ended far too early."

"I remember him, too," said Ara. "Something strange happened with his body, but I don't remember what."

"That would be because his body was never found," Prang told her. "Along with the bodies of several other crew members. The rescue team searched the area thoroughly, but they never recovered all the bodies. They did find one still alive, though. A man named Roger Howard had stayed safe by sealing himself away in the ship's storeroom. By the time the 4S found him, he had clearly suffered some kind of psychological trauma. He would babble on about nonsense like 'the shadow' or something 'rising'. It got to the point where he was no longer able to carry on with his usual tasks. Howard was eventually medically discharged, and he's passed on since, but the memory of his words has stayed with all those who heard them."

"So how does this all relate to us?" asked Tom.

"Because," replied Prang, "I'm beginning to think that his words were more than just nonsense. Most of the things he would ramble about made little to no sense, but sometimes he would begin to speak about a 'source' and how someone would eventually come for it. We soon realized that he was too far gone to provide us with any real answer as to what he was talking about, and yet now that we know the 4S has enemies targeting the source of our Eden Project, it seems to me that perhaps his words were more than coincidental."

"With all due respect, that seems kind of far-fetched," said Jax. "If there were people trying to take down the project back then, why did they wait so long to make their next move? And how could that man have known about it? It sounds like he didn't know much of anything by the end."

"I'll admit, I don't have your answers," Prang told him. "By the time I rose to the rank of admiral, the entire incident had long since been hushed up. To this day, the public only knows that the research team suffered a tragic accident which only one of its members survived. During his psychotic fits, the moments in which he seemed most grounded in reality were those when he talked about something coming for the 4S."

"But you have to know you're being ridiculous. You think this man was, what, some kind of a prophet? Some herald of things yet to come? How often does something like that come around?" Jax shot back.

"It's a long shot for sure, and we have no way of proving or disproving it. For now, I won't bother to ask that you believe me. I only brought up the story because your words reminded me of the research team's fate," said Prang.

"But, sir, what about our fate?" asked Ara. "What would you like us to do now?"

"Return to *Home Base* as soon as possible," said Prang. "I need to know everything that happened aboard the solar station, but this is hardly the place for that conversation. After we've spoken, you four will be free to go about your assigned tasks until I call upon you again."

"Yes, sir. I'll lay in a course back to the cruiser right now," said Billy.
"Thank you, Ensign Vurk. That would be most appreciated." Prang faced the others. "I'll look forward to your return." His hologram fizzled away.

Billy headed off toward the cockpit, but he paused at the other end of the room. He glanced back to see Jax sharing a look with Tom and Ara.

"Now I know he's losing it," said Jax.

"Be nice," said Ara. "Can you blame him for being concerned? It's a scary thought that someone might have predicted the problems we're having right now, even if the idea of it is outlandish."

"I'm not putting too much stock in it, either," Tom said. "It's a very long shot. If Prang really had a warning under his nose this whole time, the guy who gave it could have been a lot clearer. Seems like a cruel joke to give us some kind of vague prophecy and only have us realize what we have when it's already too late to use it."

"Maybe you're right," Ara told him. "Maybe it's all some trumped-up story, or maybe it really was a genuine prediction of what the 4S is going through. I don't know if I fully believe in it, but I'm definitely paying attention to it. If Admiral Prang is so worried by it, then I'm worried, too. The fact that we could possibly have prevented all this, that we could have saved the lives of dozens of people … it's haunting. The kind of thing that stays with you forever."

"Would it really make a difference?" Tom asked. "Whether we knew about them thirty years ago or just yesterday, these things are still happening right now. I don't want to distract myself with questions about the past when there are people in the present who've shown themselves to be completely willing to stab our backs the second we turn them."

The argument continued as Billy walked out of the room and into the cockpit. The sounds of his friend's voices faded as he strapped himself into his pilot's chair.

Billy had never been the kind of pilot who viewed flying as a form of escape. He loved the Earth—no, he loved the entire galaxy—and he wanted to experience as much of it as he possibly could. To him, seeing the planets blur as they whizzed by at thousands of miles per hour seemed somehow more beautiful than they were when they were stationary. Joining the 4S and learning to operate their space shuttles had always been his dream.

And yet …

The same expanse of stars and planets that had once seemed to be boundless now felt like it was tightening like a noose around Billy's neck, choking the life energy out of him. Even the wide open spaces between celestial objects made him feel confined, trapped with nowhere to go. As Billy watched the current coordinates of the *Home Base* scroll across his screen, he fought to keep his breathing under control.

The story of the lost research team would have been tragic on its own, but the revelation that the sole survivor could have had a premonition warning him of the 4S' current struggles added to its weight.

The kind of thing that stays with you forever, Ara had

called it, and Billy had to agree.

So many dedicated 4S personnel had already been lost. Billy and his team had come close to joining their number, narrowly escaping with their lives.

Our enemies won't be satisfied with small-scale attacks forever, Billy thought. *Soon they'll go for the big prize. What will we do then?*

Then there was no more time for introspection. Making a conscious effort to stay in the moment, Billy pushed the ship's throttle as far up as it would go, and the shuttle leapt back into lightspeed.

CHAPTER THIRTEEN

GYMNASIUM—4S COMMAND CRUISER *HOME BASE*— DEEP SPACE

Jax closed his eyes, hoping that the repetitive motions of his feet on the treadmill would lull him into relaxation. When he opened his eyes a minute later, he found to his disappointment that he hadn't succeeded.

Nine whole days had passed since he and the others had returned from the solar station, and yet sometimes it felt as though no time had elapsed at all. Jax didn't know about Ara, Billy, or Tom, but each night in his dreams he found himself back in the thick of the fight against those masked strangers. Unlike the real event, his nightmares never ended with him pulling off a clever escape. Each night he woke up covered in cold sweat, and each night he dreaded the thought of going back to sleep and reliving his worst fears.

Few people would have called Jax introspective, and fewer still would have called him philosophical. And yet, Jax found himself thinking thoughts of life and death with surprising depth.

On the morning he had stood before his parents' corpses, crying tears of rage and grief, he made a promise to bring about vengeance for their untimely deaths, and he still had no intention of reneging on his vow. He was, however, coming to appreciate the full scope of exactly what that vengeance would cost him. He had rushed into his vendetta without a clear path to fulfilling it. If the 4S hadn't come along and offered him a place among them, he might still be wandering aimlessly around the city of Chicago, unsure of what to do with himself.

What had he expected? That the killers would just shrug their shoulders and turn themselves in? That the legal system would take care of the problem before Jax had to lift a finger? No. Whoever the people under the black masks were, they would face the punishment of the law one day, but as long as they roamed free among the stars, it would be Jax's job to root them out. Perhaps it was not his job alone—after all, the 4S had lost people too, and had given Jax access to the resources he needed—but business concerns shrouded their interests in the matter. For Jax, the quest was entirely personal.

Even so, Jax's desire for vengeance hadn't been enough to carry him through. If Tom hadn't figured out how to disable the solar module's gravity generator, Jax's story would have likely ended that day. Before that day, he had never considered that he might be taking on more than he could handle. If he went into another fight against the 4S' unknown enemies, he didn't know if he could make it out.

Doctor Fletcher had made it quite clear that Jax's physical skills were little more than painfully average. He performed well enough that Admiral Prang felt comfortable employing him, but he barely scratched the surface of the level and amount of training full-time 4S agents like Ara, Billy, and Tom enjoyed.

And so he had come to the *Home Base*'s onboard gymnasium, hoping that he could train his body to be stronger. The 4S lacked the equipment or instruction for hand-to-hand combat, so a regular regimen of exercise would be the next best thing. Every day since the fight, he had run himself through a gauntlet of workouts. Each night he fell asleep almost the moment his head touched his pillow—which might have been a blessing had it not provided him more time for nightmares.

Jax roused from his thoughts as the timer on his treadmill signaled the end of his workout. He dismounted from the treadmill, headed over to the water fountain to fill his 4S-issued canteen, and wiped his face with a towel. His panting breaths slowed as he ran himself through a series of cool-down stretches, and by the time he walked out of the gym his legs felt steady underneath him once again.

Jax wasted no time in heading up to the dormitory for a cold shower and a change of clothes. By 1800 hours, he made it down to the cafeteria, where he sat with his tolerable Instant-Meal casserole for a full fifteen minutes before Ara, Billy, and Tom showed up. He even had time to surprise himself by going back for seconds.

When the other three arrived, they found Jax sitting alone at a corner table and settled into the remaining chairs. Billy was in the middle of entertaining Ara and Tom with some kind of story. They laughed heartily as the tale came to an end, but Jax tuned it all out.

Moments such as those were stark reminders for Jax that these three people had a connection to the 4S and to each other that he didn't share. While Jax had been pushing himself to sweat off the pain of his dreams, these three had had all kinds of work and activities to bury themselves in and take their minds off their collective near-death experience. Even though he would never have admitted it out loud, he envied them that.

As far as Jax was concerned, meeting the three ensigns and later joining their squad had been little more than a convenience. His place among them had afforded him access to the vast resources of the 4S so he could finish the quest he could never have finished alone. Jax could admit to himself that he might be beginning to like them, or at least to appreciate the ways their minds worked, but he knew it was far too early in the game for him to call them his friends. Perhaps someday, though …

No. Jax knew his boundaries. Even if they were waiting to accept him, he would always feel like he was holding a part of himself back, out of their sight. And it would all be moot in the end anyway. As soon as their enemies were vanquished, Jax would leave, and the others' careers would carry on without him. Maybe that was for the best.

"Jax? Jax!"

Jax snapped back to attention at the sound of Ara calling his name. "You okay there, Jax? You don't look too good."

"I'm fine," Jax said. "Just spacing out a little is all."

She looked like she might argue, but decided to take his

word for it. "If you say so."

"We were talking about our assignment," cut in Tom. "We were wondering when Admiral Prang will need us next. What do you think?"

"I don't know," Jax replied. "If it were that predictable, we wouldn't be sitting here wondering about it, would we?"

"Good point," said Tom.

"I'm not in any hurry to get out there again," Billy admitted. "We all remember what happened last time."

"Last time was a deliberate trap," said Tom. "We should have noticed it long before we did. Now that we know their tactics, we can avoid it in the future. We won't be caught off guard next time."

"If they did it once, they can do it again," said Billy.

Jax just scowled.

"Are you sure you're okay?" Ara asked. She rested her hand on top of his where it lay on the tabletop. "These people did kill your parents. They pretty much destroyed your whole life. You're allowed to stop and be emotional about that, even if it's just for a minute."

Jax pulled his hand away. "What difference would it make? What would it change? Yes, people I loved are dead. That just gives me more reason to concentrate on bringing their killers down."

The look she gave him wasn't unsympathetic, but Jax got the impression she wished he had said something else. Her jaw was set a little too squarely, and her posture was a little too rigid, for him to think she was entirely comfortable with his words.

"But what will you do when you have?" she said gently.

Jax went silent. It was a question he had wrestled with several times over the past weeks.

Back when he had lived on Earth, when he had still thought his life was normal, Jax had never felt an urgent need to plan out his future. He had always known that he wouldn't always have his parents to rely on, but he had been young enough that he hadn't yet considered striking out on his own. The events since the night his parents died seemed to have aged him ten years in that many weeks, leaving him no time to truly grapple with the ramifications of all that had occurred. When his crusade finally ended and the threats to the 4S were gone, what did he even have to go back to?

"You don't know, do you?" Billy said into the silence. He ignored Jax's glare as he went on. "Jax, you don't have to be alone. Even if you're trying to close yourself off from us, we want to help you."

Jax glanced away. If even Billy could pick up on his thoughts, he must not have been doing as good a job of concealing them as he had thought.

"He's right, you know," said Ara. "We know this must be hard for you, and we do want to help you through it as much as we can. If that's something you want, of course. But we need you to meet us halfway if it's going to work. Can you do that?"

Can I? Jax wondered. Blocking them out wasn't exactly something he wanted to do, but it seemed to be happening anyway. He had attempted to rationalize it, telling himself that they would never understand what he was going through, but taking it all upon himself hadn't worked either. One way or another, he would break eventually. Would it be better to just have that moment over with?

"I don't know," he admitted honestly. "You're asking me to do a lot. Everything that happened when I came here was just so sudden, and I'm only now getting around to processing a lot of it. Even I don't completely know how I feel. Do you know how crazy that is?"

The words had tumbled out of him before he had even planned to say most of them. Realizing how he must have sounded, he looked down at his hands in embarrassment.

"I'm sorry," he said quickly. "Forget it. It doesn't matter."

"Look, Jax," said Tom. "We meant what we said. The reason the three of us have been friends for so long is because we're not afraid to tell each other when we're hurting, and we help out the ones who are. If you're going to be part of this group, you can have that help too. We won't force you, but we don't want to see you in pain. If there's ever anything we can do for you, just let us know, okay?"

Lost for words, Jax simply nodded.

"Good choice," said Tom.

His conversation with Billy and Ara resumed, turning to far lighter topics. Jax joined in a few times, offering his thoughts on this thing or that, but he spent most of the remaining mealtime deep in thought as he picked away at his Instant-Meal.

What do I do now? He had aired his feelings to the others, and they had expressed an honest wish to listen. He sensed that they truly wanted to help where they could, or at least that they had no intention of turning him away. The problem lay with him. Would he ever be able to let his guard down? What was he so afraid of? These people had been nothing but kind to him, yet he kept them at arm's length. They may not need him, but he was beginning to understand more and more just how much he needed them.

At that, Jax felt a light beginning to break through his funk. What had he been thinking? Giving in to his darker thoughts wouldn't help him. It wouldn't help anybody. It didn't matter whether or not he stayed or left, or what the others did without him. They were all together in the moment, and that moment was all he needed.

Jax had survived the assault on his parents lab and the trap the raiders had set for his team on the solar station. He didn't let himself believe that he had survived because of anything more than dumb luck, but the important thing was that he had survived. Every day his life went on was a gift, an opportunity for him to rededicate himself to his pursuit of the justice his parents had been denied. As he sat on the metal seat in the cafeteria, amidst the bustling crowd of hungry 4S agents, Jax renewed his promise to himself and his parents' memories that he would seek out that justice. He would end the killers' reign of terror if it was the last thing he did.

And he would keep his newfound teammates by his side for as long as he possibly could.

*

Admiral Prang took advantage of a rare uneventful day in his schedule to travel to Voyager Station with Vice Admiral Pitt. In a secure chamber with Chief Research Officer Fletcher, they studied a map of the solar system. Several blue dots scattered across that map signified the locations of research stations for the Eden Project. Two of those dots—one on Earth marking Theta Outpost and one in space marking Epsilon Station—had changed color from blue to red, as those two stations were no longer operational.

"The attack on our team of ensigns proves that our enemies can anticipate our moves," Prang said. "I suggest we see if we can anticipate theirs."

"And how do you propose we do that, sir? Unlike those lowlifes, we don't have a helpful source of information to tell us what's going to happen next," said Pitt.

"Yet there are still things we can be sure of," replied Prang. "They've taken out two of our stations thus far. We should look for any connections that might exist between those two stations."

"I'm afraid you won't find much to go off of there, Admiral," said Doctor Fletcher. "Beyond the fact that they both served our Eden Project, there is very little to link those stations. Theta Outpost made use of the cosmic energy collected by Epsilon Station, but, then again, so did many other stations, and all of those have remained safe."

"If their goal were only to take out as many stations as possible, many more stations would have been attacked," Prang said. "As of now, however, only two have suffered that fate. Why would our enemies have chosen to go after those first? That is the question."

"Theta had the Nurmens," said Pitt. "Those two were just about the strongest supporters of the Eden Project, and we all know they would have fought to the end to protect it. Perhaps whoever is hoping to destroy the project wanted to spare themselves a bit of trouble down the road."

"That may be the case," said Doctor Fletcher, "but Epsilon Station had no personnel with such a strong commitment to the project. Its workers were dedicated, of course, but none of them were as dedicated as Rebecca and Albert, may they rest in peace."

"So maybe they weren't targeting any specific researchers," Pitt shot back. "Maybe their only goal was to cause destruction and destabilize our work. They've certainly accomplished that."

"That may be," chipped in Prang, raising a finger as a thought occurred to him, "but I think there may be something even more sinister afoot. After all, Epsilon Station experimented with collecting cosmic radiation, and Theta Outpost focused on how to redirect that energy to provide electrical power. I hope I'm wrong on this, but I believe our unidentified terrorists could very easily have attacked the stations they did in the hope of seizing the research data for themselves."

"Sir, I don't think that's likely," Pitt said. "What reason would they have to do that? Do they think they can do it better? Besides, if we decided that they knew not only where each station was located but also what specific research each one did, we'd be admitting that the leak in our information runs deeper than we previously assumed. Personally, I refuse to believe that a group of lowlifes could worm their way that deep into the restricted sections of our archives."

"Perhaps your less-than-optimistic outlook has rubbed off on me, then," Prang replied.

Pitt let out a grunt of indignation, but the admiral went on.

"I don't want to assume the worst before we have evidence for it. The last thing we need is to be hurling around baseless accusations. We will have to look both inward and outward before we get to the heart of this problem."

"Well spoken, sir," said Doctor Fletcher. "Might I suggest that instead of spending time trying to figure out why the Epsilon and Theta outposts were attacked, we figure out how to prevent future attacks from occurring?"

"You're absolutely right," agreed Prang. "The Eden Project is too important to lose. Before any more stations can be lost, we have to—"

The beep of his personal communicator cut him off. Removing the device from its holster on his belt, he glanced down at its screen.

"Speak of the devil," he murmured.
"What was that, sir?" Doctor Fletcher asked.

"I'm being hailed on a secure channel," said Prang. "One of the ones we use to communicate with the Eden Project research stations."

He opened the channel on his communicator, and immediately they could all hear the voice of a man.

"This is Doctor Brian Han from Rho Station calling Admiral Prang!" he said frantically. "Can anyone hear me?"

Prang thumbed the button to respond. "This is Admiral Prang. I hear you, Doctor Han. What's your situation?"

"Sir!" The man sounded breathless and immensely relieved that his call had been received. "The station … crazy masked lunatics … came out of nowhere … three scientists already gone—"

Admiral Prang raised his head to share a look with the others. They all knew what Doctor Han was implying.

"Slow down, Doctor." Prang kept his voice level. "We can't understand you. What exactly is happening on your station?"

The man took a deep breath. "My apologies, Admiral. We've been overrun. This ship appeared out of nowhere, and these strange people boarded, and then—"

Prang thrust the communicator away from his ear as the sound of an explosion and rupturing metal erupted from the device, followed by a much quieter intake of breath from Doctor Han.

"They've found me," he said. "Admiral, please. We need—"

They heard the sound of a sharp object entering human flesh, then the thud of a body against the floor. The transmission from Rho Station dissolved into the crunching of metal followed by the buzz of static.

Prang placed the communicator close to his mouth. "Doctor Han? Doctor Han, what is your status? Please respond!"

He waited several minutes, and attempted to reestablish contact several more times, but no answer ever came.

"It seems another station has been lost to us," Doctor Fletcher observed.

"Indeed." Prang toggled a few controls to change the dot that represented Rho Station on the holomap from blue to red.

"We can't let this keep happening," Vice Admiral Pitt growled. "We're losing ground fast, and if we can't regain it, everything will go up in flames."

"Calm down," Prang said. "This will not stand. I have a plan."

"With all due respect, Admiral, anything you could do would likely be too late," Doctor Fletcher said. "By all accounts, the raiders are already on the station. By the time you mustered any form of aid, they would likely be gone."

"That doesn't change the fact that we have to try," argued Prang. "There may be clues they left behind."

"Of course," said Fletcher. "What would you have us do, sir?"

"We need to get men on the scene as soon as possible," replied Prang. "Call in our team of ensigns," he ordered Pitt. "And get me two—no, three full search and rescue teams. Have Captain Ramón assemble them in a briefing room on the *Home Base* so we can speak to them by holomessage. I want them ready in one hour."

"That's a bit of a tall order," replied Pitt. "But I'm sure they'll manage. What will you have them do?"

"Isn't it obvious, Vice Admiral?" asked Prang. "We're going to save some lives. And if we can't, we'll find a way to avenge them."

CHAPTER FOURTEEN

BRIEFING ROOM 175—4S COMMAND CRUISER *HOME BASE*—DEEP SPACE

Jax, Ara, Billy, and Tom clustered around the table in the center of the room, observing Captain Ramón as he paced close by. Unlike their last official briefing, they were not alone with the captain. A full three dozen other 4S agents of varying age and rank stood around them. With so many people around, even one of the larger 4S briefing rooms began to feel crowded.

A woman with dark skin and wavy black hair fixed Ramón with steel-gray eyes. Her rank patch marked her as a Commander, which made her the second-highest-ranked individual in the room, subordinate only to Captain Ramón.

"Why have you brought us here, Captain?" she asked in a heavily accented voice. "What's so important that you had to gather three whole teams for one mission?"

"Teams?" Jax whispered into Ara's ear. "What kind of teams are these?"

"Search and rescue, most likely," Ara whispered back. "That woman is Commander Ellen Sullivan. She's the head of that division."

"Then why are we here?" asked Jax. "We aren't trained for that kind of mission. Do you think we're going to be?"

"I don't know," she said. "Admiral Prang will probably want us to stick with our current assignment. Whatever we're here for must be connected to that in some way."

Meanwhile, Captain Ramón had answered Commander Sullivan's query. "I'm not exactly sure myself. My orders to gather all these agents together came from higher up the chain of command."

"Oh, yeah?" Sullivan shot back. "Just how much higher up, exactly?"

"From the highest possible point," came a voice. "From me."

Jax and all the others in the room spun around to see that a life-sized holographic image of Admiral Prang had materialized in the space behind them, accompanied by similar projections of Vice Admiral Pitt and Doctor Gregory Fletcher.

"At ease," Prang told the gathered crowd after they saluted him.

"Admiral!" Commander Sullivan gasped. "My sincerest apologies, sir. I had no idea—"

"It's all right, Commander." Prang gave her a knowing nod. "You have nothing to be sorry for. It is I who should be apologizing, for keeping you all waiting."

"We haven't been waiting long, sir," Sullivan assured him. "Maybe five minutes at most. Calling in from—well, wherever you are—"

"Voyager Station," Prang said.

"Calling in from Voyager Station takes a bit of time," she finished. "What was it you wanted to tell us?"

"One moment," Prang said. "Captain Ramón, if you would please pull up the hologram?"

"Yes, sir." Ramón moved to the table's keypad. After he pressed a few buttons, an image of a 4S space station appeared in the air above the table. At least, Jax could guess the image was a space station, because it looked like Voyager Station without the vertical pylons.

"This is Rho Station," Prang began. "It is one of many 4S research stations throughout the solar system dedicated to conducting research for our Eden Project. Approximately two hours ago, we received a troubling call from one of its personnel."

Prang held up a communicator and played a recording for the crowd.

"The station ... crazy masked lunatics ... came out of nowhere ... three scientists already gone—" a man's voice said rapidly.

Jax tuned out the rest of the recording. As soon as he heard the words *crazy masked lunatics*, he knew exactly what the situation was. Rho Station and all its staff had met the same fate as Jax's parents. That explained the presence of the search and rescue teams, and why there were so many of them.

When the recording ended Prang spoke once again.

"We tried and failed to reestablish contact with Doctor Han or anyone else on Rho Station. While I hate to be a fatalist and assume the worst, for all intents and purposes, we must consider the entire staff of that station to be missing in action."

Missing. Not *killed*. Jax wondered if there was still a difference between the two.

Commander Sullivan stepped forward. "How can we help, sir?"

"I'm glad you asked," said Prang. "I want you to lead your teams to Rho Station and sweep the area. Searching for survivors will be your first priority, but I also want you to bring back as much data on the state of the station as you can, as well as any clues you may uncover as to the identity of the attackers."

If Commander Sullivan was fazed by the idea of attackers and survivors, she didn't show it as she nodded assertively. "It'll be done, sir."

"Thank you, Commander," said Prang. "I'll have Doctor Fletcher here send the station's coordinates to your personal holopad. Captain Ramón has procured a shuttle for your teams in Docking Bay Fifty-Five. You are to leave as soon as possible. Any questions?"

"I have one, sir." Ara stepped into the admiral's field of vision. Commander Sullivan moved aside to accommodate her.

"What do you want the four of us to do?" Ara asked, gesturing to where Tom, Billy, and Jax leaned against the wall.

"Your task will be the observation I mentioned earlier,"

said Prang. "While the search and rescue squads perform their work, you four will be the ones gathering information on what happened to the station. Stay close to Commander Sullivan and her team, and don't go into any areas they haven't declared safe, but be observant. I want to know about anything at all that could potentially be useful, and I'm trusting the four of you to be my eyes. Can you do that?"

"Yes, sir." Ara saluted. Jax, Billy, and Tom did the same to show their sincerity. "You can count on us."

"Wonderful," said Prang. "Commander Sullivan, these ensigns are under your command for the duration of this mission. As I reminded them, you should all be wary. The station may no longer be structurally sound, and we don't want any accidents. Stick together and watch each other's backs. If you see any of those 'masked lunatics', do not engage them unless it becomes absolutely necessary. Am I understood?"

All the 4S agents in the room responded with, "Sir, yes, sir."

"Then you had best be on your way," Prang told her. "There is no time to lose. Stay safe, and bring back whatever you can."

"If there's anything left to bring back," Jax muttered.

No one heard him.

*

The space around Rho Station was utterly devoid of ships, 4S or otherwise. Unlike Epsilon Station, Rho Station seemed to have remained largely intact despite the recent attack. There was no massive gaping hole in the side, at least. If Jax didn't know what had just occurred aboard the research station, he might well have been fooled into thinking everything was completely fine.

Jax, Ara, Billy, and Tom gathered with the search and rescue crew in the shuttle's common area as Commander Sullivan walked in from the cockpit to address her team.

"Right," she said briskly. "We've completed our initial scans of the station, and there are a couple things we should all watch out for. Docking bays seem to be in working order, so we can land the ship. The rest of the station also looks stable, so we don't have to worry about it falling apart on us."

The entire crowd relaxed a little as she brought up an image of the station above the room's holotable. The first stage of their operation had proven easier than expected.

"Since we brought three teams, we'll split the search grid into three sections," Commander Sullivan continued. "I'll lead Team One to sweep the top third. Lieutenant Commander Braun's team will take the middle, and Lieutenant Commander Goodman will take the bottom. Braun, you'll handle Levels Six through Ten. Goodman, you'll handle Levels Eleven to Fifteen. My group will handle Levels One through Five."

Two lieutenant commanders, one a tall ginger-haired man and the other a shorter blonde woman, stepped forward and saluted in acknowledgement of their orders. As they stepped back into the throng, Ara took their place in the colonel's line of sight.

"Excuse me, ma'am," she began, "but what about us?" She nodded to where Jax, Tom, and Billy stood nearby. "We aren't assigned to any of the teams."

Colonel Sullivan looked Ara up and down before she responded. "Oh, yes. You're the ones Admiral Prang sent along, aren't you? He wants you to observe, so you'll observe. I'll bring you along with my team so I can keep track of you, but you'll get your chance to get in on the action. Satisfied?"

Ara only allowed herself to be taken aback by the colonel's brusqueness for a second. "Yes, ma'am," she said.

Colonel Sullivan turned off the holoprojector and addressed the entire mission team once more.

"Right. We've scanned the station for life signs, and we found a few. We won't be able to tell for certain whether any of the people are alive or dead until we're next to them, but it looks like we'll all have our work cut out for us. This isn't going to be like it was at Epsilon. I'd wager good money that there's a reason the bodies were left behind this time. I want everyone to be on guard. If you see anything suspicious, report it immediately. Is that clear?"

"Yes, ma'am," chorused the assembled crowd.

"Good." Sullivan faced the cockpit and called, "Pilot?

Take us in."

Within moments, the shuttle was on the move again, making for the nearest docking pylon. The automatic docking procedures worked like a charm, and not long after the ship had been sealed into the hangar, the crew stepped off into a fully oxygenated atmosphere. All three search and rescue teams moved as a pack through the hangar bay and the sterilization chamber until they were spat out into the station proper. Colonel Sullivan led them to the hub at the center of the station where its elevators were housed, where she gave her final orders before splitting them up.

"You know your assignments," she said. "Remember to be on alert. The station itself hasn't been compromised, but all manner of things could still have been happening. I know I for one don't like how easily this mission's gone so far. I don't want to think it's a trap, but we can't afford not to consider the possibility."

Everyone else agreed.

Lieutenant Commander Goodman's Team Three was the first to board the elevator. Once they had begun their descent toward Level Eleven, Colonel Sullivan led her team and the four tagalong ensigns into a second elevator car bound for Level One. None of them spoke for the entire two-minute trip, until they stood at the very top of the station, where four separate hallways branched off from the elevator hub.

Colonel Sullivan's team consisted of twelve members, including the colonel herself, and she sent one team of three to scope out each hallway. She sent one ensign along with each team, and Jax joined Sullivan's group.

Slowly and methodically, the search and rescue operatives made their way through the top five levels of the station. The first two contained bunkrooms, dining rooms, communal areas, and all the other facilities necessary to support Rho Station's apparently quite large crew complement.

The next three levels were divided into smaller laboratories. Some of those labs were clean and empty, while others had been set up for ongoing experiments, the interactive holoscreens on their walls covered in all sorts of data tables and mathematical calculations. Colonel Sullivan's team tested each lab before they entered to make sure there were no hazardous materials out of containment, but each room proved safe.

The team found a number of lab personnel—eight in total—as they carried out their search. Of those eight people, three were already dead, and their bodies were respectfully laid in black bags for transport back to the shuttle. The other five had managed to cling to life, but some had survived more easily than others. Two had to be placed inside medical pods for a more advanced treatment, while the other three got by on basic first aid. Only two of those remained conscious, but all three were in stable condition. As the team picked up more scientists, their efficiency took a hit, but they still managed to complete a thorough sweep of the top third of the station in just under two hours.

The whole time, Jax, Ara, Billy, and Tom remained on the lookout for signs of anything suspicious. Even so, just like its exterior, the inside of Rho Station appeared remarkably undamaged considering the attack it had just undergone. Aside from the dead and injured laboratory workers, and the numerous cases of minor property damage, it almost looked as though no attack occurred.

Ara was the first to comment on that strange phenomenon.

"It's uncanny," she said to the others. "At Epsilon Station, the raiders made a pretty big display of their intentions. Here, they were a lot more subtle about it. I don't know if I could make a guess as to what their ultimate goal could be."

"I can," Jax said darkly. "They're killers. Just because they spared some of the people this time doesn't change that. All these people want is chaos and destruction."

"But that still doesn't make any sense to me," said Billy. "What kind of deranged psychopaths would want to destroy a project with such a noble goal? It's not like the 4S is weaponizing the Eden Project, or hoarding the benefits."

"Some people are just wired wrong," Tom observed with a sad shake of his head.

At last, when the team had peered into every nook and cranny in their portion of the station, they all met up in the elevator hub on Level Five. Commander Sullivan took advantage of the lull in her squad's work to contact the other two teams and attain an update on their progress. Both Lieutenant Commander Braun and Lieutenant Commander Goodman reported that their searches were well on the way to completion. Like Sullivan's team, they found survivors and victims of the enemy raid.

Comfortable for the moment that her mission team was doing its work well, Commander Sullivan sent half of her squad down to their shuttle with the body bags, medical pods, and conscious and unconscious scientists they collected. The six men and women made three trips before they finished their task. Once they returned and stated that everything aboard the ship was in order, Commander Sullivan gave them a satisfied nod.

"What do we do now, ma'am?" asked her second-in-command, Lieutenant Commander Ashton. His light brown hair, cut just an inch below regulation length, slid from side to side over his broad shoulders as he scanned their surroundings.

Commander Sullivan raised a finger, her eyes flicking back and forth as she scanned the room around her, taking several seconds to scrutinize each of the four branches it split into. When her personal communicator began to beep, however, her eyes flicked downward to the device on her hip. She unclipped it from her belt to receive the message she had been sent.

"Commander Sullivan?" came a man's voice from the unit's speaker. "This is Lieutenant Wilcox with Team Three. Do you copy, ma'am?"

"I copy, Lieutenant," said the Commander. "What's the sitrep?"

"We … we found a body," the man said hesitantly.

Commander Sullivan sighed theatrically. "Then what are you calling me for, Lieutenant? We have protocols for that. Put it in a pod if it's breathing, or a bag if it isn't."

"All due respect, ma'am, it's more complicated than that," Lieutenant Wilcox answered. "I really think you should come down and see this for yourself."

"And why would I do that?" Sullivan shot back. "How am I supposed to sweep the station properly if I'm always getting called away to watch everyone's menial tasks? What's so special about this body?"

Several moments passed before the lieutenant replied, and the entire group clustered around Commander Sullivan could hear his audible swallow. When he finally spoke, Jax shared a look with the others on his mission team—a look that confirmed they all understood the implications of the lieutenant's finding.

"It's not one of ours," Wilcox blurted out at last.

*

When Commander Sullivan and her team reached Lieutenant Wilcox's team, they found six of the other search and rescue agents in one of the larger lab rooms, standing in a circle around a pile of collapsed metal rails and girders. By the looks of it, a catwalk running along the edge of the room had been blown apart, trapping the dark shape of a human figure beneath it.

When Jax caught up with the others, he saw that the human shape wasn't dark only because it had been swathed in shadow. The figure was dressed all in black, right down to the hood obscuring its face. Jax's blood ran cold as he realized what that meant. Next to him, Ara, Billy, and Tom, pulled up short as they, too, recognized the importance of the discovery.

"And what exactly is this, Lieutenant?" Commander Sullivan directed her question toward a heavyset man with curly auburn hair standing at the edge of his group.

The man greeted his commander with a salute. "We're not quite sure, ma'am. We called you as soon as we found this body. It can't be 4S; none of us would ever have any reason to cover our face like that. My guess is that it's one of the 'crazy lunatics' who broke into this station and started hurting people."

Commander Sullivan turned to Jax and the other ensigns. "Admiral Prang tells me you've seen these 'lunatics' before. Does this look like the rest of them?"

Jax, startled to be asked, took a moment to compose himself. "Uh … yes, ma'am. They all covered up like that."

"Then we'd best uncover this person and see what we can find," said Sullivan.

She turned back to Wilcox, who stared at her as though awaiting instructions.

"Well, what are you waiting for?" Sullivan said. "Get that mask off!"

While the commander and lieutenant had been conversing, the rest of the search and rescue crew extricated the body from under the collapsed catwalk. As they laid it in the middle of the room, Jax saw that the figure was a woman, shorter than most of the other masked foes he and his squad encountered.

Two of Colonel Sullivan's men carefully pried the mask off the woman's face. One of them took a look inside the piece of cloth.

"There's some serious tech in here," he reported. "Looks like a voice filter, and some kind of eyepiece."

"There'll be time to examine that later," Sullivan said. "What's the deal with this woman?"

The woman had a freckled face and short, close-cropped hair dyed a vibrant lime green. Her eyes were closed, blood trickled from her broken nose, and her lower lip had been split open.

The other man pulled out a holopad and flicked through the 4S' personnel records. After a few minutes, it became clear that he had come up short.

"I can't find a match in our listings," he told the commander. "She isn't 4S."

"Is she alive?" asked Sullivan.

"Yes, ma'am," answered Wilcox. "We detected a pulse, but she's still in critical condition. Her face alone took a beating, and I wouldn't be surprised if she had a few broken bones or internal bleeding as well. We won't know for certain until we've checked her over."

Commander Sullivan brought her fingers to her chin as her eyes clouded in thought.

"Ma'am?" Wilcox spoke hesitantly. "What do we do? What's the protocol here?"

Instead of answering, the commander whirled around to face two of the members of her team.

"Get a medical pod!" she barked. "Now!"

The two agents hurried out of the room. Sullivan returned her attention to Wilcox.

"I'm making an executive decision," she said. "We'll bring her back to the 4S with us, and let Admiral Prang have the final word on what to do with her. If she makes it, she could provide us with some pretty valuable information."

She pulled out her personal communicator and opened a channel to Lieutenant Commanders Braun and Goodman.

"This is Commander Sullivan. We're pulling out. The entire station's staff is accounted for, and we've picked up a … an unexpected addition as well. I'd say our job here is done. I want every team member back at the shuttle as soon as possible. We have injured scientists who need real medical attention as soon as possible."

The lieutenant commanders gave their assent. By the time Commander Sullivan ended the conversation, the medical pod she requested had arrived. The search and rescue agents took great care lowering the unconscious woman into the floating metal pod, closing the opaque lid to give her some measure of privacy. Commander Sullivan led the way out of the room and back to the elevator with Lieutenant Wilcox, followed by four team members guiding the medical pod, then by the rest of the team. Jax and the other ensigns brought up the rear.

As he walked and brooded, Jax allowed himself to think that maybe the 4S was finally getting somewhere.

We've been reacting for so long, he thought. *It's high time we took some steps forward instead of staying on the back foot.*

He only hoped that Commander Sullivan's 'unexpected addition' would truly prove to be the lucky break the 4S desperately needed.

CHAPTER FIFTEEN

DOCKING BAY 322—4S COMMAND CRUISER *HOME BASE*—DEEP SPACE

Tom, Ara, Billy, and Jax were among the first members of the search and rescue crew to disembark from their shuttle in the *Home Base*'s hangar. As they milled about, waiting for the rest of the team to join them, they took the time to have a quiet but meaningful conversation among themselves. They had avoided broaching the topic ever since they had found the green-haired woman on Rho Station, but after that woman had managed to remain in stable condition for the duration of the trip back to the *Home Base*, the ensigns couldn't put it off any longer. Tom had hoped that they could leave the matter to the proper authorities, but Jax raised the loaded question right off the bat.

"What happens now?" he asked. "We got more than we bargained for back on that station. Where's this woman going to end up?"

"It's up to the admiral, isn't it?" said Billy. "He'll decide if she stays or if she goes. But she has to stay, doesn't she? What other choice is there? Throwing her out into space?"

"Admiral Prang would never do that," Tom said. "Even if she's one of our enemies, she deserves a chance to rehabilitate. Maybe if she helps us, and we track down the rest of those masked people, she'll see she chose the wrong side."

"Be patient," Ara urged them. "She's still in pretty bad shape. We don't even know if she'll recover to tell us anything."

"Then let's just hope she does. We went to all this trouble for her; the least she can do is pay some of it back," Jax said grimly.

Tom didn't like that sentiment at all. "It's not a transaction. We shouldn't save her just because she has information we want. We should save her because she's still a person, and she has as much of a right to life as any of us."

Jax shrugged. "Okay. If you say so. But don't tell me you don't want to hear what she might have to say."

Tom opened his mouth to respond, then closed it again. He couldn't bring himself to disagree with Jax's statement.

At last, the final four search and rescue squad members bustled down the shuttle's ramp, guiding a hovering medical pod between them. The mystery woman rested comfortably inside, hooked up to a series of tubes to supply her with the fluids she would need to stay alive until she could receive real care from one of the 4S' physicians.

All of the other medical pods and body bags had already been offloaded, along with the scientists whose injuries hadn't been serious. Commander Sullivan's search and rescue teams worked quickly and efficiently to move them all into the *Home Base*. Commander Sullivan tasked Lieutenant Commanders Braun and Goodman with taking the injured up to the sick bay while she and the team of ensigns met with Admiral Prang to receive his verdict on what would be done with the green-haired woman.

Tom and his squad passed through the hangar's sterilization chamber, accompanied by Commander Sullivan and four members of her team handling the medical pod. They lowered the pod onto the tram when it stopped at their platform, then took a seat in the next car with their commander and the ensigns.

Once they reached the *Home Base*'s Beta Hub, they found Admiral Prang himself there to meet them.

"Commander Sullivan," Prang greeted the search and rescue team leader. "Welcome back. I assume this is the woman you messaged me about?"

"Yes, sir," she replied. "She's stable for now, but she might not survive unless she gets checked out soon. I didn't want to make too many assumptions, so the final decision is yours. What would you like us to do with her?"

Prang laid a hand on the commander's shoulder. "You made the right choice. She may yet be crucial to helping us understand the logic behind her group's recent raids. But either way, if we let her die without trying to save her, we'd be no better than they are."

"Yes, sir," Commander Sullivan said, more fervently this time. She turned to her four agents. "Let's get this pod up to the sick bay on the double!"

As the group moved into an elevator, Admiral Prang turned his attention to the ensigns. "Walk with me."

He beckoned them into another elevator. They only traveled up one level, exiting into the bustling hubbub of the massive space cruiser. Prang turned his head as the ensigns trailed after him. He ushered them into the closest empty briefing room and closed the door behind them.

"What did you see?" he asked.

"It didn't seem to fit with anything our enemies have done before, sir," said Tom. "They only caused minimal damage, and they left most of the scientists alive. This attack wasn't about total annihilation like the other two."

"Hmmm …" Prang mused. "Interesting. It does beg the question of why they would make such a change. You're right, Ensign Ubert. It doesn't seem to fit the pattern."

"One more reason to keep that woman around, huh?" said Jax.

Tom shot Jax a dirty look.

"You may be right," responded Prang. "That might just be the most intriguing fact of the matter. Why would the raiders leave one of their own behind?"

"They might have thought she was already dead," said Ara. "She was in pretty bad shape, and she might have died if we hadn't found her when we did."

"I don't know," Tom said. "It seems a bit too convenient to me. If these people can kill an entire station's worth of scientists, and if they can put so much effort into staying off our radar, they could definitely go to the trouble of making sure that woman was dead before she could tell us whatever she might know. But they didn't."

"Who knows why these people do what they do?" said Billy. "Personally, I think it's a good opportunity, regardless of how we got it. We need to seize the moment while we still can."

"Quite right," said Prang. "I agree that these changes in our enemies' methods are disturbing, and they do leave room for further debate. For now, though, I've learned all I need from you. You four are free to go. Wash up, eat something, get some rest. I have a feeling that the next few days will be trying for us all, in one way or another."

As the admiral took his leave, the group of ensigns headed back toward the elevator. Boarding the first available car, they ascended until they had reached the cruiser's dormitory level. There, they split up, each going to recover from the mission in their own way.

Tom stepped into his bunkroom, but he found himself too restless to focus on anything at all. He paced for a few minutes, then, finally admitting to himself that he was utterly exhausted, sat down on the edge of the bed to think. One thought quickly rose to the forefront of his mind: Admiral Prang's last words to his team. *The next few days will be trying for us all.*

Tom decided that he believed Prang wholeheartedly.

*

The next twenty-four hours passed in a tense blur. Tom spent his day working in the cruiser's repair bay, waiting for news of their prisoner's condition. During those moments when his work became especially monotonous, he took some time to dig deep into his conflicted feelings regarding the whole affair.

On the one hand, he hoped the woman would recover. Not because she could offer the 4S valuable information, not because she could help them end the threat to the Eden Project, but simply because a life saved was a life saved, regardless of which side the person went on to choose. It wasn't Tom's place, or even Admiral Prang's, for that matter, to decide who lived or died.

On the other hand, if she did survive, what would her fate be? She would more than likely remain on the cruiser even after she had fully healed. The 4S would want to keep her around to answer its many questions. Tom didn't think for a second that Admiral Prang would allow the woman to be tortured for information, but he couldn't trust any other 4S officers to have the same moral scruples. Perhaps it would be more merciful to let her slip away.

In the end, Tom still felt conflicted. There was only one thing he could be absolutely certain of.

It isn't right. She's a human being, but everyone here can only think of her as a tool.

Lost in thought, Tom hardly noticed as his grip on the socket wrench he was holding started to loosen. He jolted back into the moment when it slid out of his hand and clattered to the floor.

His supervisor, a burly raven-haired woman, whirled around from where she had been standing nearby, deep in conversation with a supply officer.

"Ubert!" she barked. "Keep your tools in your hands!"

"Y-yes, ma'am," said Tom, chagrined.

Bending down to pick up his wrench, Tom returned to his work. *Forget about that woman. You can't do anything for her. It's out of your hands.*

But he couldn't forget so easily.

For the first time in a long time, Tom found himself directing his thoughts toward a higher power. Back on Earth, his parents had been among the last holdouts of a culture where religion still flourished. Although their devotion to a deity had not stuck with Tom, the lessons he had been given on how to live righteously had.

He had long since forgotten any scripted prayers he had ever been taught, so he improvised.

Whoever you are up there, he said in his mind, *please let there be some resolution to this situation. How much longer before the 4S does something it can't take back? If you're out there, and if you have any real power at all, help us make it through this with our humanity intact.*

Tom couldn't know if he had reached the ear of any cosmic being, and he didn't really feel much better for having tried. He supposed blind faith wasn't for everyone.

Tom returned to his work on the engine block. In almost no time at all, he had isolated the issue, found a replacement part, and restored the engine to working order. He wouldn't know if it truly worked again until it was placed in a ship, but there would be time for that later.

As Tom moved on to his next repair job, he allowed the routine maintenance to take his mind off his worries. Life was always so much easier when he had problems he could identify and fix. The trouble, of course, was that the universe was rarely so straightforward. Regardless, he finished his shift with no further slip-ups, and when he punched his timecard at the end of the afternoon, his mind felt considerably lighter.

Tom had no issue with Prang's choice to keep the woman in the 4S sick bay and help her recover. In the admiral's shoes, he would have likely done the same. His thoughts on the plan to question her for information were less clear-cut. He knew the 4S needed more intelligence on their enemies' operations, and that the woman was their best option for getting it. He had full confidence in Admiral Prang's upstanding ethics, and he knew the woman wouldn't be mistreated. By all accounts, the plan seemed both practical and moral.

So why did Tom still feel like something about it was horribly wrong?

*

Another week went by with no news of the mysterious woman's condition. Tom and his squadmates did their best to go about their daily tasks as though nothing had changed. Some of them succeeded more than others. The subject came up in conversation more than once, but it was always quickly dropped. Ara and Billy largely moved on from the topic, and Jax remained as stoic as ever. Tom kept his thoughts on the woman mostly to himself.

He spent his days toiling away in the repair bay. The work was often dreary, but Tom enjoyed it. He would take installing new fusion converters onto shuttle engines over fighting for his life any day. Meanwhile, Billy found time to fly two separate supply runs—one to Voyager Station and one to the lunar colony—while Ara went to work in the archives and Jax did whatever he did when the others weren't around.

All four were surprised and slightly apprehensive when a message from Admiral Prang upended the newfound predictability of their lives. They found it on their holopads eight mornings after their search and rescue mission. Prang had simply invited them to his office for what he termed 'a talk'. His words contained no hint of what that talk might be about.

By the time Tom, Jax, Ara, and Billy stood before him, the serious expression on Prang's face was the first thing they noticed. Prang sat in his chair behind his desk with Vice Admiral Pitt standing by his side, but he rose to his feet as the ensigns walked toward him.

Once everyone was settled in a chair, Prang got down to business.

"I thought you would like to know that the woman you helped recover from Rho Station is on the mend. She came out of her coma three days ago, and she was cleared to leave the sick bay this morning. It appears the extent of her injuries was not as severe as Commander Sullivan initially believed. Aside from a broken leg and a smashed nose, the debris that fell on her didn't deal too much lasting damage."

The ensigns glanced at each other as they took in Prang's news, then back at the admiral.

"With all due respect, sir, why are you telling us all this?" Ara asked. "It hardly seems necessary for us to be involved in this discussion. We're all just ensigns."

"Ordinarily, I would agree," said Prang. "But we are in desperate times, and desperate times mean that some of us must rise to the occasion in ways we never would have otherwise. I assume you are all aware of my intent to interrogate that woman and see what she can tell us?"

"Yes, sir," said Tom. "We all heard about that."

"Good," Prang replied. "That is why I have called you four here today. The results of that interrogation may well lead to a new special assignment for your team."

His use of the words *special assignment* was not lost on anyone in the room.

"I am choosing to keep you in the loop," continued Prang, "because you may have a part to play in this situation before it is all over. Make no mistake, your services thus far have been immensely helpful, and you've all proven yourselves to be a credit to the 4S and the Eden Project. However, I must admit that the risk factor has proven to be considerably higher than I first anticipated. And, if I send you out again, that risk would only increase. You wouldn't simply be searching for lost ore transports or rescuing injured scientists. You might very well be heading into the heart of our enemy's operations. I'm not sure that I could conscience sending agents so young as you into that sort of danger."

Tom couldn't help but agree. As much as he and all his squadmates wanted to help the 4S defeat its enemies, the fact remained that the four of them alone would always be outclassed in that fight. None of them had received any formal instruction in combat or self-defense, and neither they nor any of their ships were equipped with weapons to even their odds.

As soon as Tom had thought all that, Jax stepped forward.

"These people killed my parents," he said. "They ruined my life, along with who knows how many others. I don't care where I have to go, or what I have to do. I won't stop until the threat is gone."

A small appreciative smile interrupted Prang's neutral expression, before his face visibly fell. "That's a noble sentiment, Jax, but I need to know that you can keep a clear head. I need to know that you won't go dashing off on some half-cocked revenge attempt before you know what you're getting yourself into."

"I know exactly what I'm getting into," replied Jax. "Is there really any outcome to this situation that doesn't end with me fighting those masked people again sooner or later?"

"Be that as it may, one man does not constitute an entire mission team. There isn't much point in you continuing your team's mission if you'll be doing it alone," said Prang.

Tom's next words seemed to go against every sentiment he had previously held, and yet he found himself unwilling to take them back.

"He won't be alone, sir. I'll stand with him."

Ara and Billy each placed a hand on one of Tom's shoulders.

"We'll all stand with him, sir," said Ara.

"I see," said Prang. "I do have to admire your dedication to your teammate."

"Jax is more than just our teammate, sir," said Billy. "He's our friend."

Jax glanced back at his three squadmates with an expression Tom couldn't quite decipher. Was it surprise? Appreciation? A bit of both, perhaps?

"Well, then," said Prang. "As I said, your dedication to your mission and to each other is commendable. But whatever that woman tells us, investigating it would most likely be the single most dangerous task of your careers thus far. Before I can even think about sending you on such an assignment, I need to know that you're all fully conscious of the risks involved."

"With all due respect, sir, we're hardly inexperienced at going into danger," said Tom. "We all know what could happen to us out there. It's already happened once, and we got away. I don't think any other 4S team can say that. You don't need to worry about whether or not we understand the risk of what we're doing. You can trust me when I say that the answer to that is yes."

"Hmmmm," said Prang slowly. "You do raise a good point."

As the ensigns looked on in varying degrees of apprehension, the admiral looked down at his hands in his lap. At last, a look of acceptance spread across his face, and when he finally spoke again there was no doubt in his tone.

"I won't lie to you," said Prang. "You four have impressed me today, so I'll hold off on passing judgment on your futures for now. I won't dissolve your squad, but I also can't guarantee that I'll keep using you. Until the 4S has learned whatever there is to learn from the mystery woman, you can consider yourselves to be in a state of limbo. I'll still expect you to go about your official duties, of course, but anything else has yet to be determined. I'd say that's fair, wouldn't you?"

"Yes, sir," the four ensigns replied.

Tom glanced down at his hands where they hung by his sides. Prang's decision was indeed a fair compromise, and yet something was still nagging at him.

He raised his head. "Permission to ask a question, sir?"

"Please do," said Prang.

Tom spoke with some hesitation, giving voice to every fear he had had over the last few days. "What are you going to do with that woman, sir? Is she a prisoner?"

Prang breathed a deep breath before he replied. "If it puts your mind at ease, Ensign, I strongly dislike thinking of her that way. I have no wish to turn into a cruel warden. I see her stay merely as an extension of the hospitality we have already offered. She will be afforded every comfort we can provide."

Tom plucked up the courage to ask another question. "But where would she stay? We don't have any cells. Is it … is it wise to just let her roam around on board the *Home Base*?"

"We have elected to keep her in the officers' lounge for now," Prang said gently. "That part of the *Home Base* is the most secure, and only people with the proper clearance will be able to enter. Our guest will be isolated but still comfortable."

Tom nodded. It seemed like a good plan, under the circumstances.

"We will start questioning her soon," Prang said. "Nothing is certain until we know the results of that questioning, but I wanted you all to be prepared. You may well be needed sooner rather than later."

"Does that mean you will use us?" Billy asked.

"Right now, I just don't know," Prang told him. "You've all argued well on your squad's behalf, but if the risk factor proves to be too high, I'll have to send in trained professionals instead."

Trained professionals, thought Tom. *Ha. If the 4S had any trained professionals for this kind of thing, we wouldn't be in this situation.*

"I wouldn't advise you to get your hopes up," continued Prang. "I know you want to help, but I would rather keep you grounded than have you put your lives on the line when it can be avoided."

"We understand," Ara assured him. "We all believe in the Eden Project as much as you do, but it really is starting to seem like this is all beyond us."

"I'm glad you can see things my way," said Prang. "For now, you may return to your normal lives. You all have my respect and gratitude. When we next convene, I will have a final verdict on the operational status of your team."

"Yes, sir. We'll be ready for whatever you decide," said Tom.

"I would expect nothing less," said Prang. "Until then, you four are dismissed."

With the admiral's words of special assignments and prisoners echoing inside all of their heads, the ensigns left the room and made their way to the elevator that would return them to their so-called 'normal lives'.

*

Later that afternoon, in the 4S officer's lounge a few levels below Admiral Prang's office, Captain Carson of the 4S Security Force swiped his key card in the scanner that would grant him access to the room where the green-haired woman was being held. As he strode through the door, ducking his unusually tall head, he cast a surreptitious glance into the corner of the room, where a small metal sculpture on a table concealed a hidden camera. He knew that the admiral and vice admiral would be watching the interrogation, learning everything Carson learned in real time.

The woman looked up from her position on one of the room's wide couches. Her broken leg had been wrapped in a metal brace, and her nose was still bent out of shape. Other than that, she had recovered well from her near-death experience.

"What are you doing here?" she asked. "What do you want?"

"My name is Captain Darryl Carson of the 4S," he told her. "We have some questions for you, if you're feeling up to it."

"Whatever," she said. "Do your worst. You can't make me talk."

"I don't think you quite understand," said Carson evenly. "This is an open conversation. We have no wish to harm you. We merely wish to have a civil discussion. After we nursed you back to health in our very own sick bay, some might say it's only fair that you help us out a little."

"So that's your angle?" she said. "You think you can butter me up by telling me how you 'graciously saved my life' until I tell you everything out of gratitude? I don't crack that easily."

Carson sighed. "Let's try this again. Forget expectations. How are you feeling?"

"You know how," she said. "I can't use my leg, and I can't do much of anything else, but as long as you all keep the painkillers coming it's not too bad. The second I get out of this brace, though—"

"Can we do anything to make you more comfortable?" Carson asked, heading off the threat he anticipated she would speak.

The woman swept a hand around the entire room. "How could it get any more comfortable than this?"

"Very well," said Carson. "Let's talk about you. Do you have a name? Some way you'd like to be addressed?"

"Why do you care?" she asked bitterly.

"Trust me, I'm only trying to be polite."

She considered his words for a moment. "The people I work with don't have much use for names. It's been a while since I've needed to tell anyone mine."

"But surely you have one," Carson prompted. "Someone must have given you one when you were born."

"Ugh!" she groaned. "My parents called me Jess, all right? That's all you need to know about me."

"Jess, huh?" Carson repeated.

"Yeah," she snorted. "Don't wear it out. We're still not friends or anything, okay?"

Carson remained unperturbed. "Whatever makes you feel comfortable."

"I might be comfortable, but I'm not stupid," she said.

"No matter what you say, you definitely have some agenda you're running. Are you going to keep tabs on me once I'm gone? Are you going to track me and see where I go, just so you can swoop in heroically and take us all out at once?"

"Not at all," he said. "If anything, we want to help you. We don't want to see you throwing your life away like this. We want to help you be better."

"Yeah, not gonna happen," the woman said. "I don't need to 'be better'. Just get on with the interrogation we both know is coming. I'm sure you have places you'd rather be."

"Fine," said Carson. "If that's what you want. Why don't you start by telling me how you came to be on Rho Station when it was attacked?"

"Simple," she replied. "I had a job to do. We all did."

"But what job was so important that it was worth attacking not only one, but three, 4S stations and murdering or attempting to murder dozens of our staff?"

"We did what we were ordered."

"And who gave those orders? Or who gave you the data on how to find and access 4S stations? Do you have a mole inside our organization, or just really good hackers?"

"How should I know? They didn't tell me where that information came from. They just told me to use it."

Carson sighed again. This was going nowhere. "Let's get back to my original question. Why did you do it at all? What are you getting out of this?"

"Like I said, it's necessary," she told him. "We're bringing about a new order. You 4S people can sit up here in your cushy lounges and tell yourselves that you know what you're dealing with, but you've barely scratched the surface, and you're deliberately holding yourselves back from going any further. You can't comprehend the true power of what you hold in your hands. It belongs with the people who can really set it free."

"What are you talking about?" Carson asked, even though he had a sneaking suspicion he already knew. "What is it we're dealing with?"

"Power," she said simply. "Strength. You're dealing with the greatest force in the universe, and you don't even care."

"The 4S isn't interested in power," said Carson. "We only want to be the second chance our world desperately needs."

"Spare me the lecture. Save it for someone who cares," she retorted with a dismissive wave of her hand.

"You clearly cared enough to attack Rho Station and harm so many of its personnel, whatever your reasons were. If you did it to bring about this new order of yours, then who's going to wind up at the top of that order?"

"Someone who understands the way things really are," she said. "We've seen it already, and believe me, others will, too. We did what we did because we couldn't let your negligence go on."

"But you still aren't telling me anything," said Carson. "What's this thing you're claiming to have seen? Even if you disagree with the 4S in some way, surely there isn't cause for violence."

"Really?" she asked. "What did you think was going to happen? We'd just come out with our hands up?"

"Despite what you might think, the 4S only wants to help you," Carson told her. "You don't have to go back to your old life, whatever they told you. We can get you out for good. We could set you up with an entirely new identity. You don't have to be one of them. You can be better."

"I've already told you, I don't need your help!" she growled. "You can pretend all you want that you only want what's best for me, but we both know better. Someday, you'll come for repayment. And I don't even want to think about what that might look like."

With a snort, she made a deliberate show of turning away from the captain.

Carson wasn't fazed. "All right, then. You don't have to take our offer. We'll respect your wishes. But even if you don't want our help, we need yours."

"Ha," she muttered. "So you admit it."

Carson chose not to rise to the bait. "We really do believe that your group can be saved, and turned away from the path you're on. We don't want to hurt you if we can avoid it. All we need is a location, or even just a name. Something to help us find them. I promise you, we'll do all that we can to resolve this situation peacefully and make sure everyone walks away happy."

"Jeez. You really don't know anything, do you?"

"That's … one way to phrase it, I suppose. Anything you say could go a long way. Even just one name, if you can find it in you to confess it."

"A name, huh …?" She seemed to be considering that, but without seeing her face, Carson couldn't gauge exactly what she was thinking.

After a few seconds, she began to lightly chuckle.

"What's so funny?" Carson asked casually.

"You know," she told him, "you do have some compelling points there. I might have been too hasty at first."

"Then you'll give us what we need?"

She turned around to face him once more, and he saw that a glint had come into her eye.

"Maybe. I could give you some pretty juicy stuff, couldn't I?"

A new look came over her face. Where before she had been guarded, refusing to reveal even the smallest detail, now it almost looked as though she was considering spilling something big. Had Carson finally worn her down?

No. He didn't believe for a second that it would be that easy for him. But he had to let this play out and see where it went. Whatever this woman was trying to do, he had to stay on his toes.

"Then what can you tell us?" he asked, trying to keep a straight face despite his rising misgivings.

"There's one name I can give you, free of charge," she said. She chuckled again at the end. "Pay close attention. I'll only say it once."

"I'm listening. Say what you need to say."

"Be sure to include this in your report. Your admiral will probably get a kick out of it."

"What are you talking about?"

"You can tell your admiral," she said, "that Doctor James Simmons sends his warmest regards."

<u>CHAPTER SIXTEEN</u>

ADMIRAL'S OFFICE—4S COMMAND CRUISER *HOME BASE*—DEEP SPACE

Jax shook his head. "She has to be wrong. Or misleading you somehow. You said yourself that James Simmons died on his last mission."

"He only said they never found the body," said Billy. "Haven't you ever watched any movies? If you don't see a body, the person isn't dead."

"This isn't a movie," cut in Tom. "This is real life, and we have a really big problem on our hands."

"Ensign Ubert is right," Admiral Prang spoke up from behind his desk. The four ensigns in the room snapped to attention as he went on. "There is a part of me that hopes James Simmons survived, and yet if our guest's words can be believed, it may not be such a blessing after all. But regardless, we cannot allow our emotions or personal opinions to dictate our actions. We have to proceed with extreme care until all the specifics of our situation have become clear."

"So what do we do, sir?" asked Ara. "Like we said, we haven't seen a body. How are we supposed to know if this woman is telling you the truth?"

"I'd bet she isn't," said Jax. "She probably wants to keep you second-guessing yourself so her group has more room to operate. Don't believe her for a second."

"Thank you for your insight," Prang said, neither reprimanding nor truly congratulating.

"The last time we spoke, I mentioned a potential special assignment for you all. That assignment has now arrived. I need you four to investigate that woman's story and see if it checks out."

"I don't understand, sir. Where would we even start?" said Tom.

"It just so happens that we do have some idea of where to begin," Prang replied. "When Captain Carson spoke with that woman, she did provide a few tidbits of further information. Most notably, she gave him a set of coordinates where she implied that some major operation was taking place. She even hinted that her group's mysterious leader, whoever they may be, would be there."

"How much did you have to pressure her before she gave that up?" Jax asked flippantly.

"Not much, actually," Prang told him. "She essentially volunteered the information."

"All the more reason to be suspicious, then," said Jax. "Last time those people gave us an obvious trail to follow, they tried to kill us at the end of it. How do we know they're not setting us up for another situation like that?"

"In short, we don't," Prang admitted. "You're completely right, Jax. We won't have any idea what's happening at the location she gave us until someone goes out there and takes a look at it. That is why it's more important than ever that you stick to your mission of observing without engaging. I'm sending you four because you've all voluntarily chosen to participate, even after I made you aware of the risks. But I'll remind you that you'll very likely be traveling into enemy territory. If any of you wish to back out, this is your last chance. I can assure you that no judgment would be cast if you did."

"We all know what we're getting into, sir," said Ara. "We'll be careful. You can count on us."

Prang folded his hands atop his desk. "Very well. If you four truly believe you can carry out this surveillance mission and make it back in one piece, the 4S and I will honor your commitment. But surveillance is all I'm clearing you for. All you need to do is confirm whether or not something is out there. You don't need to be the ones to discover exactly what that something is. If you see anything out of the ordinary, come back to base at once, and I'll send in a more qualified team to perform the full investigation. Do I make myself clear?"

"Yes, sir!" the four ensigns replied in unison.

"Just what I wanted to hear," Prang said. "Now then, let's get down to business. As soon as we're done here, I want you all to head down to Bay Four-Seventy-Four. You'll find a shuttle there with the coordinates already uploaded, ready for you to fly out on your mission."

"But where are you sending us, sir?" asked Tom. "You never actually told us that."

"Ah, yes," Prang said. "My apologies. I had a tech team analyze the coordinates, and the location you're headed for appears to be right in the middle of an uncharted sector of space not far beyond our solar system. Because we don't have any reliable maps of the area, you'd be flying in blind."

"I can handle it, sir," said Billy. "How different can it really be?"

"Don't get cocky," Prang advised. "Many more experienced pilots than you have been lost to unfortunate accidents because they tried to fly in unknown space. You'll need to be extremely careful, and ready to run at the first sign of trouble. That means no reckless maneuvers, and no crazy shenanigans. If you see anything amiss, I want you to turn your ship right around and return here. Whether you're facing enemy forces or even just unsafe flying conditions, you are not to endanger yourself in any way. That goes for all four of you. Am I understood?"

"Yes, sir," they said again, more subdued this time.

"That's good," said Prang. "If you all understand the severity of your situation, I won't waste time rehashing it. Any further questions, Ensigns?"

None of them had any.

"Then you're dismissed," Prang said. "Please hurry to

your ship. Your mission awaits."

*

When Admiral Prang had said that the sector of space where the woman's coordinates lay was unexplored, Jax hadn't expected it to also be completely empty.

As soon as their scout shuttle came out of lightspeed, all four gathered in the cockpit, on alert for any danger. As the blurred stars beyond the windshield came back into focus with the ship's deceleration, however, they saw that those stars were all that lay in the space ahead. There were no planets, moons, or chunks of space debris as far as the eye could see. Jax gazed straight ahead and couldn't help but feel all that empty space pressing in on him.

"I can see why Prang wasn't in a hurry to map out this part of space," he said, trying to lighten the mood. "There's nothing here. He could probably just keep the maps he's already got."

Tom scoffed. "Stay alert, everyone. Just because we can't see things doesn't mean they aren't there. We've already learned that the hard way. Billy, how far off are we from the coordinates Admiral Prang gave us?"

"Pretty far, actually," replied Billy. "Since Prang told us we'd be flying blind, I brought us out of lightspeed close to the boundary of space charted by the 4S. We'll have to approach the location at realspeed, but we'll be able to react in real time to whatever pops up."

The others found this acceptable. Jax was less amenable, however, when he learned that it would take them just over two hours to reach their destination.

"You're telling me you couldn't have gotten us any closer?" he asked Billy. "Even just a little bit?"
"Not without more reliable navigational data," Billy said. "Would you rather we hit a star, or crash into a planet? If we were moving at lightspeed, the results would be catastrophic."

Jax accepted Billy's reasoning and subsided.

As the shuttle began to move again, its occupants stayed at the windows, watching for signs of danger. As time went on, however, and the view they had to look at remained largely the same, their assignment quickly turned from duty to drudgery. With little to break up the monotony, Jax find himself growing more and more bored with the whole thing.

"This is what most space is like," Tom told him. "Just barren and desolate. That's why they call it space."

His words didn't make Jax feel any better.

After an hour and forty-five minutes of staring out at empty space, Jax's concentration waned. He didn't realize just how deeply he had fallen into numbness until Ara, sitting at the window on the opposite side of the cockpit, gave a start and called out to the others.

"Asteroid field dead ahead!" she said.

"I see it," Billy called back from his pilot's seat. "Looks like we have to go through it."

With a flick of the joysticks, he turned the ship to the right until its nose pointed toward the scattered space rocks.

"Hold on," said Jax. "You're seriously going to fly into that? Can't you just go around?"

"Not unless you want this mission to be even longer," Billy replied. "I'm just taking the most direct route to the coordinates Admiral Prang gave us."

"We should check it out while we're here, anyway," said Ara. "There could be all kinds of things hidden in those rocks. If I wanted to conceal a secret lair, a place like this would be exactly what I'd use."

"Can't you just scan them?" asked Jax. "Find out what's inside?"

"Not from here, we can't," said Billy. "There's too much interference from all the metal in the asteroids for me to get a reliable scan out of any one of them. If we want to find out what's going on in there. And we'd have to go in either way, because the coordinates Prang gave us are—"

"Let me guess," Jax muttered. "Right in the center of the asteroid field?"
"Pretty much, yeah," said Billy. "So there's nowhere to go except forward."

Finding the closest gap between two asteroids, Billy slowly took the shuttle deeper and deeper into the cluster. Jax kept his eyes on the space in front of the ship as it twisted and turned its way through several tight squeezes, but there was nothing to see except more and more asteroids. A few of the smaller ones drifted slightly too close to the shuttle for Jax's comfort.

"Is this safe?" he asked. "What happens if one of those things hits us?"

"Don't worry about that," said Tom. "4S ships have thick hulls to defend against possible breaches. And if it looks like we're in trouble, we do have at least one way to save ourselves. 4S ships also come equipped with one small plasma cannon to break apart any random pieces of debris before they can collide with the hull. We'll be perfectly safe as long as we keep our eyes open."

Tom's words calmed Jax immensely. As their ship continued its voyage through the asteroid field without incident, Jax let himself relax. The asteroids were spaced far enough apart that it was easy for the light and fast scout shuttle to slip among them. A few smaller chunks of detritus impacted the ship's hull, but true to Tom's assessment, the metal plating held strong. Jax, Ara, Billy, and Tom kept their eyes peeled the whole time for any signs of an enemy trap, but there were none to be seen.

Soon, they arrived at the coordinates Admiral Prang had supplied them with. As they gazed upon the massive asteroid that lay before them, Jax found himself feeling strangely disappointed. He didn't know what he had been expecting to find, exactly, but just another space rock wasn't it.

"Oh, boy," he said sarcastically. "This sure is impressive. Really glad we came all this way."

"Will you stop being so pessimistic?" asked Ara. "This is serious. We shouldn't pass judgment until we know there isn't something going on beneath the surface here."

"Beneath the surface?" echoed Jax. "It's a rock! The only thing below the surface is just gonna be more rock."

"Not necessarily," said Ara. "If the 4S can have asteroid bases, anyone can."

"Okay," Jax shot back, "but the 4S' bases aren't actually *in* the asteroids."

"Fair point," conceded Ara. "We should still check this one out, though. That woman gave up these coordinates for a reason."

"Yeah," said Billy. "Give me a minute to scan it, and we'll see what we've found."

He set the shuttle in motion again, making three full circles around the asteroid. When he stopped in the same spot he had started from, he leaned his head closer to his screen to view the sensor readings.

"Huh," he said.

"What is it?" asked Tom.

"I'm reading a large amount of life signs," said Billy. "This thing is practically crawling with people, and it looks like they've managed to bring in a good amount of technology, too."

"Are you sure?" Jax asked. "This isn't exactly prime real estate."

"But it really is a good place for an evil gang to hide," Tom said. "It might be a bit cliché, but still. They're already in a sector the 4S hasn't expanded into yet, and the asteroids provide a good cover against scans from any ships that do wind up out here. It still doesn't explain how they got all the stuff out here to set this up in the first place, though."

"Let's not worry about that for now," Ara advised him. "That's a problem for the team Prang sends in later. We've done our job here, and we've found what we expected to find. Let's get out of here before things get hairy again, just like Admiral Prang told us to."

Tom nodded. "You're right. Take us away, Billy."

But Billy didn't move. He stared at a screen on his control panel as though he had been transfixed by it.

"Billy?" asked Ara. When he still didn't respond, she called out again with a little more trepidation. "Billy?"

Jax rose from his seat and took one step toward the pilot's chair. "We have to get out of here," he urged Billy. "You remember what Prang said. That could be the enemy base right there. If they see us—"

"Oh, they've seen us," Billy said without turning around.

At that, Tom shot to his feet beside Jax. "What? Tell me you're not serious. How can you possibly know that?"

Only then did Billy turn to face his comrades. His fearful expression shot down any further questions.

"We've got a problem," said Billy. "That asteroid's opening up."

They crowded closer to the ship's windshield, trying to see what Billy saw. Near the equator of the asteroid, a gaping hole had mysteriously opened. Squinting, Jax could barely make out the shape of something detaching from the asteroid and beginning to move in their direction.

"Holy crap," said Billy.

"What do you see?" asked Ara.

"Something just launched out of that asteroid," Billy reported. "Multiple somethings. Three small ships. Like, really small."

"He's right." Tom glanced at the readout. "Energy readings are consistent with some kind of spaceship, but these things are smaller than any shuttle I've ever seen."

"Can we tell whose they are?" Ara asked.

"Not as far as I can tell," said Billy. "Scanners aren't picking up any identifying markings or registry codes. I can't find any life signs aboard them, either. They're probably drones."

"Look, that's interesting and all, but I'd say this is a pretty big violation of Prang's do-not-engage rule. We should get out of here," said Jax.

Billy turned their shuttle one hundred and eighty degrees and made for the edge of the asteroid field. "Maybe we shouldn't have stuck around."

"You think?" asked Jax.

"Save it," Ara told him. "The mission comes first. We have information the 4S needs, and they can't get it if we're dead. We have to get back to the *Home Base*."

"We won't get away that easily," said Tom. "Looks like

they've locked onto us. They're heading this way."

"Hold on," said Billy. "I'll try to lose them."

With that, he took the shuttle into a dive. He slipped between two asteroids and weaved in and out between several more. All the while, the pursuing ships matched the shuttle's every movement in perfect synchronicity. They flew in a triangular formation, with one drone in front and the other two behind. Even with Billy flying as fast as he safely could, the drones began to close in on their target.

"Get us out of here!" Jax yelled, his calm and composed demeanor melting away in the heat of the moment.

"I'm trying!" Billy shouted back. "If I had more space, it would be easier. And we can't go to lightspeed until we've cleared the asteroid field."

"What about the plasma cannon? Could we use that?" asked Ara.

"It isn't powerful enough to destroy other ships. The best we could do would be to overload their circuits for a short time. If we were really lucky, they might not even recover."

"So we can fight back?" broke in Jax.

"I didn't say that," said Tom. "That cannon wasn't designed for situations like this. We don't know what would happen if we tried to use it in live combat."

"We have to do something!" called Billy.

Jax glanced over to see Billy's panic-stricken face reflected in the windshield. Then he looked toward the back of the shuttle, where the drone ships tailed them. Their enemies would soon be within firing range of the 4S shuttle, and if the weapons they were charging were any more powerful than the plasma cannon ... Well, it wasn't a pretty picture.

"Fine," said Tom at last. "Do it. What have we got to lose?"

Everything, Jax thought.

As Billy continued driving the shuttle, he touched part of the control panel Jax had never seen him use before. Once he flicked a switch and tapped a few keys, the humming of the shuttle's inner workings gradually but steadily rose in volume.

"Plasma cannon's online," Billy said.

As the whine of the newly online weapons system continued to mount, a small holopad popped up from a slot atop Billy's control panel. Billy shoved the device into Tom's hands.

"It's charging now," he said. "Take this, Tom. You'll need it in a few minutes."

"What is it?" Tom asked.

"Firing controls," said Billy. "I can't fly and shoot at the same time, can I?"

Tom glanced down at the image on the holopad. "Why me?" he asked incredulously.

"You know the most about this thing," Ara said.

"But— we shouldn't—" Tom stammered.

"Get over yourself, Tom! It's not like there are people on board those ships. They're drones! So either take the shot or pass that tablet over here," said Jax.

Tom shook his head emphatically as his confidence returned. "No, Ara's right. It has to be me."

"There, see?" said Jax. "That wasn't so hard, was it?"

The two men scowled at each other until Billy broke the silence.

"You'll need to be quick," he warned. "Even at our fastest safe speed, the drones will catch up with us before we're in open space. You'll probably only have time to get off one good shot."

"You're going to have to widen the plasma radius," put in Ara. "Hit them all at once."

Tom whirled to face her. "But the shot would be weaker. We could hurt them, but there's less chance of immobilizing them."

"Still, slowing them down would be preferable to them catching us," said Jax.

"All right, all right," agreed Tom, adjusting the controls on the holopad. "Billy, are we ready to fire?"

"Any minute now!" Billy assured him.

As the shuttle kept pushed toward open space, its occupants waited tensely for the moment they would be able to take action. The overall mood in the cockpit was one of anticipation until Tom took another look at the holopad and groaned in dismay.

"I'm getting some abnormal energy readings from the front of these drones. It looks like … well, they look more like the energy that comes out of our plasma cannon."
"So these ships have plasma cannons of their own?" asked Ara. "Is that a real problem, though? I mean, are they big enough to muster up the kind of firepower we have?"

"Maybe not if we were only facing one of them," Tom said gravely. "But there's three ships out there, and they each have two cannons. That could potentially be enough to match what we've got."

"Then we have to get out of here," said Jax. "If they can kill our electronics, we'll be dead in space, and I don't want to see what would happen after that."

"What do you think we're trying to do?" asked Tom. "But we can't outrun them, so we'll have to try and outgun them."

Jax turned to Billy. "How long until our cannon finishes charging?"

Billy glanced at his control panel. "About fifteen seconds."

"Good," said Jax. "Let's get them before they get us."
"It's not that easy," said Tom. "I have to wait until they're within a certain range before I fire. Otherwise, the plasma would dissipate and lose its charge before it could do any damage, especially with a shot as wide as the one I'm using."

Jax gritted his teeth in agitation. "This thing makes a terrible weapon."

"Don't be too hard on it," Ara told him. "We built it for use on asteroids. This is the first time I've ever heard of anyone having to use it against another ship."

"Whatever," said Jax. "Can we try to lose them in the asteroids?"

"No," said Billy. "The best thing for us to do is to stay on course."

"Then are you sure you can't go any faster?" asked Jax.

"I can try," replied Billy, "but if I increase the speed too far, we'll lose maneuverability. If an asteroid came at us, we might not be able to dodge, and the plasma cannon's occupied."

Despite his dire warning, Billy set his jaw and pushed the shuttle's throttle a little further forward. The humming of the engine mingled with the buzzing from the plasma cannon as the ship shot forward, gunning for open space. They still had a ways to go, but they were closing the gap quickly.

Even so, Billy had little room to maneuver, hindered by the asteroids all around him. The light, fast, and agile drone ships slipped effortlessly between the rocks while Billy was forced to take his time and go carefully. Nonetheless, Billy stayed just ahead of them, and as the 4S shuttle neared the edge of the asteroid field, Jax let himself think they just might make it.

Then that hope was shot out from under him.

"We're out of time!" Tom called out suddenly. "The drones' weapons are really heating up. Either they'll fire soon, or they're about to short themselves out."

"And I guess it's too much to hope for the second option," said Jax.

"Have we been that lucky so far?" asked Tom.

"So take your shot!" Jax yelled back. "Shut them down!"

"I can't!" said Tom. "They're still out of range!"

"Well, do something!" Billy chimed in. "We're still nowhere near the edge of the asteroid field."

Just then, the drone ships loosed their weapons. The 4S shuttle gave a great shuddering heave, and all its systems went dead at once. The cockpit lights went dark, all the instruments on Billy's control panel fizzled out, and the hum of the plasma cannon was abruptly silenced.

All the ship's forward momentum ground to a halt, throwing everyone in all directions except Billy, still strapped in his pilot's chair.

Jax barely had any time to register what had just happened before his head collided with the wall. His vision blurred, and he saw stars, then nothing at all.

CHAPTER SEVENTEEN

SECURITY CONTROL ROOM—4S COMMAND CRUISER
HOME BASE—DEEP SPACE

Admiral Prang gazed intently at the screen as he watched Captain Ramón make his way into the officer's lounge, where Jess lounged on the couch.

After the last revelation she had dropped on them, Prang had planned to see if Carson could squeeze any more details out of her. However, Ramón had come to Prang and requested that task before the admiral could make his intentions public. Prang had been surprised and a bit skeptical that Ramón had suddenly wanted to speak to Jess after he had previously been quite content to let the Security Force handle the situation, but he hadn't been able to find a reason why he shouldn't agree with the Captain's proposal.

Beside Prang, Vice Admiral Pitt watched the proceedings with a deep scowl.

"Have I mentioned that I don't like this?" he asked.

"Several times now, Vice Admiral," Prang replied. "Your complaints are most definitely on record."

"It's more than that, sir," said Pitt. "I worry that you're overstepping your authority. Keeping a hostage aboard the *Home*

Base? It's unheard of."

"That woman is not a hostage. We aren't planning to hold her for ransom. She is our guest, and as long as she is with us we may as well take advantage of the opportunities that presents."

"The Council may not see it that way."

"The Council is free to see things as they please," said Prang. "I am of course beholden to their will. However, until they see fit to give their opinion on this matter, as the acting commander on location, I'll decide how we should proceed."

"You're twisting the rules," Pitt said, but he subsided at a glance from Prang.

Both men turned back to the screen. Down in the officers' lounge, the woman had just noticed Ramón's arrival. A flicker of surprise appeared briefly in her eyes. Clearly she hadn't expected to be visited again so soon, but it almost seemed as though her reaction ran deeper than that—as if somehow, it was connected to the specific man she saw before her.

You're reading too much into this, Prang thought. *Of course she doesn't know him. They're on opposite sides, aren't they?*

"Another interrogator?" she spat, her voice tinny as it passed through the monitoring room's speakers. "What do you people want now?"

"I only want to talk," Ramón assured her. He set a dish of Instant-Meal rations on a nearby table. "Are you hungry?"

"Like you really care," she scoffed, but she still crossed the room to take the food.

Ramón allowed her a few minutes to eat. She took slow, tentative bites at first, then began shoveling the food into her mouth when she accepted that it hadn't been tampered with. When she pushed the bowl away from her, satisfied for the moment, Ramón started in with his questions.

"You certainly gave us a shock yesterday," he told her. "Any chance you could elaborate on what you said?"

"I told you one of your lost sheep is alive," she replied. "Shouldn't you be thanking me instead of pestering me more?"

"You have to understand that it's hard for us to believe," said Ramón. "Doctor James Simmons has been presumed dead for over three decades by now. We'll need more proof than just your word if we're going to believe that presumption was wrong."

"I've told you everything I know. I gave you coordinates. Go there and check it out."

"You must know more than just that," Ramón argued. What is your group's ultimate plan? What did you hope to achieve by attacking three research stations and stealing some ore?"

The woman laughed bitterly. "It's bigger than that. Bigger than us, or our hopes. The shadow will rise, and all will be consumed."

Ramón's eyebrows rose; his interest had been piqued. He dipped a hand into his pocket to appear more casual. "The shadow, you say …"

As he watched the somewhat grainy footage on the monitor, Prang couldn't tell for sure, but he thought he saw Ramón's eyes darken for just a moment.

"That's right, and it's coming," she replied. "All that we've done up to this point has been prelude. When the shadow rises—"

She froze abruptly and keeled over.

A second later, Prang and Pitt's camera feed went dead. The audio feed cut out with it.

"What happened?" Prang asked Pitt. "Why can't we see what's going on down there?"

"I don't know," said Pitt. "Let me try and get it working again."

Prang watched intently as Pitt sent his fingers flying across the keyboards, though none of his commands seemed to have any effect. At last, Pitt gave the system a hard reboot, and the dark screen finally came back to life. Prang and Pitt could see into the officer's lounge again.

What they saw there wasn't good.

Ramón knelt before the prone form of the prisoner, attempting to resuscitate her.

"That's not a good sign," said Prang. "What happened down there?"

"I'm not sure," answered Pitt. "It looks like she's going into cardiac arrest. There's still a chance we can bring her back before—"

On the screen, Ramón pulled his hands away from the woman's body. He turned to face the camera and shook his head with a regretful expression on his face.

"She's dead."

"Scratch that," Pitt told Prang. He rested his forehead in the palm of his hand. "There had better be a very good explanation for all this."

*

Later that night, Pitt made his way across the sick bay waiting room, having just concluded a debriefing with the doctors who had examined Jess' body. From what little those doctors had discovered so far, the explanation Pitt had hoped for was still long in coming. But Pitt felt confident that all would be revealed sooner or later.

Prang and Ramón stood in the far corner of the room and, as Pitt strode over to meet them, he could hear them conversing in hushed tones.

"She died in seconds, sir," said Ramón. "I didn't know what was happening until it was too late."

Admiral Prang raised his eyes from his holopad and the report the captain had just quoted almost word for word. "There was no warning?"

"None, sir," Ramón replied. "If I had known what she was about to do—"

Prang held up a hand. "No apology necessary, Captain. This clearly wasn't your fault." He dropped his hand and groaned in frustration, a rare occurrence for him. "I'd just like to know how she did it."

"I may have some answers for you, Admiral."

Prang and Ramón turned as Pitt reached them, subdued expressions on all their faces.

"The autopsy has concluded?" Prang asked, a slight note of surprise in his tone. Three hours had elapsed since the prisoner's untimely death, enough time for Ramón to compose his report, but the doctors had only been operating on the body for about half that time.

Pitt shook his head. "Not quite, sir. The doctors are still working, but they found something I thought you should see immediately."

Prang motioned back the way Pitt had come. "Lead on."

Pitt headed back across the room, followed by Prang and Ramón.

"The head physician is beside herself, sir," Pitt reported as he walked. "I think she might be in shock. She swears that the prisoner was on the road to recovery when she was discharged from the sick bay, with no underlying conditions."

"Then it seems I'll have to have a word with her as well," said Prang. "I don't want any one of us to blame themselves for events outside of our control."

The trio of officers passed through the door into the sick bay proper: a long corridor with a row of wards on each side. Pitt led the way down the hall, not breaking stride as the simple hospital rooms gave way to larger operating theaters.

They entered a small room, sparse and unfurnished save for a metal table around which five 4S technicians bustled, poking and prodding at a pile of spare machine parts. The technicians all straightened up at the sound of the door sliding open, and they saluted as they saw their superiors enter.

"As you were," Prang told them, and they returned to their busy work.

Prang strode across the room until he stood next to one of them. "Please, explain this to me," he said warmly. "What am I looking at here?"

The technician turned to face him. "We're not entirely sure, sir. The doctors found this pretty quickly when they opened up that woman's chest cavity. It may be small, but it still packed a punch. This thing generated a pretty strong short-range electrical pulse. I probably shouldn't say this, sir, but I have to give the builder credit for their ingenuity. For something so small, it sure had a lot packed into it. Not just circuitry, but cloaking tech as well. It never showed up on any medical scans."

"So that explains how the security cameras were shorted out," Prang said, sharing a look with Pitt. "But how would such a thing have been triggered?"

"Again, sir, we can't be sure," answered the technician. "There wasn't a timer, so it wasn't preprogrammed. The trigger must have been external."

"Maybe a code word?" Prang wondered aloud.

Pitt raised a finger in thought. "The word 'shadow' got thrown around a few times, if I recall. But why wouldn't the device have just killed her the first time anybody said it …?"

"Either way, we haven't actually found any audio receptors on this thing," the other man said. "If there was a code word, I couldn't tell you how the device picked up on it."

"That's quite all right, technician," Prang soothed. "Keep working, and let us know if you make any further discoveries."

"Yes, sir," the technician replied, then went back to his task. Prang returned to the other side of the room where Pitt and Ramón still stood.

"What now, sir?" Ramón asked tentatively. "Where do we go from here?"

"We should head up to my office," suggested Prang. "I think it would do us all well to get away from this place and remind ourselves that life still goes on."

With those words, Prang swept from the room, striding briskly back down the corridor, through the waiting room, and out into the belly of the massive cruiser, with Pitt and Ramón close behind. Together they took the elevator up to the highest level of the administrative suite, all the way to the admiral's office.

The receptionist glanced up from his desk in the antechamber as the elevator doors swished open. The young man gave a curt nod and a salute as he recognized his superiors. "Good afternoon, sirs."

"Good afternoon to you as well, Benson," Prang returned the nod.

Pitt and Ramón followed Prang into his spacious office. They waited for him to take up his position behind his desk, then seated themselves when invited.

"I would welcome your thoughts on this matter," Prang told them. "I'm not entirely certain what to make of it myself. Please, speak freely."

"Something seems off to me," said Pitt. "It's all a little too convenient. She gives us one hot tip—which we still don't know was true—and then, when we try to coax some more information out of her, she drops dead. If she always had the ability to pull that off, why wouldn't she have done it sooner? Why would she have cooperated initially only to reverse her stance later?"

"It's not uncommon for prisoners to want to escape by any means necessary," argued Ramón. "She could easily have decided that death was the only way out. We tried to put her at ease, but some people just can't trust anyone else to want what's best for them."

"I don't think it was that simple," Pitt said. "If she didn't want to be a captive, she wouldn't have let us capture her in the first place. Besides, she gave up too much information for me to accept that she never wanted to say anything. If that were the case, she wouldn't have told us about James Simmons or given us his coordinates."

"Unless she was leading us into a trap. We still have no evidence that the information she gave us is valid."

"True, but we can't discount it either. Whether she lied to us or not, we still have to consider all the facts."

"We can't go on debating this, or we'll just keep going in circles," Ramón argued. "How are we supposed to know what made her do what she did when none of us noticed she was doing it until it was already too late?"

At those words, an idea suddenly came into Pitt's mind.

"Hold on." He rose from his chair and turned his back to the desk, pacing a few steps toward the door with one finger raised in thought. "You're right, Captain. We never saw what happened, because all the security cameras in the room were knocked out. I wonder why that was?"

"Uh … what do you mean?" Ramón asked.

"It seems like overkill, doesn't it?" Pitt went on. "If she wanted to die, a much smaller pulse of electricity would have done the job. But she still used enough to short out the camera so we couldn't watch her final moments. The only reason for her to do that would be …" His voice trailed off.

"You're reading too deep into it," said Ramón. "I think it's more likely she wanted to ensure the trick would work. The pulse needed to be strong, or it wouldn't do much for her."

"No. She wouldn't have disabled the cameras unless she had something to hide."

"But what could she possibly have wanted to hide? She didn't move again after she fell."

"It's too convenient," Pitt said. "The camera failure must have been meant to cover something up. And if it wasn't something she did—" He stopped cold as a new thought struck him. "It must have been something you did."

Prang had been placidly watching his subordinates debate for the last several minutes, but Pitt's accusation forced a reaction out of him. Prang's face turned a shade whiter, and his mouth began to curve downward in a concerned frown. As the seconds ticked by and Ramón didn't reply, the tension between the three men thickened and thickened.

"Is this true, Captain?" Prang asked. Did you have a hand in that woman's death?"

"What makes you think that?" Ramón's voice rose. "I tried to save her! I wanted her to stay alive as much as you did!"

"Calm down," Prang urged him. "We aren't making an accusation right now. We just want the facts."

"I'm giving you the facts," Ramón insisted. "That device inside her stopped her heart, and it stopped the cameras too. But nothing nefarious happened, I swear."

"Vice Admiral Pitt," said Prang, "why do you believe that Captain Ramón was involved? What do you think he would stand to gain by killing that woman?"

"I'll admit, I can't come up with a plausible motive," Pitt said. "But something still seems fishy about all this, even if I can't quite put my finger on it."

"You're being paranoid," said Ramón. His voice had taken on a new inflection. Was it exasperation? Resentment? Pitt couldn't tell.

"Am I?" Pitt asked. "That woman died under our watch. How many of her fellow masked people have the ability to pull off a stunt like that? What if it isn't just an electric shock next time? What if it's a bomb? If we can't figure out how this woman got away with doing what she did, then the next person who tries it might kill more people than just themself."

Ramón held up his hands. "Okay, okay, I see your point. I want to be careful, too. But I think we already have all the facts we need. That device in the woman's chest shocked her, and she died. Why go spinning tall tales out of thin air when there's no need for it? What else is there for us to figure out?"

"The trigger, for one thing," said Pitt. "We know how that thing worked, but we don't know why it went off when it did. We know it wasn't on a timer, and we can presume it wasn't voice-activated because it didn't have sensors for that sort of thing. That only leaves one option: remote activation."

"Like a remote control?" Ramón asked. "I can tell you she definitely didn't have one of those on her. I would have seen it."

"She has to have activated it somehow," said Pitt. "It's the only way this makes sense. You must have missed it."

"How could I have missed it?" Ramón said. "It would have been obvious. You would have seen it on the cameras. And she didn't look like she was doing it deliberately. She looked as surprised as we were when it happened."

"So it must have been someone else," conceded Pitt. "But a device like that would have to be activated from up close. And there was no one else close enough ..."

Everything coalesced in the vice admiral's mind.

"Except for one person," Pitt said. "You."

"Yes." Ramón spoke with the resignation of someone who had realized his jig was up. "Me."

Pitt didn't turn around immediately. He did his best to control his tone as he asked, "So you did do it?"

"You got it in one," said Ramón. His tone had turned ice-cold.

Pitt's mind raced, trying to adjust to this new revelation. "But how? Like you said, we would have noticed."

"I wasn't being entirely honest," Ramón admitted. "It's actually remarkably easy to conceal a device like that. A person with long sleeves such as myself could hide it with no trouble."

"But why would you do it?" Pitt asked. "I've known you for years, Captain, and I've never seen you have a single violent thought."

"Things change," Ramón replied offhandedly. "People change."

"How long have you been planning this?" said Pitt. "Before you volunteered to talk to that woman? Or before she even came here? How much do you know about them? And more importantly, how much have you told them about us?"

"I haven't told anyone anything," said Ramón. "I don't even know who they are. I did what had to be done. Just like I'm about to do now."

As Ramón spoke those words, Pitt felt every hair on the back of his neck lift.

Slowly, planting his hands on his hips, Pitt finally turned back to face the other two men in the room.

Captain Ramón had crossed the space between himself and Admiral Prang to grab hold of the older man's arm and pull him out of his seat. Now, Ramón stood with his left arm wrapped around Prang, his mouth twisted in a sneer, and a pistol held against his superior's skull.

"You're astute," the captain said. "More astute than I gave you credit for. I had hoped to keep you in the dark for a while longer, but I can work with this."

"Stand down, Captain," barked Pitt. "That's an order."

"Sorry, Vice Admiral." Ramón shook his head. "You can't give me orders anymore."

"What are you talking about?" Pitt asked. "Don't act stupid. I'm your commanding officer."

"I've seen the light." Ramón let out a short cackle. "Or perhaps the shadow would be more accurate. Either way, I know things. I know secrets. Secrets of the universe itself."

"Stop talking nonsense and lower your weapon," Pitt said sternly. "I'll give you five seconds."

"How about I save you the trouble of waiting?" said Ramón.

He leveled his gun at the vice admiral and fired.

Pitt collapsed to his knees, clutching at his side as blood soaked into his uniform. Ramón released Prang, shoving the admiral towards Pitt and keeping his weapon trained on the pair.

"Are you okay, John?" the admiral asked, bending to look his second-in-command in the eye.

Trembling, Pitt struggled to his feet. Even as he fought to stay upright, he placed himself in front of Prang, making himself a shield for the admiral. "I will be," he said shakily. "Let's get him."

Ramón shook his head. "Oh, no. I don't think so. There'll be none of that today, unless you want more lead in you."

"What the devil are you playing at, Captain?" asked Prang.

"It's like that woman said," answered Ramón. "The shadow will rise, and all will be consumed."

"The shadow ..." Prang repeated. "Then the warnings were true."

"Warnings?" Ramón asked. "I have no idea what that's about, but it doesn't matter. We've already almost won."

"We?" Pitt asked. "Who is *we*? Who else are you—"

Ramón raised his gun and fired a single bullet into the ceiling. "That's enough out of you. All you need to know is that your time is over." He leveled the weapon at his admiral again. "But don't worry. You aren't totally useless yet. Our leader really wants to speak to you. You'll meet him soon enough."

"Admiral Prang won't be going anywhere," Pitt grunted through gritted teeth. "And there's only one place you're going—"

"Where?" Ramón taunted him. "You can't possibly hope to hold me."

"You'll be court-martialed for this," Pitt warned him. "The 4S won't take you back."

"Haven't you been listening?" Ramón asked. "I don't need the 4S. I have something better to believe in."

Keeping one hand pressed against his bleeding wound, Pitt stood as straight as he could. His eyes blazed with fury as he swept them around the room.

"Enough," Prang whispered to Pitt. "I appreciate your devotion, but he has the advantage. We need to get away and regroup."

Pitt took one step forward, continuing to shield his superior with his body. "Last chance, captain," he said, using as grave a voice as he could muster. "Whatever is going on in your mind right now, we can get you help. You don't have to escalate this any further. For your own sake, stand down."

"You just don't know when to quit, do you? Lucky for me, the shadow doesn't need you." Ramón trained his gun on Pitt, aiming for the head. "I'm going to enjoy this."

Pitt lunged for the desk, plucked a small metal instrument from its surface, and chucked it at Ramón. The projectile struck Ramón above his left eye, blinding him for one critical moment. As his arms flailed wildly in the air, his finger found the trigger of his gun. A bullet ricocheted off the roof before hitting the frame of one of Prang's wooden shelves.

Pitt took advantage of the distraction to get Prang to safety. Supporting each other, they stumbled through the door and let it slide shut again behind them.

Benson looked up from under his desk where he had been cowering as the door to Prang's office slid open. His skin had gone white as chalk. Pitt guessed that he must have heard the gunshots and decided to take cover. Prang gave him a friendly nod as he and Pitt passed.

"It's all right," he said. "Everything is fine for now."

Benson didn't look convinced, but there was no time for Prang to comfort him further. Pitt hurried Prang into the elevator, and once the door had closed behind them he pressed the button that would take them downward two levels. Letting go of Prang as soon as the elevator car was in motion, Pitt leaned against the wall to steady himself.

"We need to take action," he said. "We need to gather our forces and stop that man before he can cause any more damage."

"No," Prang told him. "If Captain Ramón was compromised, anyone could be. We don't know who we can trust aboard this cruiser."

"Then what are we going to do?" Pitt asked. "Surely we aren't going to let a maniac like him run around unchallenged?"

"We won't, I assure you," Prang said. "I already have a plan in mind. He will be brought to task for his crimes."

"Fine," Pitt huffed. "At least allow me to call in some of our security officers to detain him."

"Go right ahead," said Prang. "We need to keep him isolated until we can figure out if his corruption has spread among the 4S."

"And just how are you going to do that?" Pitt had already pulled out his personal communicator and selected the frequency for the commander of the *Home Base*'s security force.

"There's only one man I know we can trust. We'll need to travel to Voyager Station and enlist the aid of Doctor Fletcher. We can't do it without him."

"Very well," said Pitt. "How soon did you want to leave?"

"As soon as possible," Prang replied. "This is a matter of utmost urgency, after all." His eyes flicked to the large bloodstain on Pitt's uniform. "How are you holding up? Be honest with me, and don't try any bravado. Can you stay with me?"

Pitt stood up straight, saluting with one arm while the other remained pressed to his side. As long as his admiral had need of him, he would serve until his dying breath.

"Always, sir."

*

Captain Ramón leaned back in the leather chair and propped his feet up on Admiral Prang's desk.

"This is the life," he told himself smugly. "Being a big man in charge has its perks. Too bad this particular big man won't be in charge much longer."

Pushing the chair back and letting his feet fall back to the ground, Ramón swiveled in his seat in time to see the shape of the admiral's shuttle fly past the window and vanish into lightspeed.

The captain watched the ship until he could see it no longer, then he returned to his previous position with his feet atop the desk. Pulling his personal communicator from his belt, he tapped a few buttons to open an encrypted channel.

Before he could speak, however, there came a loud and insistent banging on the locked door, followed by a gruff male voice.

"This is Captain Carson of the 4S security force!" it boomed. "Captain Ramón, we've come to take you into custody for your assault on Admiral Prang and Vice Admiral Pitt. Open this door and come out with your hands up!"

Ramón simply shook his head in amusement. Raising his communicator to his lips, he sent a brief audio message along the frequency he had chosen: "Phase One is complete. The admiral is on his way. Be ready. The shadow will rise."

Outside the office, Captain Carson and his men hammered on the door again.

"Captain Ramón!" Carson bellowed. "Open this door immediately, or we'll blow our way in! This is your last chance to come quietly!"

Ramón stood, pressing the key on the admiral's desk to unlock the door. "All right, then," he muttered to himself. "Have it your way."

As the 4S security officers hurried into the room and fanned out into a defensive wall, Ramón turned his back to them in a deliberate show of disinterest.

"Turn around slowly," Captain Carson ordered. "Let me see your hands!"

Discreetly, Ramón dropped the communicator under the heel of his boot.

"Hands up now!" Carson yelled from behind him. "Don't make us get physical!"

Ramón crushed the communicator under his boot and scattered the broken pieces across the floor. Then he turned to meet the oncoming security forces with raised hands and a surprisingly clear conscience.

CHAPTER EIGHTEEN

UNKNOWN LOCATION

Jax came to with a strange feeling of deja vu. Hadn't he been in this exact situation before?

Yes. He remembered. He remembered a hidden facility and a spaceship above the Earth. He remembered three young people trying to take him to their admiral.

Then he remembered another spaceship—not the same one, but one still crewed by himself and the three 4S ensigns, following a trail laid out by the green-haired woman they had found on Rho Station to the hidden asteroid base. He remembered being chased by the drone ships, their plasma cannons disabling the 4S shuttle's systems, but discovered he remembered nothing else.

How much time had passed? Was he still on the ship, or had he been taken somewhere else? And where were the others? Could they still salvage some measure of success from the disaster their mission had become, or had they arrived at the end of the line?

Jax opened his eyes to find that he had definitely been moved somewhere else. Instead of the cockpit of a 4S shuttle, he was now in a small room with gray-paneled walls. He lay on a low cot near the center of the room. A corner of the room had been walled off, sealed with a closed door. Jax contemplated standing up to check out what was behind that door, but stopped when he heard a voice from behind him.

"You don't want to go in there. That's the toilet, and it stinks like you wouldn't believe."

Jax rolled onto his other side and saw Billy sitting up on a cot positioned not far away from Jax's own. Ara and Tom were sprawled on their own cots, still unconscious.

"Toilet?" Jax repeated, dumbfounded. "This is all wrong. What is this place?"

Billy jerked a pointing finger over his shoulder. "I'll give you one guess."

Jax followed Billy's finger and saw that the wall behind him wasn't really a wall at all. Off-white plaster covered three sides of the room, but crosshatched iron bars stretched across the fourth side.

"Huh," said Jax. "Figures we'd wind up in a place like this eventually." He swung his head around to look at Ara and Tom still sprawled motionless. "What about the others?"

"Don't worry about them," said Billy. "They're still alive. Their pulses have been pretty regular this whole time. If you're awake, I bet they'll wake up soon, too."

"Good" Jax maneuvered himself into a seated position. "That means we can turn our attention to more important things."

"Like what?" asked Billy.

"Like, what is this place? And how did we get here?"

"I know as much as you do," said Billy. Then he seemed to reconsider. "Well, maybe a bit more."
"What do you mean?" Jax asked.

"The rest of you got knocked out when the ship shut down," Billy began, "but I didn't. Since I was buckled into my chair, I didn't fly into anything." He rubbed at his neck. "Those straps can still give you some serious whiplash, though."

"Get to the point," Jax urged him.

"Right. Point is, I was pretty dazed, but I was still awake. I remember some of what happened right after the drones shot at us, but it's all kind of jumbled."

"Still better than what I remember," Jax said grudgingly. "Go on."

"I can remember the ship starting to move again. I don't remember how, because the electronics never came back online. Those drones must have towed us somehow, or something bigger came to join them. Next thing I knew, we were back at that big asteroid. You know, the one with all the life signs? I think this cell has to be inside it somewhere, because that's where our shuttle went. Inside, I mean."

"Uh-huh," said Jax. "You saw all that? What happened next?"

"This is the part where it gets really weird," said Billy. "Or maybe not. I was drifting in and out of unconsciousness by then, but I heard the shuttle's hatch open, and a bunch of people came in. They checked you three over and said some things about taking you alive, but when they got to me and found I was still awake, they jabbed some kind of needle into my neck, and that's the last thing I remember before I was here."

"Who were these people?" asked Jax. "Did you get a good look at them?"

"Not for very long," said Billy. "I was already kind of out of it, and the drugs they gave me didn't help either. But I don't think it would have mattered, because they were all wearing those black masks anyway."

"Of course they were," said Jax. "I should have guessed. Did you find out anything else?"

"Not much," said Billy. "When I woke up again, I was already in here. I didn't want to try anything until I knew for sure that you were alive. Piloting is my skill, not breaking out of jail."

"Well, they say it's never too late to learn something new," said Jax. "But I see your point. How about we table the planning session for now until Tom and Ara can join us, and then we all figure something out together?"

"Sure," replied Billy. "At least things probably can't get any worse."

"That's the spirit," said Jax.

Jax rose from his cot on wobbly legs and began to pace. He squinted at the walls and tried to imagine what lay beyond them. Were they really inside of an asteroid? Even if they got out of the cell, how far would they get before their black-clad foes found them? And what would happen if they did? Jax had a horrifying vision of himself and his teammates, unceremoniously tossed out into the vacuum of space, unable to do anything but wait for its cold embrace to claim them …

He shivered. *No.* He wouldn't let that happen. There had to be some way out of their predicament. The 4S was depending on them. Admiral Prang was depending on them.

On Jax's fifth pass by their cots, Ara and Tom stirred. He paced by them three more times before they had fully come to.

"Wh-where are we?" Ara asked groggily.

Jax and Billy filled the other two in on the situation as best they could. Once they were all up to speed, the four of them convened in the center of the room to formulate a solution.

"We need to get out of here," said Jax. "We need to find our ship and get back to the 4S."

"How?" Tom objected. "We don't know the layout of this place, or even if that shuttle is still here."

"We have to try," said Ara. "This is the most important mission we've ever been given. We can't fail if we can help it."

"That's just it," said Tom. "Maybe we can't help it this time. There aren't any reinforcements or antigravity tech here that could get us out of a scrape. We're on our own, and we have literally nothing to work with. Maybe we should give up."

"Are you listening to yourself?" Jax asked. "How can you suggest we just give up? You were the one who got us out the last time we were in a hairy situation."

"This isn't that!" said Tom. "Then, we had a clear path to escape. Now, we don't. I can't make something out of nothing, Jax."

"Uh, guys?" Billy cut in.
But Jax and Tom weren't paying attention.

"I've come too far to give up now," said Jax. "We all have."

"I respect your conviction, but how is it going to help

us get out?" Tom jabbed a finger at the bars. "Hope can't get us through this. We need a tangible solution."

"Oh, calm down, both of you," Ara huffed. "You're both acting like children."

"Guys?" Billy asked again.

Tom crossed his arms over his chest. "I don't hear you offering any brilliant ideas."

"I know," Ara replied. "That's because none of us are going to have any unless we all work together."

"That's cool and all, but it doesn't really help us," said Jax. "I say we should—"

Billy lost his patience and shouted, "Guys!"

The other three turned to him, shocked into silence

"What?" Ara asked.

"I might know a way for us to get out of this cell," said Billy.

"Oh," said Jax. "Well, why didn't you just say that?"

Billy groaned in exasperation.

"Whatever," Tom said. "We're listening now. What do you mean, you know a way out? What are we supposed to use?"

"That's the beauty of it," Billy told him. "If I'm right, we should barely have to do anything."

"Okay, now this I have to hear," Jax muttered sardonically.

"I'm serious!" Billy protested. "But you all need to be ready to move when it's time."

"When it's time?" Ara echoed skeptically. "Billy, if we can escape, we need to do it now. Or at least as soon as possible."

"I know that," said Billy. "But I can't control the timing of this. I'm not even sure it'll happen at all."

The others stared in bewilderment, unsure what to make of their comrade's rambling.

"I think you should start explaining," said Tom.

"Okay, okay," said Billy. "So while I was waiting for you all to wake up, a good amount of time passed. I think it was about fifteen to eighteen hours in all. Somewhere in the middle of that time, one of those freaky masked dudes came along in the hall outside. I guess he was trying to check on us or something, you know, make sure we hadn't gotten out. Anyway, he opened the cell door and came in so he could walk around and take a good look at us. I just pretended to be asleep so he wouldn't bother me, and he didn't. He saw that we were all still accounted for and went right back out."

"And?" asked Tom.

"And," Billy said, "if someone came back here one time, it stands to reason someone might do it again later, right? Now that we're all up and back to full strength, we could take them out if we're ready for them."

"I mean, it sounds good," said Tom. "But are we really willing to stake our fate on the fact that these people *might* have a schedule? I still think we need more solid intel."

"And where are you going to get any of that?" Jax asked. "Not everything is an exact science. Sometimes you have to jump before you know where you'll land."

"You're both missing the point," said Ara. "I wish we knew more, too, but this isn't just about us. We came all the way out here on Admiral Prang's orders, and he's depending on us to report back. We have to do that as soon as we can before our enemies attack another research lab or something."

"I get that, but we still have no idea if Billy's actually right," said Tom. "If no one comes, we're all going to look pretty stupid."

"Looks will be the least of our worries," Ara broke in.

"Fine," said Tom. "Just tell me this—is this really what we're going with? What happens if they just chucked us in here and forgot about us? It could be hours or even days before they come back."

"Then we wait," said Jax. "It's not like we have much else to do at the moment."

"I agree," said Ara. "It's clear to me that we can't do

anything to help ourselves so long as we're all on our own. If Billy's plan has a chance of working out, we should take it. But like he said, we're going to have to be ready at a moment's notice."

"Hold on, though," said Jax. "What are we even going to do if we do get out? We don't know the layout of this place. If we came across any of the guys in the masks, we'd be goners for sure."

"It's worth considering," Ara replied. "But it would hardly be the first time we've worked things out on the fly."

"And what happens if we fail?" asked Tom. "That's got to be worth considering, too. If these people catch us trying to escape, what will they do? Would they let us walk away in one piece?"

"That's a question for the future," Ara told him. "We're still in the present, and in the present we don't have any other choice. For better or worse, we have to try something."

Billy gave voice to the all-important question. "So we're going with my plan?"

"Looks like it," Tom said grudgingly.

"Yes," Ara agreed. "You might just be onto something. I'm willing to see how things go."

"Then all we have to do now is wait," said Billy.

"Wait and hope you're right," added Jax. "If you aren't, I don't want to think about what might happen."

*

They set up a system of shifts, where each one of them took a turn keeping watch while the others did their best to relax and think about something other than the 4S' potentially impending doom.

Several hours later, Billy was on lookout while Ara, Jax, and Tom tried to formulate some kind of strategy in case they got out.

"There's no reason for us to push our luck," Tom said. "Admiral Prang himself told us to get out of here the second we saw anything suspicious, and we definitely have that covered.

We should find our ship and book it out of here. The 4S will send in a more professional team later."

"But if we can get them some kind of idea of what this place is like, they'd be better prepared for that," said Jax. "Don't you want to know what these people are trying to hide?"

"We all do," said Ara, "but I'm sure we'll hear about it soon enough once the 4S blows the whole case wide open."

"But we'll already have been here," said Jax. "Anything we find out now could be usable information for later."

"I don't disagree," replied Ara, "but going out of our way to collect any more data than what we see with our eyes is too dangerous. We'd be risking ourselves when the specific orders we were given explicitly told us not to do that. If we don't make it out, no one will have any idea this is out here. It's our duty to make sure they know."

"Yeah. Putting self-preservation above the mission makes sense in this case," said Tom.

"All right, I'm outvoted," said Jax. "Settle down. It was only a suggestion anyway."

"We already have one impossible task to accomplish," Tom reminded him. "Getting whatever secret plans these crazy people have won't do us any good if we don't have a shuttle to fly them away. And then there's the matter of the asteroid field. We have to make sure we don't get pinned down like last time—"

"Shhh!" called Billy. "I can hear something!"

The others listened and heard it too: the clatter of footsteps, followed by the whir of an opening door.

It didn't take long for the mystery visitor to come into view. Unsurprisingly, it was yet another of the masked raiders who had already attacked the 4S so many times. This man was taller and thinner than most of his people. That was good, Jax thought. They could work with that.

"What did I tell you guys?" asked Billy. "Here he comes, like I said."

"Yes, you're very smart," Jax told him. "Is that what you want to hear?"

"Hey, go easy on me," said Billy. "I'm just saying, I told you this would happen."

"You made a lucky guess," said Tom. "That's different."

"All of you, be quiet," hissed Ara. "Stay focused. This is gonna take some precise timing."

The man carried a tray containing four bowls of generic Instant-Meal protein mush. As he stopped outside the 4S agents' cell, he shifted the tray to one hand while he retrieved a key card from his pocket.

"I've brought you food," he told them, in a voice carefully disguised by his group's characteristic modulation. "See?" He indicated the tray with a tilt of his head. "It's all perfectly healthy. You can eat it, and regain your strength."

"Since when do you care about our strength?" cut in Jax. "I bet you're just trying to fatten us up for later. You've tried to kill us all before, so why stop now? We're all locked up in here. Why don't you come and get us?"

"We have no wish to harm you," the man said. "We do have to keep you inside your cell for the foreseeable future, but you will all be well taken care of. If there is anything we can do to make you more comfortable, now is the time to let us know."

"Getting out of this cell would make us comfortable," grumbled Tom.

"Unfortunately, we can't allow that," said the man. "There will be a time when there won't be a need for cells or hostilities, when everyone will see our new world and rejoice in its glory. Surely a short period of solitude is a small price to pay for such an opportunity."

"Oh, shut up," said Jax. "Spare us your speeches. Find someone who cares."

"Very well," the man said. "If you won't listen to our truth now, you'll hear it sooner or later anyway."

"We'll just see about that," said Ara.

Instead of arguing further, the masked man swiped his key card in the mechanism. The cell unlocked with a loud clunking noise.

"I'm about to open the door," he said. "Please do not make any attempt to escape. If you lay a hand on me, we may be forced to rethink our leniency toward you."

Wow, thought Jax. *Do these people ever talk normally?*

"Step back from the bars," the masked man ordered. "Stand against the back wall, and don't move until the door has closed again."

"All right, all right." Jax stepped backward and motioned the others to follow. When they didn't at first, he beckoned them more urgently.

The masked man lifted a short baton from his belt. "Stand against the back wall. If anyone moves or attempts to escape, there will be consequences."

Jax moved back until he reached the wall. The others did the same.

The masked man yanked the door open and strode into the cell. The door swung closed behind him, but he hadn't locked it yet. Jax and the others had a shot at getting past him, if they were quick.

The masked man's head swiveled as he scanned the room, checking that each prisoner was still in their place. Nodding once when he saw they were, he walked into the center of the cell, where the cots were. Bending over at the waist, he began to set his tray of food down on one of those cots.

Jax watched all the man's movements with narrowed eyes. So far, everything had played out even better than he'd dared to hope. Their enemy was inside the cell, within their range. He had come alone and he had let down his guard. Jax and the others could take him out easily.

They had to move now, while they still had a chance. How long would it be before that chance would come again?

Jax looked to Billy on his right. He locked eyes with him and slowly turned his head toward the masked man in a clear signal of intent. They had planned for this. Now was the time to put their plans into action.

Billy extended one leg, peeling away from the wall.

The masked man's head snapped around at once.

"Remain in your place. No harm will come to you if you comply."

Yeah, right, Jax thought.

The masked man set his tray fully on the cot and rose to his full height, smacking his baton into the palm of his hand. "This is your final warning."

Billy refused to cower under the threat. He took three more steps in the masked man's direction.

Sidestepping the cots, the masked man held his baton above his head.

"I warned you," he boomed. "You brought this on yourself. This is for your own good."

And he started to cross the distance between himself and Billy.

Jax's heart leapt. Was this really going to work?

The masked man focused on Billy as the two of them closed in on each other, so much so that he had forgotten the other three 4S agents in the cell.

Jax turned to Ara and Tom, silently mouthing one simple word: *Now!*

Tom and Ara charged at the masked man, circling around to attack him from behind. Ara swung a punch into the soft flesh of his neck while Tom lashed out with a sweeping kick that the masked man barely avoided. Billy joined the fray, and the three 4S agents battered the lone enemy from all sides.

With the masked man completely distracted, Jax made his move. Racing over to the fight, he grabbed the masked man's arm and twisted the baton out of his grip. Ara, Billy, and Tom disengaged as Jax clobbered the man over the head with his own weapon. He fell to the floor and lay unmoving.

The entire scuffle was over inside of two minutes. Jax felt almost disappointed, like he had more frustration to work out. He almost hoped the masked man would stand up again and continue the fight. But he didn't, and Jax had to move on to bigger and better things.

"I'll grab his key card," Ara said, reaching down. "We

might need it."

"Good idea," said Tom, who had already swung the door wide open.

Jax, Billy, and Ara followed Tom out into a short corridor lined with six prison cells on each side. Their cell sat at one end of the hall, where a sliding door restricted access to the rest of the facility.

Billy ran down to the other end of the hall, but he discovered only another wall.

Jax and the others looked at the door at their end of the hallway. It seemed to be controlled by another key card reader, but the card Ara had just swiped should allow them access.

"We made it," breathed Jax, almost disbelievingly. "Last chance to back out."

"No chance," said Tom. "We need to get out now."

Ara raised their stolen key card and was about to scan it to open the door.

"Hang on," Billy shouted from behind them. "There's someone down here."

Jax, Ara, and Tom spun around to see Billy at the other end of the hallway, peering into another cell. None of the other three could make out from their vantage point exactly what he was looking at, so they all walked over to join him.

In the cell at the opposite end of the block, an elderly man sat hunched over on a cot pressed up against the back wall. At the sound of Billy's voice and the others' footsteps, he glanced up, fixing them with dull, sunken muddy brown eyes. A scraggly unkempt beard hung from his chin, and his graying hair hung down to just beneath his shoulders. He seemed to be somewhere between the ages of Vice Admiral Pitt and Admiral Prang. When he lifted his head off his chest, he allowed his onlookers a glimpse at a uniform they all instantly recognized—the uniform of the 4S.

The man wasn't any 4S agent or officer Jax had ever come across on *Home Base* or Voyager Station. That was hardly surprising, though. Judging by the man's appearance, he had clearly been in captivity for far longer than Jax, Ara, Billy, and Tom had.

"Huh," said Tom. "Now that is interesting."

The man blinked as though he had just woken up from a long nap. When his watery eyes landed on the people standing before him, he sat up straighter and came fully to attention.

"You four," he called. "You're 4S?"

"That's right," Ara replied tentatively.

"But what are you doing here?" the old man asked.

"We wish we could tell you," said Jax. "Until five minutes ago, we were in the same position as you."

"You're the ones they brought in the other day, then?" the man said.

"Um … yes," Billy said tentatively. "Unless they've got any other 4S agents here."

"No, no," said the man. "You're the first ones I've seen in … oh, it's been so long. I had almost given up hope."

"Hope of what?" asked Tom.

"Don't get too chatty," said Jax. "We still don't even know who this guy is." He turned to face the man in the cell. "Care to comment on that?"

"Ah, yes," the man said. "How rude of me. My name is Doctor James Simmons. Pleasure to meet you all."

CHAPTER NINETEEN

CELL BLOCK—ASTEROID BASE—DEEP SPACE

"You're James Simmons?" Tom asked. "As in, *the* James Simmons?"

The man behind the bars let out a hollow laugh. "Everyone always told me I was a brilliant scientist, but I never thought I'd be that well-known."

Ara stepped back, quickly followed by Billy. Jax and Tom stayed rooted to the spot.

The man just stared at them, bemused. "What? Was it something I said?"

Jax crossed his arms. "Maybe."
"What are you talking about?" the man asked. The look of relief and hope in his eyes had begun to shift into something new, something more guarded.

"There's no easy way to say this," Tom said at last. "We were led to believe you'd be running this whole show."

The man raised his arms in disbelief. "Look around you, boy! Look at where they've stuck me! Do I look like I'm running anything?"

"I don't know," Jax said. "Maybe if you were, you could have done something about that beard."

The man stiffened indignantly and put a hand to his chin. "I'd like to see you do better after so long without a razor," he muttered.

Ara retrieved her holopad and pulled up a photograph.

"It does look like him," she whispered to the others. "He's older now, obviously, but he could easily be the same man."

Jax took a long look at the image Ara had called up, then took a long look at the man in the cell. In the end, he had to agree that both people were one and the same. James Simmons' hair had gone gray, and he sported his unkempt beard where once he had been clean-shaven, but the overall structure of his face had remained the same, with its square jawline and piercing eyes.

"It doesn't make any sense," whispered Billy. "Even if he isn't leading the bad guys, he hasn't been seen for decades. He's supposed to be dead. What is happening here?"

"Isn't it obvious?" Tom asked in the same hushed tone. "They wanted to catch us off guard. All they had to do was insinuate this guy was out here, and what did we do? We rushed off, right into their trap. These people fed us lies, and we just ate them up."

"Apparently, not all of it was a lie," said Ara. "He's here in front of us, isn't he?"

"Is he?" asked Jax. "All we have to go off of is his word. There has to be some better way of verifying his story."

"We could do a DNA test, like we did when we first found you," said Ara. "But we don't have the proper equipment on us, and we're kind of strapped for time."

"Can we leave him?" Jax asked. "He wasn't part of the plan."

"Our ship could carry an extra passenger, no problem," said Tom. "But every second we spend in this hall is another second those masked crazies could send more goons after us. I don't think they'll be so … what did he call it? … lenient the next time."

The man calling himself James Simmons watched them deliberate. His eyes betrayed a hope that he was clearly trying not to show on his face.

"We can't just let him stay here!" said Billy. "He's a human being, and a 4S agent on top of that. We still have our loyalty, don't we?"

"He might slow us down," said Tom. "As much as I hate to say it, he does look weak. If we had to fight or run, could he keep up?"

"We don't even know if we'll be bringing him," said Jax. "I think there are some questions that need answers before we can decide what to do with him."

"We don't have time for that!" Tom snapped. "We have to go!"

Jax ignored Tom's outburst.

"Okay," he said eventually, directing his words to the imprisoned Doctor Simmons. "Say we believe you. Say we believe that you're really who you say you are. What exactly are we supposed to do with that information? Even if you're not the one in charge of this operation, what are you doing here at all?"

"They took me!" said Simmons. "Against my will, I might add. They took me, and they made me build things. Parts of things. They keep me on a very tight leash, though, let me tell you. Day in, day out, it's wake up, walk to my lab, do some work, walk back, sleep, repeat. I don't know if you can tell, but that sort of thing really wears a man down—"

"Believe me, I get it," said Jax. "It's terrible that they did that to you. But … Well, this whole situation is full of logistical problems. How exactly did you end up here?"

"Now there's the million-dollar question," said Simmons. "Truthfully, I couldn't tell you. I've been here for three decades and I've never learned anything that would tell me what or where it is."

"We can help you with that," said Ara. "By all accounts, this is a secret base hidden inside an asteroid. Something like that, anyway."

Simmons' eyes widened. "Inside an asteroid? Intriguing. The seer possibility—" He stopped himself. "But I digress. You were asking about how I got into this mess. The last thing I can surely recall before I was stuck behind these bars was going aboard a 4S scientific expedition to study cosmic rays."

"Oh, yeah," said Billy. "We heard about that. The ship blew up, and everyone died except one man who went completely nuts. Oh, and you, I guess."

"Is that what happened?" Simmons asked. "What a tragedy. So many good souls …"

"The ship went down with all its crew," Tom confirmed. "Multiple casualties. Until right now, everybody assumed you were one of them."

Simmons' eyes darkened, and his voice grew fainter. "It happened so suddenly. We were taking samples of radiation from deep space. We had to calibrate our instruments precisely, you see, so we wouldn't have any leakage. We carefully inspected everything before we set out, but something must have slipped between the cracks in all the fuss. It only took one flaw in the machine for things to go sideways. I never even discovered what that flaw was. I just woke up here."

"That's the thing I still can't understand," said Jax. "How did you wake up? If your ship got exposed to the vacuum, how are you still breathing? No offense."

"None taken," Simmons replied. "It's a mystery to me as well. I must have been plucked up quickly, though, since the asphyxiation didn't have much time to take effect. The next thing I can remember after the disaster is coming to in this cell. I thought it might have been a sick bay at first, but that illusion didn't take long to dissolve."

"So what have you done since then?" asked Billy. "Just sit here and let them push you around? Haven't you ever tried to escape?"

"Several times, throughout the early days," replied Simmons. "But they always kept me under close surveillance, with guards nearby at all times and cameras everywhere. As time went on, and my body grew older, I just didn't have the vitality I needed to make the attempt."

"You said you built some things for them," said Jax. "Do you know what those things were, or what they might plan to use them for?"

"I know just as much as you do," said Simmons. "My specialty was always radiation, and all the technology I've built since I've been here seems to tie into that, but I have no clues as to its ultimate purpose."

The others all looked at him, turning his words over in their minds.

"I can promise you that I never wanted to harm anybody," Simmons continued. "If the people who locked us up have used my work to do evil deeds, I would be devastated, and I would do everything I could to shut it down before it got out of control."

Ara turned to her squadmates. "His story might have some holes in it, but I don't think he's lying. If he really was an evil mastermind, why would he need to hide in a cell?"

"Then are we just supposed to accept a story that doesn't make sense just because the alternative makes less sense?" asked Tom. "He's still been working for those masked people for thirty years. Who knows what they made him do?"

"We can worry about that later," Ara said. "It was never going to be our problem to solve anyway."

Tom shrugged. "Fine. Your funeral."

Jax stared Simmons in the eyes. "We'll believe you for now. It looks like we'll be bringing you along when we fly out of here."

"Wonderful," said Simmons. "You won't regret this."

"Good," said Tom. "Now, before any other people in masks come along, we need to go."

"First, why don't you tell me a little about yourselves?" said Simmons. "It's been so long since I've met anyone new. How did you four find your way out here?"

"We don't have—" Tom began, but Billy cut him off.

"Admiral Prang sent us," said Billy.

"Good old Prang," said Simmons. "Glad to hear he's still kicking around. And as the admiral, too. When I last saw him, he was only a vice admiral." Simmons' momentary nostalgia vanished abruptly as his face fell again. "But why would he send you young people out to an asteroid? This place has never struck me as a tourist trap."

"The people running this base have been attacking 4S research stations," said Tom. "They took out three before we managed to bring one of their people in for questioning. She gave us the coordinates to this place, and we were assigned to scope it out."

"And is she the one who told you I was 'running this whole show'?" Simmons asked.

"Um … yes," said Tom sheepishly. "But that wasn't really our concern to figure out one way or another. We were just supposed to determine whether or not there was a base here before the 4S sent in a better team."

"Then I take it your mission took an unexpected turn," said Simmons, "considering you're still here."

"Yeah, you could say that," Jax said. "They shorted out our ship and stuffed us in a cell. It's a pretty massive setback."

"But perhaps it was still fortuitous in the end," said Simmons. "After all, it brought us all together. Maybe we can all help each other."

"Finding you was a happy bonus," said Ara. "Believe me when I say that we'll do our best to get you home safe again."

"I appreciate that, Miss—" Simmons broke off abruptly. "You know, it occurs to me that I never even asked your names. How rude of me. Let's start again, shall we? Just who exactly am I looking at here?"

Ara, Billy, and Tom each gave a salute as they stated their name and rank, just as they would to any 4S official.

"Ensign Ara Kendall, Records Division, sir."

"Ensign Billy Vurk, Pilots' Corps, sir."

"Ensign Tom Ubert, Engineering Division, sir."

Finally, Simmons turned to Jax. "How about you, son?" he asked. "You're wearing a 4S uniform just like them. Where do you fit in?"

Jax stood to attention but didn't salute. "My name is Jax Nurmen, sir."

Simmons' eyes went wide. "Nurmen? Any relation to

Albert and Rebecca Nurmen from the Research Division?"

"They were my parents," said Jax. "They're dead now. I'm with the 4S to get revenge."

"I'm so sorry for your loss," said Simmons. "They were several years younger than me of course, just starting out the last time I saw them, but they were still as fine a pair of scientists as you could ever hope to find. I'm not surprised that you came along, either. Most of us knew their workplace relationship was going to blossom into something bigger, and evidently it did."

Jax tried to imagine his parents as young fresh-faced agents looking to make their mark on the 4S, and found the image more appealing than he had expected. At one point, they had been like him: directionless but full of good intentions. They had eventually discovered their purpose. Would he ever be able to do the same?

"Th-thank you," Jax stammered, caught off guard by the rush of feelings flooding into his mind.

"But you have no rank?" asked Simmons. "You haven't joined the 4S officially?"

"No," said Jax. "It's a long story. My parents raised me while they were undercover doing secret research. I didn't even know they worked for the 4S until just before they were killed. Admiral Prang offered me a chance to avenge them, and I took it."

"But surely you can't expect that to fuel you forever," said Simmons. "If you're anything like your parents, you're sure to have all kinds of talents and skills. The son of two people like Albert and Rebecca Nurmen shouldn't waste his entire life on some narrow-minded quest for vengeance."

His final statement caught Jax off guard, so much so that he physically took a step back. The idea wasn't new; his teammates had raised it several times over. But to hear it from someone so much older, someone who had actually known his parents, gave it a new and impactful quality.

"Maybe ..." he murmured hesitantly.

Thankfully, Jax didn't get much time to think about it.

The entire station rumbled with the deafening sound of an explosion somewhere close by. Jax braced himself, ready for the cellblock to collapse around him, but for the moment everything still felt stable.

"What was that?" asked Tom. "Are we under attack?"

"How could we be?" said Ara. "Who would be attacking? The 4S doesn't know we're here, and they don't have warships either way."

"But what if this is someone else?" asked Billy. "Another enemy group?"

"Another one?" Jax raised an eyebrow doubtfully. "How many space terrorists can there be, realistically?"

"What if they breach the walls?" Billy asked. "We're inside a space rock. Could this place survive an explosion?"

Apparently, it could. A second blast never came, and no emergency sirens sounded either. The cell block's structure remained entirely intact.

"I guess they just hit another part of the base," said Billy. "We're still safe here."

"The asteroid was big, but not that big," said Tom. "And besides, the explosion was really close. All around us. There's no way we could be unaffected if anywhere else on this base was."

Jax spun around to face Simmons. "You've been here the longest. Has anything like this ever happened before?"

"No, never," replied Simmons. "I can't think of any reason this base would blow up, unless …"

He broke off as a stricken expression flickered onto his face.

"Unless?" Tom asked. "Unless what?"

"Oh, dear," said Simmons.

"What?" Ara asked. "What's going on?"

"They've done it," Simmons said. "They've actually done it. We're all doomed."

*

Vice Admiral John Pitt of the 4S was not a man who

tended to believe in luck. To his mind, nothing ever happened by chance. When Pitt looked at the universe, he saw something so structured that there almost certainly had to be some greater force behind it all. He didn't know what to call it—God, logic, or something else entirely—but he believed it was out there, guiding events toward some unknown but predetermined end. In Pitt's opinion, everything happened for a reason.

Despite all his convictions, he still found it astounding that Captain Ramón's bullet had only grazed him. The injury would leave a scar, but it would heal. Pitt would live to fight another day.

He would have to take that as a good sign—even if only because, try as he might to avoid it, all he saw in his immediate future was fighting.

Pitt took a deep breath, only to double over as pain lanced through his freshly bandaged side. He decided to give up his existential musings for the moment. None of them would make his wound less tender, and it was best not to aggravate it this early in his recovery. Admiral Prang needed him at his best, and his best was what he intended to give.

Once the two men had extricated themselves from the tense standoff with Captain Ramón, Pitt had wanted to stay at the shuttle's controls. As soon as he had laid in their course and taken them into lightspeed, however, Prang had appeared at his shoulder and all but ordered him to go get some rest.

"Please, take care of yourself," Prang had urged. "We'll need you ready to face whatever is coming."

Pitt had protested, but Prang wouldn't hear of it.

"These ships practically fly themselves at lightspeed," he reminded. "Besides, my piloting skills are no more rusty than yours. I can handle the shuttle while you look at that wound of yours."

Pitt relented under the admiral's sympathetic gaze, but only after Prang promised to call him the second any trouble presented itself.

As Pitt had staggered to his quarters behind the cockpit, his adrenaline rush finally began to fade, and the pain of his injury leaked in to replace it. It took all of Pitt's considerable willpower to not fall flat on the floor before he could retrieve a first aid kit and sit down at the table in the shuttle's common area.

It wasn't easy for Pitt to tend to his own injury. He spent a few minutes fumbling around with a pair of tweezers before he pulled the small metal object out of the hole in his side, then pressed a cold compress against the wound until he had staunched the bleeding. He took off his ruined shirt and pants and thoroughly cleaned himself under a cold shower. It stung the whole time, but Pitt forced himself to tough it out.

An hour and a half later, with his side wound swaddled in thick gauze bandages under a fresh, crisply pressed uniform, Pitt rejoined Prang in the shuttle's cockpit for the final approach to Voyager Station.

"How are you holding up, my friend?" asked Prang.

"Well enough, considering," replied Pitt. "I can't believe Captain Ramón could be so brazen."

"I highly doubt he was in his right mind," Prang said. "I've known him for years, and he isn't usually the type to hurt anyone. Clearly this shadow he mentioned has warped his mind in some way."

"Do you think it could be reversed?" asked Pitt.

"I hope it can," said Prang. "If it really is some form of hypnosis, we'd probably be able to break it, given time. But all that is frankly beyond my scope to understand."

"Fair enough," said Pitt. "And we have more pressing matters to deal with either way. What are you going to do if more 4S personnel turn out to have been affected? How will you even know if they have? I'd rather not wait around to get shot again."

"Nor would I ask you to," Prang assured him. "I'm hoping Doctor Fletcher or someone in his department will know some way to help us ferret out the compromised agents."

He broke off to glance down at the readings on the shuttle's control panel.

"You should probably sit down," he told Pitt when he raised his head again. "I'll be bringing us out of lightspeed in a few minutes."

Pitt found himself a seat and watched the stars come

into focus. In the distance he saw the shining light of Voyager Station, but Prang didn't move any closer to it. Instead, the ship idled as the seconds dragged on.

"Shouldn't we be moving?" Pitt asked eventually.

"In a moment." Prang's hand hovered over the shuttle's comm controls. "First I want to try and contact the mission team we sent out to investigate the coordinates that woman gave us."

"The ensigns?" asked Pitt. "What for?"

"To put my mind at ease, I suppose," Prang admitted. "I don't mind saying that the whole debacle with Captain Ramón truly shook me. Who knows what other plans they've enacted? If I've sent those young agents into danger, wittingly or unwittingly …"

He shuddered. Pitt had never seen him shudder before.

"Why did I ever think I could send them out alone?" Prang went on. "If something were to befall them, I don't know if I could bear it."

Pitt didn't know how to help the admiral; he only knew that he didn't enjoy seeing Prang in such an anxious state. "Well, if calling them would really make you feel better, I can't see the harm in it."

"Very good," said Prang. "Let's get right to it, then."

He tapped a few commands into a keypad and flipped the switch to open a comm channel to the ensigns' scout ship.

Pitt and Prang waited in silence for a few minutes, but to no avail. A light buzz of static issued forth from the comm unit with no ping or indicator light to show that the call had gone through. After a while, they had to agree that nothing was going to happen.

"Maybe it's just the distance causing interference," said Pitt. "We've never really tested the 4S comm network over such a long range, have we?"

"No, I suppose not," said Prang, flipping the switch down to close the connection.

"All the more reason to see Doctor Fletcher," Pitt said. "It won't do us any good to sit here and ponder conspiracy theories. We need to do something concrete before we lose ourselves to paranoia.”

“Of course.” Prang set the shuttle in motion. They sped toward Voyager Station. He turned the comm back on, keying it to the frequency of the station’s control room.

“Voyager Station, this is Admiral Prang. Do you copy?”

“We read you, sir,” came the voice of a young and slightly startled technician. “May I ask the purpose of your, um, sudden visit?”

“I’m afraid that’s just above your pay grade, my friend,” Prang replied. “Is Doctor Fletcher available? I must speak with him as soon as possible.”

“One moment, sir,” said the technician. Pitt could hear several voices murmuring indistinctly on the other side of the call. At last, the same voice they had been speaking with spoke again.

“The Chief Research Officer is on his way up, Admiral. My apologies, but this may take a few minutes.”

“I quite understand,” Prang told him. “Don’t worry. Please ask him to call me on this channel when he arrives.”

“Yes, sir,” the technician replied. “You’ll hear from him as soon as he gets here.”

Prang ended the call. He and Pitt sat in silence as the moments stretched on, staring into space and the bulk of the station that interrupted it.

Eventually, they were both jolted back to reality by the pinging that heralded an incoming call. Prang accepted it immediately.

“Doctor Fletcher, I presume?”

“Of course, Admiral,” replied the Chief Research Officer. “My apologies for the delay. Since you brushed aside my staff, can I assume you wish to speak with me in private?”

“You can,” said Prang. “I hate to impose upon your time like this, but something’s come up. I’d rather not say more until we’re together.”

“Then let’s not dally,” Fletcher said. “The hangar at the

top of the upper pylon is available for your use. I'll meet you there as soon as you've landed."

"Thank you, Doctor," said Prang. "I appreciate your accommodating me on such short notice."

"It's my pleasure," said Fletcher. "After all, it's not every day our humble station gets a visit from the admiral himself. See you in the hangar."

The call was severed, this time from the other end. The shuttle rose until it sat level with the station's topmost hangar, then moved forward until it hovered just outside the door. When Prang entered his personal clearance code, the door slid open, and he brought the ship down in the middle of the bay floor.

Once the hangar had been sealed shut and reoxygenated, Prang and Pitt disembarked. Prang brought his personal communicator to his mouth.

"Doctor Fletcher," he said, "this is Admiral Prang. I've landed safely in the hangar and am awaiting your arrival. Do you read me?"

"I read you, sir," Fletcher replied. "I'll be with you in a moment."

True to Fletcher's word, only a minute or two passed before the elevator doors at the other end of the room slid apart and the Chief Research Officer stepped out with one of his personal assistants, Doctor Melville, in tow. His other assistant, Doctor Jennings, was nowhere to be seen.

Pitt noticed the discrepancy instantly. It wasn't unheard of to see Fletcher with only one of his assistants in tow, but it was rare nonetheless. After what happened with Ramón, Doctor Jennings' absence put him on edge.

"Greetings, Admiral, Vice Admiral," said Fletcher, with a nod to each. "I've been expecting you."

"Expecting us?" Pitt asked. "We didn't tell you we were coming."

"No," said Fletcher, "you didn't."

All at once, he straightened up. "Admiral on deck!" he bellowed.

Pitt stared at the Chief Research Officer, wondering what Fletcher thought he was doing. Besides the four of them, there were no other people in the hangar.

Then he felt it: the same prickling on the back of his neck that had warned him when Captain Ramón had been about to fire on the admiral.

Pitt spun on his heels to look behind him.

All around the hangar, men and women covered from head to toe in black shimmered into existence as their personal cloaking devices deactivated. There weren't too many of them, only fifteen in all, but that number would still be more than enough to overpower Pitt and Prang. The two men could do nothing but watch as the figures closed in around them. One of the men stepped to Fletcher's side.

"They came just like you predicted," he said. "It's almost too easy."

"Yes, yes," said Fletcher. "Now why don't you take off that mask and show our guests who they're dealing with? We have no need for secrecy here."

The man reached up to pull the shroud off his face, revealing himself to be none other than the missing Doctor Jennings.

If Pitt had needed any more confirmation that something was amiss, he now had it.

"What is this?" he asked. "What's going on here?"

"Come now," said Fletcher, "you're an intelligent man. I will say, you're here a little sooner than I thought you'd be, but surely you've already picked up on the fact that you've played right into your enemy's hands."

"It's you, isn't it?" asked Prang, in an uncharacteristically small voice. "You're the ringleader of this conspiracy."

"Please, Admiral," said Fletcher. "'Conspiracy' is such a dirty word."

"Very well," said Prang. "What would you call it?"

"I'm actually still not quite sure myself," said Fletcher.

"You see, I've been so focused on planning and executing our agenda that I've barely had time to stop and consider publicity. When one undertakes a great work, he can hardly afford to let vanity get in the way. You above all should be able to understand."

"No, I'm not sure I do," Prang said defiantly. "I've never lowered myself to consorting with villains in the name of my 'great work.'"

"I'd say you have some explaining to do, Doctor," Pitt said.

"You're certainly owed that much," agreed Fletcher. "However, before I fulfill your request, allow me to make one of my own."

"Oh, no," said Pitt. "You don't just get to—"

"Let him speak, Vice Admiral," interrupted Prang. "Whatever he wants, we'll deal with it."

"Thank you, Admiral," Fletcher said. "I appreciate your willingness to listen."

"Speak carefully," said Prang. "I haven't guaranteed you anything."

"Let's get you back aboard that shuttle of yours," said Fletcher. "There's so much I'd like to show you."

"And why would we go anywhere with you?" Pitt asked. "If anything, you're coming with us, Doctor. The authorities need to know about what you've done."

"Oh, you could certainly try to take me in," Fletcher told him. "But just look around you. Do you really think you could manage to fight your way through all of my associates and get to me? And what would happen to Admiral Prang if you left him all alone?"

"What's the alternative?" asked Pitt. "We do what you say, you cart us off to dispose of us in secret, and we're never heard from again?"

"I'm afraid I agree," said Prang. "You've essentially admitted to your being the head of … whatever this is, and now you're asking us to venture off into the unknown? I wouldn't be doing my due diligence if I didn't point out how suspicious that makes you.”

"Oh, don't be like that," said Fletcher. "If you come quietly, I'll even tell you all about the shadow …”

CHAPTER TWENTY

CELL BLOCK—ASTEROID BASE—DEEP SPACE

"What do you mean, 'they've done it'?" Jax asked. "What do you know?"

"Not much, admittedly," said Simmons. "Just the bits and pieces I've picked up from the guards over the years. I always knew they were using me to build them some kind of radiation collector, but I never knew why. All I really know is that they were very interested in the practical applications of cosmic rays."

"What did you tell them?" asked Ara. "What practical applications are there? Admiral Prang tried to use cosmic rays to provide power for our ships and colonies, but what else could they do?"

"You don't even want to know," replied Simmons. "Their effects are still largely untested. Humanity just didn't have the equipment to harness their power until quite recently. They could provide clean energy, yes, but they could just as easily cause a lot of destruction if they weren't handled properly."

"Destruction?" Billy repeated. "Like some kind of weapon? How would that even work?"

"Like I said, it's impossible to know for sure," Simmons said. "Cosmic rays can have all kinds of crazy effects on the human body. That's why 4S ships are designed with radiation shielding. It's possible that, if enough cosmic energy was concentrated around a human being, it could really mess with their DNA and genetic makeup. If that effect could be multiplied to cover a wider area, it could cause a lot of damage."

"So not something we want our enemies to have access to," said Jax.

"Not something we want anyone to have access to," said Simmons. "Mankind has made too many mistakes with science and arms races. We researchers gave them greater energy efficiency, and they used it to build bigger bombs. The 4S was meant to be a fresh start for humanity, away from war and death and slaughter. But somewhere along the line, someone else must have decided they knew better."

Tom's face hardened into a scowl as he made a noise of disgust in the back of his throat. "Typical. Just typical."

Billy looked at Simmons. "There has to be something we can do. Some kind of way we can turn this around. If you built it, you can undo it, right? Right?"

Simmons sunk down onto his cot, laying his head in his hands. "It's all my fault," he said softly, his voice barely carrying to the others' ears. "All my fault. What did I think was going to happen? Why didn't I do something sooner?"

"Sounds like that'd be a no," Jax said to Billy.

Billy's face fell.

"Oh, pull yourselves together!" snapped Tom.

His outburst stunned all the others into silence.

"I've said it before, and I'll say it again. This isn't the place for chitchat," Tom began. "Our enemies' threat level just went up from mass murder to potential nuclear armageddon. Now more than ever, it's imperative that we get to our ship, get off this asteroid, and get back to the 4S."

"Hold on," said Billy. "We're just going to cut and run? I know I'm not the bravest person here, but is leaving really the best thing we can do right now?"

"It's not 'just leaving'," argued Tom. "If anything, it's a strategic retreat. What would happen if we stuck around? Or if we tried to escape and the people here decided we're more trouble than we're worth? Without any advance warning, the 4S would be a sitting duck against whatever weapon the enemy's cooked up."

"And how is a warning going to help solve that?" Jax asked. "Are they going to fight back? They don't have any weapons of their own. Whether they knew the enemy was coming or not, they'd still be helpless against them."

Tom glowered. "You might have a point."

"The least we can do is find out exactly what we're dealing with here," said Jax. "If the 4S isn't going to be able to outgun this weapon, disarming it would be the next best thing."

"Then what do we do?" said Ara. "Tom was right about one thing. We can't stand around and wait for them to kill us, or anybody else."

"We have to stop them," said Simmons. "If they've found a way to weaponize my research, they can't be allowed to use it. The results could be disastrous."

"How are we supposed to fight a weapon like that?" asked Tom. "What would it even do?"

"I don't know," said Simmons. "Without proper schematics or diagrams, I couldn't tell you for certain. But I can say that turning harmful radiation on human beings might be more cruel than just killing them outright. It would be like an atomic bomb that only spread nuclear fallout instead of an explosion. There are no laws or conventions to govern this sort of chemical warfare. It's never been attempted on such a scale."

"With all due respect, we don't need a lecture on ethics right now," Jax told him. "We already know that what's going on is bad. We need you to tell us, once and for all, whether or not you can actually stop it."

"Like I said, I really don't know," Simmons replied. "Cosmic rays are always tricky to work with. We might try to disable the weapon and end up letting the radiation leak out into this base. If I wanted to find a safe way to neutralize the weapon, I'd need access to its official schematics."

"Then let's get you those schematics," said Jax.

Billy spun to face him. "You can't be serious!"

"I am serious," said Jax. "I'm not going to sit around and wait for these people to turn their weapon on me. I say we take action while we still can."

"I don't much like the idea of doing nothing either, but we need a plan," said Tom. "These people won't just have left their top-secret plans lying around where anyone can find them. So how exactly are you suggesting we find them, Jax?"

"I may be able to help with that," Simmons said. When the others all turned to him, he shrugged. "Okay, okay. I don't know where the actual plans might be, but I know how we can find that out."

"What do you mean?" asked Ara.

"I can get you to my lab," Simmons replied. "There's a rudimentary computer system set up in there. It's a long shot, but I think I can use it to hack into the mainframe of whatever this place is and download its layout. If we know where they'd keep secret plans, we could go there and get what we need."

"So we have to find some schematics before we can find some schematics?" asked Billy. "How many steps are there going to be?"

Jax chose to ignore the question. He didn't have the patience for Billy's hyperbolic complaints just then.

"You really think your plan could work?" he asked Simmons.

"Like I said, it's a long shot," Simmons replied. "But I find it hard to believe that any base hidden inside an asteroid could be large enough to support two independent computer systems. Even though my lab's module has been locked out of the overall network, there should still be a backdoor I could use to sneak my way in."

"It's the best chance we've got," said Ara. "I say we go for it."

"Great," said Jax. "Doctor Simmons, it looks like you'll be coming with us."

"Wonderful," replied Simmons. "I can't thank you four enough."

"Saving us all from certain doom would probably cover

it," Jax remarked. "Ara, can you set him free?"

Ara pulled out her pilfered key card and swiped it in the lock of Simmons' cell. The mechanism unlocked with a click, and Ara swung the door wide open. Simmons rose from where he had been sitting to join the others in the hallway.

"Okay," Jax began. "Now we just have to—"

"Wait a minute," cut in Tom.

Jax spun around. "What now, Tom?" he snapped irritably.

"Take it easy," said Tom. "I'm on your side now. I'll follow the plan. But I do have one suggestion."

Jax shrugged. "Go on. But be quick."

"Like I've been saying, this place is probably going to have a lot of guards," said Tom. "It's a wonder more haven't come down here yet, and if we go to this guy's lab we'll almost certainly run into some. There's only five of us—four, really, since we still don't know if Simmons is in any shape to fight. We need to make sure we can get to the lab and complete the plan without getting stopped along the way."

Jax fought the urge to groan. Tom was irritating, yes, but he was also right. Jax didn't much enjoy the thought of being annihilated, either. Still, their little band of heroes didn't have any armaments of its own. What could they really do to achieve Tom's idea?

On a sudden whim, Jax glanced back down the hallway to the cell where they had left the masked man unconscious on the floor. As he thought about the man's prone form, noting how it had been completely covered in black fabric, an idea flew into his mind. He turned back to face the others with a new light in his eyes.

"I have a plan," he told them. "But you might not like it."

*

They didn't like it, but none of them could come up with anything better.

Fifteen minutes later, with the unconscious man's clothes

pulled over his 4S uniform and the man's mask pulled over his head, Jax led the others through the door at the end of the hall.

"Do you remember the route to your lab?" he asked Simmons.

"Of course I remember," Simmons replied. "Walking back and forth from there was the only exercise I got for three decades."

"Good," said Jax.

Hearing his voice as it filtered through the mask's built-in modulator still made him shiver. He kept wanting to look over his shoulder for an approaching enemy, and he had to constantly remind himself that he was the only black-clad figure around. Paranoia at this stage wouldn't help anyone except their foes.

All the same, Jax started to question his own judgment. He couldn't get the mask off his face soon enough. It itched far more than he would have expected, and it stank of human sweat. The only real bonus he could find from it, beyond its service as a disguise, was that it hadn't left him completely blind. Thanks to cleverly disguised infrared lenses woven into the dark fabric, Jax could see in front of him almost as clearly as if his head was uncovered.

Jax huffed out a breath. He shouldn't be focusing on himself. He could bear some discomfort, if it meant that the 4S would come through its ordeal safely in the end.

And yet that in itself surprised him. When had he become so devoted to the cause? Had Simmons' words about him and his parents sunk in so deeply? Or was it the companionship he had found with his squadmates?

Forget it, Jax urged himself. It didn't matter what he was so desperate to prove. It only mattered that he had skin in the game. In the current crisis, that would have to suffice to guide him through.

"Turn right here," said Simmons as the corridor split into two. "We'll be walking that way for a few minutes."

The group's footsteps echoed off the polished walls and flooring as the five 4S agents moved off down the hall Simmons had indicated. They walked in a small cluster, sticking close to each other and keeping a lookout on all sides. Jax walked slightly in front the others, to keep up the impression that he was leading them somewhere. He clutched the small baton the masked man had carried, smacking it into the palm of his hand every so often. If any of their masked enemies had done the same, it would probably have been menacing, but Jax just felt a bit stupid when he did it.

The group walked for several minutes, passing through a strangely deserted space. The walls were colored the same dark gray as their cells had been, with few doors to interrupt their monotony. Jax thought they must have been somewhere deep within the base, because he couldn't see any windows that might help them pinpoint their place in the wider universe. They didn't have the time or desire to look into any of the rooms they passed; instead, they remained laser-focused on their goal of reaching Simmons' laboratory as fast as possible.

Tom looked around. "This is weird. Where is everybody?"

"I'm not going to complain," Ara said. "This is better than anything we expected."

"Yeah, but it won't last forever," said Tom. "If they haven't come for us yet, that just means they're keeping their forces in reserve for something else. We'll meet them sooner or later, and if they're all together when we do, nothing good is going to happen."

"You can be a real downer sometimes, did you know that?" asked Ara.

Tom scoffed and turned away.

Once again, Jax's thoughts drifted. He knew he couldn't take on more than a few of their enemies at one time, even with his team by his side. And they didn't even have the advantage of disguises like he did. If worse came to worst, all their skills would be put to the test. But what else was new?

"Hey!" Billy whispered urgently. "Do you all hear that?"

They listened, and they did. Somewhere in front of them, where the hallway began to curve to the left, footsteps marched in their direction, loud enough to signal more than one person coming, but quiet enough that it couldn't have been a very large group.

"All right," said Jax. "You all know what to do."

The four others did their best to appear dejected and helpless, as befit the roles they were playing.

The next moment, a man and a woman covered fully in black came around the corner and halted in front of the group.

"What's going on here?" the man barked. "This is highly unusual."

"Why are the prisoners out of their cells?" the woman asked.

"Uh …" Jax thought fast. "I'm taking them to the scientist's lab. Lots of work to get done."

The woman wasn't convinced. "On whose orders?"

"The boss," said Jax, praying he sounded confident enough. "You know, the one in charge. They won't like being delayed."

"Sure," the woman replied doubtfully.

The man craned his neck to see the others lined up behind Jax, almost as if he was looking for something. Jax tensed, waiting for his verdict.

The man straightened up to gaze at Jax. "We captured four new 4S agents. So where's the other one?"

"Other one?" Jax tried to sound innocent. "What other one?"

The man didn't reply; he just took two threatening steps forward.

Jax decided it would be best if he quit while he was still ahead.

"Oh, well," he said with a shrug. "We were never going to keep you fooled forever."

"Fooled?" the woman asked. "What do you—"

Ripping off the stolen hood from his head, Jax hurled it into the masked man's face. The man dodged out of its way, forcing the woman to leap to the side before they crashed into each other.

Jax swept his arm forward. "Go!"

Ara and Billy leapt forward to tackle the masked woman, while Jax joined Tom in going for the man. Simmons hung back for the moment.

The fight ended almost as soon as it had begun, with the mystery man and woman knocked out and sprawled across the floor. Jax wanted to tell himself that perhaps his concerns had been exaggerated, but then he remembered Tom's earlier claim of a vast enemy force lying in wait and decided instead that complacency was the last thing they needed just then.

Ara opened the nearest door with her key card, and Jax and Tom shoved the two limp bodies inside the room on the other side. Billy wrung his hands together as he watched them.

"Okay," he said breathlessly. "Now we've done it. If they weren't coming after us before, they definitely will be now."

"All the more reason to get to that lab before they can take us out," said Ara. "Which way now?" she asked Simmons.

"Keep going straight," he told her. "It'll be at the very end of the hall. You can't miss it."

They started again off at a faster pace, moving as quickly as Simmons' advanced age would allow.

Simmons' words were proven right when the hallway terminated in a set of shiny metal double doors. The dim lighting glinting off the metal contrasted sharply with the base's monochromatic design.

Jax couldn't help but think that just about anything could be concealed on the other side of those doors, and when Tom spoke he knew that he wasn't the only one.

"Perfect place for a surprise ambush," Tom said.

"Listen to yourself," Jax grumbled. "What would be the point of something like that? We're in their territory. They could just attack us head-on. They don't need to go to the trouble of setting an elaborate trap."

Tom grunted. "You're probably right. But I still don't like this."

"That's to be expected," Jax muttered.

If Tom heard him, he didn't respond.

"Will you both stop arguing?" Ara pushed her way between them. "Considering the severity of our circumstances, I think we'd all appreciate a little more cohesion right now."

"Whatever," Jax and Tom said in unison, then shared a mutual eye roll.

Ara swiped the key card. The doors slid open.

The space beyond wasn't crowded with enemies. It didn't look like the kind of place where Jax would expect weapons of mass destruction to be dreamed up and constructed. A large metal table stood in the center, cluttered with tools and equipment. The left wall was one large holoscreen with a small computer terminal beneath it. A row of cabinets and shelves lay against the right wall. The back wall was made entirely of clear glass, offering an expansive view of outer space and the asteroid field surrounding the base.

"Strange," said Simmons. "I never used to be able to see the stars."

"What do you mean?" asked Billy. "After thirty years, you'd know whether you had a window, wouldn't you?"

"Not necessarily," replied Simmons patiently. "That view used to be just more of the same drab gray that's all over this place. It was more pockmarked and irregular than the rest of the walls, maybe, but I tuned it out after a while."

"Pockmarked?" asked Ara. "Did you say pockmarked? Like … like an asteroid would be?"

"Surely you don't mean—" Tom began.

"The explosion we heard earlier!" Ara lifted a finger in realization. "We weren't instantly destroyed, so it had to be something outside the base. Like an asteroid blowing apart."

"That can only mean one thing," said Tom. "This base was never inside the asteroid. The asteroid was just a shell. Now the shell's come off."

"But what would be the point of that?" Jax asked. "This is still in the middle of nowhere. Hardly prime real estate either way."

"Who knows?" asked Billy. "None of this makes any sense at all!"

"Then perhaps I can shed some light on our situation." Simmons had already pulled a chair up to the computer and gotten right to work. "But it may take a while."

"I'll lock the door," said Ara, rushing over to do just that. "We don't want to get interrupted."

The others all moved closer to Simmons, forming a protective circle around him. Jax took the opportunity to strip off the rest of his disguise, letting out a massive sigh of relief as he returned to the 4S uniform he had been wearing underneath.

Simmons worked diligently, his efforts occasionally punctuated by grunts of satisfaction or frustration. Both seemed to come in equal measure.

The minutes ticked slowly by, full of mounting tension. Simmons typed furiously, pulling up the computer's internal code and isolating various sections of it for examination.

"I think I'm close," he said eventually. "I'll need a holopad for this next bit."

"I've got one," said Ara. She pulled out her holopad and strode up to Simmons' chair.

Simmons handed her a cable attached to his computer. "Hook it up. I'm going to send over some data. If I've done this right, that data package should contain everything we need."

Ara did as he suggested, and Simmons resumed his feverish typing.

The other three searched for something to do with themselves. Tom's mechanical expertise didn't extend to computers, and Jax and Billy knew even less on the subject. All they could do was keep a good lookout.

Since they were all locked inside the lab, that lookout proved uneventful until Billy glanced toward the window and gasped.

"Um, is it just me, or are those asteroids moving?" he asked.

Tom and Jax followed his gaze and saw what he had

seen.

"I don't think it's just you," said Jax.

Tom ran to the window as the sound of another explosion boomed from close by.

"One of the other asteroids just blew up!" he called to the others. "Some kind of plasma shot fired from the base."

He flinched as a bolt of white light streaked across the space in front of the window, colliding with a large asteroid and shattering it. All the while, the view outside the laboratory continued to shift as the asteroids filling it continued to detonate. Either the asteroids were moving, or the base was.

"It looks like they're trying to blow their way out of the asteroid field," Tom reported, moving back to where his friends stood around Simmons' computer.

"But how are we moving?" Billy asked.

"What is this place?" asked Jax, looking around the room. "Some kind of mobile space station?"

"Close," said Ara, still bent over the computer beside Simmons. "Take a look at this."

She pointed to the screen, where Simmons had pulled up a single image: a map of some sort of spaceship, its interior hollow to display the various rooms it contained.

The ship's design was unfamiliar to Jax. It certainly didn't resemble anything the 4S used. Boxy and square, it tapered to a point at the front and housed three propulsion engines at the back, with one stubby triangular wing extending from the middle of each side. On the top of the ship, a small tower containing what appeared to be the bridge jutted upward between the wings.

The 4S agents all examined the picture in silence.

"What's that?" asked Tom.

"It's the base," said Ara. "Except I don't think 'base' is actually the correct word." She pointed to a large open space located near the rear of the vessel in the blueprint. "That's the lab."

"Hold on," said Billy. "If that's us—"

"This is a spaceship?" Tom asked incredulously. "Well, that complicates things."

"In what way?" Jax shot back. "It doesn't change anything. We still have to shut the weapon down before it can hurt anyone. That hasn't changed."

"But we have to be careful not to take out the whole ship when we do it," Ara warned him. "Or do you want to be floating out there in open space without an oxygen tank?"

Jax took one step back. "No, thanks."

Tom turned to Doctor Simmons. "Can you take out the weapon without blowing this whole ship out from under us?"
Simmons set his jaw in a determined stare. "I won't know for sure until I see it, but I'll do my best."

"So what now?" asked Ara. "Do you know where the weapon plans will be?"

"Yes, I do," said Simmons. "You may want to brace yourselves. It's exactly what I was afraid of."

"What are you talking about?" Tom asked.

"Let me explain," said Simmons. "This ship is big, yes, but it's still not on the same scale as the 4S' *Home Base*. It's small enough that all its major systems will be centralized in one location. If you want to find any files, weapon designs or otherwise, you'll have to take them from the ship's central data drive. And in order to get to that, you need to go to the place where the ship is controlled."

"Of course," Ara said. "The bridge."

"The bridge?" echoed Billy. "But that place'll be crawling with those masked people!"

Jax set his jaw in a stare of determination. "We can do it. We have to."

"It's a suicide mission!" exclaimed Billy. "I know what I said earlier, but I'm starting to think this whole 'let's stick around' plan might not be the best bet after all."

"I agree with Billy," Tom said. "If we go to the

bridge, we'd be walking straight into the heart of the enemy's operations. If they're going to congregate anywhere, it'll be there. They wouldn't have to set a trap for us. We'd basically be setting one for ourselves."

"Get over yourselves," Jax said. "This isn't just about us anymore. We can't let these people take the 4S down. If that means we have to walk into danger, then we walk into danger. Admiral Prang is counting on us."

"I'm not saying we don't have a duty here," said Tom. "But I am saying that maybe you're being too impetuous. Since when are we qualified to act as crisis control?"

"Since we have the one person who can conceivably still stop the carnage before it starts," answered Jax.

"It's not that simple!" Tom was beginning to raise his voice. "Why are you so focused on having some big heroic moment? We don't need to be everyone's last line of defense!"

Jax just let out a low growl.

"Er, if I may?" interjected Simmons.

Everyone looked at the scientist.

"Go ahead," Tom said.

"There's an elevator up to the bridge not far from here," said Simmons. "We actually passed it on our way to the lab. But, if you want to leave, the hangar isn't too far away, either. And it looks like there's one 4S-model shuttle docked there. I'll let your squad make the final decision on which way we go, but you need to decide quickly."

"The data download isn't complete," said Ara. "We won't be able to move out for another twenty-five minutes or so. But Doctor Simmons is right. You two have to make a compromise here. So where are we going?"

"Hangar," said Tom.

"Bridge," said Jax, at the same time.

The two of them locked eyes and stared intensely at each other, both refusing to look away.

Ara huffed. "Are we really going to do this?"

"Yeah," said Billy. "We need to make a decision, or they're just gonna kill us all, remember?"

Something jolted beneath Jax. The ship didn't shake, but his stomach churned slightly nonetheless—a feeling he was getting to know all too well. Breaking his eye contact with Tom, he looked to the others for confirmation of his suspicions.

"Was that what I think it was?" he asked.

"We've entered lightspeed." Tom pointed to the window, where the stars had all blurred into streaks. "Wherever this ship is heading, I don't think anything good is going to happen once it arrives. I don't know what we're going to do here, but we're running out of time to do it."

"Tom's right," Ara said. "It's now or never."

"Then we go for it," Jax said. "We don't really have another option."

"So we're going to the bridge?" asked Billy.

"It's a moot point now," said Tom. "We can't launch our shuttle from a ship that's moving at lightspeed. The physics doesn't work. As long as we're stuck here, we might as well do something useful with it."

"There we go," said Jax. "Onward and upward, am I right?"

With their action plan decided, all they could do was wait for Simmons and Ara's data dump to finish processing. It seemed to take an interminably long time, but at last, Ara held up her holopad and stared at its screen.

"The data package just finished downloading," she said. "I now have access to this ship's plans and maps. I can navigate us wherever we need to go."

"All right," said Tom. "Looks like I'm outvoted. Let's head for that elevator."

Ara unhooked her holopad from the computer cable and unlocked the lab door. The entire group jogged back down the corridor. Fortunately, they didn't run into any more masked assailants, and they made it into the elevator safely.

Jax wished he could trust the bridge to be so peaceful.

But he didn't dare get his hopes up. That place would be swarming with black-masked people—more than he had seen on the night his parents had died, or on the solar power station. Barring some miracle, Jax's squad would be in for the fight of their lives.

Jax set his face in a stern, resigned expression as the elevator doors opened. *Bring it on.*

CHAPTER TWENTY-ONE

HANGAR BAY U-01—UPPER PYLON—VOYAGER STATION

Admiral Prang stared into the face of his Chief Research Officer as the circle of black-clad figures tightened around them. Still flabbergasted by the revelation that Doctor Gregory Fletcher had been behind the actions of those masked people from the start, Prang's mind barely registered the other man's request that they all take another trip aboard the admiral's shuttle. He only stirred back to life when Vice Admiral Pitt took a step forward from beside him.

"He isn't going anywhere," Pitt said. "And I'll take on everyone in this hangar if I have to to keep it that way."

No, Prang thought urgently, but he hesitated to speak the word aloud. A fight was the last thing they needed. With Pitt already injured, and Prang past his prime, they were outclassed and outnumbered by the men and women surrounding them.

Prang pushed his way in front of Pitt once more. The vice admiral tried to take up his defensive stance again, but Prang held out an arm to hold him where he stood and spoke before Pitt could make any more threats.

"I accept your proposition, Doctor Fletcher," he said.

"What?" exclaimed Pitt. "Sir, I must insist—"

Prang ignored him for the moment and continued to look at Doctor Fletcher.

"I will accompany you," he said, "but only if you can guarantee the safety of myself and the Vice Admiral until we reach your proposed destination."

"Do you think so little of me?" Fletcher asked. "I told you I would explain everything, and I will. Whatever will happen after that is largely up to you."

"A fair compromise," said Prang. "I suppose I'll simply have to make the right choice at the end."

"Yes," Fletcher said darkly. "Let's both hope you will."

Pitt moved back into his position next to Prang. "Admiral, with all due respect, what are you thinking? How can you trust any promise he makes? Everything he's ever done has just been called into question."

"I've made my decision," said Prang. "I'm prepared to live with whatever consequences it may bring."

"If you die—" Pitt began.

"If *we* die, the 4S would be rudderless," said Prang. "But this isn't a situation where we have the luxury of dictating terms. We really have nothing to lose by simply taking the option that keeps us alive the longest."

"That's the spirit," said Fletcher. "And, Vice Admiral, you don't have to accompany us. If you would prefer to stay behind …"

"No," said Pitt. "Wherever he goes, I go. That's non-negotiable."

"If you insist," replied Fletcher, glancing down at his watch. "But we had best get underway if we want to be on time."

"On time for what?" Prang asked.

"Trust me, you'll see," said Fletcher. "Once our journey is over, you'll have all the context you need to understand why we've done what we've done."

"Then shut up already and let's get going," Pitt grumbled. "If we have to listen to your blabbering, you could at least tell us something useful."

"Yes, let's get going," said Fletcher. "A wonderful idea,

if I do say so myself."

He turned to Doctor Jennings and snapped his fingers.

"I think they understand their position," he said. "We shouldn't need to intimidate them any further."

"You heard him," Jennings called to the rest of the men and women surrounding them. "Fall out!"

The circle of masked enemies formed two lines, creating a tunnel leading to the boarding ramp of the shuttle.

Doctor Fletcher gave a satisfied nod to his two captives. "Shall we be going?"

"By all means," said Prang. "Lead the way."

If Fletcher had any concerns about letting Prang and Pitt out of his sight, he didn't display them outwardly. His expression remained placid and unperturbed as he turned and walked over to the ship. Doctor Melville and Doctor Jennings shoved the admiral and vice admiral after him.

Once everyone had climbed aboard the shuttle, Fletcher glanced around and appraised their surroundings.

"Let's all retire to somewhere more comfortable," he said as he walked into the ship's common room. "I hope I can put your bodies as well as your minds at ease while we speak."

Prang could have said that there was no need for him to be invited into any area of his own private shuttle, but he chose not to make a big deal out of it.

Fletcher pulled out a chair at the common room's table and gestured for the others to join him. His assistants herded Prang and Pitt toward him. Once all three officers were seated, the rest of Fletcher's masked goons took up positions around them. Some moved to block the exits and the rest stood guard around the table.

"Doctor Jennings, Doctor Melville." Fletcher nodded to each one in turn. "Go to the cockpit and get this ship ready to depart. Transmit my clearance code to Hangar Control, and once we're in open space, you know where to go."

After they left to follow his instructions, Fletcher returned his attention to Prang and Pitt.

"Now, then," he said. "How about we get down to business?"

"Before you begin, there's one thing I need to ask," said Prang.

"Of course." Fletcher spread his arms wide in a parody of Prang's trademark jovial greeting. "Ask away."

"The woman Commander Sullivan's team discovered on Rho Station died yesterday," said Prang. "She went into cardiac arrest after a hidden device in her chest administered an electric shock to her heart."

Fletcher sadly shook his head. "Really? A terrible shame, for anyone to go out that way."

"Like you care," Pitt muttered under his breath.

"Of course I care. Sacrificing one's own agent is not a thing one can ever take lightly. Or maybe you've forgotten that, after how many times you sent those innocent ensigns into mortal peril," said Fletcher.

"But why would you kill her?" asked Pitt. "Why would you order the death of one of your people? Especially since you were too late. She already told us where your secret base is."

Fletcher smirked. "You presume too much. She only said what I wanted her to say. Her death simply made sure that she couldn't reveal anything more. Our plan relied on the 4S only knowing exactly what we wanted them to know at any given moment. The longer she remained on the Home Base, the more of a liability she became."

Pitt seethed with barely repressed indignation. "So a woman's life is just something for you to throw away the second you feel like you're finished with it?"

Fletcher didn't answer.

"Calm down, my friend. We should keep our heads clear," Prang urged Pitt.

Pitt's glare didn't disappear, but his voice was more controlled as he said, "One of these days, Fletcher, you'll get what's coming to you."

Fletcher allowed a few seconds of Pitt's heavy breathing

to pass before he spoke. "Have you gotten all that out of your system? Are you ready to listen now?"

"Only if it means we can get to the part where we put you away for a very long time," said Pitt.

"As if you could," Fletcher shot back scathingly. "The pious 4S, jailing a man? How would you even go about doing a thing like that?"

Prang broke into the conversation before Pitt could make any more threats. "There's more we need to know, Doctor, if you'll be willing to tell us. The device was activated by Captain Ramón. He killed her in cold blood, and apparently just for the fun of it. But he also claimed to be serving some higher power. Now that I know you're the one leading our enemies, I need you to answer just one question for me. Did you order Captain Ramón to kill that woman?"

To his credit, Fletcher didn't try to deny it. "Yes. The captain acted on my orders."

"That's impossible!" said Pitt. "Even if the 4S condoned murder, the Chief Research Officer doesn't have that level of authority."

"Perhaps not," replied Fletcher, "but therein lies your problem. You've shackled yourself to your comfortable ideas of power and security, but soon enough it won't be your authority that matters anymore. It will be mine, and that of the forces I speak for."

"So how deep does your authority reach? How many men and women have you convinced to betray us?" Prang asked.

"Not nearly as many as you might think, I assure you," said Fletcher. "I had to be practical, you see. The more 4S agents I suborned, the more likely it became that my activities could eventually be traced back to me."

"Still, we'll need names," said Prang. "Names, and positions. We have to root out your corruption before it can spread further. I'm sure you understand."

"Calm down," said Fletcher. "There's no need for a witch hunt. Aside from Captain Ramón, I haven't employed anyone of consequence. Just a few supply officers and accountants, and a construction team here and there. Even with the considerable leeway my position allows me to allocate the Research Division's resources as I see fit, you can probably see why it was best that certain decisions remained off the record."

"Then where did you find so many people to follow you?" asked Prang. "Any 4S personnel abandoning their regular duties would have been noticed, so how did you manage to gather enough forces to attack our facilities?"

"My converts come from many places," said Fletcher. "Not everyone is completely enamored with your vision of a bright and shining future. The more you look to the stars for hope, the more people you leave behind on a dying Earth, grasping for even the smallest scraps of optimism. Amidst so much hypocrisy, can you blame the people you've kept marginalized for wanting a way out?"

"The 4S has never marginalized anyone," said Prang. "There are several services across the globe to help people who've been displaced and impoverished. Our place has always been out here in space."

"Which makes for a convenient excuse, doesn't it?" Fletcher asked scathingly. "*Of course* you don't have time to spare to fix the problems in society. You're too busy building a better one—but it's one that nobody alive right now may ever get to see. Now how do you imagine that sounds in the moment to someone who's been living in squalor for so long?"

He took a deep breath. "But I digress. Either way, you can trust me when I say that the 4S isn't in any danger of fracturing. My double agents served their purpose well when I still had to keep my cards close to my vest, but now I have something far more effective than even the most well-placed infiltrator."

"Yeah, right," said Pitt. "You'll have to forgive me if I say I don't trust you as far as I could throw you. What could you possibly have that's so much better? Go on. Out with it."

"All in good time," said Fletcher. "But first, I have a question for you, Admiral. When Captain Ramón executed the woman, can I assume she mentioned something about the shadow?"

"Just that it was supposed to rise, whatever that means," replied Prang. "The woman he murdered mentioned that as well. Can I assume that this shadow of theirs is the same one that the sole survivor of the Simmons expedition disaster used to rant and rave about?"

"The very same," replied Fletcher. "That man was truly ahead of his time."

"But we all dismissed his words as nonsense," said Prang. "Clearly we shouldn't have been so hasty."

"No," said Fletcher, "you shouldn't have. But it's far too late by now."

"And the shadow drove you and all your foot soldiers to destroy so much 4S infrastructure?" Prang asked.

"Yes," said Fletcher. "Each station we raided was strategically chosen because it had been researching a specific aspect of cosmic rays and we needed the data for our plans. Of course, I could simply have used my authority to access whatever information we needed, but it was better if the 4S was too focused on an exterior threat to notice its own staff making shady deals right under its nose. And it worked, didn't it?"

"Justify it all you want," said Pitt. "You've still killed people. You've still ruined so many lives. You may not have always done the deed yourself, but in the end, you're still nothing more than a sadistic, delusional murderer."

"I am what the shadow commands me to be," said Fletcher.

"Nice copout," Pitt harrumphed. "Go ahead. Make up some random scapegoat out of thin air—something we can't even see or hear—and tell us that it's the one responsible for everything you've done, not you. Seems a bit suspicious, doesn't it?"

Prang, meanwhile, decided to entertain Fletcher's ranting for the time being. He didn't believe in the shadow any more than Pitt seemed to, but he thought they should at least find out why Fletcher was so enamored with it.

"It's past time you explained to us just what this shadow actually is. Isn't that what you wanted to do when you caught us in your trap?" Prang asked.

"Of course, of course," said Fletcher. "Perhaps it would be best if I began at the absolute beginning. Or as close as I can get, anyway. I don't know exactly when or from where the shadow originated, but I can pinpoint almost the exact day it started to speak to me."

"It speaks to you?" asked Prang. "How?"

"Not in the conventional way, that's for certain," said Fletcher. "For a long time now, I've been able to hear its messages in my mind. The ideas enter my head, and I'm simply compelled to carry them out."

"So the shadow made you betray the 4S?" Pitt asked. "The shadow turned you evil? Do you realize how stupid that sounds?"

"To think in terms of good and evil would be an oversimplification," said Fletcher. "I've always been ambitious. I've always wanted to excel in my field, and I've always been willing to do whatever it takes to get ahead. In fact, I think it's exactly those qualities that attracted the shadow to me in the first place."

"Yes, yes," said Prang, "but what does the shadow actually do?"

"I'm actually still quite fuzzy on the details myself," Fletcher admitted. "It would seem our connection only works one way. The shadow can worm its way into my mind, but I can't follow it back to its source. From what little I've been able to glean, the shadow is a primal cosmic force that's existed in tandem with our universe since the dawn of time, just outside of our mortal perceptions. If I follow through with the things it wants me to do, the shadow will be able to mingle with the makeup of our universe at the subatomic level and change things drastically from there. Again, I don't know the full extent of its designs, but I've been able to parse out that much."

"Then why are you listening to it?" asked Pitt. "If you don't know what the outcome is going to be, why are you going along with it? You could have stopped. You could have averted so much senseless bloodshed."

"It's not that simple," Fletcher said tersely. "Our world is deeply and irreparably broken. You know that. It's why the 4S is working so hard to find a new one. But deep down, we all know humanity would just wind up repeating its past mistakes sooner or later. The cycle has to end somewhere.

"That's where the shadow comes in. Through its power, we can build the utopia that Earth never turned out to be. The shadow will put everything in order. Society will be productive, and people will live in harmony with their environment. No one will have to suffer pain or senseless violence again. Everything will just be better. I've been assured of that much."

"Did I mention that you're delusional?" Pitt asked.

"You might mock me now," said Fletcher, "but I dare you to look me in the eyes and tell me you fully believe that what you're doing isn't futile."

Prang sat up a little straighter so he could fix his fierce glare on Fletcher. "All your flowery rhetoric won't change our minds. We fight for humanity not because it's perfect, or because it ever will be. We fight to give it the chance to be better."

"Then why wouldn't you jump at the chance to perfect this disordered universe in one fell swoop?" Fletcher asked.

"Because we don't know if anything will be better," said Prang. "Some of us are wise enough not to take chances on supposed cosmic forces that may or may not exist, or hold any power at all."

"Oh, it holds power, all right," said Fletcher. "Everything it's ever told me will happen has come to pass, with uncanny accuracy. From the very moment when I began to hear its voice during my work with cosmic radiation, I've followed all its instructions, and not once has it failed to deliver on its promises. It whispered to me exactly what I should say and do to get selected as head of the Research Division. It showed me how to sabotage James Simmons' scientific mission and fake his death so I could snag his vast mental prowess for my own purposes. It laid out every step of the way that led to this moment."

Pitt grunted dismissively. "I'm not convinced. It wouldn't be the first time someone's invented an excuse to justify their depraved behavior."

"Is it depraved to want the best for humanity?" Fletcher asked. "We both want the same thing, but you're deliberately holding yourselves back. What would happen if you let the power inherent in the space around you loose? Are you truly being careful? Or are you just afraid that I might be right?"

Prang and Pitt shared a confused glance, neither one quite knowing what to say. The back of Prang's throat suddenly went dry. *This is the most insane thing I've ever heard, he told himself. He's clearly gone mad. So why can't I come up with an argument against him?*

Fletcher's personal communicator began to beep, saving him from. Fletcher pulled the device out and opened the channel.

"This is Doctor Melville calling Chief Research Officer Fletcher," his assistant's voice crackled from the speaker. "We're almost at our destination, sir."

Fletcher thumbed the button to reply. "Thank you, Doctor. We'll join you in a moment."

He pushed back his chair and stood, gesturing for Pitt and Prang to follow suit. "Won't you accompany me to the cockpit?"

Four of the black-clad guards fell into step behind the three 4S officers as they headed past the shuttle's crew quarters and into the cockpit.

Doctor Melville sat in the pilot's seat while Doctor Jennings stood beside him. Outside the windshield, the stars raced frantically by.

Doctor Jennings offered a detached nod to the newcomers. "Everything is running on schedule, sir."

"Five minutes to breakout," Doctor Melville reported.

"Wonderful," said Fletcher.

Everyone took a seat, to better weather the rapid deceleration. They sat together in a silence punctuated only by Doctor Melville's occasional announcements counting down to their exit from lightspeed.

When the stars settled into their fixed positions, Prang and Pitt noticed another celestial body among them: round and painted in splashes of blue, green, and brown.

"Earth," said Prang. "This is Earth. Why have you brought us here?"

"To make a rendezvous," said Fletcher. "I told you I would tell you everything, and I will. We just have to wait a little longer for the rest of my forces to arrive."

"The rest of your forces?" Pitt asked. "How many of you

are there?"

"Uh-uh," said Fletcher, waggling his finger in the air. "I won't spoil the surprise. Just wait and see."

Prang and Pitt kept their gazes locked on the space directly outside the shuttle's windshield, and it didn't take long for them to see what Fletcher was talking about.

As they watched, another spaceship popped into view not far in front of them. If its black paint hadn't been reflective, they might have missed it entirely. The starlight bending around it gave away its shape, and it was clear from the first glimpse that this ship was far more than a mere transport shuttle.

The ship was easily three or even four times larger than Prang's shuttle. It almost looked more like a submarine than a spaceship; with a rectangular body, pyramidal front end, rear engine thrusters, and a protruding superstructure on top. Its wings were the only indication it had been designed for flight.

Pitt spun to look at Fletcher. "This is what you wanted us to see?"

"That's right," said Fletcher.

"So you have your own cruiser," said Pitt. "Big deal."

"I'm glad you think so," Fletcher said. "Seeing as that cruiser is the base from which we'll be bringing about the shadow's new order."

"Don't get too cocky," said Prang. "From all we've heard, we don't think too highly of that new order, or even of this cruiser of yours."

"Really?" Fletcher asked in mock offense. "You'd reject it so quickly? But I haven't even told you its name yet."

A few moments passed in silence before Prang replied. "Very well, I'll bite. What do you call this … vessel?"

"Why, this is our warship," Fletcher said proudly. "We call it *The Shadow*, of course."

Pitt buried his head in his palms.

"A warship," repeated Prang. "Then you truly have betrayed everything the 4S stands for."

"Oh, don't be so dramatic," said Fletcher. "I'm not a traitor; I'm a liberator. When will you learn to look beyond this dichotomy you've boxed yourself into? A shadow isn't inherently evil. After all, everything has its equal and opposite. Who are you to say that the universe we've been living in is the best possible version?"

"You really are crazy," said Pitt.

"All progressives are regarded as crazy in their own time," said Fletcher. "But the shadow is bringing about a necessary change. Eventually, the world will understand that we're doing this for its own good."

"Or maybe it'll decide you're a lunatic, and expose you for the fraud you are," said Prang.

"That's still up in the air, though, isn't it? Both our ideas could still happen. How about I bring you aboard the warship, and you can decide what you think once you've seen it from the inside," said Fletcher.

"Do we really have a choice?" Prang asked.

"Not much of one, no," Fletcher replied. "It's best for you if you comply. But don't worry. You'll have front-row seats for our restructuring of the universe."

He turned to Doctor Melville, who hadn't moved from the pilot's seat. "Signal the *Shadow*'s docking bay and bring us aboard."

"Right away, sir," Doctor Melville replied.

He tapped a few keys on the command console, and a few seconds later his comm unit pinged with a response. The shuttle's engines gunned into life as Doctor Melville brought the ship under and around the massive cruiser. On the other side, a docking bay door opened to admit them.

The shuttle touched down on the hangar floor almost before Pitt and Prang had any time to react. They could only watch as the bay door closed again, trapping them in the strange spaceship.

"Landing gear is locked and secured," Doctor Melville announced. "Hangar atmosphere should be breathable in four ... three ... two ... one ... and we're good to go."

"Thank you," said Fletcher. "Now let's get going. We

have a schedule to keep."

A few of his men yanked Pitt and Prang to their feet and shoved them down the boarding ramp. Fletcher followed with the rest of his group. Then he took the lead, moving at a brisk pace into the rest of the cruiser's cavernous interior.

As they walked, Prang's eyes roved around the room, and he quickly noticed one very interesting fact. His shuttle wasn't the only 4S craft in the hangar; a smaller scout ship sat tucked away in the far corner.

Prang looked over at Pitt and knew instantly that the other man had seen what he had seen.

"We're not the only 4S agents here," Pitt observed.

"Indeed," said Prang. "And we sent the ensigns out in a ship just like that."

"But they weren't going anywhere near this sector of space. It could just be more of Fletcher's turncoats."

"We're on a cruiser. It's not impossible that they made a stop somewhere else before coming here."

"We still shouldn't get our hopes up. If the ensigns are here, where are they?"

"That's enough talking back there!" Fletcher snapped from the front of the group. "Let's keep moving. I wish we had the time for a grand tour, but we really should get to the bridge."

His guards shoved Pitt and Prang into motion. After spending a few minutes in a sterilization chamber, the entire party trudged off down a long, gray-walled corridor and piled into an elevator at its end.

Their upward ride deposited them in a sparsely furnished room. The only real decoration was the double doors directly across from the elevator. Doctor Jennings swiped a key card in a reader to open the doors and Fletcher led the group through.

On the other side of the doors lay the ship's bridge. In the center of the bridge sat three rows of two consoles each with an aisle down the middle. The helm stood alone at the very front of the room, just behind the windshield. A person covered from head to toe in black cloth manned each station. Others walked up and down, checking the machinery.

Gazing through the thick glass pane above the pilot's seat, Prang could see Earth turning not far away. But he didn't have time to appreciate the view.

"Well, now we're all here," he said, speaking directly to Fletcher. "What is it you want from us?"

"Relax, Admiral," said Fletcher. "You don't need to do anything. All you have to do is watch."

"If you think we're going to just stand around while you unleash whatever murder weapon you've cooked up, you've got another thing coming," said Pitt. His arms flexed as he glowered at all the enemy crew members around him, as though he was tempted to take them all on at once.

"You should be more proud. You two made this whole thing possible," said Fletcher. "You've both played your parts admirably. By encouraging the 4S to study cosmic radiation, you accelerated the speed of the shadow's rise. Your Eden Project was an admirable one, and you're still going to get to watch it come to fruition—in a way. We will build a better society, but it'll be based on the shadow's vision, not yours."

"So your plan is to destroy everything the 4S has been working to create?" said Prang. "I'm afraid we can't stand for that."

"And just what do you expect to do?" Fletcher shot back. "Please, Admiral, be realistic. Do you really think you could make it past all of us? No, all you'll be able to do is watch as the world is remade."

"Remade? What do you mean, remade? Stop monologuing and get to the point, dang it!" barked Pitt.

"Have you not figured it out yet? Are you really that dense?" Fletcher shot back.

"Insults won't help anybody, Doctor," said Prang. "Whatever mess you've gotten us into, I'm still your commanding officer. So why don't you enlighten us?"

Fletcher sighed. "Must you take the fun out of everything? Very well. My plan is this: the shadow will overtake the universe, and everything will finally be as it was meant to be."

Prang glanced around the bridge. He couldn't see

anything that could confirm Fletcher's ramblings, but he couldn't see anything they could do to stop him, either. Fletcher's supposed ultimate plan was so nebulous that there was nothing they could do to stop him until he revealed more of it. Whatever happened next, Prang and Pitt would just have to wait and watch.

Is this it? Prang thought desperately. *Is this how the 4S comes to an end?*

CHAPTER TWENTY-TWO

BRIDGE—WAR CRUISER *THE SHADOW*—HIGH EARTH
ORBIT

The elevator ride up to the bridge was short and uneventful. When it ended, Jax and his team found themselves in a small antechamber with another set of double doors opposite them.

Jax took a deep breath. "We're not going to be any more prepared than we already are. Let's get those doors open and get this over with."

Ara walked over to the key card reader beside the doors. She hesitated for only a few moments before swiping the card.

The five 4S agents watched in anticipation as the doors to the bridge swished open.

Nothing could have prepared them for what they found on the other side.

As the doors to the bridge slid apart, Jax, Ara, Billy, Tom, and Doctor Simmons ducked back against the wall, out of sight of anyone who could have noticed their arrival. The unspoken understanding passed between them all that revealing themselves too early could be fatal.

Jax carefully peered into the other room, and was initially taken aback by how mundane it looked. On the bridge, men and women clad completely in black walked briskly up and down, checking their screens and making minute adjustments to their instruments. None of them exuded any obvious aura of menace. Their work seemed as organized and methodical as anything he had seen among the 4S. If Jax hadn't been fully aware of these people's evil intentions, he wouldn't have given the scene a second glance.

Then, Jax noticed something strange. Looking around at his squadmates' faces, he could tell they had noticed it, too. For as large as they knew their enemies' vessel to be, they saw a surprisingly low number of personnel on the bridge.

"Are they running this ship with a skeleton crew?" Tom whispered.

"Apparently," said Ara. "At least that explains why they couldn't spare anybody to put us back in our cells."

"A few people deciding the life or death of hundreds," said Jax. "If that isn't sadistic, I don't know what is."

"Uh, guys? I hate to interrupt the big moment, but have you noticed who else is here?" said Billy.

They looked onto the bridge and nearly did a collective double take when they noticed the man standing in the center of the hustle and bustle.

"Doctor Fletcher?" Ara asked incredulously. "What's he doing here?"
Beside him, Simmons stirred in recognition of the name. "Fletcher? Surely you don't mean Gregory Fletcher?"

"You know him?" asked Jax.

"We were colleagues in the 4S Research Division once upon a time," said Simmons. "I remember him being a good man, even if he could be a little cold at times. To see him in a place like this … I won't lie. It's disconcerting."

"It gets worse," Tom told him. "These days, he's the Chief Research Officer. He runs the entire division."

"And that's not even the weirdest part," said Billy. "Look who's with him."

When he took a second glance, Jax could make out two more familiar figures standing beside Fletcher: Admiral Prang and Vice Admiral Pitt.

Something was very definitely wrong.

"You're right," Jax said. "That is weird."

He took a second to think, and a new thought came into his mind.

"Worse than weird," he amended. "If Admiral Prang is mixed up in all this, everything we thought we knew goes out the window. Was he ever telling the truth about these people? Did he set us up?"

"He would never do that!" said Ara. "Admiral Prang is one of the most dedicated men I've ever heard of. He cared so much about the Eden Project and the 4S' mission."

"That's always how they get you," Jax retorted dryly.

He didn't mean to be so harsh—at least, he thought he didn't. But being here among their enemies, the people who had killed his parents, and seeing the 4S' leaders, whom he had almost been growing to trust, standing in their midst, chilled him to his bones. He didn't know why any of the three officers were there, that was true, but if any of them were mixed up in this conspiracy, he would be forced to reevaluate everything they had ever told him. Had Prang ever truly been upfront with him? Had Pitt? Had Fletcher?

Tom rounded on Jax. "Don't even say that! It can't have been them. They wouldn't have waited to spring their trap."

"Are you sure?" asked Jax. "Remember what happened the first time we went out on a mission? At the solar station? That seemed pretty much like a trap to me."

"But then why would Prang have sent us out there at all?" asked Tom. "If he wanted to keep his secret plans protected, not bringing us into them at all would have been easier than initiating us and then getting rid of us right away."

"You do have a point," Jax conceded. "But still, should we really discount the possibility that he was only ever putting on appearances?"

"No," Tom said firmly. "I refuse to believe that our leaders are against us."

"You might be right. Look at their body language. They're as confused as we are," said Ara.

The admiral and the vice admiral stood with hunched shoulders. Jax couldn't see their faces, but he could recognize their despondent posture. Of the three 4S leaders standing together on the bridge, the Chief Research Officer was the only one experiencing any sense of victory. He appeared to be in the middle of an animated speech, one that included a fair amount of gesticulating.

"Hold on," said Billy. "Does that mean Doctor Fletcher is the actual bad guy? Because that's not much better."

"I hate to say it, guys, but even that may not be the worst part," said Ara.

"What could be worse than our Chief Research Officer having a big energy weapon he can aim at the organization he's supposed to be helping?" asked Tom.

"Maybe if he doesn't actually intend to aim it at the 4S," replied Ara.

"What are you talking about?" Jax asked.

"Look out the windshield," said Ara.

Jax peered through the wide glass panel at the opposite end of the bridge. While his team had been busy making its way up to the bridge, the enemy ship had come out of lightspeed. In the center of the view from the ship's windshield floated a familiar blue-green sphere.

"My goodness," said Simmons. "It's worse than I imagined."

"Hold on a minute," said Tom. "Is that—"

"Yep," replied Ara. "That's Earth."

"Wow. I guess these people really don't have any shame," said Jax.

Ara's concerned expression deepened into a full scowl. "Training a weapon on the 4S is one thing. But training it on the entire planet? That's much, much worse." She turned to Simmons. "Isn't it?"

"Oh, it is," Simmons replied. "Even without discussing morality, science alone could tell us that. A blanket of cosmic rays around the planet could cause unprecedented catastrophic effects, not the least of which would likely be a horrifically torturous death for everyone present."

"Oh, great," said Billy. "This just gets better and better."

"So what are we still standing around for?" asked Tom. "We still need to stop this weapon. There aren't a lot of people on that bridge, and two of them are on our side. If we rush in and don't give the rest a chance to regroup and adjust, we can maximize the chance that one of us will get to that central data drive and find the information that will let us put an end to this once and for all."

"We wouldn't stand a chance," said Jax. "They'd be on us in seconds."

"This was your plan!" Tom did his best to keep his voice low so it wouldn't carry onto the bridge, but he could barely conceal his anger. "You were the one who said we should come up here. What did you think would happen?"

"I never said we'd just go charging in blindly," Jax reminded him. "If I recall, you were the one who didn't want to throw our lives away."

"That's not important right now," said Tom. "And you're the one who said this wasn't about what we wanted. Make up your mind, Jax. Are you all in on this or not?"

Jax turned away and stared back into the crowd on the bridge. Tom had been right about one thing: they had to do something. But what could they do, when they didn't know the layout of the bridge?

We need more information, and we need it fast.

As Jax debated with himself, Fletcher stopped pontificating to Prang and Pitt. His head tilted to one side, then swiveled to look out through the open doors, his eyes landing almost directly on the spot where the 4S agents stood just beyond his line of sight.

"It seems we have guests!" His voice carried all the way out to the antechamber. "Why don't you all come out and show yourselves?"

Jax and the others glanced around themselves in panic.

"How did he know?" Billy asked.

"Does it matter?" Tom said. "He obviously does. Otherwise he'd just look stupid for pointing out something that wasn't there."

"Are we going to go in there?" asked Ara.

"What do we have to lose?" said Jax. "If they're going to bring us in, I'd rather have that happen on our terms."

"That barely makes any sense," said Billy. "But I still don't want them to beat me up, so whatever."

"Forget this," said Tom. "I'm not waiting around to get captured again."

He took a step in the direction of the bridge doors, and the others reluctantly followed him. With their hands raised high into the air, they strode into the midst of their enemies.

Every head in the room turned to gaze at them, though most were veiled and indiscernible. Fletcher looked every bit as self-assured as Jax had guessed him to be, and Prang and Pitt's eyes had widened in shock.

"Can … can it be?" asked Prang. "James Simmons? Is that you?"

Simmons stood a little straighter. "In the flesh, sir. And, if I may say so, congratulations on your promotion to full Admiral. I always thought you would be well suited for the job."

"Thank you, my old friend," replied Prang, nodding in humble acceptance of the compliment. "I'm glad to see you're still alive. And yet …"

"Don't worry, Admiral," Ara told him. "He wasn't the one behind any of this after all. They had him locked up just like they tried to do to us."

"Thank you, Ensign," said Prang, "but in fact I already knew. Doctor Fletcher here was *kind* enough to explain the entirety of our current predicament." He emphasized the last words with a cynical disdain Jax had never heard from him.

"Did he now," said Simmons. "I don't suppose he'd be kind enough to explain it all again for a poor old latecomer like me?"

"Have you not pieced it together yet?" asked Fletcher.

"I'm disappointed. I expected better from a man of your intellectual caliber."

Simmons sighed. "No, I know what you've done. My work was highly specialized, after all."

Prang's gaze swiveled to Simmons. "He made you work? What have you been doing all this time?"

"The same thing I did for you, I think," said Simmons. "They made me design a machine to capture cosmic radiation, just on a much larger scale than anything the 4S ever attempted. And under harsher conditions, of course."

"I can't imagine that was a very pleasant experience," said Pitt. "We'll just have to add it to Fletcher's ever-expanding list of crimes. To think that he let you suffer so much for so long …"

"Yes, yes, this is all very sentimental," cut in Fletcher. "But let's not forget that we haven't all come here for a meet-and-greet."

"Could have fooled me," muttered Jax.

"No," said Fletcher. "We're here to bear witness to a new world order."

"Great," Pitt grumbled. "This again."

"I suppose you young ensigns must be wondering why I didn't spare any of my agents to imprison you again," Fletcher went on. "Truthfully, I just didn't feel the need. It's actually quite fortuitous that you all made your way here on your own. Of course, I would have eventually wanted you here either way."

"You wanted us here?" echoed Ara.

"I did," said Fletcher. "Not at first, I'll admit. Your team nearly ruined all my plans, but I was never able to talk Admiral Prang out of bringing you together. Since I couldn't have you revealing our operation too early, I arranged for you to be conveniently disposed of at one of the old solar stations. But when you managed to escape that trap, I decided that I might as well dictate how and when you discovered us while I still had the opportunity. It was extremely fortunate that the shadow's master plan came fully into fruition at the same time."

"But that doesn't really answer the question," said Ara.

"Why are we here?"

"Why else?" said Fletcher. "To witness our final victory, and the rise of the shadow."

"The shadow?" Tom asked. He turned to Prang. "Like when that scientist—"

"It certainly appears that way," said Prang. "By all accounts, Doctor Fletcher is referring to some kind of cosmic force, one which apparently drove him to manipulate and exploit every tragedy that has befallen the 4S since the accident with James Simmons' research expedition."

Simmons stepped forward until he was almost nose to nose with Fletcher. His eyes betrayed his anger and hurt.

"Is it true?" he asked. "Did you sabotage my mission?"

"The shadow willed it to be done," Fletcher said. "I simply executed its will, as I have so many times since. As I am about to do once again. But you should be grateful. The shadow has given you the chance to perform a great service. Through your work, we will cleanse the universe."

"You're wrong," said Simmons. "My work helps people. That's the 4S' way. You may have lost sight of that, but I never did."

"Are you so sure?" Fletcher asked. "Let's take a look and see exactly what your help has led to."

He walked over to the wall on his right and tapped a command into a keypad mounted on it. A holoscreen unfurled itself from the ceiling. When Fletcher input another command, the screen lit up and came to life, displaying the same cross-section diagram of the space cruiser that Jax and his teammates had already seen in Simmons' lab.

"As you can probably tell, this image represents the warship we're standing in right now. It may look unassuming, but trust me, it won't be for much longer." Fletcher tapped a finger against the bridge tower in the picture. "We're here"—he moved his finger to indicate a room deep in the lowest level of the ship—"but the action happens down here."

He strode over to one of the consoles nearest the pilot's seat. "Why don't we show them what we've cobbled together?" he asked the man sitting at that console.

"Yes, sir," the man replied, and he tapped a few commands into his keyboard.

As the 4S agents and officers watched the image of the warship, a new attachment shimmered into existence on its underbelly. With its long cylindrical barrel and its, everyone knew instantly what they were looking at.

"You built a gun," said Tom. "I mean, it's a big gun, but …"

"You make a good point," said Ara. "Even with all the 4S satellites and platforms orbiting the Earth, there's nothing around here that would require that amount of firepower."

"Maybe he's compensating for something," Billy suggested, the shadow of a grin crossing his features.

"Yeah," said Jax. "Compensating for a lame and underwhelming plan."

"Enough!" snapped Fletcher. "You might mock our vision now, but we'll see who's laughing once the weapon has been activated."

"Oh, come on," Jax said. "I can't be the only one who sees how dumb that is. You schemed for months, you tricked us all into trusting you just so you could betray us, and now you're just going to start shooting things? Seems like a step down."

"This is no ordinary gun," said Fletcher. "It doesn't fire bullets, or cannonballs, or even plasma. In fact, it's not really a gun at all. It's more of an energy projector. Using James Simmons' expertise, combined with more modern research done by the 4S, we've constructed a machine that will allow us to not only capture cosmic radiation, but also channel it into a specific localized area. In this case, the atmosphere of the Earth."

"You're sick," Tom spat. "Don't you have any morals? Or did your shadow burn them all away?"

"Hardly," Fletcher said. "It might be hard to believe, but the shadow is the only moral thing that exists."

"We'll see about that," said Pitt. "Why don't you tell us what exactly you'll be using those morals to accomplish?"

"Gladly," said Fletcher. "We're going to do something no one before us has ever dared to attempt. We're going to create a singularity."

"A singularity? Like a black hole?" asked Ara.

"Precisely," said Fletcher.

Jax stared stone-faced into Fletcher's eyes. "Wow. That's even dumber than I thought. Instead of just dousing everyone with cosmic rays, you're going to sink the Earth into a freaking black hole? You do realize that'll just kill everyone, right? Including you. How can you have a new world order without a world?"

"You're being reductive," said Fletcher. "The shadow merely aims to reshape the world, not end it. It would not have advised me to take this action unless it was certain of the result."

"But you're not denying that you want to open up a giant void right next to a planet where billions of people live and just trust the voice in your head that it won't suck everyone inside it?" asked Jax. "Again, dumb plan."

"Hardly," said Fletcher. "I'm doing so much more. All these years, we've been looking at black holes in completely the wrong way. We know they suck matter inside them, but we've never given much thought to what happens afterward."

"What are you getting at?" asked Prang. "I'm afraid I don't understand."

"And I'm afraid I do." Simmons looked at Fletcher. "You're referring to the gateway theory, aren't you? The idea that they're portals to other dimensions?"

"There we go," said Fletcher. "Someone gets it."

"How is that even possible?" Simmons asked. "That theory was always impossible to prove."

"Not by conventional science," Fletcher said. "Luckily, I have something far better: divine revelation."

"Have you gone mad?" said Simmons. "What are we supposed to believe that means? A disembodied hand writing on the wall? Or maybe a man in white robes floating down from the sky?"

"Neither," said Fletcher. "My new commandment was etched directly onto my brain."

Simmons scoffed. "Listen to yourself! This goes against everything empirical research is based on! In my opinion, you should go see a psychiatrist for a full examination."

"That would be a waste of valuable time," said Fletcher. "It would be quicker for me to simply prove the shadow's authenticity by opening the gateway to bring it into our world."

"Wait," said Billy. "Slow down. I don't get it. What is it a gateway to?"

"All right, then, perhaps gateway isn't the best word we could use," said Fletcher. "Maybe calling them doorways would be better. We aren't trying to force our way through to something on the other side. We're trying to help what's on the other side force its way through to us."

"But how can you possibly know what's on the other side?" asked Ara. "Once something goes into a black hole, it's pretty much gone forever, right?"

"Not entirely," said Fletcher. "Matter cannot be created or destroyed, as we know. It can only be converted into some new state of being. Even a black hole can't erase it from existence entirely. So it follows that whatever goes in must be converted—or, if the shadow is to be believed, subsumed."

"Subsumed?" Tom said skeptically. "Subsumed into what?"

"Think about it," said Fletcher. "Like I said, matter cannot be created or destroyed. And yet the prevailing theory to explain the creation of our universe is the big bang, when all the matter and energy in existence exploded into being all at once. The question is, where did all that energy come from?"

"I don't know, but I'm sure you're about to tell us," said Jax.

"The age of religion did get a few things right," Fletcher said. "Namely, the existence of some higher power responsible for the creation of everything around us. That power most definitely exists, and the right people can indeed commune with it, but it isn't interested in any of our delusions of mercy or idealism. And you had best beware, because it's coming back with a vengeance. All it needed was a little help from someone on the other side."

"And you call yourself a scientist," said Simmons. "Now you're talking like some sappy hermit monk. Are you going to tell us you're off to go live in a mountain cave and put on a hair shirt so you can get more in touch with this shadow of yours?"

Instead of responding, Fletcher strode over to a console midway along the right side of the bridge.

"This conversation is going nowhere," he told the woman operating it. "I think it's time for a demonstration. The shadow will rise."

"Right away, sir," she said. "The shadow will rise."

She tapped a few commands into her computer, then pressed a button—

And nothing happened.

The 4S agents and officers all looked around in bewilderment. Jax had just started to allow himself to think that all Fletcher's words had been nothing more than grandstanding when Billy raised a trembling finger to point toward the ship's windshield.

"Um, guys?" he said meekly. "I don't want to alarm anyone, but what's going on out there?"

Everyone looked, and they all saw the same thing. Jax had to rub his eyes a few times before he was convinced that what he was seeing was real, but he couldn't keep denying it forever.

A menacing red-orange glow enveloped the planet Earth.

"Well, that wasn't there before," said Tom.

"No, it wasn't," said Jax. "So why is it there now?"

"An excellent question." Prang spun around to fix his gaze on Fletcher. "What have you done?"

"I've proven a theory," said Fletcher. "The Research Division always knew that enough concentrated cosmic rays could form a singularity, and so many of us also speculated that it would even be possible to do so inside the atmosphere of a planet. I must say, I'm feeling quite vindicated."

"That's all well and good, but you could have picked a

better planet for your trial run," said Pitt.

"Nonsense," said Fletcher. "What you see before you is no mere 'trial run'. Every aspect of this process has been carefully calculated and arranged according to the shadow's precise specifications. There will be no need for do-overs."

"I think he's referring more to the billions of lives your little stunt is going to cost," Simmons cut in.

"Little stunt?" Fletcher feigned offense. "Obviously none of you understand what's happening here. No one is going to lose their life, but their world is about to undergo an irrevocable metamorphosis. If they're still able to remember the way things used to be when it's all over, they'll recognize that it had to happen this way."

"And who's to say it has to happen at all?" Jax asked. "Seems to me like you haven't actually done anything you can't take back. If your weapon has an on switch, it's got to have an off switch."

Fletcher shook his head. "It hardly matters now either way. We built our device specifically to magnify the latent cosmic energy around the Earth, not to absorb it. What we've just done is irreversible."

Jax fixed his gaze on Simmons. "I don't know. I'd say there's one person who could still fix this."

Simmons took a step back in surprise. "Me? But—"

"Yes, you," Jax said. "You built this. Can you disable it or not?"

"I don't know," said Simmons. "They might have made modifications to my original machinery when they repurposed it for offense. I'll need to get a look at the technology they've built before I can say anything for sure."

"It's always something with you," said Jax. "But if we can get you to the weapon, can you at least promise us that there's a chance you can reverse all this?"

"Of course," said Simmons. "There's always a chance."

"Then that's all you had to say," said Jax. "Let's get down there already."

"It won't be as simple as you think," said Fletcher. "Even if you did have a grasp on the technology, you'd still have more issues to contend with."

"It doesn't matter," said Tom. "We'll find a way. We always have."

"Don't be so sure," Fletcher said. "You might just find that the shadow's plan includes a little extra … shall we say, insurance. You could turn off the weapon, but not without a cost. Are you sure you'd be able to bear it?"

"I don't know," said Jax. "I guess we'll have to figure that out for ourselves. We can deal with whatever you have to throw at us. Count on that."

"Suit yourself," said Fletcher. "I'd be interested to know whether you're singing the same tune after you've tried it."

"You can't possibly expect us to believe that," said Jax. "You're going to have to come up with a better reason if you really want us to stop. Don't you know not to make threats you can't make good on?"

"If it would make you feel better, you can go on assuming that I don't," said Fletcher. "I would never dream of using any unnecessary force on you. I only wanted to make sure you understand the risks of what you're proposing."

"Stop!" Jax said forcefully. "No more mind games. You can't talk us out of this."

Turning his back on Fletcher, he swept his gaze around the other members of his squad.

"I'm going to find this weapon and shut it down," he told them. "Who's with me?"

Within just a few seconds they had all stepped to his side. Watching from nearby, Prang and Pitt didn't speak but looked on in obvious pride and satisfaction.

Jax turned to Simmons. "We'll need you, too. Are you in?"

"Absolutely," said Simmons. "I'll stop this weapon if it's the last thing I do."

"All right," said Jax. "Let's go nip this thing in the bud."

With Doctor Simmons and his team behind him, Jax raced back off the bridge. They piled into the elevator.

*

Doctor Fletcher watched the young ensigns and the old scientist leave, shaking his head and clicking his tongue.

"Such a shame," he said. "I really was hoping they'd stick around to watch the fireworks."

"Should we go after them, sir?" one of his masked men asked.

"No, let them go," Fletcher said. "I told them they'd be too late. If they want to speed up their demise by rushing headlong into certain doom, we can afford to allow that."

Vice Admiral Pitt had heard enough. Grabbing hold of Fletcher's shoulder, he spun the other man around to face him.

"How could you?" he growled. "Those are young people, with their whole lives and careers ahead of them! You've just sent them all to die!"

"I haven't sent them anywhere," Fletcher replied. "They've sent themselves. I explained the futility of their current endeavor, and they chose to attempt it anyway. Whatever happens to them is on their own heads."

"Don't aggravate him, John," Prang warned from somewhere behind Pitt. "Stay calm."

"This isn't the time for calm, sir!" Pitt shouted. "This man needs to be brought to justice! Why shouldn't we get aggravated?"

"Because being violent would leave us little better than him," replied Prang.

Prang never raised his voice, but Pitt could detect a note of steel in it nonetheless.

"Yes, sir," he said. Still gripping Fletcher's shoulder, he let the fire in his eyes speak for him.

"You worry too much, Vice Admiral." Fletcher spat out the last two words as though they tasted vile. "It won't matter what they do. No harm will come to the weapon. Our plan will proceed."

"Oh, yeah?" asked Pitt. "And just what makes you so sure about that?"

"Do you really think I would create a weapon of this magnitude without installing safeguards against tampering?" Fletcher shot back. "Nothing will interrupt the shadow's grand design. Certainly not some gaggle of misguided fools barely out of basic training."

"Safeguards?" asked Pitt. "What do you mean, safeguards?"

Fletcher didn't answer. He wrenched himself out of Pitt's grip and strode over to one of the consoles near the front of the bridge.

"Give me a status report," he said. "How is everything looking?"

"The gateway is holding stable, sir," the woman working the console reported. "It should be fully open in about forty minutes."

"Good, good," said Fletcher. "Keep monitoring the status readouts, and alert me immediately if anything changes. The shadow will rise."

"Yes, sir," she said. "The shadow will rise."

Pitt didn't like the sound of that. He looked to Prang for guidance, but the admiral seemed anything but decisive. His mouth hung slightly open, and his eyes kept darting around the room, as though he could barely comprehend what was going on in front of him.

"We're just going to let this happen?" Pitt asked.

"I don't see anything we can do from up here," said Prang. "Our best hope for neutralizing Fletcher's weapon lies with Simmons and the ensigns. James Simmons would never have built any kind of weapon without some kind of emergency killswitch. His conscience simply wouldn't allow it."

"Thank the universe for moral men," Pitt said dryly. "Where would we be without them?"

"Now, now," said Prang. "Sarcasm won't help us out of this bind."

"No," agreed Pitt. "Only James Simmons' conscience can do that, as you so eloquently put it."

"The 4S will prevail," said Prang. "I have absolute faith in our agents. They've come through difficult circumstances before. I know they'll do it again."

"They'd better come through," said Pitt. "Too much is riding on this gamble."

And with that, the two men fell silent, having both run out of comforting words to speak to each other.

Pitt stared into the dark void forming above the Earth and searched for the light of hope.

CHAPTER TWENTY-THREE

LOWER DECKS—WAR CRUISER *THE SHADOW*—HIGH
EARTH ORBIT

As the elevator carrying Jax's squad descended, Ara pulled up a map of the ship on her holopad. "Looks like it's a straight shot down to the reactor. We'll just turn right out of the elevator."

"That's good," said Tom. "It'll give us an easy escape route when things go wrong."

Billy looked at Tom bemusedly. "When did you suddenly become so negative?"

"Probably about the time death and destruction started lurking around every corner," Tom grunted.

"Okay, we're not starting this up again," said Jax. "How about we stay focused and just shut this weapon down already? Maybe then Tom can stop being so depressing."

Tom opened his mouth to reply, but then decided against it. With a huff of annoyance, he made a point of turning away from the rest of the squad.

Simmons glanced up at the screen above the elevator doors, where the number four slowly faded out to be replaced by the number three.

"Perhaps you could save this for some other time," he suggested. "We're nearly there, and we'll need to be focused.

Squabbling among ourselves won't help anybody."

"Fine by me," said Jax. "That's all I've been saying this whole time."

Tom crossed his arms and glowered.

"Stop," said Ara. "Just stop, all of you. Even if this wasn't how we imagined things would go, this is where we are. No one else is available, so it's up to us to complete this mission. I don't enjoy that thought either, but this isn't the time to let personal opinions get in the way of saving literally the entire universe. Got that?"

The other three glanced at each other in a mix of shame and reluctant acceptance as they recognized the truth in Ara's words.

The number above the doors ticked down from two to one, then the screen went black. The elevator's gentle downward motion came to a stop, and with a faint but pleasant chime the doors parted to let the team out.

On the lowest level of the cruiser, the ship's internal systems were far more exposed than on any of the levels above. Metal piping and electrical wiring ran along almost all the available wall space. By the look of it, the cruiser's inner workings had been cobbled together, either as repairs necessitated new parts or as the builders made do with whatever material had been available to them.

Additionally, this deck wasn't as expansive as the others, with wider corridors the 4S agents could run through without getting in each other's way. The hallways never twisted or split in two, and there were no side rooms to distract visitors. Jax and his teammates reached the reactor core without running into any complications.

Just under ten minutes after they had left the bridge, they skidded to a halt in the middle of a large room. In front of them stood a door marked with a large biohazard symbol, and a single control console took up the center of the room, with a computer screen in its center surrounded by all kinds of gauges, buttons, and dials.

The lone masked man sitting at that console was so absorbed in his work that he didn't notice the 4S team's arrival until Jax, Billy, and Tom shoved him roughly out of his chair and dragged him off into the corner, where they knocked him out and left his body propped in a seated position against the wall.

James Simmons took the freshly vacated seat at the console, and Ara stood beside him as he did his best to puzzle out how it worked.

When the other three rejoined them, they found Simmons staring intently at the diagrams and data streams scrolling across the screen.

"Well?" Jax asked. "How's it looking? How soon can we be done with this?"

"I'm not entirely certain," Simmons replied. "For now, I have good news and bad news."

"Good news first, please," said Billy, stressing the last word.

"The good news is, the weapon isn't wired directly into the cruiser's main power core," said Simmons. "It looks like they've built an entire secondary reactor for it. Both reactors appear to be completely redundant, so each one can run without affecting the other."

The four ensigns just stared at him in confusion.

"And that's good news, why?" asked Jax.

"I get it," Tom said a few seconds later. "Taking out the weapon won't take out any of this ship's other systems. We wouldn't have to worry about not being able to breathe, or about the cruiser falling out of orbit."

"I couldn't have put it better myself," said Simmons. "Any collateral damage we incur could be kept to a minimum."

"That's all well and good, sure," said Jax. "But it doesn't answer my question. Can you, or can you not, shut this thing down?"

"That's the bad news," said Simmons. "I still don't know. If this weapon were entirely based on my radiation-capture technology, maybe I could. But they've expanded so much on my original work that I hardly recognize it anymore. I've tasked this computer to do a diagnostic search, so we should have more clarity in just a few moments."

"How optimistic should we be, though?" asked Tom. "The way Doctor Fletcher was talking, it sounded like he still had some kind of ace up his sleeve to stop us."

"Don't listen to him," said Jax. "He's probably just bluffing. He knew we'd put a stop to his evil plan, so he made up some vague excuses to make us think twice. But we aren't stupid."

"But if that were the case, why wouldn't he have just tried to stop us from leaving the bridge?" Ara cut in. "They had the numbers."

"Yeah," said Billy. "He just let us go. Doesn't that seem suspicious to anyone else?"

"Who knows?" said Jax. "He's been messing with us for months. Why wouldn't he try a little more deception on top of all that?"

"If I may," interrupted Simmons.

When the others turned to look at him, he went on.

"When I worked with Doctor Fletcher, he was never the type to mince words. Everything he said had a clear purpose behind it. I can't believe that a man like that would ever make a baseless claim. If he said he had something up his sleeve, we should all be wary of the moment he reveals it."

Almost as soon as he finished speaking, the computer pinged twice.

"And that'll be our results," said Simmons. "What say we stop debating and get some answers?"

He bent over the console's screen, his eyes flicking from side to side as he read. Jax couldn't see his face anymore, but from Simmons' occasional sharp intakes of breath he got the impression that the news wasn't all good.

At last Simmons straightened up, and Jax could clearly see the new unease in his eyes.

"Uh-oh," said Billy. "That doesn't look good."

"What is it?" Ara asked. "What did you find?"

"Trouble," Simmons replied simply. "Some of the

scans are still running, but we've already come across our first problem."

"Which is?" Jax prompted him.

"This console doesn't control the weapon," said Simmons. "Well, more accurately, it doesn't control the reactor that powers the weapon. It contains the primary targeting systems, yes, and it allows the user to monitor the weapon's energy output, but in order to shut the weapon down we'd have to access the reactor itself."

"But what's stopping us from doing that?" asked Tom. "I don't see what the problem is. Just point us at the reactor, and we'll trigger an emergency shutdown. Nothing to it."

"The problem, my friend," said Simmons, "is that there may very well be something to it."

"Like what?" said Tom. "Everything you said goes against that. If you know something, just tell us what it is."

"I can't," said Simmons. "Not yet. Not until the second scan I set up is finished. I can't confirm anything until then."

Several long seconds passed in silence before the computer pinged twice more.

"Well, there it is," said Jax. "So what exactly are you trying to prove?"

Simmons bent down to read the screen again, then looked up. The mild concern in his expression had nearly escalated to full-blown horror. At the sight of it, all Jax's irritation quickly melted away. Simmons had obviously been on to something after all.

"So this is what Fletcher was talking about," said Simmons.

"What is it?" asked Ara. "What did he do?"

"He's sealed the reactor controls behind that door," said Simmons, pointing to the door marked with the black-and-yellow triangular sign.

"That door?" asked Billy. "The one with the universal symbol for radiation on it?"

"There isn't any other door within at least a hundred yards," Simmons replied dryly.

"Tell me you're joking right now," said Jax.

"I wish I could," said Simmons. "But Fletcher did mention a cost we'd have to pay, and now we know what it is. No one who goes in there could possibly come out unscathed."

"But what's the alternative?" asked Jax. "The world is doomed if we abandon our mission now. Can we really say that any cost is too high to pay?"

"You can't possibly be suggesting—" Ara began, but Billy's next outburst cut her off.

"Nuh-uh," he blurted out. "I'm not going in there. Not in a million years."

"Even if it was the only way to stop Doctor Fletcher?" Jax asked.

"Yes!" said Billy. "We've been told over and over that cosmic radiation can be really, really bad. And now you want us to just walk into a whole cloud of it?"

"Oh, when will you man up?" Jax asked. "No one ever got to be a hero without paying some kind of price."

"Jax, that's uncalled for," said Tom. "He isn't wrong about how dangerous this could be. I'm honestly worried that you don't seem to care about that."

"You think I'm not scared?" Jax asked. "You think I don't realize what could happen if somebody went in there? It's like Ara said earlier. I can't let my feelings get in the way when the fate of the world is on the line!"

"Well, whatever you decide to do, your window of opportunity to actually do it is closing rapidly," Simmons put in from his chair. "If we don't take action soon, the singularity will open."

Jax looked imploringly at the others. "You see? Everyone on Earth right now is probably terrified out of their mind. How would you all feel if something bad happened to them, and we could have stopped it, but we didn't want to go out of our comfort zones?"

"Something bad will definitely happen," said Simmons. "Even without the black hole, the weapon's radiation output alone is cause for concern. Anyone who didn't die immediately would be torturously sick for the rest of their lives—which wouldn't be too long."

"But we still have a chance to stop the weapon?" asked Jax.

"Yes, you do," said Simmons. "As long as you're fine with suffering acute radiation poisoning, actually turning off the reactor would be a completely simple endeavor."

"Then the way I see it, there's only one thing for us to do," said Jax.

"What?" shouted Billy. "Are you crazy? There has to be something else we can do. Something that doesn't involve one of us losing their life. What if we took out this ship's other reactor?"

"No dice, Billy," said Tom. "That would kill the engines and the life support, and since we're already inside the Earth's gravity well, we'd crash for sure if we couldn't keep ourselves in the air. Besides, if the reactors are redundant, the one controlling the weapon would keep running, and even without taking the black hole into account, a cruiser with so much concentrated cosmic radiation emanating from it would pose a danger to humanity no matter where it landed."

"Sounds like Fletcher covered all his bases," said Ara.

"You can bet he did," said Simmons. "We're dealing with one fiendishly crafty man here."

"So targeting the weapon's reactor really is the only thing we can do," Jax said. "At least that way, only one of us has to put themselves in danger."

"All right, I get it," said Billy. "You make a compelling case. I'll shut up now. But at this rate, how do we know the black hole won't gobble us up before we have a chance to do anything about it?"

"Good question." Ara looked over to Simmons. "Does that computer tell you how long we have before the singularity finishes growing?"

"You have twenty minutes," said Simmons, glancing

down at the screen. "By the time one of you made it to the reactor, you'd only have a narrow window of time to switch it off."

"And there's really no way to switch it off remotely?" Ara asked. "There's nothing we can do other than heading into the reactor core?"

"No," said Simmons. "Clearly Fletcher was gambling on the fact that you four would be either too scared or too closely connected to one another to take that step."

"Well, he forgot one important thing," said Tom. "The will to do good triumphs over fear any day."

Jax groaned. "Oh, come on. If we're going to save the world, can you at least not make it so cheesy?"

"I regret nothing," Tom said quickly.

"Will you all be quiet for just ten seconds!" Ara said in exasperation. "The clock is ticking. If we've committed to taking out the weapon reactor, then we have to do it now, while we still have the option."

"Fine," said Billy. "If you think that's what's best, I'll go along with it. I don't want to die, but I also don't want to watch anyone else die."

"At last, you're all in agreement," said Simmons. "The only thing left is to choose which one of you will sacrifice themselves for the sake of their planet."

"Can you please not phrase it that way?" asked Billy.

Simmons didn't take his words back. He just watched the ensigns as a charged silence fell around them all.

"I'll go," Tom said eventually. "I know the most about machinery like this. I could shut it down the fastest."

"Well, I'm not going to do it," said Billy. "Not because I'm terrified, but because machinery isn't my specialty. And besides, you're going to need someone to fly you out of here if it all goes south."

"I hate to say it, but I think you're right, Tom," added Ara. "Any knowledge I would have would be purely theoretical. Unless I had exact specifications or a user's manual for this weapon, it'd be touch and go for me. And we don't have time for me to read through a bunch of technical documents."

"Those documents don't really exist, either," said Simmons. "The reactor is mostly standard, but a good bit of the technology is still one-of-a-kind. There's nothing else like it anywhere in the universe."

"Then I guess this is it," said Tom. "It's definitely not how I would have preferred to go out, but if I can save all those people in danger, then it'll be worth it."

As Tom spoke, something about the whole situation began to feel suspiciously familiar to Jax. It took a few seconds for the details to coalesce in his brain, but when they did, the realization was staggering.

The last time anyone had rushed into danger on Jax's behalf had been the night he had lost his parents.

He remembered it all too well: the pounding of battering rams against the walls of their home, then the stale air of their escape tunnel, then the crunch of leaves under their feet as they sprinted through the woods. He remembered the scratchy tree bark digging into his back as he had crouched unseen and watched the last moments of his parents' lives.

And then Jax's mind made a new connection, one that he had always been aware of but rarely acknowledged.

His birth family had been all but wiped out, but he had still found a new family here among these 4S ensigns. They weren't bonded by blood, and they argued almost as much as they agreed, but they shared the kind of closeness that only mutual adventuring could create. Jax wasn't always sure whether he hated these people's guts or admired their virtues—in fact, he was pretty sure it was both at once—but they were his best friends, even if only by default.

Jax didn't know if he had failed his parents, necessarily, but he had always felt like he should have done more for them. The masked attackers had made him helpless, and he never wanted to feel like that again. Now here was a chance to give them their comeuppance, and to not only avenge his birth parents but also to save not just his new friends, not just the 4S, but the entire human race, and potentially the very essence of the universe itself.

There, in the tensest moment of Jax's life, all he knew

for certain was that he wasn't about to lose another family.

"No," he said, taking a step forward into the middle of the group. "It has to be me."

"You?" asked Tom. "No offense, Jax, but … why?"

"I'm just the only one who can," Jax said. "You all have too much to lose. You've got your careers ahead of you. You deserve to experience them. But what do I have? I'm not one of you. Admiral Prang can't keep me around forever, and let's not pretend like I have any other big prospects waiting for me after this is over."

"Jax," said Ara, "if this is about some kind of death wish—"

"It isn't, I swear," said Jax. "It just feels like … like this is something I'm meant to do."

"You cannot be serious," said Billy. "You're really okay with dying?"

"Yes, if it helps you all live," said Jax. "Fletcher wants to tear you apart. He wants to tear the entire 4S apart. What better way to stick it to him then for you three to come out of this safe and sound?"

"He'd still be tearing us apart," said Ara. "You're one of us, Jax. Don't you know that by now?"

"Maybe I am," said Jax. "But not in the ways that count. What happens after this mission is over? I'll leave, and you'll never see me again."

"You don't know that," said Tom. "And we wouldn't say you were one of us unless we thought it mattered."

"That's nice," said Jax. "Really, it is. But you three trained together. You were a team before I ever met you. I'm always going to be just the auxiliary."

"No," said Ara. "You have your own skills. This team wouldn't be the same without you."

"Then why am I not part of a specialized division like any of you?" asked Jax. "Maybe this is my purpose. I'm not super connected to anything, so I can put my life on the line when the rest of you can't."

"Stop talking like that," said Tom. "Stop putting yourself down. You're as important as we are."

"Oh, for the love of—" Jax muttered. "That's not what I—"

"Fifteen minutes," interjected Simmons. "I hate to do this to you, but whoever is going to the reactor needs to go *now*, before it's too late."

Jax looked at his squadmates, silently imploring them to see his point.

"Please," he said. "This isn't bringing me any joy. I wish it didn't need to be this way. But logically speaking, I'm the best suited for the job. Forget what I said about not having talents. I'm just the most expendable either way."

"Maybe so, but you'd still have the same problem Billy and I have," said Ara. "You don't know the technology. Not like Tom does."

"How hard can it be?" Jax asked.

"It can be very hard, actually," said Tom. "We're taking a big gamble. If the reactor didn't work like a normal one, would you be able to figure it out in time?"

"I have a comm," said Jax, pulling the small personal communicator unit from his pocket. "We can keep in contact, and I'll let you know if anything out of the ordinary pops up."

"Yes, but the radiation may very well interfere with the comm signal," said Simmons. "You may not be able to maintain contact for as long as you might like."

"Fine," said Jax. "But you said this reactor was a standard model, right?"

Simmons nodded.

"So how does the killswitch usually work?" asked Jax.

"The reactor will be housed inside a large cylindrical casing," Simmons replied. "Somewhere around that casing's midsection, you'll find a very obvious red button inside a plexiglass casing. Your task will be to break the glass and press the button. That will be enough to trigger the reactor's failsafe mechanism."

Jax strode across the room to the masked man he and the others had roughed up earlier, removed the baton from the man's belt, and strode back over to Simmons.

"Consider it done," he said.

"Very well," replied Simmons. "But know that we can't predict what's going to happen to you in there with any certainty. No human being has ever been subjected to so much cosmic radiation contained within a small area. There's a chance you could expire before you ever reach the reactor. But there is a way to keep you moderately protected, as a bit of extra insurance."

"Lay it on me," said Jax.

"The first thing you'll find behind that door is a sterilization chamber," said Simmons, pointing to the door. "Within that chamber, you should be able to find a couple hazmat suits. There's more than one size in there, so you should be able to find yours. The suit won't offer complete protection from the cosmic radiation, but it should stave off enough of the negative effects for you to shut the reactor down before your body gives out on you."

"Great," said Jax.

Simmons looked at the screen once again. "We're down to ten minutes," he reported. "By the time you're out of the sterilization chamber, you'll have an extremely small window in which to shut the reactor down."

"Then I won't wait any longer," Jax said.

He moved a few steps toward the door, then turned around to face his friends.

"Looks like this is it," he told them. "Thank you so much for everything."

"No problem," said Billy. "But we had so little time together, and it's already ending."

"Don't think of this as an ending," said Jax. "Nothing is going to end today. Think of it as me giving you a chance at a fresh start."

"Call it whatever you want," said Tom. "This still doesn't feel right."

"It shouldn't," said Jax. "It's not right. But it was also never going to be."

He spun around, and pressed the button to open it. Once it had opened, he stepped into the sterilization chamber and looked back one last time at his squadmates. They had a few seconds in which to converse before the door closed again.

"Remember me," Jax said. "If I don't see you again, keep my memory alive, okay?"

"Of course we will," said Ara. "As long as you make sure we're still around to do it."

"Sounds good to me," said Jax. "Whatever's about to happen, I'll see you on the other side."

He kept his eyes fixed firmly on his squad until the door slid closed and cut them off from each other.

While he waited for the sterilization chamber to do its work, Jax looked around and saw a rack of hazmat suits on the wall to his left. Rifling through them, he found the one closest to his size. He pulled the rubbery material over first his shoes, then his pants, then his shirt. He zipped up the zipper in the front and pulled the hood down over his face. Unlike the black mask he had donned not long before, this hood was transparent in front, with an air filter attached to its lower half for ease of breathing.

Once he had slipped into the complete suit, Jax pressed a button on the neck to make it skintight. With a puff of air, the bottom of the hood sealed itself to the material around his shoulders, creating a virtually airtight barrier. It wouldn't keep all the cosmic rays out—not according to James Simmons—but it would ward off some of them, and that would have to be enough.

Jax made sure to affix his comm unit to a clip on the hazmat suit's waist, along with the masked man's baton. He knew he'd be needing both of them later.

Jax was ready not a moment too soon, for just after he had slipped into his suit the door at the opposite end of the room slid open to grant him access to the reactor.

This is it, Jax told himself. *The point of no return.*

A wave of mild nausea swept over Jax almost as soon as he stepped into the next room, as though he had just stepped off of a speeding rollercoaster. He could tolerate that, though, and he refused to let it stop him. He gritted his teeth and fixed his eyes on his goal.

The reactor room wasn't especially large, and it couldn't have been more than fifty yards in length. The walls were lined with hexagonal designs resembling solar panels, which must have been used to absorb the radiation. Periodically spaced thin metal pipes along the walls funneled the energy into a divot in the center of the floor, where they connected to the main weapon on the underside of the cruiser. At the opposite end of the room, Jax could see the cylindrical reactor housing Simmons had told him to look for, with another long pipe attaching it to the weapon it powered.

Jax would have to pick his way through the cluster of pipes, but they were all close enough to the ground that they wouldn't give him much trouble. He took one step forward, then another, and for the first few seconds he almost thought that everything would be all right.

But the closer he got to the reactor, the stronger his discomfort became. The radiation remained invisible to Jax's naked eyes, but he had no doubt that it was there.

He made it approximately a third of the way across the room before his arms and legs started to feel weak. Jax told himself to keep moving, to push through the pain, but he couldn't deny that it was becoming harder and harder.

Just over halfway to the reactor, Jax's limbs started to shake. His legs felt like jelly beneath him, and every so often he would shiver and stumble. He almost tripped over two separate pipes, but both times he managed to regain his footing.

By the time he crossed two thirds of the room, Jax didn't know how he was still going. Simply being near the reactor was causing him unspeakable agony, and the pain was only growing by the second.

The third time his foot caught on a pipe, Jax fell and hit the floor. He lay there for several moments, desperately trying to rally himself and stand up again. He was so close; he couldn't stop now.

Jax's comm buzzed, and he gingerly reached down to grab it and bring it to his lips. "Jax here," he mumbled deliriously.

"Jax, this is James Simmons," came the old researcher's voice. "We only have five minutes before Fletcher's black hole is fully formed. If you don't stop it now, before too long it'll be irreversible. You need to—"

Whatever he would have said next was cut off by a sharp burst of static.

Five minutes, Jax repeated in his mind. *Get back up! You have to!*

He maneuvered his hands underneath him and tried to rise to his feet, but at first he couldn't. It felt like there was a huge weight pressing down on his back, as though a thick beam had fallen on top of him.

Get up! Jax urged himself frantically. *Get up, get up, get up!*

But it was all to no avail.

Jax would never finish the job on his own. What had he been thinking? He would never make it to the reactor, and in a few minutes Fletcher's singularity would consume everything.

Then, just as it had when Tom had offered to sacrifice himself, Jax's mind transported him back to the night his parents had died.

He could see them in front of him, telling him to go. But that one word contained a vastly different meaning in that moment than it had when they had last spoken it. Now, instead of telling Jax to get as far away from the situation as possible, they were urging him on to complete a very specific task.

Jax shook his head limply back and forth, but the images of his father and mother refused to fall away. Jax knew they weren't really standing there before him, and he knew that the radiation was probably starting to go to his head, but none of that mattered.

Jax had been drifting, aimless and unmoored, ever since he had lost his parents. Now, at long last, he finally knew what he had to do. And nothing was going to stop him from doing it.

With his parents' imagined presence lending him new strength, Jax pushed himself up and staggered over to the reactor casing. Mercifully, there were no pipes in the way to trip him up again. Jax leaned against the cool metal cylinder and tried to get his breath back. He could only afford to devote a few seconds to that effort before he had to get moving again.

Wrapping his arms around the reactor for balance, he made his way around to its backside, where he finally found the killswitch he had been looking for, exactly as Simmons had described it to him.

With the last of his energy, Jax released his arms from the reactor. He swayed back and forth for a few seconds, but his legs held steady beneath him. Shifting his comm from his right hand to his left, Jax used his newly free hand to take his purloined baton and, drawing on one final burst of strength, smashed the button's plexiglass case. As its shards fell to the floor, Jax dropped the baton, curled his fingers into a fist, and leaned forward to punch the big red button in its direct center.

He had done what he had been told to do, but he had no idea if what he had done had actually done anything.

Jax brought his comm back up to his mouth.

"Guys?" he asked. "Can you hear me?"

This close to the reactor, even with it presumably powered down, Simmons' answer could barely pierce the static occupying the frequency. Jax could only make out a few of his words.

"We read … Jax," Simmons said. "What's … status?"

"I did it," Jax mumbled into the comm. His words slurred, and he had to clench his sweaty, shaking fingers together as tightly as he could so he didn't drop the device. "At least, I think I did it. How's it looking out there?"

"You did it," came Simmons' garbled reply. The audio issuing from Jax's communicator fluctuated between clear words and fizzing bursts of static. "The weapon … levels dropping … singularity probably … away."

Jax couldn't help but grin. He hadn't caught everything Simmons had said, but from the gist of it, their plan had succeeded flawlessly.

"So … we won?" Jax asked tentatively, almost not daring to believe it.

"Yes, Jax," came the short reply, and somehow this one

was perfectly clear. "We won."

"But … what do I do now?" Jax asked the scientist.

"Stay where you are," Simmons said hurriedly. The static returned, preventing Jax from hearing all his words. "The radiation … dissipating but … attempt a rescue … dangerous. Right now … best thing … stay put … hurts, but … we'll try … get you … soon as we can."

By then, Jax couldn't blame them for not wanting to come in. He wanted to vomit, but it had been so long since he had eaten that all he experienced were dry heaves. His vision blurred at the edges, and stars danced before his eyes. He made a last futile attempt to remain standing, but at last, he had to admit that he wasn't strong enough. He staggered over to the wall, slamming clumsily into it and barely remaining on his feet. He tried to keep his eyes open, to not black out, but it was all in vain.

For the second time in as many days, and potentially for the last time ever, Jax crumpled onto the floor and closed his eyes.

<u>CHAPTER TWENTY-FOUR</u>

BRIDGE—WAR CRUISER *THE SHADOW*—HIGH EARTH
ORBIT

Doctor Gregory Fletcher stood slightly behind the warship's pilot's chair with his hands clasped behind his back, gazing out upon the beautiful, massive black hole he had created.

Just look at what we've accomplished.

The prideful thought flickered into existence, and only a fraction of a second after it crossed his mind, an answering thought that was not his own came to him.

You have done well, my vessel. When I reform this tired universe in my image, rest assured that you will be elevated to a place of great prominence.

Fletcher allowed a wide smile to spread across his face. After all, why shouldn't he gloat? From the very first day he had heard the shadow, after the experimental nuclear reactor accident that had claimed the use of his legs, he had followed its instructions to the letter and without question. He hadn't batted an eye when it had told him to stage an even more catastrophic accident for James Simmons' mission, or when it had told him to scoop up the team's leader from the scene and subject him to decades of forced labor. He hadn't doubted its judgment when it had sentenced dozens of Research Division scientists to a largely needless death. He had trusted it implicitly when it had ordered him to saturate the Earth with potentially harmful cosmic rays. And, by all appearances, his gamble had paid off.

By now, the orange glow that ringed the Earth had spread out to encompass a large radius around the planet. Between the circle's fiery outermost layer and the spinning blue-green ball, there was only black. All the myriad stars that had previously occupied that area had been blotted out.

Fletcher let his voice ring out across the bridge. "How long until the singularity has fully formed?"

"Less than five minutes, sir," the woman he had spoken with earlier reported. "It's already beginning to develop its gravitational pull. Not enough to shift the position of the Earth, but still enough to prove that this whole operation is more than just a fancy light show."

Fletcher's smile spread even wider. "Then it's all happening exactly as I predicted," he said. "Or should I say, as the shadow predicted. The calculations it revealed to me were entirely precise, down to the last digit."

"That's good, sir," another woman sitting on the opposite side of the bridge chimed in, "but what exactly did it calculate was going to happen? I mean, what's the shadow rising actually going to look like? Are we going to go into the black hole? Or is something going to come out?"

Truthfully, Fletcher didn't know how to answer that question. The shadow had always managed to be impressively vague whenever it had spoken to him about what life after its rise would look like. The only thing it seemed willing to admit was that everything would somehow be better than it currently was.

Other men, ones with weaker wills or less vision than Fletcher, might have seen this as a reason to reject the shadow and its message. Fletcher himself harbored no such compunctions. He had always known that the world was a broken place. He had been willing to work with the 4S to change that, even while he secretly wholeheartedly believed that their goals didn't go far enough. Even if he had to impose it over the chaos of the modern age by force, Fletcher would see that order and unity were returned to the universe.

And so it was that all he told the woman was, "We won't have to wait long to find out. Just keep watching. You can be sure that it will be a spectacle you can't afford to miss."

Fletcher didn't know if the woman believed him, given that he couldn't see her face underneath the black hood she wore, but she didn't question him again, and that was enough.

Fletcher had to admit, even if only to himself, that he was as curious about what was about to happen as anyone else on the bridge. He joined the rest of them as they all fixed their collective gaze on the cruiser's windshield, where the artificial black hole had nearly reached the average size of its naturally occurring counterparts. For the moment, everything still seemed to be indeed proceeding as it should.

Then something caught his eye—something decidedly out of place.

The orange light at the edge of the singularity—was it flickering?

"Sir?" called one of his men. "We have a problem."

Fletcher spun around and hurried to the man's side. "What? What is it? Talk to me. Now."

"I've been monitoring the energy readouts from the projector," the man replied, "and they're dropping fast. It almost seems to be shutting down."

Fletcher glanced back to the windshield, where the black hole was now starting to dissipate and break apart like a high-resolution image dissolving into its composite pixels.

"Well, what are you sitting around blathering at me for?" he shouted. "Bring it back online!"

"That's just it, sir. I can't," the man replied. "Not from this terminal. My best guess is that someone hit the killswitch on the weapon's main reactor. We can't do anything about that except go down there and manually restart the whole thing."

"I see," said Fletcher. "Clearly those ensigns were more tenacious than I gave them credit for."

"What are we going to do?" the man asked.

"You said it yourself," said Fletcher. "Someone will have to go down there. And we'll take care of those ensigns. No more cushy prison cells for them. Their insolence calls for a more permanent solution."

However, before anyone could follow through on Fletcher's instructions, another one of his masked followers spoke up with more bad news.

"Four ships approaching from the rear!" she shouted. "4S scout models, all of them!"

"What?" roared Fletcher. "How is this happening?"

"They're hailing us, sir," said the pilot. "Pretty insistently, too. I guess they aren't too happy with us."

"You think?" Fletcher muttered.

"Should I reply, sir?" asked the pilot

"No," said Fletcher. "They can be made to wait a few moments. Patience is a virtue, after all."

He reached out to the shadow in his thoughts. *Guide us!* he pleaded. *Surely you can't abandon us now! I did everything you ever asked of me! We were so close! Don't give up on us yet!*

But the shadow didn't answer, and eventually Fletcher had to give up trying to persuade it. There were more immediate matters at hand.

Fletcher sighed. With his weapon offline, there was nothing he could do. "Patch those ships into the bridge speakers," he ordered.

The man at the console tapped a few keys and a loud, authoritative voice filled the room.

"This is Captain Carson of the Society for the Settlement and Security of Space! Under the authority of the United Nations, I'm ordering you to disable all weapons aboard your vessel, shut down all nonessential electronic systems, and stand by for our boarding."

Fletcher spun on his heels to face Prang and Pitt, his face beginning to redden with rage.

"What have you done?" he shouted. "This was my triumph! Mine!"

Prang glanced over at Pitt with a wry smile on his face.

"Dare I suppose this was your doing?" he asked slyly.

Pitt couldn't help but smile himself. "You got me, sir," he replied. "I won't deny it."

"I see," said Prang.

A look of shame and sheepishness flitted across Pitt's features. "I saw the situation starting to go south and I couldn't help but try to correct its course."

"Hmmm," said Prang.

"I only did what I thought was necessary, sir," said Pitt. "If you want to tell me I overstepped, I'm prepared to accept any disciplinary action you might deem necessary."

Prang shook his head fondly. "I keep telling you, things like this are exactly why I chose you for the vice admiral position. You've always provided a vital counterbalance to my own soft-spoken approach to leadership. And how could I not agree that justice must be dealt in this situation?"

A relieved and satisfied smirk came over Pitt's face, but if he was going to respond to Prang's compliments, he never got the chance.

Fletcher stomped over to his superiors. "How dare you? You have no idea what you've done. The Council will see you hanged for this, Admiral. The shadow will rise again, and we'll see what happens when the 4S doesn't have you around to—"

But Fletcher didn't get to finish his threat before Vice Admiral Pitt landed a strong right hook to his jaw.

The Chief Research Officer staggered backward, arms flailing as he tried to regain his balance. In the end, his heavy metal leg braces worked he collapsed against one of the consoles and slid to the floor.

"And there's more where that came from," said Pitt. "So tell your shadow that the 4S will always be ready to hit back."

He strode purposefully into the center of the bridge.

"Who here controls access to the hangar bay?" he asked.

"I—um, I do," a black-clad man said timidly from his console near the bridge doors.

Pitt stepped over to join that man. "All right, why don't you be a gentleman and get the bay doors open so our friends can dock? Or do I have to throw a few more hands?" He raised his fist.

The man hurried to enter the relevant commands, and as he did, Fletcher could feel the situation quickly slipping out of his control.

Desperate, too weak to get back on his feet, he lay slumped where he had fallen and tried once more to reestablish contact with the shadow.

Nothing came of this second attempt, just like nothing had come of the first.

"No," Fletcher mumbled to himself. "No! Where is it? Where did it go?"

A new thought came to him, and he couldn't tell if it was the shadow's or his own.

You have failed.

No! he mentally pleaded. *It isn't over yet! We can still repel this 4S boarding party. We can get our weapon back up and running. We can still help you rise! You can still cleanse the universe!*

But the fateful three words entered his mind again, and this time he knew that they were exclusively from him and for him.

You have failed.

Doctor Gregory Fletcher, Chief Research Officer of the 4S and a man who had once been described as the greatest living intellect in the universe, was out of ideas. He had absolutely no idea what to do next.

He had almost forgotten what that felt like.

Those blasted ensigns! he thought. *Prang should never have brought them into the Eden Project. Or, even better, they should have been wiped out in the trap I set for them when I arranged for that ore shipment to get waylaid. I was a fool to think they'd ever just stand idly by and watch their doom arrive. Now the universe will be fractured forever. They've ruined everything, and they don't even know it.*

As the final realization of a plan more than fifty years in the making slipped further and further out of his reach, the only thing that brought Fletcher any comfort was his hope that whichever young idiot had been foolhardy enough to walk into the cloud of cosmic rays had met an especially painful end.

*

Jax floated on a sea of black, borne along by soft, warm currents. His eyes were closed, and his bare face was exposed to the elements, and yet he was as relaxed as if he were sitting outdoors in a lawn chair on a hot summer day.

Then, all of a sudden, Jax's eyes shot open, and a billion pinpricks of light twinkled into existence all around him. It was the most beautiful sight he had ever seen, and he would definitely have taken more time to bask in its glory were it not for the horrible thought that almost immediately crossed his mind.

Jax was in space. Somehow, he had wound up out among the stars. Where was Doctor Fletcher's warship? Where was the planet Earth? Where were his friends?

And not only was Jax in space, he was in space without a spacesuit. Out of a dozen terrible realizations, the most terrible of all was the fact that he shouldn't have survived long enough to have any of the others.

Jax's head darted from side to side as he frantically searched for some safe haven, some place he could crawl into to slow his otherwise inevitable demise. He tried to force his body into motion, to propel himself through the open space around him, but nothing he tried worked.

Would this be his fate? Was this really how it would end? After all he had done, after how he had helped bring the 4S back from the brink of destruction, would he die all the way out here, all alone, with no one to mourn or remember him?

Then a strangely familiar female voice echoed hauntingly through the emptiness.

Stop struggling, Jax, it said. *Everything is alright.*

Jax's mind registered the voice, but his body continued to flounder. By all appearances, he should be dead. No one could survive in space without oxygen. So why didn't he feel colder? Why didn't his lungs feel emptier? What was going on?

A new voice spoke up, this one the gruff voice of a man. As Jax listened, he swore to himself that he knew this second voice, just like he had known the first. If only he could remember the names he should have been able to attach to them.

Don't worry, said the man's voice. *You won't be hurt here. We'll make sure of it.*

Gradually, Jax's initial panic began to abate. As unprotected from the vacuum he was, he didn't seem to actually be in any danger of asphyxiation. He let his flailing limb go limp, forcing his emotions back down to a manageable level. If he wasn't going to die, and he didn't have anywhere else to go, the least he could do was hear these mysterious voices out.

And that was when he realized who the voices belonged to.

Jax tried to speak, but he couldn't move his mouth. But, even as he strained to open his lips, he could hear his thoughts echoing in the still void as if he had spoken them aloud after all.

Mom? he asked. *Dad? Is ... is that really you?*

Yes and no, the voice of Albert Nurmen replied. *Doctor Fletcher's mad experiments broke down the barriers between dimensions. For a time, our two planes of existence were able to overlap. But the tears in reality are already being stitched back together. I'm afraid we don't have much time to talk.*

Planes of existence? asked Jax. *What do you mean? Where are you guys?*

We still aren't entirely sure ourselves, Rebecca Nurmen said. *We don't know if we'll ever be sure. But we're okay, Jax. We miss you, and it broke our hearts to leave you behind, but it doesn't hurt where we are now. The pain of our death, the pain of our secrets—it's all just gone. Like it never even happened.*

That's good, said Jax, and he truly meant it. *But what about me? What about my friends? They could be in trouble right now. I have to get back to them!*

And you will, his mother told him. *This liminal space we're in is only temporary. You'll be back to your own body soon enough.*

You don't get it, said Jax. *The weapon—and cosmic rays—and—and—*

We know, said his father. *We saw it all. But Doctor Fletcher won't be hurting anyone anymore.*

What makes you so sure? Jax asked.

Trust us, said his mother. *The 4S has the situation well in hand. You played your part beautifully, but they can take it from where you left off. The most important thing for you right now is to just rest.*

Rest. The word seemed somehow foreign to Jax. When was the last time he had truly let himself rest? He couldn't recall.

For months now, he had kept himself going out of a combination of spite, stubbornness, and righteous rage. But, by all accounts, he had just accomplished the revenge he had been seeking. Doctor Fletcher would be brought to justice for his crimes, and Jax's parents had already indicated that they now knew only peace. Was it time for Jax to discover the same for himself?

It's—it's over? He didn't realize the thought had passed through his mind until he heard it uttered aloud.

It's over, his mother told him. *You're free to chart your own path in life.*

I can't do it. Again, Jax's speech moved faster than his brain could process. *I'm not ready. I don't have you. Soon I won't have the 4S. I'll have to start all over again.*

No one can ever have their whole life planned out in advance, his father soothed him. *We were both like you are now, once upon a time. We had no idea what we wanted to do either. But the 4S gave us the opportunity to find out. Who's to say they can't do the same for you?*

Because I'm not one of them, said Jax. *I never really was. Any link I had to the 4S died with you.*

Perhaps, his mother conceded. *But you've already forged new links, haven't you? Those three ensigns who took you into their squad consider you their friend. Even the admiral and the vice admiral think quite highly of you, if you can believe that. And after the sacrifice you made, your credibility with them has already risen.*

Big whoop, said Jax. *But I'm still not a scientist, or a mechanic, or a librarian, or a pilot. I'm not all that smart, and I don't work with my hands all that much. I don't really think I have any of the skills the 4S is looking for.*

Skills can be taught, said his father. *It's up to you to

decide what kind of job you want to take up. But not everyone working for the 4S fills such a specialized role. *They're always looking for people to staff their manned expeditions, or to take jobs managing the facilities in their biodome colonies.*

The question is, added his mother, *what appeals to you the most? What do you like to do?*

Jax didn't have an immediate answer ready to go. He would be lying if he said that his parents' comments hadn't made him think, or that he hadn't already been thinking about the same things for a while, even if he hadn't focused too much attention on them.

I—I'm not sure, he said haltingly. *Can I think on it some more?*

That's all we're asking, replied his father.

Great, said Jax. He didn't know whether he was being sarcastic or not. But he also wasn't going to waste this valuable time of reunion with his dead parents being introspective. He decided to change the subject.

But enough about me, he said. *What about you?*

What about us? asked his mother. *What do you want to know?*

We never really got a chance to talk the last time we were together, Jax explained. *I just have so many questions. Like, why did you do what you did?*

We did a lot of things, replied his father. *What specifically are you referring to?*

Any of it! exclaimed Jax. *Why couldn't you tell me who you really were in the first place? Or why didn't you fight harder to have us moved to a safer place? Why did you have to go and get yourselves murdered?*

Some of that was beyond our control, his father said. *If you want to complain about the secrecy, you'll have to take that up with Admiral Prang. He thought that, if news of the Eden Project got out before it was completed, it wouldn't take long for nefarious forces to come for it. In retrospect, he was right about that, but to many of us scientists at that time it didn't seem like true, respectable 4S behavior.*

We hated it, his mother said. *We hated the thought that you'd grow up never knowing what our work was really going towards. The only bit of consolation was that one day you'd be able to live in a more peaceful, harmonious world.*

Oh, yeah, and that worked out real well, didn't it? Jax cut in.

Don't be like that, his father gently admonished him. *As for the rest of it, there simply wasn't time to inform you of anything after the fact. We were on the run. Going to the lab, going to the city, sending you on ahead—all of those were snap decisions. There was never an opportunity for a family meeting. We were always on the back foot, right up until we were caught. But we don't regret what we did. We only regret that it took us away from you.*

It was a simple choice, really, added his mother. *Saving our own lives wouldn't have been worth it so long as yours would still have been in danger.*

But ... but how can you just be so calm about it? Jax blurted out. *You left me alone! What made you so sure those goons wouldn't have just turned around and gone after me the second they finished with you?*

I'll admit we took a big risk, said his father. *But it was a very calculated one, Jax. We had to believe that we were the only ones the 'goons' were after. They had no reason to seek vengeance against you. No one did.*

And even though we left you alone, we had faith that you'd be safe, his mother said. *Admiral Prang knew what was happening, and even though he was half the solar system away from Earth we knew that he would do everything in his power to keep you safe and solve the crime that killed us.*

Well, thought Jax, Prang had undeniably done that. Pacifistic though the admiral was, he had still relentlessly kept up his pursuit of his enemies until they could be cut off at the source. In the end, justice had won the day, even though so much and so many had been lost before it could.

Even if Jax didn't agree with every choice his parents had made, he couldn't argue with the fact that all those choices had brought him to the point where he had been ready to give up everything for the sake of the cosmic balance of the universe. And no one could say that he hadn't preserved that balance. After all, didn't everything always have a silver lining?

You sure left a lot up to chance, though, he said. *Everything you did, you did on faith.*

The sound of chuckling drifted through the void into his ear, and Jax almost choked up as he recognized his father's characteristic unbridled laughter.

Maybe we did, said Albert. *But believe me when I say that we could not be more proud of how well you handled yourself under all the pressure we left you with, and we are so sorry for heaping all that pressure on your shoulders. If we could have had it happen any other way, we would have.*

As he spoke, his voice started to get quieter and quieter, as though he was moving further and further away from Jax. As he continued speaking, Jax had to strain to hear him.

What's happening? Jax called. *Why can't I hear you so well anymore?*

We're almost out of time. The universe is settling back into its usual arrangement. You'll be back among the living in just a few minutes, his mother replied. Her voice echoed as though he were shouting across a vast divide.

You can't go! cried Jax. *I have so many more questions! What if I never see you again?*

You will see us again, his father told him. *All in good time.*

But you have a long life to live before we'll meet again, his mother said. *Try not to waste it, okay?*

How? Jax asked. *You still haven't told me what to do!*

Oh, Jax, said his mother. *You can't rely on us forever. You're an adult. And look at what you've already accomplished. If anything, we should be taking guidance from you.*

Yeah, but all that's over now, said Jax. By this point he was drawing the conversation out as much to find the answers he wanted as he was out of desperation not to lose his parents again.

Stop, Jax. His father's voice wasn't stern, as if he were disciplining a child, but compassionate, as though he were offering guidance to an equal.

You can't run from destiny, he continued. *Maybe yours is with the 4S, and maybe it isn't. That's entirely up to you. But if you can't face that choice head-on and make your own decision, someone else will choose for you.*

I'm not running! Jax objected. *It's not like I know what I'm supposed to do and I'm going out of my way to avoid it. I have no idea what my destiny is.*

What did we just tell you? his mother asked. *Nobody does, at first. It takes a lot of trial and error before they ever get to that knowledge. But you've faced your fair share of trials, and made a few errors along the way. Now is the time for what comes next.*

Their voices mingled as they uttered one last crucial sentence:

And we will always be with you, every step of the way.

Jax's parents' voices had already fallen to the level of whispers, and by their last four words they sounded like little more than puffs of air, futilely being flung into a great empty chasm that had no place for them.

Jax could barely hear his parents anymore. And, surprisingly, he didn't feel like that mattered anymore. He was now totally at ease, as if he had just disposed of a heavy burden he had been carrying over a great distance. And maybe he had. Without the resentment that had fueled him for months, he felt strangely hollow, but in a pleasant way, like he was simply waiting to be filled back up with something far better.

As the last scraps of his parents' spirits faded away, Jax closed his eyes, and his starry surroundings fell away.

CHAPTER TWENTY-FIVE

ROOM B23—SICK BAY—4S COMMAND CRUISER *HOME BASE*—DEEP SPACE

When he opened his eyes again, Jax found himself in a completely different location.

The soft, yielding surface he could now feel beneath him was a jarring contrast to the hard metal floor where he had passed out. With a thin sheet of fabric draped over most of his body and his head popped up on what seemed to be a fluffy pillow, Jax guessed he was in a bed somewhere, though his eyesight was still too blurry for him to discern any of the room around him.

Strangely enough, he didn't feel any discomfort. Waking up in this bed felt exactly like waking up in his bed on any old morning.

But how was he even in a bed? Once again, he had fallen unconscious in one location and then been transferred to a completely different place. He really had to stop doing that.

"Where … where am I?" Jax croaked through his dry, chapped lips, not really knowing whether he expected anybody to respond.

"He's alive!" came a shout from somewhere nearby. It didn't offer Jax much in the way of answers, but it reassured him nonetheless.

As Jax turned his head toward the source of the voice, his surroundings belatedly started to settle into focus.

His bed sat in the center of a small, austere room, surrounded by four walls painted in a soothing sky blue. A small night table stood to his right, within arm's reach. The tabletop sat empty save for a small communicator unit and an untouched glass of water. On his left stood a cluster of chairs.

But Jax wasn't alone in this strange new place. At the foot of his bed, halfway between him and the door, stood his three teammates—Ara, Billy, and Tom. It had been Billy who had shouted out that Jax was alive.

Jax tried to raise himself up, but all his muscles screamed in protest, and he slumped back down. The others crowded around him, moving nearer to the bed while still remaining at a respectful distance.

"How are you feeling, Jax?" Billy asked. "Anything we can do? Anything we can get for you?"

"Shhh!" said Tom in a low voice. "Don't overwhelm him. Let him get adjusted to this place first."

Jax's dry lips smacked together as he struggled to form words. "Wh-where am I?" he stuttered.

Ara took two steps toward him. "Don't worry," she said. "We're on the *Home Base*, in the sick bay. You stopped that nasty weapon Doctor Fletcher's gang made, and we all lived to tell the tale."

"It was a near thing for you, though," added Tom. "Even with the radiation suit you had, the cosmic rays around that machine should have burned you to a crisp, and then atomized that crisp."

"That's right …" muttered Jax, wincing as the memories flooded back into his mind. He could all too clearly recall the nausea he had felt from the second he had stepped into that reactor core, and how every single step had pained him beyond belief. As he remembered it, he seemed to experience all the agony all over again.

Jax moved his head slowly from side to side, and the mental reconstruction fell away, the phantom pains vanishing as quickly as they had come.

"But … how am I here?" he asked.

He broke off as a new, horrifying thought struck him.

"You didn't walk into that radiation to get me, did you?"

"No, no," said Ara. "Nothing like that. Fletcher's warship was moved into the 4S' junkyard to be decommissioned. They sent in some drones to open it up and pull you out."

"And then they brought me here?" Jax asked. "What if I'm still contaminated?"

"Relax," said Tom. "You aren't. They don't even really think you ever were."

"What are you talking about?" asked Jax. "That place was saturated with radiation. I felt like I was going to puke my guts out."

"The radiation was definitely there," said Ara. "But it's like it was reflected off of you. It's like you had some kind of shielding we didn't know about."

"That's impossible," said Jax. "Simmons specifically said that the hazmat suit I was using was inadequate. I shouldn't be feeling as good as I am."

"Are we really complaining, though?" asked Billy. "I've seen what radiation can do to people. We all have. Would you rather be sick for the rest of your life? Or mutated?"

"Of course not!" said Jax. "That isn't what I'm saying. I got a lucky break, and I'm grateful for it. But that doesn't mean it isn't completely absurd."

"Well, I'm sorry, but that's the way it is," said Tom. "It's a mystery. Nobody fully understands cosmic rays."

"Nobody …" Jax muttered softly.

He thought of his parents, existing somewhere out there in the dimensions beyond his own. What grand secrets had they learned after their deaths? Did they know anything about his miraculous fate? They had certainly hinted that they did. Would Jax ever ascend to that level of awareness?

"What was that?" asked Ara, oblivious to Jax's introspection.

"Nothing," said Jax. "It doesn't matter. Let's talk about something else. Why didn't Doctor Fletcher just turn his weapon back on and keep doing what he was trying to do?"

"He couldn't," said Billy. "The 4S Security Force showed up not long after you passed out. Apparently Vice Admiral Pitt had some contingencies in place."

"Good for him," said Jax. "So he's … what? In jail?"

"Pretty much," said Ara. "The 4S doesn't have a brig, so they transferred him to some maximum-security facility on Earth. The exact location is above our clearance to know. Oh, and Captain Ramón went with him."

"Captain Ramón?" Jax repeated incredulously. "Why? He seemed like such a good guy."

"He fooled us," said Tom. "He fooled us all. And he killed that woman we brought back from Rho Station to cover his tracks."

"Oh." Jax was dumbfounded. He had almost forgotten that woman. But she had been the reason he had been aboard Fletcher's warship and in position to stop the weapon in the first place. And he didn't like to think of anyone dying, even one of his enemies. After his talk with his parents, he couldn't find it within him to hold a grudge anymore.

A thought occurred to him. "If Captain Ramón was evil all along, does that mean anyone else was, too? How do we know we don't still have traitors in the 4S?"

"We don't," said Tom. "But Admiral Prang has begun an inspection of every 4S staff member—every rank and every division. If he finds anything out of order, he'll deal with it."

Jax opened his mouth to speak again, but his attention was diverted when the door of his room slid open and Admiral Prang walked in.

"Speak of the devil," said Tom, apparently almost without meaning to. He quickly clamped his mouth shut in chagrin.

He needn't have worried. Prang appeared to be as utterly good-natured as ever.

"Ah," he said. "Talking about me, were you?"

Rather than replying directly, the three ensigns saluted him crisply, and he acknowledged them with a nod and an "At ease".

"Good afternoon, ensigns," he said as he joined them

by Jax's bed. "I hope you don't mind if I drop in. I was passing by the sick bay, and I received the news that Jax had regained consciousness."

"It's not a problem at all, sir," said Ara.

"That's a relief," said Prang. "I always hate to intrude."

Jax detected both genuine sincerity and determined lightheartedness in Prang's tone, each seeping in in equal measure.

Prang walked over to stand at the foot of Jax's bed. "How are you feeling?" he asked. "Your doctors tell me that you're on track to make a full recovery within just a few days, but I want to know how things are looking

Jax took a few seconds to stretch all his muscles, rolling his shoulders and flexing his toes. They felt just the slightest bit stiff, since he hadn't been using them recently, but that could easily be taken care of. Nothing felt out of the ordinary beyond that.

"I think I'm going to be alright, sir," he said. "Weird as that may be."

Prang clapped his hands together once, clasping them together briefly before letting them fall back to his sides.

"Ah," he said. "Wonderful. Ordinarily I'd say that our fine medical professionals have done it again, but this time I don't think there was much for them to do."

"Apparently not," Jax agreed.

Prang turned to the others in the room. "I suppose this must all be a relief for you three," he said. "Your friend has been brought back from the brink of death. Or maybe he was never on the brink at all. Who can say?"

"Not us, sir, that's for sure," said Tom. "But I know I'm not going to look a gift horse in the mouth."

"I think that's a fine idea, Ensign," said Prang. "And I'm rejoicing with you. Having Jax with us once again is the perfect symbol of our victory. Doctor Fletcher's machinations may have put a dent in the 4S, but our future is secured with young agents such as him at our disposal."

"I don't know if I ever agreed to stay, sir," said Jax. The words had slipped out almost before he thought them.

"Respectfully," he hastened to add.

"Of course," said Prang. He turned to Jax and looked at him apologetically. "Please forgive me."

"It's okay," said Jax. "Let's just take it slow, if that's alright with you."

"As you wish," said Prang. "You've earned that much. Even if you choose not to continue working with us, you should know that we greatly appreciate everything you've done."

"You're welcome," said Jax.

Prang seemed eager to move past that awkward interaction. He turned back to the ensigns.

"Now then," he began, "as happy as we all are, let's not forget that some of us have duties to attend to. I've been generous, and I allowed you to take a few hours off here and there while Jax convalesced, but now that he's conscious again, the work of the 4S must go on."

"I don't get it, sir," said Billy. "Are you saying—?"

"I'm afraid I am," said Prang. "If you want to spend time catching up with your friend, you'll have to come back later. For now, if you'd kindly leave us, I'd like to speak to Jax alone."

The three ensigns didn't complain, and they didn't look dismayed. They only said, "Yes, sir". Turning sharply on their heels, they left the room.

As the door closed behind them, Prang took one of the vacated chairs near Jax's bed.

Jax stared into Prang's eyes, but he found the admiral's expression too reserved to decipher. Still, his face was somber enough for Jax to tell that his visit wouldn't just be a social one.

"Is there something I can help you with, sir?" he asked.

Prang sighed heavily. "Frankly, I'm not sure, but I appreciate your willingness nonetheless."

"Uh … anytime," Jax said quickly.

Prang chuckled. "Relax, my young friend," he said. "This isn't a test, and it isn't an interrogation. This won't even go on any record. I wanted to have a conversation with you that wasn't hampered by our power dynamic."

"About what?" Jax asked. "I don't want to be rude, but there isn't a lot we both have in common. What could you possibly want to talk to me about as 'just friends'?"

Prang swallowed, then followed that up with a deep breath. "I'll admit, this is more than a friendly chat," he began at last. "But I wanted you to know that I'm not speaking to you as an admiral, or at least I won't be giving you any direct orders. What you do after this conversation is entirely up to you."

"Okay," said Jax. "Go on."

"The United Nations' Oversight Council for the 4S has opened an inquiry into the recent events surrounding Doctor Fletcher's weapon," Prang began. "I've been summoned to a hearing at their headquarters in Geneva. It's expected to last for a week at least, and they've subpoenaed testimonies from everyone involved in the incident."

Suddenly, Jax could see all too clearly where Prang was going. "And they want me to be one of those."

"Along with your teammates, Vice Admiral Pitt, and myself, of course," said Prang. "The Council can be tedious, yes, but that's the cost of being thorough. And we'd all like to know more about exactly what happened with that weapon."

"Yeah, I guess we would," said Jax. "What should I do?"

Prang had to compose himself for a while before he answered.

"Jax, I want to be absolutely clear here," he said eventually. "Your testimony in particular has the potential to make or break the Council's verdict. I can't force you to speak in my favor, and I won't stoop so low as to try. All I ask is that you answer the questions they ask as honestly as possible."

"You aren't trying to save your own skin?" Jax asked in astonishment.

"The charges against me are completely fair," Prang said. "The Council exists to monitor the 4S' activities, and I obstructed their duty by not reporting everything to them. And that's without even bringing up the whole legal mess I tangled myself in when I brought you onboard the Eden Project. Hiring a complete outsider could potentially be forgiven, but to send you into danger is another thing entirely. And there are those who would argue that I took advantage of you when you came to me in a state of grief. Whatever happens next, my moral character has already been thrown into question."

"I see," said Jax. "That doesn't sound good."

"No, it doesn't," Prang agreed.

Neither man spoke for several moments before Jax changed the subject.

"So you just want me to get on the stand and testify?" he asked. "That shouldn't be too hard."

"It might have been, if your condition had been worse," said Prang. "I did try to get the Council to relieve you of your obligation, but they just couldn't do it, what with your story being so integral to their case and all. I was able to convince them to move your testimony to the final day of the hearing, so you'll have some time to recuperate before they hear from you."

"That would be nice," said Jax. "That radiation really did a number on me, even if I can't feel it anymore. Which sure is a relief, by the way."

"Yes, it is," said Prang. "If you had died, or been crippled in some way, the Council would probably have fired me on the spot."

A sheepish look came over his face. "Look, Jax, I don't want to seem like I'm being self-centered here. I just want you to know how severe the situation is."

"Nothing's changed, sir," said Jax. "We're just facing paperwork and bureaucracy now instead of a horde of criminals. You know, I actually think I might like this better."

Prang chuckled. "I'm glad you can still look on the bright side of all this. You should know how grateful I am to see that, even after all I've put you through, I haven't beaten it out of you."

"You didn't put me through anything I didn't want to do," said Jax. "You didn't even have to direct me at the enemy. I was already gunning for them, ever since they killed my parents.

All you did was give me easier access to them."

Prang didn't respond out loud, but he looked at Jax with a new light beginning to kindle in his eyes.

"I was afraid of that," he said. "Violence often tends to beget more violence."

"That isn't what I meant—" Jax began, but he was quickly interrupted.

"Stop," said Prang, holding up a hand. His voice sounded gentle but tired. "Save it for the hearing. Your testimony should be one hundred percent your own. I don't want to say anything that would skew it one way or the other."

"But why?" asked Jax. "Why wouldn't you try to protect yourself?"

Prang didn't answer the question outright; instead, he posed his own.

"Jax," he asked, "do you remember the conversation we had when I first introduced your team to the Eden Project?"

"I don't know," replied Jax. "You said a lot of things that night. What specifically are you asking me to remember?"

"I began that briefing with a story," said Prang. "It was the story of a dream. The story of humanity hoping against hope that even with all its faults, and all its ignorance, it wasn't licked yet. The dream was the dream of a new start.

"And ever since I was mature enough to know it, that dream was my dream too. Yes, humanity has made mistakes, and yes, we've hurt our planet just like we've hurt each other, but if we don't have any hope of coming to our senses, then what will we become? I wasn't the man who instituted the Eden Project, but it always had my full support. How could I not throw my belief behind our best attempt to buy a fresh, clean start for the human race?"

"But did you?" Jax asked. "No offense, but it seems to be like you might just have made everything worse. Doctor Fletcher and Captain Ramón still got corrupted, and they managed to corrupt a whole bunch of other people. They used your research to do the exact opposite of what it was meant for. How can you look at that and still be so optimistic that humanity can resist its greed for power?"

Prang took a few deep breaths before he answered.

"You're right," he said. "You're absolutely right. But those men clearly weren't in their right minds. Their actions and intentions were being warped by the shadow. I have to keep believing that no one is inherently evil, and that no one is beyond salvation, or else I might as well just give up and wait for death to take me."

"Hmph," said Jax. "Fair enough."

"Your parents believed too, for what it's worth," Prang said. "As long as I knew them, they always stood with me at the forefront of the change we wanted to bring about. My only regret is how much of a curse that change turned out to come with."

"Curse is right," said Jax.

"It certainly looks that way," said Prang. "But, by all accounts, the shadow has been dispelled, and we can begin. Perhaps this time we can finally get it right."

"Then I'll wish you luck," said Jax. "Something tells me you'll need it."

Prang nodded gratefully. "Thank you," he said.

They spent the next few minutes together in silence, neither one knowing just what to say to the other.

"So," Jax said at last. "The Council is just going to ask me some questions, right? Nothing too intensive?"

"No," replied Prang. "It's fairly straightforward. You'll go before them, and they'll ask for your account of what happened on Doctor Fletcher's cruiser. All you need to do is answer as honestly as you can, with whatever feels truest to you, and they'll let you go. It's as simple as that."

"Sure," said Jax. "I think I can do that."

"Very good," said Prang. "Vice Admiral Pitt and I will be leaving for Earth in two days, along with the rest of your squad. Unless your health should somehow take a turn for the worse, the doctors have cleared you to join our delegation at that time. For now, just stay here and get some rest. The worst thing you could do would be to strain yourself too much too early. Your friends will be able to come and visit you again, and you can use the room's intercom to call for food or drinks when you want them."

"Okay," said Jax.

"Well, it seems we're on the same page for now," said Prang. "I hope I've made my position clear, and if I kept talking I might say something that would change your mind one way or the other. I want your testimony—including your bias for or against me, whichever way you decide to lean—to be free of my influence."

"Even if it gets you fired?" Jax asked.

"Even if it gets me fired," said Prang. "Every accusation the Council has leveled against me is

"Then it's settled," said Prang. "I'm glad to see you're okay, and I wish you a speedy return to full strength, but just like your teammates, I have work to do. I need to put the 4S in order before we go to meet the Council."

"That's fine," said Jax. "Go do what you need to do. I'll be fine here."

"That's just what I like to hear," said Prang. "I'll look forward to seeing you in the hangar bay when it's time to leave. Spend some time thinking about what kind of angle you want your testimony to take, and please know that no matter what you say, I will not hold any grudges against you. Good day, Jax."

With that, he turned and walked out of the room, leaving Jax with a lot to think about.

*

For the rest of the day and into the night, Jax mulled over Prang's words. The admiral had clearly believed in everything he had said, both the reasons he had given for his choices and the punishment he thought he deserved for them. And yet, he had also admitted to using Jax for his own purposes—or at least he had admitted that it might look that way to an outsider.

The question therefore became, should Jax play up that interpretation of events in order to gain sympathy? Or should he try to help get Prang exonerated? Did he owe the man his loyalty or his contempt?

At long last, he made up his mind. He knew what he would say to the Council. He still hadn't quite figured out what his life would look like afterwards, but he'd already been making it up as he went along for months. What were a few more days in the grand scheme of things?

Besides, in a strange way, it didn't matter what he did. Whether Jax's words helped Admiral Prang lose or retain his position, either way the hearing would mark the end of an era.

<u>CHAPTER TWENTY-SIX</u>

4S OVERSIGHT COUNCIL CHAMBER—UNITED NATIONS HEADQUARTERS—GENEVA, SWITZERLAND

"Admiral Alpheus Prang." The woman sitting directly in front of the 4S leader spoke in a slow drawl, accentuating every other word with a shake of her head.

"What are we going to do with you?" she asked.

Seated before the hastily convened United Nations tribunal, Admiral Prang fought the urge to squirm. It was a foreign urge, the sort of thing he had long believed he had left behind in his younger days. He had learned to make himself appear comfortable in all situations, as befit his position at the head of one of the world's most prestigious organizations. Even people such as himself had to occasionally be held accountable, though, and as he sat in the room where his fate would be decided, all Prang could think was that he would rather be anywhere else.

Fletcher's massive warship bombarding Earth's atmosphere with cosmic rays and nearly opening up a gigantic black hole above the planet had stirred up chaos that had extended into every corner of the globe. Naturally, the 4S had come under scrutiny for its failure to prevent the incident in the first place, even though the agency as a whole had been largely unaware and uninvolved. Naturally, as the man in charge of the 4S, Prang had borne the brunt of his superiors' fury.

The United Nations Oversight Council, made up

of representatives from the twenty-four nations which had collaborated to bring the 4S into being, had been debating for days over just how much Prang should be brought to task. While none of its members had gone so far as to blame Prang himself for the actions of Doctor Fletcher's splinter group, Prang was all too aware that he had made mistakes. He had prioritized the privacy of the 4S over the safety of the human race, and for that he was all too culpable.

And yet, no matter how much time Prang spent blaming himself, he couldn't see anything he could have done differently. The 4S' infrastructure hadn't been built to account for high-level officers going rogue under the influence of primordial cosmic forces. Prang knew that, and he knew the Council knew it as well. Given the unconventional circumstances, they would have to carefully consider how much punishment they wanted to assign.

So Prang sat there, with the Council's round table wrapping almost all the way around him, waiting for his trial to get underway again. His own small table stood in front of him, with a chair on either side of Prang's own. The Council had allowed him to keep his dignity by not stationing any guards in the room, but given the hard stares at least half of its members were shooting at him, he might as well have been handcuffed to an electric chair.

The woman in front of him slammed her gavel down on the table three times. The thuds of wood hitting wood echoed loudly around the large room.

"As chairwoman of the United Nations' Oversight Council for the Society for the Settlement and Security of Space, I hereby call this session to order," the woman declared. "I'm sure I don't need to remind any of the honorable representatives gathered in this room why we're all here."

No one challenged her assertion.

"I didn't think so," she said. "Now, let's get down to business. Admiral Prang, you stand accused of gross negligence, dereliction of duty, and criminal endangerment of your entire agency. You've pled guilty to all the charges thus far, and yet every witness we've brought forward has stalwartly defended you. I'll ask you one more time: do you wish to change your plea?"

Prang fought to stop himself from sighing. They had

started every day of the hearing this way, and every day he had offered the same answer. He knew the Council had its formalities, but he wasn't going to deny that he had made several poor choices.

"No," he said. "I won't be changing my plea. I appreciate the witnesses' efforts to stand by me, but I won't try to sweep my mistakes under the rug. I'll leave that decision up to you."

"Very well," said the chairwoman. "Your plea is noted. Would you like to use this time to make any statements regarding these accusations?"

"I would, ma'am," replied Prang. "I did what I thought was best to mitigate casualties, prevent mass panic, and keep our mutual interests intact. But I did ignore the Council's authority on several occasions, and so I have come here before you of my own volition to accept whatever ruling you see fit to lay down."

"You say you wanted to protect our interests, yet you also claim you deliberately withheld vital information from us," said a woman sitting on the left edge of Prang's vision. "How can you explain that contradiction?"

"It's like I said," said Prang. "I didn't want an uproar. I admit I wasn't truthful with you, and I'm not trying to justify that. Still, at the risk of sounding pretentious, I don't think you'll find any precedent for an event like this anywhere in the 4S' bylaws."

"That may be the case, but you have to understand that exploiting legal loopholes won't help strengthen your position," the chairwoman said. "The Council doesn't have to approve every decision you make, yes, but your Eden Project looks to have been somewhat dubiously organized even before the attacks on it began."

"The 4S has been experimenting with the ambient energy of the universe since its inception," said Prang. "Our purview to study the galaxy around us almost obligates us to do so."

"That's not the point, and you know it," she said. "We aren't here to debate the mission statement of the 4S. This hearing is solely focused on the steps you yourself took to carry it out. Your secret research stations and your formation of a special operations unit of inexperienced young recruits would suggest some level of disregard for consequences. I hardly think it would be advantageous for you to be glib right now."

"My apologies," Prang said. "I meant no offense. I only wished to say that I did what I thought was best to protect the 4S' mission."

"Objection!" called a councilman from somewhere to Prang's right.

Everyone in the room swiveled in their seats to face the man.

"On what grounds?" the chairwoman asked him.

"The Society for the Settlement and Security of Space is not a judicial force!" the man shouted, slamming a hand down on the table. "The admiral can argue whatever semantics he likes, but he has never had the freedom to act with impunity. If he sensed an imminent threat to the security of his operations, he should have expressed it to this council immediately."

The man was not the first council member to speak out in opposition to Prang, nor was he the first to raise that argument. Prang hadn't sat in on enough of the Council's deliberation to know exactly where each individual member stood on the matter, but he knew that their discussion had been down this particular route several times already.

Evidently the chairwoman thought so too. "Your point, Councilman?"

"This farce has gone on long enough." The man's face began to redden. "Why must we keep wasting this council's valuable time? Madam Chairwoman, I move that we strip Admiral Prang of his command and get back to more productive business."

"There are procedures that must be followed," the chairwoman said. "This council still believes in justice, and the admiral has the right to a fair and complete trial. Your objection is noted, but we cannot compromise our principles just because we find them inconvenient."

The councilman subsided, and the hearing went ahead.

"Admiral Prang, do you have anything else you would like to add?" the chairwoman asked.

"No, ma'am," said Prang. "I merely hope I've made my intentions clear."

"Then would any other representatives like to make a statement?" the chairwoman said.

Once more, the room was silent.

The chairwoman nodded once. "Very well. In that case, we'll continue with our proceedings. We only have one more testimony to hear, and by all accounts this one should be quite inflammatory."

She raised a personal communicator to her mouth. "Send in the witness."

Prang could hear the swish of the meeting room door opening and then closing behind him. A few seconds later, Jax Nurmen stepped around Prang and stood at the admiral's shoulder. He had been escorted in by one of the Council's aides, who turned and walked back out of the room after the chairwoman waved a hand to dismiss him.

"Welcome, Mister Nurmen," the chairwoman said. "Please, take a seat."

Jax sat next to Prang in the chair the aide had pulled out for him.

"Do you know why you are here?" the chairwoman asked him.

"Yes, ma'am," Jax said. "You'll be asking me for my account of what happened with Doctor Fletcher's black hole."

"Indeed we will," the chairwoman replied. "You've been assessed and declared mentally fit to testify, and so long as you understand what's happening I see no reason not to go ahead with this. Do any council members know any reason why Jax Nurmen should be unable to take the stand before us today?"

None did.

"Then the testimony will begin," she went on. "Mister Nurmen, so long as you are speaking here, do you swear to tell the truth, the whole truth, and nothing but the truth? If so, then place your hand over your heart and reply, 'I do'."

"I do," said Jax, laying his right hand atop his chest.

"Then state your name for the record," the chairwoman instructed him.

"Jax Nurmen," Jax replied.

"And you are the son of Albert and Rebecca Nurmen of the 4S Research Division, are you not?" the chairwoman asked.

"Yes, ma'am."

"Then you must be aware by now that your parents are merely two names on a list of dozens of casualties that Admiral Prang's decisions have incurred."

"I am," said Jax, after only a second's hesitation. "But the admiral didn't kill them himself, and he didn't order them to be killed. He didn't order any of those casualties."

"Perhaps not," the chairwoman conceded. "But that is not the matter we have come here to debate. Not all the people Admiral Prang directly or indirectly endangered are now dead. You yourself were one of them. How is it that the admiral convinced you to fight his battles?"

"We were never supposed to fight any battles," said Jax. "We were a reconnaissance team. Nothing more. Admiral Prang always made it clear that we were to steer clear of any conflict. He put our safety above our mission every time."

"An interesting distinction," a councilman chimed in, "considering that many if not all of the places you were sent to perform reconnaissance led you directly into conflict."

"That wasn't anyone's fault except Doctor Fletcher's," Jax said. "None of us ever knew what we were going to find on any of our missions. By the time we found out, it was too late to avoid the traps. We always did our best to escape as quickly as we could to report back to Admiral Prang, even if we had to do a bit of fighting along the way. If any of us had known what was actually happening at any of the sites we visited, we never would have been sent to them in the first place."

"The danger should have been clear from the start," a councilwoman argued. "The people working against the 4S were obviously all too willing to commit mass murder. With that in mind, it shouldn't have mattered what your mission objectives were. Agents so young as you should never have been put at risk."

"I agree," the chairwoman put in. "Whatever you were told, can you truly say that you and your fellows were the best suited for the task?"

"We weren't," Jax said. "The 4S could definitely have found hundreds of people more skilled than we were. But it was partly because of that that Admiral Prang chose us. We could slip under the radar and do the work that others couldn't, all because we were so unassuming."

The Council pondered this for several seconds.

"I think we're asking the wrong question here," said a councilman. "Let's forget about the others for now, and let's talk about you specifically. Regardless of the nature of your work, the fact that you came to be working for the 4S at all is highly suspect. Your parents were legitimate 4S officers, with all the training and documentation to prove it. You, meanwhile, never were. What I'd like to know is, what possessed the admiral to recruit you? What made him think it was a good idea?"

"I can't speak for the admiral," Jax said slowly. "But I think he did know what he was doing. If I were just a random person he plucked from the streets, it would have been different, but I always had a vested interest in what was going on. I think he chose me because I wasn't as deeply rooted in the 4S' traditions as the others were. My thought process would have been clearer in crisis situations."

"And yet, by all accounts, you were clearly in a state of grief when he recruited you," said another council member. "It could easily have compromised that thought process. One could even say that Admiral Prang took advantage of that for his own ends. How would you respond to that?"

Jax didn't answer immediately.

"No," he said eventually. "They were my own ends too. Admiral Prang never forced me to do anything I didn't want to do. All the choices I made were my own."

Prang quietly let out a breath he hadn't realized he'd been holding in.

"And it never occurred to you that the admiral could easily have found many people more qualified than you?" a councilman asked.

"Maybe he could have," Jax conceded. "But I don't think that would have done him much good. He already had the three other ensigns on the team lined up, and originally he was going to bring in my parents instead of me. When they died, a spot on the roster opened up and needed filling. I consented every step of the way, even when Admiral Prang was very explicit about the risks."

As Jax spoke, Prang tried to catch his eye, without much success. He wanted him to see the gratitude that had bubbled up within him. If even Jax, the most reluctant of Prang's agents, could offer such a staunch defense of the admiral's actions, then Prang might have a chance at fending off the allegations against him after all. But Jax was so focused on answering the questions being flung at him that he failed to notice Prang's sideways glances, and eventually Prang had to give up. Whether or not the Council dropped its charges, Prang would make sure that Jax knew just how much his support was appreciated.

The Council's cross-examination of Jax dragged on for two more whole hours. Once it became clear that they had exhausted every line of questioning, and that Jax's testimony wouldn't change no matter what they threw at him, they thanked him for his cooperation and dismissed him from the room.

Prang remained behind and found himself subject to a new barrage of queries as the Council attempted to determine whether Jax's testimony had affected Prang's own. Prang told them that he had already said everything he wanted to say back on the first day of his hearing, and eventually the Council was satisfied and dismissed him as well.

In the waiting room outside the Council's chamber, Prang met up with Jax, James Simmons, Vice Admiral Pitt, and Jax's three teammates, all of whom had given their testimonies over the previous five days. They each offered their friendly greetings, but a somber atmosphere hung over the group. Everyone was aware that, now that the Council had collected all the evidence they had been looking for, it wouldn't be long before they delivered their ultimate verdict on Prang's fate.

Nonetheless, Prang still made an effort to appear optimistic. He tried to make small talk with Pitt about the 4S' future, but that quickly became depressing. He watched the young ensigns awkwardly chatting amongst themselves, but all he felt was sorrow for the terror he had put them through. He ate his dinner from the buffet the Council had provided, but he discovered that his stomach didn't feel any more at ease once he had.

The others respectfully left him alone, sensing that he needed some time with just his own thoughts for company. But that got old quickly.

Prang had always been aware that someday it would come to this. The Council had tolerated his establishment of covert facilities for the Eden Project, fearing as he did that the research might be corrupted by some misguided person. But when he had set up the special team of ensigns, he had known even as he was doing it that he was crossing a dangerous line. Had the ends truly justified the means?

It didn't matter, Prang decided. He had promised himself that he would honor the Council's decision, and he wasn't going to renege on his vow.

At last, roughly forty-five minutes after the sun had set outside the building, one of the Council's aides finally stepped out into the waiting room.

"Admiral Prang?" she called. Her neutral voice had been modulated so as to give him no foreshadowing of what was about to happen.

Prang stepped forward into her view. "Yes, I'm here."

"The Council has reached its verdict," she replied simply. "They're ready for you."

"Then please, lead the way," said Prang.

He followed the aide back into the council chamber, and sat down in his chair when he was invited to do so.

"The Council has examined all the evidence and all the testimonies of the involved parties, and we have come to a decision," the chairwoman began.

Prang stayed quiet as he waited for the words that would either condemn or commend him.

"Admiral Prang, you failed in your duty to report the threat to the 4S," she told him. "On top of that, you put the safety of several inexperienced ensigns in jeopardy, as well as the safety of one man who was entirely untrained and outside your authority to command. While your reasons for your actions have been well established, the actions themselves are still extremely problematic. This Council cannot and will not set a precedent allowing you to be selective in fulfilling your commitments to us."

Prang's heart started to sink. He had expected such an outcome, but that didn't help it hurt any less.

But the chairwoman wasn't finished talking yet.

"However," she continued, "there were several extenuating factors present in this situation. Doctor Fletcher concealed his actions well, and you couldn't have been expected to know just how close your enemies actually were to you. And you were right in saying that a thing like the so-called 'shadow' was completely unanticipated and unpredictable. You lacked much of the information that would have been necessary for you to mount a better defense of your organization."

Prang didn't dare speak. He didn't dare hope. He just sat patiently and waited for the chairwoman to finish.

"Therefore," she said, "the Council has decided not to press charges against you. You will remain in full command of the 4S."

Prang's chest swelled with renewed exhilaration, and he struggled for a moment to maintain his composure.

"Thank you," he said. "I swear that I will strive to follow your directives more closely from here on out."

"See that you do," she told him. "You won't always have madmen and cosmic forces of destruction to take the blame for you. The Council will be watching, and any further missteps will be dealt with on their own merits. I'll repeat that we are absolutely not creating a precedent for leniency with this decision."

"I understand," said Prang. "It was never my intent to oppose you, or to exploit any aspect of the situation to my advantage. Moving forward, I will be more transparent and upfront."

"Good," she replied. "I see that you understand where you stand."

"I do," said Prang. "I serve at the will of the Council, now and always."

"Then, with that, our business here is complete," the chairwoman announced with a nod and a bang of her gavel on the table. "Admiral, consider yourself dismissed. You and your entourage can return to the 4S and resume your regular business. But, if I might offer a bit of friendly advice, I would advise you to be prudent in how you proceed with your Eden Project. Perhaps clandestine outposts and secret experiments are no longer the way to go."

"Of course," replied Prang, with a respectful dip of his head. "I will certainly take that into consideration."

"Then go to it," she said. "And remember that even you are not above judgment."

"Yes, ma'am," said Prang. "Right away."

And he walked out of the room to share the good news with his agents and officers.

*

Jax sat with Ara, Billy, and Tom when Prang stepped out into the waiting room once again. Pitt and Simmons stood closer to the door, talking quietly together. All six of them looked toward the council chamber's door expectantly as their admiral rejoined them.

"Well?" asked Simmons. "What did they say?"

"They acquitted me," replied Prang. "All the charges have been dropped, and they've let me keep my position."

The gathered crowd broke out into a flurry of applause, each person offering their heartiest congratulations.

"Thank you, thank you," said Prang. "Your support means more to me than any of you will ever know. But this isn't my triumph. It was your words that helped the Council make up their minds

"Nonsense, sir," said Pitt. "The Council was never going to convict you. They had to put on a show for appearances' sake, sure, but nothing that happened was ever your fault. The real culprits have already been dealt with."

"Of course," said Prang, "but let's not act as though I never made any bad choices of my own."

"That's different, sir," said Tom. "You were doing what you thought was best, and unlike Doctor Fletcher, you weren't trying to hurt anybody."

"Besides, it's over now," put in Ara. "And we stopped the bad guys. Surely they can't say that your choices were entirely bad."

"Maybe …" said Prang, and his voice trailed off.

The conversation continued as more of the 4S agents joined in. Eventually, all except one had stated their opinion.

In all of the clamor, no one noticed Jax hanging back.

It wasn't that Jax wasn't happy for Prang. He wouldn't have given the testimony he did if he had wanted Prang to be penalized. Even so, Jax's relationship with the admiral had always been strictly professional, nothing like the kind of near-reverence all the 4S agents seemed to have for him. Jax had testified in Prang's favor not because he was especially close to the older man, but because he hadn't found a good reason not to.

So Jax moved away from the others for the moment, finding a place on the opposite side of the room where he could be alone with his thoughts. It worked out well until he heard a voice calling his name.

Jax looked around to see that the admiral had broken away from the group of his admirers and was heading toward him.

"Is there something I can do for you, sir?" Jax asked.

"I just wanted to thank you for what you said in the hearing," Prang said.

Jax gazed at him skeptically. "Really? I mean, you're welcome, but I didn't think I would have made that much of a difference."

"No, you misunderstand me," Prang said. "That wasn't what I was referring to. When your parents died, I was devastated. Not nearly as much as you were, I'd wager, but they had always been good friends of mine."

"Okay," Jax said tentatively. "So how does that relate to today?"

"Albert and Rebecca made great sacrifices for which I will be forever grateful," said Prang. "I know it hurt them to lie to you, and it hurt me every time I had to ask them to keep up the ruse. But I took it too far. I advised them to remain undercover on Earth, to keep watch over the lab. I thought they had distanced themselves from it enough that they wouldn't be targeted. I was wrong. Your parents died because I was shortsighted, and I'll live with the guilt forever. In the hearing, when you told the Council you didn't think it was my fault—well, it made me feel a lot less guilty for everything that's happened to you."

"It wasn't your fault. You didn't know that Doctor Fletcher's people knew as much as you did."

"No, we didn't. But I still couldn't help but blame myself. I should have seen the signs."

"What signs?" Jax asked. "Maybe he was a bit standoffish, but he always seemed to be loyal. I mean, I didn't really know him that long, so maybe I'm not the authority on that, but I know that I never thought he could be a traitor. And there were definitely reasons why I could have."

"Yes, yes," said Prang, "but either way, I still ordered your parents to stay put. However well Fletcher disguised himself, they were always in his line of fire. I should have recalled them to *Home Base,* or to Voyager Station, where they could have been safe."

"Safe from what? Fletcher would have found them and killed them no matter where you sent them. He was probably one of the people who advised you to have them stay on Earth, wasn't he?"

"Yes, he was," Prang admitted. "It should have been suspicious to me from the very start. I should have recognized his ulterior motives."

"How could you have?" Jax asked. "It made sense, from a certain perspective. If the three of us had disappeared from that Roamer camp overnight, that would have turned some heads. Staying in town undercover was the best way for them to stay safe. And it wasn't your fault that it didn't work out. The only reason they were still in danger after they cleaned out their lab was because of Doctor Fletcher, not because of you."

"You're sure?" Prang asked. "Are you sure you feel that

way? If you're trying to spare my feelings, please don't. You could never blame me more than I blame myself."

"With all due respect, Admiral, this isn't about your feelings," Jax said. "It's more about mine. If I keep looking for vengeance, if I keep assigning blame where it isn't due, then I'll never be able to be happy. The criminals have been punished, and the way I see it, we should let that be the end of things."

"I understand," said Prang. "That's a very mature thing to say. Your parents would be proud of how much you've accomplished.

"Seriously, don't worry about that," Jax assured him. "I don't hate you. I never did. Fighting among ourselves doesn't help anyone. We saw that with what Fletcher made Captain Ramón do."

"You're certainly right about that," agreed Prang. "To think that he was ever able to spread his evil ideology among our officers … Even the fact that he himself believed it is cause enough for revulsion."

"Do you think he was onto something?" Jax asked. "Or did he just make it all up?"

"Who can say? Perhaps he did hear the voice of a cosmic entity, or perhaps he was merely acting on some perverted desire that was entirely his own. But I don't plan to dwell on that question for long. If the shadow wasn't real, then we won't have to worry about it ever again. And if it was, then we'll all have to pray as hard as we can that it never chooses to take control of anyone else."

"Yeah, that sounds like a good idea," said Jax. He paused for a moment, then asked, "What are you going to do now that it's over?"

"The 4S' mission hasn't changed," said Prang. "I'm still as dedicated to humanity's future as I ever was. Shadow or no shadow, I'm going to fight for that future until my dying day, because if we can't have hope that things will get better, we might as well just lay down and die right here."

Then it was his turn to pause for a moment, before he posed a question of his own.

"And what will you do, Jax? You're a free man. You can

go where you want, do what you want, and I won't bother you again. The 4S is grateful for your service, and you've earned the right to live your life however you please. Just say the word, and I'll arrange transport for you to wherever you want to go. I'd even help you get settled, or maybe even endorse you on a job application. It's the least I could do."

A new start. It was everything Jax wanted, or it should have been. With Fletcher imprisoned, his black hole destroyed, and the 4S enduring to continue its work, no one could say that Jax hadn't done his part for the universe. Jax's lust for revenge had been sated, so he could finally honor his parents' last wishes and move on.

And yet, looking into Prang's tired but hopeful eyes, he just couldn't bring himself to take that option.

In that moment, Jax could see something in Prang that he never would have expected to see in a 4S admiral—a kindred spirit. In his own way, Prang had lost almost everything he had previously taken for granted. Here, even after the Council had exonerated him, Prang was at his lowest. His every action would be viewed with suspicion, maybe for the rest of his career. He may have been cleared of all charges, but he had still been irrevocably humbled, in much the same way that Jax had found himself freshly aware of life's risks after his parents had been murdered.

Leagues apart in age, experience, and rank, Jax and Prang had nonetheless been united in their mutual realization that they could never take the comforts of their stations in life for granted ever again. Jax could never go back to being an oblivious young layabout, while Prang could never return to his previous level of faith in the universe's innately good nature.

Jax knew that an unassuming, ordinary life was no longer in the cards for him, and the words he spoke next would change the course of his destiny.

"No," he said. "I want to stay."

Prang's face betrayed his surprise for several seconds before he regained his composure.

"But the last time we spoke, you were so adamantly against that," he said.

"I wouldn't say that," said Jax. "I was still figuring things out back then. But now I have, and my mind's made up."

"Are you sure?" asked Prang. "It's a big commitment. You'd essentially be signing the rest of your life away."

"No big deal," said Jax. "I never had any real plans anyway."

"You'd have to go through a lot more training," said Prang. "Given all the experience you've already acquired, I could put you on an accelerated path through the academy, but it would still be at least two years before you'd be back in the field."

"I'll do whatever training you want me to," Jax said. "If I'm going to take this job, I might as well be qualified."

"Good man," said Prang. "But I must say, this turnaround does still seem rather sudden. May I ask what brought it on?"

"Well …" Jax began.

Then he stopped. Should he tell Prang about the mystical interaction he had had with his parents? Would the admiral even believe him? No, Jax decided, he would keep that part of the story to himself.

"I guess I got attached to the 4S," he finished plainly.

"Ah." Prang looked across the room to where Ara, Billy, and Tom stood. "I suppose the friendships you forged were stronger than you might have imagined."

Jax shrugged. If Prang wanted to believe that interpretation, there was no harm in letting him do so.

"You could say that, sir," said Jax. "But it's also more than that. I don't think I could have fought to protect the Eden Project for as long as I did without believing in it for myself."

"The Eden Project's future is far from certain right now," Prang informed him, "but I'm sure we can find you something to do."

"That's fine," said Jax. "I can do whatever needs doing."

"Then I'll tell you this just one more time," said Prang. "If you joined the 4S, you would be making a lifelong commitment to our organization. You've been well informed by now about what would be required of you, so I won't waste your time explaining it again. I'll just ask you one simple question: are you prepared to make the commitment, and to honor it for as long as you are able?"

Jax didn't even hesitate for one second. "Yes, I am."

"Very well," Prang said. "In that case, it would be my honor to have you aboard … Ensign Nurmen."

Jax stood a little straighter and gave a salute. "Good to be here, Admiral. Let's get to work."

EPILOGUE

NURMEN FAMILY HOME—ROAMER CAMP IL-048—
OUTSIDE CHICAGO, ILLINOIS, USA

Jax stood on the front steps of the house where he had spent his childhood, debating whether or not he should take the final step forward.

He hadn't returned to this place since the night he had been forced to leave it, and for the most part it looked as though no one else had, either. On the outside, the building appeared untouched. Its attackers hadn't bombed it or burned it, and the structure remained completely sound. The front door, which had been jerked halfway open and wrenched off its tracks so that it couldn't be fully opened or closed, represented the only sign that the masked raiders had ever been there at all.

Three days had passed since Admiral Prang's hearing had ended, and Jax's 4S team had remained on Earth with their organization's leaders while Prang had made arrangements for Jax to join the next class of cadets entering the 4S Academy. When Jax's enrollment had been finalized, Prang had granted him permission to take some time to visit his childhood homestead and commemorate his parents' deaths once more before he shipped off to begin his formal training.

Jax didn't know exactly what he had expected to find when he had arrived at the house near the center of the Roamer settlement, but a mostly unchanged exterior wasn't it. Would the inside also be the same as it had been when Fletcher's goons had left it? If no one else had disturbed it since that night, then entering the house now almost felt like a sort of sacrilege.

Jax raised a finger to scratch at his chin as he tried to puzzle out the newfound dilemma.

"Well?" Billy called from behind him. "Are you going inside or not?"

"Shhh!" Ara whispered to him hurriedly.

Jax turned around to face his friends, and found that Billy had taken a few steps back from the house's front porch, as if to keep himself out of range of Jax's fists.

The Jax of several months ago, who had still been grieving for his parents, might have been frustrated with Billy's oblivious impatience and lack of subtlety. A part of him still was. But, if their friendship was going to work out, both of them had to give a little. Jax couldn't expect to have everything exactly the way he liked it all the time, but maybe he could learn how to like what he had.

As the seconds ticked by and Jax remained calm, Billy seemed to relax as well.

Jax smiled benignly. "You know what? Why don't we all go inside?"

"Are you sure?" asked Tom. "I mean, are you comfortable with us poking around inside the place?"

"I don't see why not," Jax replied. "There's nothing in here that I'd mind if you saw. The laboratory was where all the secret stuff happened."

"Okay," said Tom. "As long as we're all here."

Even though none of the ensigns could move it from the place where it had stuck, the front door had still opened wide enough for a person of average height and build to squeeze themselves through the crack. Jax, Ara, Billy, and Tom all accomplished it with ease.

In the foyer, a narrow hallway leading to a staircase across from the door, Jax could barely find anything amiss. Then again, that particular space had always been empty and mostly unfurnished, with no spaces where human beings could truly conceal themselves, so it made sense that the raiders wouldn't have spent too much time there.

Jax peered into the living room, the kitchen, and the dining room, and he found all three in a much more sorry state. All the cabinets in the house had been thrown open, their contents scattered across the floors. The living room couch had been tipped onto its back, and the kitchen table had been knocked over as well. The whole house had been thrown into disarray, as though a tornado had swept through it.

Jax even took a look into the garage, where he just encountered more of the same disorder, with everything strewn everywhere. He noticed that the floor panel covering the secret escape route had been opened up, but he had no interest in entering the underground tunnel again. From what he could remember, everything in the lab at the other end had already been removed or dismantled.

Jax had been given some indication of what the house might look like before he had arrived there, and so far he had to admit that it had been fairly spot-on.

Apparently, just as Jax had predicted it might, the Nurmens vanishing nearly without a trace had indeed raised some suspicion among their local community. The small police force attached to the Roamer settlement had received four separate reports of a disturbance the night it had all gone down, although they had arrived on the scene too late to witness it playing out in real time. The story had been recounted to Jax by Admiral Prang, whom Jax would also learn had intervened to ensure both that Albert and Rebecca Nurmen received an honorable burial and that their home—which had actually been purchased in perpetuity by the 4S as employee housing—would not be repossessed. The only people who had been inside since the attack had been a group of investigators, who would of course have been careful to preserve the crime scene as cleanly as possible.

After all that, the Nurmens' house had effectively been set apart as a memorial to the fallen husband and wife, left alone to honor the couple who had lost the chance to inhabit it ever again. As Jax made his way through the various rooms, he moved slowly and carefully, not wanting to make any impressions of his own that might forever spoil the delicately preserved state of the. It certainly felt strange, feeling like a trespasser within the home where he had grown up, but he didn't mind. It was a painful reminder of what he once had, but so long as he didn't let it defeat him, and so long as he stayed focused on what he had found since, he could bear a bit of melancholy.

Billy, Ara, and Tom followed Jax at a respectful distance, and when he led them back into the foyer they all looked to him expectantly.

Throughout the whole experience, Jax had done his best to remain passive and not let his emotions overwhelm him. He had succeeded somewhat, in that he hadn't broken down sobbing as he had half expected he might, but as he watched them all staring back at him in silent contemplation he knew that something must be showing on his face.

"It's a nice place you've got here," Billy observed. "If you don't mind how messy it is. No offense."

"None taken," said Jax. "I completely agree, actually. But that's just what you get when a bunch of henchmen suddenly show up uninvited."

"Yeah," said Billy. "You're probably right about that."

"What are you going to do now?" Tom asked.

"I'm going to head upstairs," Jax told them. "If you three don't mind, I think I'd like to be alone for this part, at least for the first bit."

"Go ahead, then," said Tom. "We'll be here when you're ready."
"But don't take too much time," Ara warned him. "I know this is sentimental for you, but we do have transports to catch. The 4S' flight schedules wait for nobody."

"It's fine," Jax replied. "I get it. Orders are orders. All I'm asking for is a couple minutes."

That seemed to satisfy Ara. She nodded once. "Then go. Just call us if you need us."

"Sure," Jax said. "Will do."

As Jax began to mount the stairs, he paused halfway up to glance back at his friends.

Once, he had told himself that the relationship they all shared could never last for very long. He had always kept a part of himself locked away, closed off from them, because he had thought that sooner or later he would have to go his own way and leave them behind.

How had he ever been so misguided?

His lack of a genuine place within the 4S hadn't been a reason for him to deliberately weaken the friendships he made there. Those friendships had become strong even despite his recalcitrance, forged in the fires of the trials they had undergone, and in the end they had given him cause to carve out a place for himself in the 4S, bringing the group even closer together.

I don't need to keep withdrawing, Jax told himself. *Whatever will happen will happen, but we made it through the whole thing with Doctor Fletcher, and we all lived to tell the tale. If we didn't give up on each other then, how could we give up on each other now, when we've finally found peace?*

As spur-of-the-moment as it had been, Jax still had no intention of going back on the promise he had made to his friends. He would stand by them, just as they had stood by him. They would face the future unapologetically, and they would never look back.

*

After the hearing had ended, and Jax had concluded his conversation with Prang, the admiral had walked away to discuss business with Pitt and Simmons, leaving Jax to figure out just what to say to his squadmates.

Ara, Billy, and Tom stood in a cluster on the other side of the room, talking animatedly about something or other. Jax didn't want to interrupt them, but when they noticed him moving toward them with introspection written all over his face, their conversation had come to an end either way.

Tom beckoned with his hand to invite Jax into their circle. "Don't just stand there. Come on over."

Jax joined them, and for the first several seconds no one seemed to know what to do.

"That was some trial, huh?" asked Billy, in a commendable attempt at small talk. Jax still felt as though Billy was only trying to prolong their togetherness, but he played along for the moment.

The group kept up a stream of forced chatter about Admiral Prang and the 4S for an impressive amount of time before Ara finally cracked and made what she thought was the obvious remark.

"Well, then, I guess this is goodbye," she said.

For a second, Jax was taken aback.

"What?" he asked.

"You're leaving, aren't you?" she replied. "You'll go back to your home on Earth, and we'll never see you again."

Jax couldn't blame her for her confusion. Until just a few minutes ago, even he hadn't known what career choice he would make. When he had awoken that morning, he had anticipated that this present occasion would indeed be a farewell.

Even as he thought that, however, he realized that it still was—just not in the way he had first imagined. Rather than him and his friends saying goodbye to each other, they had all been united in marking the end of the man that Jax could never return to being.

Jax knew it; it was time the others knew it, too.

"You've got it all wrong," he told Ara. "I'm not going anywhere. I'm going to be one of you from now on."

They all turned to him in shock.

"Seriously?" asked Tom. "You … you're not joking?"

"Nope," Jax replied.

"But why?" asked Billy. "Don't get me wrong, I'm happy for you, but you just never seemed to care before."

"What can I say?" Jax said. "Sometime during that crazy adventure we all just had, you guys convinced me that this whole 4S thing was worth it after all."

"Well, that's great!" said Tom. "You'll love it here."

"Whoa there, cool your jets," said Jax. "I have to spend some time at the academy first. Apparently the mishmash training I got on the fly while I was constantly fighting for my life isn't good enough or something."

"Well, the 4S is pretty choosy," said Ara. "You can't expect to just waltz in and get a job without the proper qualifications."

"I don't know about that," said Jax. "Admiral Prang hired me without any qualifications, didn't he?"

"You know what I mean," Ara huffed, but she still smiled and choked back a laugh.

"And why do you think he went in for that hearing?" Tom asked. "That isn't how things work. The Council won't let him get away with it again. If you want the credentials, you're going to have to put in the work."

"Fine by me," said Jax. "Honestly, I can't wait to get started."

And he wouldn't have to wait long before he could.

Since that day, much had changed in a short time.

The Eden Project remained mostly in limbo, its various research stations operating at a vastly reduced capacity while Prang worked to restructure its approach. James Simmons had been offered the position of Chief Research Officer to help oversee those efforts, but the elderly man had instead opted for a quiet job educating up-and-coming 4S scientists while he spent time discerning whether he himself would ever return to full-time research. Prang had respected his old friend's choice, and he and Pitt had made plans to find another officer who could step in to fill Doctor Fletcher's position.

Jax and his friends had still had goodbyes to say. Ara, Billy, and Tom had jobs on the *Home Base* that they had already been away from for too long. Prang had opened preliminary talks with the 4S Academy, which had agreed to accept Jax on a specially altered curriculum that would account for the experience he had already gained. The four teammates would be apart for a good amount of time, but they all felt confident that their friendship would survive.

Jax had gone into his testimony thinking that he would do what he could for Prang and end his time with the 4S on as high a note as he could manage. He had been fighting for the 4S for months, and no one could say that he hadn't done his part. He had thought he had earned a rest.

But there would be no rest for him. He wouldn't be in constant mortal danger anymore, but he wouldn't be able to slow down just yet. He still had a debt to repay—no longer a debt of revenge upon those who had wronged him, but a debt to the friends who had accepted him even in his broken state and to the organization that had taken him in and given him the chance to make something of himself.

Just like he had said, he couldn't wait to get started.

*

Jax reached the top of the stairs and turned right, pausing respectfully right outside his old bedroom.

Jax raised his foot and placed it back down squarely on the threshold of the door that his father had flung open when he had come to alert Jax to their enemies' presence. The door was even half open, resting in more or less the same position it had taken in that instance.

As Jax stepped fully into the room, the first thing to catch his attention was the blank gray panel where his window usually nestled. If Jax hadn't known that the panel was only a metal shutter, he would never have guessed that the room had ever had a window at all.

Thinking back to that fateful night, Jax could recall that the first clue he had gotten that something was wrong had come when that shutter had slammed closed. He remembered how quickly the events had escalated from there, how he and his parents had been forced to evacuate their home only minutes after they had sighted their enemies.

Jax also remembered how confused he had been throughout the whole ordeal, a feeling that had only heightened every time a new development had arisen—the reveal of his parents' secret lab, the destruction of their escape vehicle, and finally, their deaths.

Now, however, Jax's confusion had been entirely dispelled. He wasn't the man he had been all those months ago any longer. Until he had been absorbed into the 4S, Jax had never been particularly driven or opportunistic. When his parents had died, he had found a purpose, but not a sustainable one. Now, finally, he had found the best of both worlds, the ability to be happy and content while also actually doing something productive.

Jax had to admit, it felt good to finally know what he was meant to be doing.

He picked his way through the clutter of clothing and

personal knickknacks that littered the floor. He had never had a lot of possessions, but the way his things had been strewn haphazardly across the floor made the meager amount he had owned seem greater than it had really been.

In roughly the center of the room, Jax's toes brushed up against something orange and blue. He bent down to pick it up, turning it over in his hands until he could make out just what it was: a small scale model of a 4S shuttle. It had been dented in a few spots when it had hit the floor, and one of the wings had snapped off, but it was a toy shuttle all right.

Jax knew that model. His parents had bought it for him to occupy his time while he had recovered from an illness at age twelve. Jax had always seen it as nothing more than a novelty, but now, with the benefit of hindsight, he could recognize it as the foreshadowing none of them could have known it to be.

Jax lingered in the room for a few minutes more, taking in the atmosphere of simpler times gone by. At last, he had to admit that he had put himself through all the nostalgia he could bear.

"Hey, Jax!" Tom called from downstairs. "We should get going soon, or we'll all miss our flights."

"I'll be right there!" Jax called back, taking one last look around the room.

He had already seen everything in here anyway, and he was sure that Prang would take good care of it when he had it all sent into storage. For now, Jax had new memories to make.

Jax rejoined his friends, and together the four of them walked back out into the late afternoon air, heading for the spaceport where they would finally be forced to part with each other for the foreseeable future.

As they walked through the streets, the sun going down behind them and casting them in its fading orange glow, Billy raised a hand to his chin in thought.

"You know what I just realized?" he asked.

"No, I don't," said Jax. "And we won't know until you tell us."

"Fair enough," said Billy.

"Well, don't leave us hanging," said Tom. "What are you thinking?"

"We had our own squad going for a while there," said Billy. "And we were in space. And since Admiral Prang told us to keep it quiet, you could even say it was a super-secret squad."

"I don't get it," said Ara. "What's your point?"

"We were a super-secret space squad," said Billy. "Get it? It's like it was our own little 4S."

"Super-secret space squad," muttered Jax. "Yep, there's four S's in there, all right."

"I just thought it was funny," said Billy. "Because we work for a 4S, and we were a 4S, in a weird way."

"Heh," Tom said. "Yeah, I guess it is pretty funny."

"Too bad it's over now, though," said Ara. "Jax is going off to the Academy, and we'll be back on the *Home Base*. By the time we can all get together again, we'll all have new jobs for ourselves. We can't be a squad forever."

"Oh, no," said Jax. "You aren't getting rid of me that easily. If you think I'll let you get away without keeping in touch, you're dead wrong."

"That isn't what she meant," said Tom. "You have our personal comm frequencies, and we'll keep you updated on the 4S so long as you promise to tell us any funny stories from your training."

"Deal," said Jax.

"We'll miss you, though," said Ara. "We'll almost certainly be busy while you're gone, and by the time you come back we might not even be in the same jobs anymore. Any chance we have of working together on a mission again might have slipped away by then."

"It'll be weird for sure," agreed Jax. "It feels like we only just met, and now our mission has come to an end."

"But it hasn't," said Tom. "Not really. It's like you said back on Fletcher's ship, Jax. This isn't an ending; it's just a fresh start."

Yeah, Jax mused. *More than you even know.*

But he chose to keep that particular thought to himself.

All he said out loud was, "You know, you're right, Tom. Something tells me that me joining the 4S is just going to give us more chances to get up to new shenanigans."

"Sounds good to me," put in Billy. "As long as they aren't as deadly as the last set."

At that, Tom let out a chuckle. As the chuckle went on, it quickly grew into a hearty laugh, and the laughter became contagious. Ara, Billy, and even Jax joined in, and the friends' laughter mingled and rang through the evening air.

Jax's eyes followed the sound into the sky, where he could see the stars beginning to shimmer into view.

Somewhere out there in that field of stars lay his future. Somewhere out there lay his destiny. Somehow, he felt he had always known that, even if he had only discovered it half a week earlier.

And, if the strange otherworldly encounter he had had while comatose was anything to go by, somewhere out there his parents were still watching him. Would he see them again, or hear their voices? Did he even really want to?

From the night they had died to the time he had spoken with them again, Jax had thought that the thing he wanted most was more time with his father and mother. He had told himself that nothing, or at least nothing less than making their killers hurt as much as he did, would ever alleviate the pain their loss had brought on. But he knew now just how shortsighted he had been. As long as Jax devoted himself to the dream they had fought for—the dream Admiral Prang had described to him, the dream of a utopian future for mankind—his parents' legacy would never completely die.

Besides, he would most definitely be reunited with them again someday, but he had a long and fulfilling life to live before that moment ever came.

For now, Jax was with his best friends, and he had gained a new purpose, and that was enough for him.

After so long being stuck in a rut, Jax was finally moving up in life, and now that he was officially part of the 4S, not even the sky was the limit.

ACKNOWLEDGEMENTS

Writing a novel is exhausting. This truth has been handed down time and again by authors far more accomplished than me, and I won't dispute it. From the moment I committed to putting my words on the page, an entire horde of stumbling blocks threatened to sap every last ounce of my willpower. High school senior year, the transition to college, and the fallout from a pandemic would have been challenging enough on their own. However, I will freely admit that it was my own mental struggles—both innate procrastination and a constant battle with anxiety—that came closest to shutting this whole thing down. It didn't matter that this book was a passion project I had been sitting on for years. I was massively afraid of rejection, or of not measuring up to some predetermined standard, and it would hold me back for days or even weeks at a time.

Fortunately, I had an endlessly constructive cast of characters behind me the whole way. Their encouragement, and often their nagging, kept me pushing forward, even on those plentiful occasions I considered giving up. Now that this story has made it out of my hands and into yours, reader, allow me to express my gratitude to all the people who made the process possible.

To begin, these pages would be forever incomplete without a mention of my parents, Brian and Jennifer Coleman, who gave me my life and supported me in all my endeavors over its nineteen years. I would also like to use this space to honor my grandparents, Robert and Jane Baker of Woodbridge, Virginia and Thomas and Mary Jo Coleman of Pittsburgh, Pennsylvania. To all of you, and to all my various family members, thank you for always encouraging me to pursue my interests and chase down my goals. Without you, this novel and so much else would be nothing but a pipe dream.

With that out of the way …

Thank you to the students in the Creative Writing program at Colgan High School, especially those in the class of 2022. It was an absolute pleasure to learn and grow with y'all. Whether we were pumping out literary journals, or just hanging around with snacks, I could count on having a blast. As a collective, you truly broadened my worldview, and I wish the best of luck to every single one of you, wherever your future paths may lead.

Thank you to Marco Haase and Serena Morris, who served as my main workshop group in this book's earliest stage and helped me refine many of its details. Your contributions were instrumental in turning this story from a barely-thought-out concept into a text worthy of publication, and for that you will always have my appreciation.

Thank you to Zachary Malich, who bears the double distinction of being both my best friend of thirteen years and the talented artist who turned this book's cover from a crude pencil sketch into a full-on 3D render. We've had some good times, you and I, and you've been part of several of my greatest accomplishments. It only seems fitting that you should stand with me at this milestone as well.

Thank you to A. Floren Jay, my editor and another fellow Colgan Creative Writing alum. Thank you not only for critiquing my drafts but also for the hand of friendship you extended while I was undergoing an intense personal crisis. Even though we have next to nothing in common, the gesture means more to me than you will ever know. I will always treasure the memories of our lunchroom conversations, our fretting over AP Microeconomics, and your ever-helpful advice for refining my writing.

Thank you to Ms. Dyche, the Colgan Creative Writing

teacher who is perhaps the most influential adult in my life outside my family. Thank you for the safe space I could always count on finding between the walls of your classroom, Room 1313. Thank you for always seeing us students as more than names on a list, and for taking an interest in not only our grades, not only our writing assignments, but in all areas of our lives. In doing so, you always made me feel validated. Thank you also for sticking with this project until the end, even after I was no longer under your tutelage. Your example is one I will always strive to emulate, and I will always credit your teachings for this novel's existence.

Thank you as well to the many people I interacted with during my work on this novel who I haven't mentioned yet. This includes anyone I knew from school, sports, scouts, church youth group, or just in passing. All those people in all those places created a culture of acceptance that enabled me to push back against my fear of failure. I address them all at once when I say that, although you likely never knew the full breadth of what I was going through, thank you from the bottom of my heart for simply being part of my life. Please never stop being yourselves.

Finally, thank you to all the readers who saw fit to pluck this book from the shelf and devour its contents. Whatever impact it left on you, thank you for taking a chance on my creation. I'd like to cap this off by encouraging you to keep looking to the stars. I hope you dream without limits and always aspire to reach new heights.

ABOUT THE AUTHOR

Born and raised in Woodbridge, Virginia, Jonathan Coleman studied creative writing at Charles J. Colgan, Sr. High School in its Center for the Fine and Performing Arts program. During his four years there, he saw several of his works published in the school's literary journals, specifically the 2022 *Siren* as well as several editions of *Megalodon* from 2018 to 2022. He also served for two years on the publications staff for those journals, first as 2020-21 Managing Editor and then as one of two 2021-22 *Siren* Editors-in-Chief. Jonathan graduated high school in June 2022, and currently attends Hampden-Sydney College in Farmville, Virginia, where he plans to major in history. Beyond academics, Jonathan's interests include running, reading, consuming carbohydrates (pasta, potatoes, etc.), and the *Star Wars* and *Marvel* cinematic franchises, from which he will admit to "borrowing" several concepts during his writing process for this novel.